"Eleanor…"

She turned her head. Slowly. As if it took all her effort of will to force her body to obey. To focus on the man who stood before her.

"Eleanor. I presume that you had no suspicion of this terrible débâcle. Not the slightest hint that Thomas might have had a liaison elsewhere."

"No. How should I? I cannot believe it…."

"Nor I. It does not sound like Thomas." Henry watched her carefully, aware of the white shade around her mouth as she skimmed the brink of control. Every instinct urged him to take her in his arms and let her cry out her frozen misery against his chest. But he could not, dared not, too unsure of her reaction to him if he made any intimate gesture. Too unsure of his feelings toward her. There was no place for pity here. And yet the bitter anger at her coldhearted betrayal of his own love for her no longer seemed to weigh in the balance. A very masculine urge to protect took precedence.

* * *

The Disgraced Marchioness
Harlequin Historical "770—September 2005

AUTHOR NOTE

In *The Disgraced Marchioness* I have recounted the intense but dangerous love affair between Lord Henry Faringdon and Eleanor, Marchioness of Burford—the widow of Henry's older brother. The possibilities in their relationship fascinated me. A tale of mistaken rejection and betrayal, but above all a family saga of searing passion and undying love.

The desire to write this first volume in THE FARINGDON SCANDALS miniseries was born out of an interest in marriage in Regency England—particularly in the circumstances that might prevent marriage between members of one family. Love decrees that Henry and Eleanor be together. The severe rulings of the law seem destined to keep the lovers apart.

Henry, with his dark good looks, must assuredly attract the interest and admiration of any woman, but he is strong willed, with more than a hint of the Faringdon pride. Beautiful Eleanor, spirited and headstrong, finds it difficult to hide a fragility that would stir the protective instincts of a lesser man than Henry. And with an intimate history between them, from which neither has emerged unscathed, Henry cannot turn his back on her.

Just how will their relationship fare when scandal erupts, to threaten Eleanor with disgrace and cause the Faringdons to be snubbed by the contemptuous *haut ton*?

The history of the Faringdon brothers doesn't stop with this book, but is continued with Nick's story in *The Outrageous Debutante*, coming in December 2005.

I hope that this dynamic, vivacious but remarkably devoted family will delight you as much as they did me!

Anne

ANNE O'BRIEN

The

Disgraced Marchioness

The Faringdon Scandals

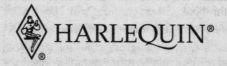

HARLEQUIN®

TORONTO • NEW YORK • LONDON
AMSTERDAM • PARIS • SYDNEY • HAMBURG
STOCKHOLM • ATHENS • TOKYO • MILAN • MADRID
PRAGUE • WARSAW • BUDAPEST • AUCKLAND

ISBN 0-373-29370-4

THE DISGRACED MARCHIONESS

Please address questions and book requests to:
Harlequin Reader Service
U.S.: 3010 Walden Ave., P.O. Box 1325, Buffalo, NY 14269
Canadian: P.O. Box 609, Fort Erie, Ont. L2A 5X3

Chapter One

The gentleman was apparently not expected by the inhabitants of Burford Hall. In no way discouraged by the silence, the lack of activity and the shuttered windows, he leapt down from the curricle with unhurried grace to stand on the gravel carriageway, as his groom ascended the shallow sweep of steps and rang the bell. With his back to the house, the visitor allowed his gaze to take in the familiar vista, noting little change over past months. Expertly and fashionably designed gardens with paved pathways and shaded walks. A rose terrace where fragrant blooms were just being tempted to open in the warm sunshine. Rolling parkland made enticing by groupings of trees, which had been planted at least a century ago for impact and perspective. All prosperous and well tended with the glaze of extreme wealth. The stables off to his left had been recently re-roofed and he could see the grazing herd of cattle, placid and fat, in one of the distant pastures beyond home farm.

He did not need to turn to face the house to appreciate every inch of the elegant façade in intimate and well-loved detail. Every pillar, portico and decorated frieze, from balustraded terrace to dominant central pediment, all constructed in glowing local stone or faced with more fashionable brick. It was a beautiful house and home, gracious and welcoming, mellow with the happy memories of a shared childhood.

Two years previously he had chosen to turn his back on it, to leave the guarantee of wealth and privilege, and social acceptance by the *haut ton*. Two years ago he had wanted to create for himself a quite different lifestyle. And nothing had given him cause to regret his choice. But now, by a mischievous and malicious quirk of fate, his life had been turned upside down.

He supposed it was all his now: house, land, title and all they could bring in terms of comfort and consequence. His brother's untimely death had, overnight, created him Marquis of Burford.

The thought gave him no pleasure. *I don't want it. I would never have wanted it.* Indeed, the deliberate rejection of his birthright screamed through his mind as he climbed the steps with outward calm to his ancestral home.

The door was flung open at the insistent ringing to allow entry to the unexpected guest. The footman, a young man in neat black, casting an envious and knowing eye over the stylish equipage and well-bred bays drawn up on the gravel, bowed the gentleman in without a flicker of recognition, but accepting of his quality and his right to be desiring entrance unannounced to Burford Hall.

'If I could take your coat, sir, I will inform Lord Nicholas of your arrival.'

The guest looked at the young footman. A new acquisition to the staff since his last visit. He smiled in courteous recognition of the offered service. 'Of course.' He handed over his tall-crowned hat and shrugged out of an eye-catching caped greatcoat.

'What name shall I give, sir?'

Before he could give a reply, hesitant footsteps echoed on the marble tiles of the entrance hall and an elderly man emerged from the servants' quarters. He hesitated on an intake of breath, blinked as if he did not quite believe the evidence of his own eyes, and then immediately quickened his steps.

'My lord, my lord. Thank God you are here. We were not expecting you.' The old man shuffled forward, in spite of the infirmities of advanced age, to take the garment from the footman, and search the face of the gentleman with eyes suddenly moist with powerful emotion. 'We did not know if the letters had reached you—perhaps you might not yet even be aware of the tragic events here.'

'They did. About two months ago.' The gentleman stripped off his leather driving gloves with brisk efficiency. 'But there have been difficulties in travelling—chiefly the vagaries of the weather—so it took me longer than I expected.'

'We are so glad to see you again, my lord. So relieved. If I may say, you have not changed in all the time you have been away.'

'Only two years, Marcle. Not so very long.' The accompanying smile was understanding but designed not to encourage further comment.

'Long enough, my lord. You have been missed here.'

'But what about you, Marcle?' The gentleman began to walk in the direction of the library, sure of his direction. 'You look well. I see that you still hold the reins, in spite of your threats to leave to live in retirement with your sister.'

'Not so bad, sir. I would not wish to leave the Hall. And certainly not now… But what a terrible occasion this is. I cannot tell you… An accident that no one could have foreseen…'

'I know.' The guest, clearly a very close and knowledgeable one, intimate with the family circumstances, touched the old man's arm in a brief gesture of comfort, at the same time hoping against hope to dam the flood of painful detail and the threat of overt sympathy. 'So Mr Hoskins informed me. And my brother. Both letters eventually found me.'

'What a terrible homecoming, my lord…'

His attempts, it appeared, had been futile. *He really could not take any more.*

'I will deal with it, Marcle,' his tone now a little brusque but not unkind. 'I presume Lord Nicholas is here?'

'Yes, my lord.' The butler concentrated on the more practical direction given less than subtly to his thoughts. 'He has spent some time in London, particularly with the lawyers, being a trustee, as you will be aware—but he returned last week. He is in the gun room, I believe. I will send a message that you have arrived.' He motioned with a rheumatic hand to the young footman. 'Silas…'

'No. There is no need to trouble yourself, Marcle. I will go to the gun room.'

'Of course, my lord. I would just wish to say that…' But he was already bowing to an empty hall as the gentleman made good his escape.

Chapter Two

The door to the gunroom at Burford Hall, deep in the west wing, opened on to a familiar and industrious scene. A young man in shirt sleeves, corduroy breeches and high-topped boots, all well suited to country life, presented his back to the visitor. A black spaniel at his feet, Lord Nicholas Faringdon leaned with hip propped against a bench on which were all the accoutrements necessary for oiling and cleaning the impressive array of sporting firearms. Head bent, he was intent on freeing the firing mechanism on a particularly fine but unreliable duck gun. He whistled tunelessly between his teeth.

'So this is how you are spending your time. I might have known it. Planning a day's rough shooting when you should be overlooking the acres!'

The young man's head snapped up and turned at the sound of the soft voice. He stopped whistling. There was a moment of stunned silence. Then he abandoned the gun on top of the rest of the detritus on the bench and pushed himself to his feet, a grin warming his features.

'Hal! I had no idea.' He approached the gentleman, hand outstretched in formal greeting, and then thought better of it and seized his brother in a warm hug, all the time firing questions. 'How long it has been! When did you arrive? Have you been back in England long? How long will you stay?'

Returning the embrace with equal enthusiasm, Henry—Hal

to those who knew him best—pushed back and the brothers, Lord Henry and Lord Nicholas Faringdon, stood at arm's length to assess each other. The family resemblance was strong. Both were true Faringdons. Dark hair, almost black and dense with little reflected light. A straight nose, lean cheeks, a decided chin and well-marked brows, they were a handsome pair. But whereas Hal's eyes were more grey than blue, stern and frequently on the edge of cynical, Nicholas, some three years younger, viewed the world through a bright optimistic gaze of intense blue. Their smiles on this occasion were also very similar, but Nicholas's mouth lacked the lines of experience, of ambition and sardonic humour that were engraved on Hal's features.

'You look well, for all your travels.' Nicholas gave his brother a friendly smack on his shoulder. 'Have you made your fortune yet? Is that why you are here, to brag of your exploits?'

'Not quite.' Hal shook his head, well used to the ribbing.

'Ha! I wager you are too fine to have anything to do with a mere landowner now. Faringdon and Bridges, is it not? Should I ask who is in charge of the business? Are you controlling New York yet?'

'No—and, no, you should not ask! Nat Bridges and I have equal shares and investment in this company. I see you haven't changed, Nick.' Henry looked at his brother, noting the faint lines of strain beside his mouth, until his attention was demanded by a nudge against his boot. 'And who is this?' He bent to pull the ears of the spaniel who had come to sit at his feet in a friendly fashion.

'Bess. She's young, but she's hopeful. As soon as she stops chasing and scattering the birds rather than collecting them.'

The dog sneezed as if knowing she was under discussion. The two men laughed.

'Hal. I don't know what to say to you about all this…' Nicholas was suddenly sober, as a cloud covering the sun, the smile wiped from mouth and eyes by a depth of sorrow.

Hal shook his head and turned away to run his hand along the polished stocks and barrels of the guns in their racks. It was all so familiar. But now it was changed for ever and he could do nothing about it. 'Any problems with the estate?' He kept his back turned.

'No.' Nicholas was relieved to return to plain reporting of facts. Emotions at the Hall were still too stark to allow for casual airing. 'All neatly tied up. The entail stands. There are no inheritance problems and Hoskins had finished his affairs when I was last in London. Thomas always was thorough, of course. He left everything as it should be.'

At that, Hal spun on his heel, his voice and expression harsh with pain. 'How the hell did it happen, Nick? A riding accident? I have never seen anyone sit a horse better or more securely than Thomas. And he was not even out hunting, if the letters speak the truth.'

'No.' Nick frowned at the problem that had faced him for the past few months. 'He went out across the estate to meet the new agent, Whitcliffe. He never arrived. His horse returned here riderless. Thomas was found later that morning on the edge of the east wood, no obvious injuries, but his neck broken. The horse was unharmed too. It must have shied—a loose pheasant, perhaps—and thrown him. His mind must have been preoccupied and…well, you know the rest.'

'Yes. Such a tragic waste of a life.'

'I still can't believe that he will not walk through that door and ask me if I wish to go…' Nick's words dried in his throat as the memories became too intense.

Hal saw and understood. He grasped his brother's shoulder, with a little shake. 'I know. Come to the library and tell me about everything. And a brandy would not come amiss, I think.'

'Yes—of course. And I would wish to know what you have been about.' Once more in command, Nicholas shrugged into his jacket and followed his brother from the room. As he turned to lock the door to the gunroom, the spaniel fussing round his feet, a thought came to him

'By the by…have you spoken with Lady Faringdon yet?'

Hal came to a halt and turned, brows arched.

'Who?'

'Lady Faringdon. The Marchioness.'

'You mean Thomas married?' Hal asked in amazement. 'I did not know…I had no idea…'

'Why, yes. And he has a son. Tom—a splendid child. Just a little more than a year old.'

'Well, now!' Hal leaned his shoulders back against the panelled wall of the passageway and let his breath seep slowly from his lungs as he felt a ridiculous sense of relief begin to surge through his body. 'So the child will inherit. He will be Marquis of Burford.'

'Of course. What else?' Nicholas eyed his brother quizzically and then his face cleared, became touched with sardonic humour as he realised. 'You didn't know! The letters after Thomas's marriage never reached you. You thought it had all come to you, the title and the inheritance, didn't you?'

'Yes.' Hal closed his eyes at the enormous sense of release from an existence that had taken on the weight of a life sentence. 'Yes, I did.'

'And are mightily relieved that it does not.' Nicholas took Hal's arm in a sympathetic grasp to urge him in the direction of the library and the brandy.

'More than mightily. It is something I would never wish for. I will happily be a trustee for the infant, but Marquis of Burford? Not to my taste at all. In America I am now used to being Mr Faringdon. And I like it.'

'Still the Republican, I see.' Nick's tone was dry, with more than a hint of amusement. 'But you are safe from the inheritance. We sent to tell you of the marriage, of course, not so long after you left. The letters must have gone astray.'

'Easy enough to do. They never reached me. I had no idea.' Hal was still half-inclined not to believe this stroke of fortune. 'Why did Thomas not tell me of his intentions before I left? I thought we were close enough. If he took a bride so soon after I took ship, surely he had already met the lady!'

Nick grinned. 'I think not, from what I remember. It must have been love at first sight. Or at least a sufficiently strong attraction. Not that you would have noticed particularly—our brother was never one to wallow in sentiment, as you know—but Thomas would have a quick betrothal and carried it all off with high-handed determination.'

'It must have been a shattering experience for him, to have fallen in love so completely.' Hal frowned a little. The picture did not quite fit with his knowledge of Thomas, his brother's over-riding interest in sport and hunting to the exclusion of almost ev-erything else.

'I know it does not sound like the Thomas we knew.' Nick shrugged in agreement, reading his brother's thoughts with un-nerving accuracy. 'But come. We will postpone the brandy and I will introduce you to the Widow. I warn you, she is taking Thomas's death hard, but she is very resilient and will come about. I expect that she will be in the blue withdrawing-room with her mother and the baby at this time of day.'

'Then lead on.'

They walked through the house in close accord, Hal's light-ness of spirit, in spite of the untimely death of his brother, a shin-ing bright strand woven through the dark skein of grief. He would not have to inherit the estates and the title. Thank God! He could return to his dealings in America with a clear con-science, leaving the care of the property with his fellow trustee Nicholas, who had no objection to rural life. The direction of his life had suddenly come back into clear focus, an enormous weight lifted from his mind. He was all set to be appreciative of and everlastingly thankful to his new sister-in-law who had pro-duced so timely an heir.

'What is she like?' he asked Nick as they climbed the main staircase. 'Is she pretty? Amenable?'

'Not so. She is a Beauty. A Diamond of the First Water! Thomas showed far more taste than I would ever have given him credit for. But you will soon see for yourself.'

Nicholas opened the door into the blue withdrawing-room, a light attractive space with azure silk hangings that matched and complimented the fashionable blue-and-silver-striped wallpaper. The room had, Hal noted, been newly refurbished, remembering the previous drab greens and ochres of his mother's occupancy.

A fire in the hearth beckoned. Sun glinted on the delicate crystal chandelier and the polished surface of a small piano. It was undoubtedly a lady's room, a lady of style and exquisite taste.

And the tableau within the room that met the critical gaze of the two men was equally attractive. A young woman was seated on the rug before the fire, her black silk skirts of deepest mourning spread around her. A baby in the experimental stage of crawling was in the act of reaching up to take a red ball from his mother's hands, then tried to stuff the soft felt into his mouth. A grey kitten curled at their side. The lady laughed at her son, face alight with pride and delight in his achievements; she reached forwards to pick him up and cuddle him against her breast, pressing her lips against his dark curls. The baby chucked and grasped her fashionable ringlets with small but ruthless fingers.

It was a scene to entrance even the hardest of heart.

Then the lady looked round at the opening of the door.

'Eleanor! I though we would find you here,' Nicholas began. 'Can I introduce you…'

The tension in the room was suddenly palpable. It tightened, brittle as wire, sharp as a duelling sword, in the space of a heartbeat. The kitten arched in miniature and silent fury at the appearance of the inquisitive spaniel. The newly widowed Marchioness of Burford, always pale of complexion, became paper white, expressive eyebrows arched, eyes widening with shock, as they fixed on the gentlemen at the door. Her smile of delight for her baby vanished, leaving her still and wary. Lord Henry Faringdon simply froze on the spot, every sense coated in ice, spine rigid. His breath backed up in his lungs.

Nicholas looked from Eleanor to Hal and back again. What in the Devil's name was wrong here? He had no idea.

For an endless moment Nicholas stood uncertain between the two, his introduction brought to an abrupt and uncomfortable halt. He looked towards Eleanor where she still knelt on the rug for some illumination, brows raised. Once pale, her face was now flushed with bright colour, but he could not read the expression that flitted momentarily across her expressive features. Embarrassment? Perhaps. A flash of anger? But that seemed unlikely in the circumstances. It did not seem to Nicholas that it was grief. There was no enlightenment to be had here.

Meanwhile Hal, he noted, had no expression at all! His face was shuttered, unreadable, his eyes hooded, an expression Nicholas recognised with a touch of trepidation from their childhood and adolescence. His brother was a past master at disguising his thoughts and feelings if he chose to do so and could quickly retreat into icy hauteur. His lips were now firmly compressed. If he had been about to say something on his entrance, he had clearly changed his mind. He continued to stand, rooted to the spot, the open door at his back.

Nicholas gave up and, for better or worse, completed the formal introduction.

'Eleanor. You must know that this is my brother, Henry. He received our sad news at last and is come to… Well, he is here, for which I am relieved.' The bland stare from the Marchioness gave him no encouragement to continue. Hal's enigmatic silence was no better. 'Hal…this is Eleanor, Thomas's wife.'

The silence stretched. The tension held.

Then good manners reasserted themselves as if an invisible curtain had been lifted. The lady placed the child back on the rug and rose to her feet with graceful composure, shaking out her ruffled skirts. Hal walked forward and bowed as the lady executed a neat curtsy and extended her hand in dignified welcome. He took it and raised it to his lips. All formal courtesy, appropriate to the occasion, all social graces smoothly applied. So why did Nicholas still feel that the banked emotion in the room could explode at any moment and shatter them to pieces?

'My lady. I am pleased to make your acquaintance, but I regret the occasion. May I express my condolences. Your loss must be very great, as is mine.'

'Thank you, my lord. Your good wishes are most acceptable. I miss your brother sorely. You must know that I have received all possible support and kindness from your family.'

All that was proper was expressed with cool, precise formality. *But it was all wrong.*

At their feet the child, tired of the red ball and lack of attention, began to fret and whimper. The lady immediately stooped and lifted him.

'This is Thomas's son.' The Marchioness turned the baby in her arms towards the visitors.

Against his will Henry was drawn to approach the child. The Faringdon line had bred true again. The infant had thick, dark curls, which would probably straighten with age. And one day when the chubbiness of babyhood had passed, he would have the fine straight nose and sharply defined cheekbones of his father. Already the dark brows were clear, arching with ridiculous elegance in the infant face. But the eyes. They were not true. They were hers, his mother's. As clear as the finest glass, as luminous as costly amethysts. The baby smiled and crowed at the attention, stretching out a hand to the newcomer. He had a dimple, Hal noticed inconsequentially as he allowed the baby to grasp his own fingers, smiling against all his intentions as they were promptly gnawed by tender gums.

'His name?' Henry had his voice well in hand.

'Thomas.' Eleanor did not. Her voice broke a little. 'He is named for his father.'

Henry stroked the baby's soft hair, his grief for his dead brother swelling in his chest.

Eleanor immediately stepped back with the child, putting a subtle distance between them. 'Forgive me—I am a little over-wrought and the baby will be tired and hungry. If you will excuse me, I will take him to the nursery.'

She turned away abruptly, never once allowing her eyes to meet Lord Henry's, and began to walk towards the door.

'My lady.' Henry's words stopped her, but she did not turn to face them as if the open door was a much-desired means of escape. 'I would request a meeting with you. A matter of business, you understand, as a trustee of the estate.'

'Of course.'

'In an hour, perhaps, if that is to your convenience. In the library.'

'Of course,' she repeated. 'An hour.'

The Marchioness left the room, taking the child with her.

Lord Henry's eyes never left her until her slim figure turned the corner round the sweep of the main staircase.

* * *

It was one of the longest hours of the Marchioness of Burford's life.

After leaving her son with a doting nurserymaid, she paced the fine Aubusson carpet in the library, oblivious to the splendour and comfort around her. The richness of the tapestries that glowed against the panelled wood left her unmoved. The leather bindings of the books with their gold and red tooling might be sumptuous, but failed to catch her eye. The polished oak furniture, well loved by generations of the Faringdon family, went unnoticed. Nor could she sit, not even in a sunny window seat with its view of woods and distant hills and the parterre which she herself was in the process of planting. Nervous tension balled in her stomach. She felt cold, yet her hands were clammy with sweat, even as she wiped them surreptitiously down her black silken skirts.

She had dreaded this meeting, fully aware that it could happen—was almost inevitable to happen—at some time in the future. But she had hoped, prayed even, that it would never come about. Or be so far into the future distance that painful memories would have faded, emotions stilled. And she had deliberately closed her mind to the consequences. But when she had looked up to see him in the doorway, tall and dark and magnificent, it was as if all time had been obliterated. Her heart had leapt. Her pulse quickened and raced before she had sternly reminded herself of the events of the past.

And as she remembered again now, anger flared, all-consuming, raging through her veins so that she trembled with the force of it. He would receive no welcome here from her.

But what would she say to him? Or he to her? On a thought she realised that he was just as shocked as she, more so since he had apparently been unaware of her marriage. At least she had known of the possibility of this meeting and had been able to prepare. From the immediate tensing of his whole body on setting eyes on her, as if facing the barrels of a shotgun, *he* had been stunned.

She laughed with bitter eyes at her own predicament. *You are*

*a fool. You were not prepared at all. It took your breath away to
see him again!*

But now she had her own secrets to keep, whatever her personal inclination in the matter. She took a deep breath to steady
her nerves. There was no room for guilt here. She would keep
those secrets until the day she died. The only one who had shared
them with her, who had understood their significance, was now
dead, and she would keep faith with the vows made.

Eleanor set her mind to rule her heart.

When he came to her she was ready, standing before the long
window, composed, confident, a glossy layer of sophistication.
She would hold this interview on her own terms as Marchioness
of Burford.

He closed the door softly, advanced and stood for a moment.
They might have been strangers, distant acquaintances at the
most, except that at least then he might have put himself out to
be sociable. As it was he looked at her with apparent indifference in his cold grey eyes and the stern set of his mouth.

And surveyed her in a detailed assessment from head to foot
with an arrogance that chilled her blood.

How right Nicholas had been, he thought. The Marchioness
was not pretty. He had forgotten how very beautiful she was.
Heart-stoppingly so. All that glossy brown hair with its autum-
nal tints, caught up in fashionable ringlets. Any red-blooded man
would dream of unpinning it, of allowing it to curl in his hands
or against his lips. He remembered exactly how it had felt. Her
perfect oval face with straight nose and sculpted lips was lovely
indeed. Calm and translucent as a Renaissance Ma-donna—until
he looked at her eyes. Amethyst fire, fringed with dark lashes,
and at this moment blazing with temper and wilful determination. Here was no simpering miss, he acknowledged. The pretty
and naïve debutante of his memory had vanished for ever. She
was tall. Taller than he had remembered, the crown of her head
reaching well past his shoulder. And the black gown, extravagantly fashionable, complimented her elegant figure and the natural cream of her complexion. Assured and polished, she had

grown into her new status since he had known her as Miss Eleanor Stamford. His brother had indeed shown excellent taste in his choice of bride.

Eleanor found herself flushing under the sustained regard. It had the whip of an insult and she raised her chin against it but she would not retaliate. She would not!

The silence between them had lasted too long for social correctness. But when the lady almost felt compelled to break it, it was he who did so.

'My Lady Burford. I believe that you deserve my congratulations as well as my condolences.' He bowed with cold grace. Another calculated insult. 'At least I now know the answer to one of the many unsolved mysteries of this world! I have clearly been lacking in my understanding of the driving ambition of some of the members of your sex. I realise that with any real understanding of human nature, I should have been able to work it out for myself.'

'My lord?'

'You look surprised, my dear Eleanor.' Lord Henry's smile was an essay in contempt. 'It is simply that I now find it perfectly plain why you chose not to respond to my offer of marriage, in spite of your previous…shall I say, *encouragement* of my suit. You had your sights set on a far bigger and more important fish in your small pond. And a far richer one.' The slick of disdain could not quite disguise the underlying pain, but the words had the bite of a lash. '*I* could obviously offer you nothing in comparison. I am sorry that my brother's death has caused all your planning to go awry, my lady! As widow of the Marquis of Burford, your social position will be far less glamorous than you had plotted and planned for—if my brother had had the consideration to live.'

Eleanor found herself unexpectedly speechless.

Whatever she had expected him to say, whatever tone she had expected him to use towards her, it was certainly not this.

'I do not understand. You will have to speak more plainly, my lord.' Eleanor managed with an effort of will to keep her response cool, with none of the confused bewilderment that resulted from his words.

'I admire your composure,' he continued in the same conversational tone, 'but of course you must have anticipated that we would meet again at some point, given the family connection. Unlike myself, who had no notion of what you had achieved in my absence. Did you perhaps expect me to have the supreme good manners not to mention our past dealings? To behave as if nothing untoward had occurred?'

Eleanor reconstructed her thoughts with a little shake of her head, trying to ignore the heavy sarcasm.

'An offer of marriage, you say? You *promised* marriage, certainly. And I believed you. But I never received such an offer. It appeared that you had changed your mind.' She held him in that clear gaze, willing him to deny her challenge. 'I could wish that you had been sensitive enough to inform me of it. Instead you left me, left the country. No word, no explanation. Nothing. I was forced to learn of your departure from elsewhere. I admit, my lord, I had expected better treatment at your hands.'

'You have a short memory, my lady.' He was implacable in his response.

'I have an excellent memory, my lord! I expected to hear from you. You promised that you would write when you had arranged your passage.' Eleanor could hear her voice rising as the past flooded back and she fought hard to keep it controlled. 'And then I was left to learn that you had sailed. To America. With no intention to return in the near future. You obviously had no thought for me at all.'

'I sent you a letter. Telling you when I would sail. Asking you to join me as we had discussed. I gave you time and place.' Lord Henry turned from her to stand before the fireplace, the distance between them a little greater. She was so lovely with the sun gilding her hair in an iconic halo. It would be so easy to believe her. And so disastrous if he allowed himself to do so. Besides, he knew that she lied. He clenched his jaw. 'Don't deny it. I know the message was delivered to your home. The groom I paid to do it confirmed the delivery.'

'I received no such letter.'

'It would certainly be more comfortable for you to hold to that fact, would it not, dear Eleanor?' Lord Henry struggled to keep his tone flat, conversational even. 'I would be the first to agree that such problems arise. It is quite possible for letters to go astray, as I discovered only a few hours ago. After all, I had absolutely no knowledge of Thomas's marriage to you until Nicholas broke the news in the gun room. And yet Thomas had certainly written to inform me of the happy event.' He picked up a fragile porcelain figure of a shepherdess and lamb from the mantelpiece, contemplated for the barest second smashing it on the hearth, replaced it gently with the utmost control in exactly the same spot. 'But I know without any shadow of doubt that *my* letter was delivered to *you,* allowing you all the time you would need to join me at the vessel. My messenger was most reliable, as you could imagine for so important a delivery.'

'Such a letter, if it ever existed, never reached my hands.' She could find nothing other to say in her own defence.

Lord Henry shrugged, a gesture of cynical disbelief. 'If you insist on holding to that, my lady… Tell me. Did you know my brother before I left, or did you wait until I had gone before you put yourself in his way?'

'I…' She could not believe that he had actually said that—that he could think so little of her!

'It would not be very difficult to lure Thomas into marriage,' he continued to taunt her. 'You have a beautiful face, as I know to my cost. And my brother found it easy to trust those he liked.'

'I never lured Thomas!' How could the man whom she had once loved more than life itself be so deliberately vindictive?

'No? But he offered you marriage.'

'Yes. He did.'

'I expect your lady mother was delighted. Your family might be respectable enough, but you had hardly been groomed for the role of Marchioness.' He lifted a hand to sweep the room in an expansive gesture. 'And here you are, mistress of Burford Hall, a town house in the most fashionable part of London and a hunting lodge in Leicestershire. Quite a killing, my lady.'

'Of course. It was more than I could ever have dreamed of.' A frown marred her forehead as she attempted to catch his meaning.

'You must have been astounded at your good fortune. A Marquis as rich as Solomon in all his glory. Instead of a younger son with uncomfortably Republican leanings and an inclination to make his own way in the colonies.'

So! He thought she had callously rejected him in the interest of wealth and social position. She caught her breath at the injustice of the veiled accusation and stepped towards him with an unconcealed passion.

'I would have risked everything to go with you if you had told me!' Her hands curled into fists, at odds with her feminine appearance. 'My home, my family. I would have followed you anywhere. How can you possibly doubt that?'

Lord Henry raised his brows in eloquent disbelief.

'Are you possibly making a play for me again, my lady—now that my brother is dead? Is the role of mother of the heir insufficient for you?' The bitter words were all that he could manage to hide the depth of hurt that still had the power to move him. He had truly thought that it had faded, that he had done with that episode of his life. Now, faced with the reality of her, knowing her rejection, it was as sharp and lethal as ever.

She could hardly comprehend his words. 'How dare you! How dare you suggest something so degrading—so despicable!'

'I dare! I dare do all manner of things!' The past swept back in a submerging wave, allowing anger, frustration, desire, all long subdued, to take hold. A desire to possess her once more filled him and, if he were honest, not a little to punish her for her treachery. She was so beautiful, and she was not his! 'Did you make a good bargain?' His demands evaded his control, even when he saw the hurt in her eyes. 'Could my brother give you pleasure to compare with that which you claimed to find in my arms? Or did you lie to me? And set your teeth when I kissed you or allowed my hands to touch your silken skin? Shall we rediscover what, if anything, was between us?'

He pounced with the lithe strength of a hunting cat on an unsuspecting mouse. His claws might be sheathed, but his dominance was lethal and dangerous none the less. His fine hands grasped her shoulders, holding her when she would have pulled away, but the initial contact startled them both, a tingle of reciprocating fire. He looked down at his hands where they grasped her shoulders. Surely he was over all that. This was not supposed to happen. Not now. Not when he had fought against it for so long, not when he believed her to be guilty of betrayal. He looked up to see her watching him with similar uncertainty, similar shock—but set his mind against it.

He would have taken her mouth with his, hot and demanding, more in punishment than passion, if his attention had not been caught by the jewel that she wore on her breast, a pendant on a fine gold chain. Small and delicate, of no great intrinsic value, yet it was beautiful and wrought by the hand of a craftsman. Its setting was gold filigree, leaves and flowers, the centre of each bloom set with a tiny diamond that glinted in the light with each erratic rise and fall of her breast. The central stone was an amethyst, clear and shining, of a depth of colour that reflected Eleanor's eyes when she was radiantly happy.

But not at this moment, when her furious glare was the stormy intensity of indigo.

'So you still wear it?' Lord Henry's tone was deceptively conversational.

'Yes.'

'It surprises me. Some would say that it was hypocritical not to consign it to the back of a drawer, since you turned your back with such ease on the one who gave it to you.'

'Perhaps, after today, I will.' She almost spat the words, shocked to the core by his accusations. 'I thought the giver had some affection for me, love even. How wrong I was! I should be grateful to you, my lord, for pointing out the error of my ways.' She angled her head, disdain writ large in her slanted glance. 'Perhaps I should return it to you. You may find some other naïve lady of your acquaintance in New York to gift it to.'

His tenuous hold on his temper duly snapped.

And he lowered his head, his eyes all the time on hers, until his mouth, hard and angry, crushed her lips. When she murmured a protest, he immediately raised his head, eyes glittering. 'Had you forgotten, dearest Nell? I thought you had enjoyed it. You did not refuse my kisses in the past.'

He slanted his head to take her mouth again, without kindness or thought for her own wishes, but forcing her lips to part against her teeth. Eleanor stood unresponsive in his hold, until on a breath, and a sob deep in her breast, her resistance melted away, her anger as insubstantial as morning mist. Instead of pushing against his chest to achieve her freedom, her fingers curled into the material of his coat and she clung to him. In response his arms tightened round her until her curves were moulded to his hard length from breast to thigh. Her mouth softened, lips parting of their own free will, to invite invasion. He groaned. And took what she was prepared to give, and more. The fire burned brightly, leaping through their veins with unexpected brilliance and heat, and seared them both.

When he finally released her, the anger had not been assuaged at all, but still surged through his blood, not even calmed when she swayed and would have fallen had she not grasped his forearms for support.

'Well, my lady?' For a brief moment he allowed her to see the temper that burned in his gut. 'What do you think? A title and a fortune balanced against the pleasures of my hands and mouth? I wager that my brother was not lacking in skills of love. But did he satisfy you?' But then the pain in her eyes, sharp and beyond her control, forced him to retreat. 'Perhaps he was kinder than I,' he murmured. 'Perhaps you were wise in your decision after all.'

Confusion swept Eleanor's features as she pushed herself to stand alone. She could not think, could not accept what had just happened between them, what she had allowed to happen. Humiliation brought its warm colour to her throat and cheeks. She veiled her eyes from him with a downsweep of lashes. Perhaps there was the merest sparkle of a tear, but he could not be sure. But it brought him to his senses as assuredly as a deluge of cold water.

'Forgive me. I should not have forced myself on you in that manner. It is unpardonable.' He stepped back from her as disgust rose in his throat at his own temper. And that she should be able to rouse such longings in him again, revealing a weakness that he thought well and truly dead. Disgust at the betrayal of his body, which was hard and demanding for her. He now kept his voice low, but with no warmth in it, simply cold acceptance of the situation. 'You would seem to have a talent for falling on your feet, my lady. I am not available to you. But I should warn you. Keep your clever velvet claws out of Nicholas.'

The lady flinched as if he had slapped her with the outrageous comment. 'I will not continue this conversation.' Eleanor choked on a sob. 'I can only be grateful that fate spared me marriage with you, my lord. I could never have guessed at your capacity for inflicting such pain.' She swept past him, but when she had reached the door his voice stopped her.

'Eleanor?'

'Well?'

'I would be interested to know if you managed to persuade my brother that you were a virgin on your wedding night.'

Her whole body stiffened under the vile cruelty of the attack. She dare not face him again for fear that he would see the tears that had begun to track down her cheeks.

'The matter is entirely none of your affair,' she managed in a voice little more than a whisper.

'Of course not, my dear. You are not my affair any longer. And I thank heaven for it. And by the by, there is no need for you to be concerned. I shall not divulge our sordid little secret to anyone. I believe it is not to the credit of either of us. We must preserve your spotless reputation at all cost, must we not?'

On which vicious parting shot, the composure of the Marchioness of Burford finally disintegrated. She wrenched open the library door to hurry from the room, slamming it forcefully in Lord Henry's face.

His lordship merely stood, head bowed, eventually returning to stare blindly into the empty fire-grate, until moved to kick viciously against a half-charred log with his booted foot.

Well done indeed!

His intention had been to pursue the interview with icy and disinterested detachment. So how the Devil had he allowed him-

self to make such unwarrantable comments? To inflict such blatant intimacies on her, uncaring of her wishes in the matter? A
despicable act, unworthy of his birth and upbringing. Conflict-
ing emotions and images warred within his brain. Of course she
deserved every accusation. Had she not rejected and humiliated
him, casting his love into the gutter as so much worthless trash?
Her promises of love, protestations of devotion and a willingness
to throw in her lot with him, had been shallow and empty. Instead, she had chosen worldly ambition. How fickle women
were! And yet…the horror in her face when he had accused her
of perfidy demanded his attention. The hesitation in her voice.
The tightening of the muscles along her jaw as she had striven,
unsuccessfully in the end, to prevent tears gathering in those glorious eyes, spilling down her cheeks. She had not been unmoved
by his words. Or by his demands on her body. He closed his eyes
as he remembered the scent of her hair, the taste of her lips as
they responded to his insistent possession. But then, women
were skilled actresses after all.

But what did it matter? Lord Henry straightened, stretching,
allowing the muscles in his shoulders to relax as his pulse slowed.
He had not realised that he had been so tense. He walked slowly
to follow the Marchioness from the library. It was all in the past.
She had what she wanted. The inheritance was secure with an heir,
albeit very young. Nicholas would more than willingly play the
interested uncle and trustee. He was now free to return to America and wash his hands of the whole situation in England unless
something unforeseen arose to demand his presence in the future.
He need trouble himself no further over Eleanor Faringdon.

And in the short time remaining to him here at Burford Hall,
he would treat her with all that damnable courtesy and good manners worthy of a gentleman. Whatever the cost!

Chapter Three

Lord Henry Faringdon settled back into life at Burford Hall in the following days with consummate ease. Casting an eye over the splendid horseflesh in the stables, he chose himself a handsome bay hunter and rode the familiar estate with Nicholas.

'This is all very impressive, little brother. The livestock looks well. And you have drained the lower pastures at last, I see. Your doing or Thomas's?'

Nicholas laughed, the shadows of bereavement lifting in response to the bright spring sunshine and physical exertion of a gallop across the open parkland. 'Do I need to say it? I may be the *little brother,* but I have an eye to the future of the family. Thomas, as you are well aware, only had an eye to the next run of the fox in winter, or the next winner at Newmarket in summer. Or a flirtation with the prettiest girl in the room.' His smile became tinged with sadness as the loss was driven home by the memories, and he changed the subject. 'The stone quarry has been developed since your day, Hal. We have improved the surface on some of the roads. And we are beginning to manage the old woodland for timber.'

Hal snorted. 'Very efficient! I will leave all such matters to you.'

Nicholas was silent for a moment as they reined in their horses to take in the fine view of the lower lake with its ornamental planting. Then he fixed his brother with a determined eye.

'Hal. I know that you can tell me it is none of my affair—but is anything wrong?'

'How do you mean?' Henry betrayed nothing by glance or voice. 'I am aware of nothing. Apart from having to share the breakfast table with Alicia Stamford and her interminable opinions on every topic under the sun. She is enough to make a saint swear—and I am no saint!'

Nick grimaced in sympathy, but refused to be put off.

'I don't know what it is, but between you and Eleanor I sense unease, some distance between you. More than that, in fact—a definite lack of…of *tolerance.*'

'How so?' Hal's expression became even more bland.

'I don't know.' Nicholas rubbed his chin with his gloved fist. 'It is nothing that you say or do. Just that—you don't seem to like each other very much. And you seem to have deliberately kept out of her way—and she out of yours.'

Henry kept his gaze fixed on the landscape, lifting his shoulders in the lightest of shrugs. 'I was not aware. Perhaps Lady Burford is just wary of men, after Thomas's death.'

'There, you see. You are all cold formality, using her title. And I had not thought that she was wary. Nell is usually approachable and friendly enough.'

Henry shook his head, teeth clenched. Nicholas had called her Nell! A spark of jealousy gripped him before he could curse himself for a fool. Such suspicions were totally unfounded as he knew very well. And what was it to him? The Marchioness was free to give her affections where she chose.

He deliberately turned the conversation back to the engaging topic of the merits of growing beet for the overwintering of cattle, leaving Nicholas with a clear conviction that his question had been adroitly evaded.

Henry's relationship with Mrs Alicia Stamford, Eleanor's ever-present mama, edged to the glacial. They were scrupulously polite to each other with no direct reference made to the circumstances of their previous encounters, when he had been regarded by her as a most unsatisfactory suitor to her beautiful daughter.

The rules were clearly laid down between them during their first meeting after Henry's arrival.

'Lord Henry. We are pleased to see you back in England.' Mrs Stamford forced her lips into the semblance of a smile and inclined her head with condescending grace, as she smoothed her satin skirts and arranged the costly and delicate shawl round her shoulders in more becoming folds. She had been a beautiful woman in her youth, shadows of it still there in the rich auburn of her hair and her elegant figure. But advanced hypochondria and a fierce ambition dedicated to ensuring the social advancement of her daughter had taken its toll. Her once-porcelain skin was now finely lined, her complexion sallow. Her husband, a country gentleman of comfortable means but no social pretensions, had been dead some dozen years. The lady was now intent on enjoying her freedom and elevated status as mother to the Marchioness of Burford, secure in the knowledge that she lived at one of the best addresses in town and had the means to trick herself out in the latest fashions.

'Thank you, ma'am.' Lord Henry raised her cold fingers to his lips with impeccable finesse. 'I see that you remember me.'

'Of course, my lord.' A flush stained her thin features. 'I remember making your acquaintance in London during my daughter's first Season.'

'But our acquaintance, as I recall, was of very short duration.' *Since you did everything in your power to keep Eleanor out of my path!*

'You were very keen to seek your fortune in America, my lord, as I recall. I trust that matters went well for you.'

'They did.'

'And how long do you plan to remain here at Burford Hall?' *A matter of days, I sincerely trust!*

'I have not yet decided.'

'I am sure the estate can manage well enough without your involvement, if business demands your presence elsewhere.' Her lips curled unpleasantly that he might be engaged in something so common as *business,* no matter how lucrative. 'Nicholas has proved himself an excellent trustee for my grandson. And Mr Hoskins, of course.'

'I am sure he has. But it my inclination to remain here for a little while.'

Which was about as much as they could find to say to each other. Henry smiled and bowed. Mrs Stamford inclined her head once more. They understood each other very well.

And Nicholas, with half an ear to the exchange, was left with the uneasy impression that there was something here which he had missed, of which he was unaware. Conversation with Nell's mama was always an adventure, bordering on the brittle. Opinionated, critical, frequently acerbic and intolerant, she took no prisoners. But here… Nick could not quite put his finger on it. The sneer on Mrs Stamford's face, the edge to her voice as the exchange drew to a close could have cut through flesh and bone. And as for Hal… There was no love lost here, despite the exquisite politeness of the little episode. But short of asking either combatant outright… One glance at the closed expressions, the barely veiled hostility, convinced Nick that no man of sense or with an eye to self-preservation would risk such a foolhardy move.

In spite of Nell's determination to keep her mind on more important issues, her thoughts betrayed her with cruel persistence. And her dreams. She relived again and again that magical Season when her mother and an aged uncle had launched her into society, the only season which was possible, given their financial circumstances. Her mother had been intent on a good match, as advantageous a marriage as could be achieved. Once she had met Lord Henry Faringdon, Eleanor had thoughts for no one else.

It was at a soirée, at the home of a distant cousin who mixed in the most fashionable of circles, an ideal opportunity for Eleanor to meet the privileged members of the *haut ton*. Her mother had managed to pull strings to achieve invitations. Eleanor could remember the occasion in perfect detail when she dared allow her mind free rein. Sitting in her bedroom with her son on her lap, she abandoned her attempts to discipline her memories and simply let them sweep back unhindered, layer upon layer. The decorations of hothouse flowers with the intense perfume of jasmine and heliotrope. The music and dancing. And the dress she wore for the occasion. White muslin as would become a débutante with a delicately embroidered hem and silver ribbons at waist and neckline. Her hair in high-pinned ringlets, falling to her shoulders, and a string of pearls, the only jewellery she possessed.

And she had seen *him* that night. He had entered the room with his brother, the Marquis, but Eleanor had eyes for no one but Lord Henry. The Marquis, for all his consequence and good looks, might not have existed. Lord Henry filled her vision and her senses. Tall, dark of hair, handsome of face, elegant of figure, impossibly attractive in the formal splendid of black satin evening clothes and white linen. They were introduced. They stood up for a country dance. And her heart was lost before she could take a breath, somewhere between the cotillion and a reel.

Her smile was wry, a little sad, as she recalled that heady moment. The merest touch of his hand had quickened her pulse and when his lips had brushed her fingers she knew that she was his for ever.

Disastrously, she was now forced to admit, Eleanor had believed that he was as captivated as she. What a fool she had been! Carried away by the romance of snatched meetings, the delicious duplicity of a few stolen moments of time when they could close out the world. She had listened to his dreams of a new life, fired by his ideas and ambitions. She had believed in him. Trusted. They would go together.

And then he had simply left her with not one word of explanation or farewell. Humiliated and heartbroken, she had hidden her grief, determined not to be an object of interest or pity. Her pride and her spirit had come to her aid when she might have been totally devastated, and she had survived. With the kindness and compassion of Thomas. Dear Thomas. But she had learned in those cold days after Lord Henry's departure that there was a high price to pay for love and she would not willingly pay it again. To show emotion, to offer love, was to put yourself into the power of those to whom it was given. And when it was not returned…

Eleanor shuddered as she remembered the exact occasion of her open avowal of love and commitment to Hal, when a soft moon illuminated the summer house, casting deep and intimate shadows within, painting the leaves of the overhanging willow that enclosed them with silver hue.

When Thomas had offered marriage, her gratitude knew no bounds. She could not love him—he both knew and accepted that. She had never tried to dissemble or pretend to an emotion that was now beyond her capabilities. Deep affection, yes, without doubt. And trust. But love…that was not possible. And he in his turn had offered her friendship, kindness, respect, a marriage based on compassion and understanding. No promises of blazing passion. But she could—indeed, wished to—live without that, and had done so comfortably for two whole years. Why was love considered necessary to achieve a satisfying marriage? When Thomas had taken her to his bed and made her truly his wife he had possessed her with such grace and sensitivity, with a depth of care and tenderness that she still felt she did not deserve. He had quite determinedly allowed no room for either discomfort or embarrassment on her part, enfolding her in warmth and a gentle humour. Her heart swelled, tears threatened as she recalled those painful early days when Thomas had set himself to comfort and reassure. And she, in recognition of her debt to him, had set herself to be a good wife and mother, equally determined that Thomas should never fault her or regret the decision that he had made that desperate day when she had visited him at Faringdon House in London to cast herself on his mercy.

Eleanor, allowing her gaze to rest for a long moment on the miniature of Thomas which stood on her nightstand, believed in all honesty that she had kept her bargain and would mourn her husband's death with genuine grief for the loss of the dearest of friends.

All passion in her life was dead.

If only Hal had not touched her beyond a formal gesture of greeting. If only he had not kissed her, held her in his arms. And she had responded, encouraged him. And wanted him. She felt the heat rise in her cheeks as her senses relived the moment.

Eleanor straightened her shoulders and lectured herself with stern words. Lord Henry must never be given the opportunity to reawaken the passion. It would—it *must*—remain dead and buried. He must never know what she had suffered for his rejection. For the future, she would tolerate her mother's well-meaning interference and devote her life to raising her beloved son. She would find enjoyment and fulfilment in that. She dashed the tears from her cheeks with an impatient hand. Of course she would. She buried her face in her son's dark curls.

On a parallel course, though both would have denied it, Henry, too, found his thoughts returning far too often for comfort to those days when he had met and loved Miss Eleanor Stamford. His courtship of her had been carried on under the most difficult of circumstances, not least the suspicious glare of her mother who desired a far better marriage for her beautiful daughter. Lord Henry, although his birth might be impeccable, was a loose cannon with a desire to make his own way in the world and an uncomfortable lack of consideration for social standing and protocol. Mrs Stamford had watched him like a mother hawk, intent on defending her chick. But he and Eleanor had found the means to meet and the memories were bittersweet.

By God, he had loved her! And believed beyond doubt that she had loved him. Enough to disobey her exacting parent and travel to the new world where they would marry and make a life not bound by rigid convention. He had sworn his undying love, sweeping her along with his dreams of the future. Made preparations. Sent to tell her of the time and place of their sailing. And waited in vain on the windswept dock as the Captain made ready to sail.

No message. No note. Nothing. The minutes had ticked by, his idealistic hopes fading with every beat of his heart, yet still trying to believe that she would arrive at the eleventh hour. And then he could pretend no more. They needed to catch the tide and he had sailed alone. He had risked one further letter when he had landed, but received nothing in return.

So Mr Henry Faringdon had set himself to building his future alone, finding the time to curse Eleanor and all women for their capricious and inconstant nature. Without doubt, she had enjoyed the romance and the excitement of his wooing, been flattered by his declaration of love, but had no intention of keeping her own promises.

Perhaps she had enjoyed the power of having him at her feet. Henry grimaced at his youthful naïvety, his black brows snapping into a firm line. Very well. He too had learnt a hard lesson and would not in his lifetime forget the painful wounds. And it would not be something that he would put himself in the way of repeating.

Thus in his dealings with women since, trust and loyalty were never an issue. Definitely not love! He kept a mistress in some comfort and enjoyed her many talents, but it was a casual arrangement, both sides enjoying the benefits but recognising the lack of commitment.

He now smiled at the thought of her accommodating bed and welcoming arms. Rosalind gave him the pleasures of light conversation, feminine company and the soft delights of her body, with no demands on his time or emotions other than those he was prepared to give. He gave her financial security—and presumably some passing pleasure. But on that windswept dock as the *England's Glory* prepared to sail from Liverpool to New York, he had vowed that he would never again give his heart and soul to any woman.

He might marry in future, of course. But he saw it as a business transaction only to achieve an heir. He would never allow memories of Eleanor Stamford to cloud his judgement or unsettle his peace of mind.

Now, back at Burford Hall, where he must see his nemesis every day, Henry closed his mind against the image of the girl who had stolen his heart, against remembering the soft seductiveness of her lips against his, her delectable curves as he drew her close to imprint her body with his own. And he found a need to discover any excuse against spending time where she might be found in the house. But he could not prevent Nell from haunting him in his dreams with her shy smile and delicious perfume, her hair unbound in glorious disorder in his hands.

He should never have allowed himself to kiss her, to reawaken the desires and needs that now snapped at him with sharp teeth.

He set his teeth against the vivid intrusion and snarled at his valet after another restless night.

On a bright morning Lord Henry, this time alone, made a private and intensely painful visit to the church of St Mary the Virgin, which served the spiritual needs of the estate and the small village of Burford. There in the graveyard, dark head bowed, he stood beside a new grave, the turned earth still raw, although now softened with a faint sheen of spring grass. A simple plinth had been erected, its clean lines topped by a classical urn. The words and dates that recorded the life of his brother were sharply incised, all very proper and tasteful, but telling nothing of the vibrant life of the young man who lay beneath the earth in untimely death. Sorrow clawed at Henry's heart, regrets flooded his mind. It felt, as the sun warmed his skin and the dappled shadows from the elm trees flirted playfully across the mown grass, that he had lost a part of himself, which it would never be possible to recover. With a gentle finger he traced the letters. The depths of the tearing grief that stopped his throat and stung his eyes shocked him as he damned the monstrous twist of fate that had robbed his brother of his life.

But at least Thomas had left a son, to carry on his blood line and the family name, so that there might always be a Faringdon living at Burford House. It was some comfort, Henry supposed, as he brushed the smooth curve of the urn. It must be.

As he would have turned away, his loss in no way assuaged, his attention was drawn to the fresh posy of primroses arranged at the foot of the plinth.

Eleanor's work? Henry hoped so. His lips curved with a cynical edge as he remounted his horse, turned his back on the calm tranquillity of the dead. Whatever motives had driven Eleanor to reject his own love, to send her headlong into marriage with Thomas, he hoped that in the end she had cared for his brother more than a little.

At the beginning of the second week, the family gathered in the dining room for a late luncheon. During the first course of a

range of cold cuts of meat, Lord Henry took the unusual opportunity to address himself directly to Lady Burford across the table.

'You should know, ma'am, that I have arranged passage for
America. I shall leave next week.'

'So soon?' Eleanor's gaze moved from her plate to his eyes
and she lifted her napkin to lips gone suddenly dry.

'Why not?' His face held no warmth, but perhaps a little surprise in the consternation that he read in Eleanor's momentarily
unguarded expression. 'My business will not prosper in my absence, whereas you do not need my help here. Nick is more than
capable and far more interested in developing the land than I. And
Hoskins has his finger on all the legal niceties. The inheritance
and your jointure are secure, ma'am. There is nothing to keep
me here.'

'Very well. I...we shall be sorry to see you go, of course.' Her
tone was low with no inflection but, to his disappointment, her
gaze now quickly fell before his. She rarely allowed herself to
look directly at him so that he had presumed her uninterest. And
yet he realised, beyond any sort of logic, that he had been hoping that she would care. It seemed from her reply that she did
not. He allowed himself a sardonic smile at his foolishness. If
Eleanor had been prepared to reject his offer two years previously
in the face of better prospects, she would hardly show any concern for his presence—or his absence—now.

But, on hearing Hal's announcement, Nell's heart had fallen
to the region of her fine kid slippers, her nerves skittering like
mice in an underdrawing. She did not want him to go. She was
afraid of him, of her reactions to him, but she did not want him
to leave Burford Hall.

Mrs Stamford took up the conversation, breaking in to her
daughter's distraught train of thought. 'I am sure that life in
America has much to entice you to return, my lord. And I expect
there are friends who will be missing you.'

'It has indeed. And, yes, there are some who will have
missed me.'

Eleanor heard and came to her own conclusions. Of course.
She should have realised. Her heart sank even lower, if that were

possible. There was nothing to hold him in England. And there would be a lover waiting for him there, a woman who loved him and fretted for his return. A woman who was without doubt beautiful and who enjoyed the intimate attention of his mouth and hands. Her own hands clenched on her knife and fork. Of course he would wish to go back. How ridiculous to think that he would even consider her own needs. Not that she had any true idea of what they might be!

She put down the knife and fork, the slices of chicken untasted, her appetite suddenly gone. And began a detailed conversation with her mama with respect to a planned visit to a neighbouring family during the afternoon. Should they take the landaulet or the barouche? And what was the possibility of inclement weather?

And Hal bitterly accepted that, yes, there was nothing to keep him at Burford Hall.

The plates from the cold collation had hardly been cleared from the table and dishes of fresh fruit and cheese set out when Marcle entered to approach Lady Burford.

'My lady. There are a lady and gentleman come here.' He frowned his disapproval of such lax adherence to acceptable visiting hours.

Eleanor raised her brows a little in some surprise. 'Now is not a very convenient time, Marcle. Perhaps you could show them to the red parlour and supply them with refreshment. We shall be finished here in half an hour.'

Marcle persisted, if reluctantly. 'The gentleman apologises for the unwarranted interruption, but claims urgent business. Of a highly personal nature, which requires immediate attention from your ladyship.'

'I see. Who is he? Do we know him?'

'Sir Edward Baxendale, my lady.' Marcle presented a neat visiting card on a silver salver. 'And Miss Baxendale, his sister, I believe.'

Eleanor looked at the tasteful lettering on the card and then across the table to Nicholas, who was in deep and detailed conversation with Henry about the merits of a favourite hunter. 'Do we know a Sir Edward Baxendale, Nicholas? Does he live locally? I think I have not heard that name, but he might be one of the hunting fraternity. In which case you will be acquainted at least.'

Nick shook his head. 'There is no one of that name who lives in this part of the county, I am sure.' He looked to his brother for confirmation. Henry shook his head, uninterested.

Eleanor decided. 'Very well. Since it is an urgent matter…' She nodded to her butler. 'Show them in, if you please.'

Within minutes, Marcle ushered the visitors into the dining room.

'Sir Edward Baxendale and Miss Baxendale, my lady.'

The gentleman was a man in his early thirties, perhaps a little older than Hal, of medium height and stocky build. Eleanor gained a general impression of quiet elegance and understated fashion in his clothing and appearance. He was without doubt a gentleman of some means. The lady who accompanied him was younger, slight of build, clothed in black as if recently bereaved, but again with a distinct air of fashion. Behind them came a young woman, clearly a companion or governess from her plain and serviceable dress, carrying a young child who squirmed to be set on his feet.

The gentlemen bowed. The ladies curtsied. Marcle hovered with interest in the background.

'Well, Sir Edward. What is this personal business that cannot wait?' Eleanor smiled to put the visitors at their ease. 'Perhaps we can offer you a glass of wine. If you would care to sit—'

'Forgive me, your ladyship, my lords.' The gentleman bowed to the assembled company, face grave, politely deferential but firm. 'I would not normally arrive on your doorstep without due notice. But this is not a social visit. Time is, I believe, of the essence. And what I have to say will certainly, I fear, be distasteful to you.' He allowed his gaze to linger on the faces around the table, his own face and voice strained with compassion.

'Then in what way can we be of help?' Eleanor approached the little group, now with some concern, noting that the young woman was nervous and kept her eyes fixed on Sir Edward, as if for guidance or reassurance.

'I fear that we are come here in some way under false pretences. This is my sister, Octavia.' He took the hand of the young woman beside him to lead her forward. 'She *was* Miss Baxendale. She is now, I must inform you, Octavia Faringdon, wife of the lately deceased Thomas Faringdon, and has been so for the past three years. She is the lawful Marchioness of Burford. And this child—' he indicated with a glance behind him '—is their son, John. Heir to the title and Faringdon estates. I believe, madam, sirs, that we have much to discuss.' Sir Edward bowed again and waited to see the impact of his declaration.

The silence that hung in the room was painful in its intensity, as enveloping as the cloud of dust motes that drifted around them in the sun's rays.

Until Mrs Stamford grasped the edge of the table and pushed herself to her feet in outrage. 'A marriage? Thomas's wife? I have never heard such disgraceful nonsense in all my life!' She glanced fiercely at her daughter. 'If I were in your shoes, Lady Burford, I would have nothing to do with this scandalous claim. It is my belief that it is merely a charade on the part of these…these *people,* to get their hands on the Faringdon fortune.' She paused to cast a look of pure disdain towards the pair, her lips curled in what, in a less well-bred lady, would have been seen as a sneer. 'If I were you, I would have Marcle show these impostors the door, on the instant!'

The company, robbed of any desire for further social platitudes, or to sample the fine array of cheese and fruit set out on the dining table, repaired immediately to the blue withdrawing-room in stunned and uncomfortable silence.

'Perhaps you would be so good as to explain your astounding claims, Sir Edward,' Lord Henry requested with remarkable calm.

The gentleman was now seated on the silk-covered sofa, his sister beside him, palpably uncomfortable with hands clasped tightly in her lap. Their companion chose to take the child into the window embrasure, away from the heart of the crisis, to look out at the park and gardens and be entertained. Eleanor had lowered herself to an oval-backed chair as if she did not trust her legs to support her. Nicholas stood behind her, Mrs Stamford took a seat at her side. Lord Henry, either deliberately or through natural inclination, took a position of authority before the fireplace. When thoughts and impressions ran riot, spiking the air with nerve-jangling tension, he took command in a cool, unemotional fashion and broached the shattering development.

'We would all be grateful if you would explain the circumstances of this supposed marriage. My family, as you must be aware, is ignorant of its very existence.'

'Of course, my lord. I can understand why you might consider it all a matter of pretence and artifice. This is not an easy situation and not one that I would naturally seek. Forgive me, my lady.' Sir Edward bowed his head to Eleanor, clear blue eyes guileless and full of compassion. She watched him with a mind frozen in disbelief, the fragile skin stretched over her cheekbones, tight with fear. It was as if his voice came from a great distance, but anguish gripped her heart at what he might say.

'My sister came out four years ago with a Season in London,' he began to explain. 'She was very young, but my mother was alive then and wished to see her daughter well established. Octavia met Burford during the Season. And then later in the summer months when we spent a few short weeks at Brighton. It is very simple. They met and fell in love, as young people may do on such occasions.' He smiled understandingly down at his sister, who continued to sit, head bent, fingers worrying at her reticule. 'And they were married, quietly, in Whitchurch, the village where we have our small estate. Their child, John, was born there the following year.'

The information, clearly and lucidly delivered, dropped into the atmosphere as hollowly as pebbles into the depths of a well. Mrs Stamford found herself lost for words.

'But why was it not made public at the time?' Lord Henry frowned as he weighed the details. 'Why did we not know of this marriage? Why did my brother not bring the lady home as his bride? I can think of no reason why he should need to keep this marriage a secret from his family and the world.'

'I know not, my lord, but Burford spoke of family disapproval. We were not to know the truth of it.' Sir Edward lifted his hands in acceptance of a difficult situation and the lowered them to cover those of his sister in warm comfort. 'My sister presumed that your family would not accept his marriage to a lady of so little social consequence. Our family is respectable enough, of course, but we have never aimed to the heights of the *haut ton*. And to enter into marriage with the Marquis of Burford was beyond her dreams, even as a young girl who did not know the ways of society.'

Henry turned his attention to the lady who sat silently, eyes on her clasped fingers. 'Is this so? Did Thomas indeed marry you, then hide you away in—where was it?—Whitchurch?'

'Yes, my lord.' She raised her eyes, not flinching as they met such stern questioning. 'Thomas and I…we fell in love and he wished to marry me, in spite of his family, he said. So we should keep it secret, he said, and I agreed. I was very young, you see, and knew no better.'

'Then why did you say nothing when my brother entered into a second marriage with…with Miss Stamford?' Incredulity coloured Henry's question. 'Surely it is beyond belief that you should simply accept such a development.' *And why in heaven's name would Thomas have done such a thing?*

'That was a mistake on my part, I confess.' Sir Edward came to his sister's rescue, taking her hand again and holding it in a warm clasp. 'My sister was very foolish and, I do not hesitate to say, is easily led. She was given to understand that his marriage to Miss Stamford—' he inclined his head towards Eleanor with grave respect '—was a matter of necessity, desired and encouraged by his family. Burford asked that Octavia keep the matter of her own marriage quiet in return for a substantial annuity settled on herself and the child. I could not persuade her otherwise. She insisted on doing what Burford wished. But now she has seen that much is due to her and wishes to make everything plain.' He smiled down at the young woman who coloured prettily and returned his clasp, nodding her agreement.

'But if he loved you and had married you, regardless of…of

the differences in your social rank,' Eleanor spoke at last to the fair lady, 'and since you had presented him with a son and heir— why would my Lord Burford consider the complications of a second marriage to me? It does not make any sense! Most particularly as—' She closed her lips into a thin line, unable to continue. *Particularly as my birth and the social status of my own family is no better!* It simply did not make any logical sense.

'My lady…' Sir Edward hesitated, all deference and concern. 'I cannot tell you… Perhaps you are the only one here who might know the reason for such an unfortunate decision.'

'But why wait to make any claim until now?' Mrs Stamford interrupted, impatient as she pinned the fair couple with an eagle stare, clearly not believing a word of Sir Edward's explanation. 'My lord has been dead for four months. Why did you not speak on hearing of his death? It has been no secret, after all.'

Sir Edward turned to face the lady with calm purpose. 'We knew of Burford's death, of course. A great shock to us all. We expected that Octavia would have been considered in the will. And that clear provision would have been made for the child— who, after all, is the heir. And so we waited in anticipation. But there was no word from the lawyers, there was no settlement for Octavia or for the child.' His voice hardened and looked down at his sister's face with concern. 'As the will stands, she has been left with no income, no security…no recognition of her position as Burford's wife. That is not right, as I am sure you will agree.' His gaze swept his audience. 'She deserves what is rightfully hers after three years of neglect, of being forced to live as if she had a guilty secret. I have persuaded her to come here today to lay the truth before you, knowing that you will not allow her to go unheard. She must receive what is due to her under the law.'

'Is this indeed so?' Eleanor appealed to the young woman who sat so blamelessly in her withdrawing-room and threatened to destroy her whole life.

'Yes, my lady.'

'Did you love him?' *And what a ridiculously inconsequential question that is!*

'Yes. I did. And he loved me. He told me so.'

'Did he…did he visit you often in Whitchurch?'

'When he could. It was not always easy.'

Eleanor's blood ran cold from her lips to the tips of her fingers. Was that why Thomas had been prepared to enter into a loveless marriage with her? Because it would have given her the protection she needed? And, more importantly, because he had already given his heart elsewhere so a union without love was of no consequence? It could be so. It could all be terribly true. The thought struck her with terrifying power. But why did he agree to marry her at all if he was already legally bound? The cool voice of common sense impressed itself on her mind, insisting that she listen to its reasoned tones. Surely Thomas, whom she had respected and married, could never have taken a decision so unworthy of a man of honour. Eleanor no longer knew what to think.

'Forgive me, Sir Edward, if I put this bluntly.' Henry broke into her thoughts. 'Is there any reason we should believe this remarkable claim?'

'Of course.' Sir Edward released Octavia's hand and stood, a deliberate confrontation now. 'I am not so foolish as to believe that you would accept my sister's claim without legal proof. I have it. I have with me the proof of the marriage of my sister and your brother. And the registration of the birth of the child. At the church of St Michael and All Angels in the parish of Whitchurch and both witnessed by the Reverend Julius Broughton who is resident there. It proves beyond doubt that the marriage predates any other agreement that Burford might have entered into and that the child was born in wedlock. Thus he is your brother's legitimate heir.'

From his pocket he produced two documents and handed them over. Henry read them, noting places, dates and signatures. And passed them to Eleanor, who did likewise, holding them with fingers that were not quite steady. Yes. There it was before her eyes. She swallowed against the tight constriction in her throat as the truth sank home. The documents predated her own marriage and the birth of her own child. She was not Thomas's wife. Her son was not Thomas's heir.

'It predates my marriage,' she stated in toneless acceptance, as if her world and that of her son did not lay shattered at her feet.

'It is as I said.' Sir Edward rescued the papers from her nerveless fingers. 'Octavia is Burford's true wife. Your marriage, I am afraid, my lady, is invalid.'

At these gently spoken but brutal words, Lord Henry took a step forward, an automatic gesture, to put himself between Baxendale and Eleanor, discovering an overwhelming desire to shield her, to protect her from these destructive insinuations, as if his physical presence could rob the words of their veracity.

It was a futile attempt. Pride came to the rescue as, choking back a sob, Eleanor rose to her feet. She could sit no longer and so walked to the window where the child chattered unintelligibly and pointed excitedly at the circling rooks. She stretched out a hand to touch his hair. Pale gold like his mother, so different from her own dark son. A lively, attractive child who clutched at the coat of his nurse with fierce fists. Then, disturbed by Eleanor's scrutiny, tears welled in the blue eyes and a wail broke the silence. Eleanor stroked his hair and the nurse shushed him, crooning to him in a soft voice until he hid his face against her shoulder.

Oh, God! How has all this come about?

Eleanor turned to look back over her shoulder at the tableau before the fireplace, with Sir Edward and Miss Baxendale—or was it the Marchioness of Burford?—at its centre. Both fair, well bred and respectable, Octavia appropriately clothed in black silk, a black satin-straw bonnet framing her lovely face—it was indeed difficult to suspect them of any degree of duplicity or trickery. And they had the documents with all the force of the law behind them...

'This is a matter that needs our consideration, sir.' Her attention was drawn back to Lord Henry, who had taken a hand in the discussion again. What were his thoughts on this untoward turn in family events? For a moment, his eyes caught hers and she thought that for that one second of contact he was not indifferent to her plight. And then he turned away. 'What do you intend now, Sir Edward?'

'It is my intention that we go to London and lay this evidence before your family's legal man. A Mr Hoskins, I understand. I would presume, in the somewhat peculiar circumstances, that we can take up residence in Faringdon House? I believe that my sister should have that right as we do not possess our own establishment in London.'

'What?' Mrs Stamford could take no more. She surged to her feet, fury on behalf of her daughter writ large. 'I think you presume too much, sir. You have no right whatsoever to take up residence in Faringdon House!'

A quick, startled glance passed between Nicholas and Henry, Nicholas astonished at the man's effrontery in demanding the Faringdon London residence for his sister's comfort, but Henry's frown prevented any comment. His lordship placed a warning hand on Mrs Stamford's rigid arm.

'Do not distress yourself, ma'am.' Turning to Sir Edward, Henry bowed his head in acknowledgement of the claim. 'Very well, sir. I shall ensure that you are expected there and given every comfort. Although I would suggest that you do not spread word of this...this unfortunate and highly sensitive affair until the legality of your claim is proved.'

'It is not our intention to provide food for the gossips, my lord.' There was the merest hint of a reprimand in Baxendale's quiet voice. He took his sister's hand once more and drew her to her feet to stand beside him. 'It would be of no benefit to my sister to be discussed in the streets and clubs more than is necessary. There will be enough scandal as it is. I shall present these documents—' he replaced them in his inner pocket '—to Mr Hoskins. I think that they will hold up under due investigation by that gentleman—and then they will ensure the inheritance for my sister and her son. The entail on the estate should confirm it.'

'Very well, Sir Edward. I must bow to your decision in this instance.'

'I must thank you for your compliance, my lord. Now. If you will excuse us. We are intending to stay the night at the Crown in Tenbury Wells. I am sure that we will be in communication again very soon to straighten out this unfortunate matter.'

'We shall.' Lord Henry's face was grim, every muscle in his body under powerful restraint. 'We too shall be in London before the end of the week.'

*** * ***

Eleanor sank down onto the nearest chair as the visitors, accompanied by Nicholas and a furious Mrs Stamford, left the withdrawing-room to continue their journey. She was alone with Lord Henry but seemed oblivious to this. Her eyes were fixed on the window where afternoon sun cast patterns on the carpet and gilded the edge of the shutters. But she saw none of it.

'Eleanor…'

She turned her head. Slowly, as if it took all her effort of will to force her body to obey, to focus on the man who stood before her. She studied his face with an intensity as if what she found there was of the utmost importance to her. But apparently she could read nothing to give her hope.

'Eleanor. I presume that you had no suspicion of this terrible débâcle. Not the slightest hint that Thomas might have a liaison elsewhere.' Henry's voice held a harsh edge, almost as if, she thought, perhaps he considered that she herself was to some extent to blame.

'No. How should I? I cannot believe it…'

'Nor I. It does not sound like Thomas.' He watched her carefully, aware of the white shade around her mouth as she skimmed the brink of control. Every instinct urged him to take her in his arms and let her cry out her frozen misery against his chest. To carry her off from this place so that she would never again have to face anything as shattering as the revelations of the past hour. But he could not, dare not, too unsure of her reactions to him if he made any intimate gesture. Too unsure of his feelings towards her. There was no place for pity here. And yet the bitter anger at her cold-hearted betrayal of his own love for her no longer seemed to weigh in the balance. A very masculine urge to protect took precedence.

'That he should already have had a wife and child when he… when he…' Eleanor swallowed hard and pressed a hand to her lips to stop the words. Then, 'I don't know what to do.'

'You do not have to do anything.' Henry attempted to reassure her. 'Now is not the time for hasty action. We need to speak with Hoskins before we accept the statements of Sir Edward

Baxendale or the weight of his documents. We know nothing of him. We knew everything about Thomas.' *I pray that we did, for your sake!*

She hardly listened, took in none of his soft words.

'How can I do nothing! I have no right to the name I bear. I clearly have no right to live here or in any of the Faringdon properties, if what Miss Baxendale claims is true. And there is no evidence to suggest that it is false. Indeed, the proof for the marriage would appear to be unquestionable.'

She rose to her feet as if she would flee the room.

'I will do all I can to help you.' Henry moved to stand in her path. 'You have only to ask.'

She really looked at him now. Contempt was clearly visible, swirled with the total despair in her eyes, their usual bright amethyst now as dark as bluebells in shaded woods.

'Will you? Will you indeed, Hal?'

'Of course. Nell…' He stretched out his hand as if to touch her arm in compassion, moved by her dignity in spite of her grief.

'Don't touch me,' she hissed the words, taking him—and herself—by surprise at the sudden vehemence. 'I do not want your pity!'

'Nell, I understand that you—'

'No, you don't. You talked of humiliation when you believed that I had rejected you. You did not know the half of it. If Miss Baxendale's marriage is indeed legal, imagine what a feast the gossip-mongers will have over that. I shall never be able to hold my head up in society again. And as for my son… I care not for myself. But what can you possibly do to save my child—an innocent victim—from the condemnation of a critical and judgmental society?'

'You must not allow yourself to contemplate such a possibility. It may yet all come to nothing.' What other could he say? He fought against self-disgust as he heard his own empty words in the face of her impossible position.

'No? But if it does stand the test of law, Miss Baxendale's document will proclaim me a whore and my son a bastard. And you tell me not to worry? You must be thanking God, Hal, for his divine retribution!' She gave a little crow of hysterical laughter. 'If I did indeed reject you in order to manipulate Thomas into marriage, as you so clearly suspect, then I have been punished for my sins beyond all belief.' The laughter shattered and she covered her face with her hands to catch the tears that began to flow.

Ignoring her bitter accusation, answering his own need, he stepped forward, intending to take her in his arms. 'Never that! Let me help you, Nell.'

'Go away!'

Logic told him that he should do as she asked, should simply walk away. To hold her would be too dangerous, reawakening the feelings towards her that he did not want to experience ever again. But conscience, instinct perhaps—and something in the depth of his soul that he refused to acknowledge—insisted that he stay and comfort. Henry went with instinct and enclosed her in his arms.

Eleanor was immediately conscious of the warmth and power of his body, enfolding her, holding her against his strength. How strong he was. How easy it would be to simply rest her head on his shoulder and allow him to lift the burden from her, to solve the whole monstrous problem for her. How tempting to curl her fingers around his broad shoulders and simply hold on, until the nightmare dissipated as disturbing dreams must with the coming of daylight. And how foolish it would be to allow herself that luxury! What a terrible mistake to allow him to come too close, to know the thoughts and feelings that assailed her heart and mind, refusing to let her be.

She froze in his embrace as if she could not bear his touch, and almost immediately fought to be free, pushing with frantic hands against his chest, lifting her head proudly, defiantly, regardless of her tear-stained cheeks.

'No. I do not think I will accept your help, my lord. I need nothing from you.' Her voice was suddenly cold, derisive even. Although it hurt him immeasurably, he had never admired her courage as much as he did at that moment, but her words struck with deliberate venom, stinging him with their power to wound. 'Go back to America, Hal. You are well out of it!'

Chapter Four

On the following morning Henry and Nicholas were the only two occupants of the breakfast table, although neither was showing much appetite. Desultory conversation occupied the first ten minutes about the value of breeding their own horseflesh. But finally Nicholas pushed the tankard of ale away across the table, leaned back in his chair and pinned his brother with an unusually stern expression.

'Do you believe it, Hal?'

'No.' His brother's uncompromising reply did not surprise him.

'Neither do I. But there is all that proof, with the power of Church and State behind it. Legal documents and such...' He frowned at Bess, who had placed one confiding and optimistic paw on his boot. 'Tell me why *you* don't believe it. The Baxendales certainly did not appear to be—'

'Rogues? Tricksters? No, they did not.' Henry steepled his fingers thoughtfully, elbows resting on the table. 'Thomas was always ripe for a flirtation with a pretty girl. And Octavia Baxendale certainly qualifies for his interest. I admit, I was surprised to know that he had married Eleanor so soon after I had left. But two wives? One of them in secret when we were all still living here under this roof? Unlikely, anyone who knew him must accept.' He pushed back from the table, and rose to his feet to pace to the windows, emotion suddenly raw in his voice as he stood with his back to his brother. 'Why did you have to *die,* Thomas? And in such a uselessly tragic fashion!' He leaned his hands on the window ledge and looked out at glorious nature with unseeing eyes. Then, on a deep breath with senses governed once more, he walked slowly back. 'Apart from anything else, as you very well know, Thomas never could keep a secret to save his life! The number of times he fell foul of our heavy-handed parent because he could not keep a still tongue in his head—he probably totted up one beating a week for one sin or another, whether it was mine or his own was irrelevant.' His smile was a mere twisting of lips. 'You were probably too young to remember.'

'So what do we do?' Nicholas prompted. 'Accept the proof and have Sir Edward Baxendale and the lady resident at Burford Hall?'

Henry eyed him with silent, brooding intensity.

'Perhaps I should sail to America with you,' Nicholas continued, 'if he asks me to move out. Which he undoubtedly will. I wager he would not want a Faringdon living under the same roof.'

'And you would be welcome,' was the prompt reply. 'The hunting is excellent—you would enjoy it.'

'That might tempt me. Is it the land of opportunity that you had hoped for, Hal? You have said very little of your life there— but then we have been taken up with other matters, have we not!'

'Very true—Baxendale has driven business from my mind somewhat,' Hal admitted. 'But, yes—the peace between Britain and America two years ago has ended American isolation, so commerce is free to develop and fortunes to be made. It is still an infant society, but progress is very rapid. New York is growing at a furious rate. Banks and businesses opening every day it seems. So, yes, the opportunity is there for those who are willing to throw the dice and bet confidently on the outcome.'

'As Faringdon and Bridges will do?'

Hal smiled, a hint of pride evident in his face, his present problems for the moment overlaid by the bright promise of the future. 'Yes…Faringdon and Bridges. It sounds good, does it not? Even if all we possess is tied up in investment, leaving us on a very uncomfortable precipice of poverty.'

'I have every confidence and shall come to you for a loan

when you have made your first fortune.' Nicholas returned the smile. 'And the women of New York?' He slanted a sly glance at his brother. 'Are they pretty?'

'I believe they would compare with London. I have found so.'

'So tell me, Hal. Is she a prime article?'

'Of course.' Hal's answer was as smooth as watered silk.

'And the name of this fair Cyprian?'

'Rosalind—and the rest is none of your affair, little brother, although she would box your ears for you if you dared impugn her morality with such a title.'

Nicholas laughed and Henry broke into a reluctant grin at the exchange but then became deadly serious again and returned to the Baxendale claim. 'But, no,. I don't think it would be politic to simply accept the story that we have been fed so far. I think—'

The door opened. The Marchioness of Burford swept into the room, carrying her son, her mother in close pursuit.

'I do not think, my dear Eleanor, that—'

'Forgive me, Mama, but I have made up my mind.'

Eleanor came to a halt before Lord Henry, mood confrontational. She had no difficulty at all in meeting his surprised scrutiny this morning, meeting it with a bright gaze that issued a challenge to anyone who might be sufficiently ill advised as to stand in her way. A sleepless night with much time for reflection had achieved a very positive effect on the lady. Yesterday, she acknowledged, she had been weak. Spineless, even. She shivered in humiliation at the memory of her tears and her outpouring of grief and disillusion in Lord Henry's presence. She must have been out of her mind to do so—to show such weakness. She had no excuse. Today she would grasp the nettle with both hands, crushing the stinging stems and leaves at whatever cost to herself. She would not meekly accept this hideous development. She would fight for her position, and, more importantly, the inheritance of her son!

Letting his gaze rest on her, Lord Henry had to appreciate that the lady had dressed for battle. The arrangement of her burnished ringlets *à la Sappho* could not be faulted, nor the quiet elegance of her high-waisted, narrow gown, long sleeved with only one row of discreet ruffles around the hem. The black silk creation, rich and costly, gleamed in the morning sunlight, undoubtedly created by the hand of an expert. Probably Eugenie in Bond Street, he thought, unless this most fashionable of *modistes* had changed in his absence.

Eleanor certainly had, he was forced to admit. Composed and sophisticated, her presence reinforced the impression that he had absorbed since his return. She had grown into her role as Marchioness of Burford and he could not fault her in it, although he felt a strange sense of loss that the young girl he had known had changed for ever.

'I have decided,' the Marchioness now announced to the room at large. 'It is my intention to go to London to confront this problem. I cannot sit here, buried in the country, waiting for decisions on my future to be made without my knowledge. I need to speak with Mr Hoskins. I *cannot* believe that Thomas had married Octavia Baxendale, visited her and had a son by her without my being aware! Certainly not for the whole span of our marriage! Such deceit is completely unacceptable.'

'But where will you stay?' Mrs Stamford broke in, continuing her earlier objections, but for once unsure of her ground. She could not but agree with her daughter's basic premise that the whole matter could not simply be ignored. 'Surely not at Faringdon House, with the Baxendales in residence. Think of the mortification of having to meet them every day, of sitting down to breakfast with them. Do think, Eleanor…'

'I have thought, Mama. I have done nothing else but think all night long! I shall not, of course, go to Faringdon House. It would not be at all suitable. I shall put up at an hotel until I can make more acceptable arrangements. But go to London I will!'

She glared at Henry as if she expected him to join her mother in condemnation of her scheme. Would he dare to thwart her? She did not care! Her mind was made up!

Henry watched her with none of the indifference he would have preferred. The anger that now drove her rendered her magnificent. She might be dressed in deepest unrelieved mourning, there might be light shadows beneath her eyes from her sleepless night, but her face was vivid and alive. Her skin glowed with delicate colour, her soft lips firm and uncompromising in her decision. The deep amethyst of her eyes was dark and turbulent, rich as glowing jewels. He was held by them, a slow enchantment which barred him from damning her hopes of success in her cause.

'Of course you must go.'

Eleanor blinked, momentarily lost for words as she marshalled an impassioned argument to use against him when he denied the validity of her plan. Lord Henry's lips curled a little at her obvious discomfort, but he had the wisdom to suppress too obvious a smile.

'But there is no need for you to consider an hotel. Nor, as you say, would it be proper for you to stay at Faringdon House in the present climate—it is not fitting. I shall myself go to London and I shall rent a house. I make you free of it. Rather than the Baxendales, you may sit down to breakfast with *me* instead!'

'You?' Her brows rose in sharp disbelief. 'But you are returning to America!'

'No. I think not. I cannot leave you with this situation unresolved. My departure for America can wait.'

'I do not need your help!' Temper flared again in the sundrenched room. She would not be beholden to this man who had kissed her into desire and then rejected her! She would not come to depend on him again!

'So you informed me yesterday. You appear to have a very low opinion of my abilities and my priorities, my lady!' Henry noted her guilty flush with some satisfaction and drove the point home. 'But this is not merely for you. My brother's good name is in the balance. And my nephew's legal recognition.' For some elusive reason, as he looked at Eleanor and the child before him, recognising her utter determination to discover the truth, he suddenly had no doubts about his own convictions. The Baxendales, for some devious reason known only to themselves, had concocted a series of lies and deceits. He lifted a hand to stroke one gentle finger down the baby's satin cheek.

The result both surprised and unsettled him. Tom ignored the gesture and continued to grasp the black satin ribbon on his mother's dress with fierce and destructive concentration. The Marchioness took the smallest of steps back, a subtle movement and yet very obvious to Lord Henry. As was the fleeting emotion that clouded her eyes. He thought it was fear—yet could not imagine why. He was no threat to her or to her son. Stifling a sigh, he accepted that it was simply another mystery in the complicated weave but must be put aside until the more immediate concern with Octavia Baxendale had been dealt with. Henry deliberately lowered his hand, but not his eyes from Eleanor's face, which was now flushed with rose.

'I need to know that the inheritance of this family is in the correct hands, you see, even if those hands are still very small and as yet incapable of handling the reins,' he stated quietly. 'And I think the matter deserves some investigation. I cannot leave.'

'But I cannot agree.' Mrs Stamford stood her ground. 'I have told my daughter that hers is a foolish idea. She could stay in residence *here*. To be turned out of her own home is insupportable. Besides, it is not seemly that she should put up in your rented property in London, my lord.'

'And why in God's name not?' Lord Henry's brows snapped into a dark bar of extreme exasperation, temper finally escaping his control. He had had enough of his family for one day and it was hardly mid-morning. 'I presume you will accompany her ladyship to London, ma'am? Does she need more of a chaperon than her own mother? And what the *devil* do you expect for her at my hands? That living under my protection will sully her reputation? The Marchioness is under no danger from me! Your comment, ma'am, is as uninformed as it is insulting, to me and to your daughter.'

The brutal statement was met with stunned silence. Nicholas turned away to hide a smile. Eleanor looked as startled as her mother. Lord Henry was not normally given to such a show of emotion.

'Well… I never intended to suggest… I did not think that… But how can you have agreed to the Baxendales taking possession of Faringdon House?' Mrs Stamford was flustered, but reluctant to admit defeat and pursued her quarry with more energy than sensitivity.

'What do you suggest?' The reply was immediate, biting. 'That we get to haggling over property at a time like this? As if we were in the market place? I think not!'

'Of course not. I never—'

'No. Perhaps you did not. But your thoughts were not complimentary to a lady who already has enough to contend with, without her mother casting doubts on the morals and motives of members of the Faringdon family!' Then, before anyone could recover from so direct an attack, Lord Henry addressed his next words to Eleanor in quite a different voice. 'I think it is an excellent idea. See to your luggage, ma'am. We leave early tomorrow morning. You, too, Nicholas,' which effectively wiped the smile from Nick's face.

'But I thought it might be better if…'

'No, it wouldn't.' His lordship's voice was now clipped. 'You are not to escape a short visit to town, so save your breath. I have need of you in London, little brother. We have a campaign to wage!'

Eleanor looked from one to the other of the Faringdon brothers. Their determination, their confident air of authority, the implacable manner in which they undertook whatever they set their mind on, touched her heart after all. Yes. She would join her efforts to theirs. They gave her more hope than she could have dreamed of. And Hal was not going back to America. Not yet! She hugged the thought to herself as she hugged her precious son, even as she reprimanded herself for her foolishness. Henry had defended her before her mother. Perhaps he would not abandon her, whatever the outcome of the case. 'I will not go without Tom, you understand,' she informed Henry, looking again for disagreement, perversely unwilling to appear too compliant. 'He comes with me.'

Henry sighed and ran a hand through his hair at the prospect of arranging transport for a large party. The unnerving experience of being regarded by two identical pairs of deep lavender eyes, one openly critical, the other innocently curious, decided the matter for him. 'I suppose you must. Very well. I will arrange for the cleaning of the chaise. Be so good as to inform the stables, Nick. Be ready tomorrow morning, ladies.'

The Faringdon family was rapidly ensconced in a smart and stylish town house in Park Lane in the most fashionable part of London. By no means as spacious or as elegantly furnished as Faringdon House in Grosvenor Square, and lacking all personal touches, of course, yet it was proclaimed sufficient for their needs, even by Mrs Stamford, who was initially prepared to dislike it on sight. The proportions and furnishings of the main withdrawing-room, smaller parlours and reception rooms were declared adequate, the bedrooms comfortable, the furnishings suitably tasteful if a little bland. The address, of course, could not be bettered. The matter of staff was ably dealt with by Marcle, who had accompanied them, despite the state of his arthritic joints, and took charge of the lower regions with seamless competence. Eleanor did not bother to marvel at the speed or the smooth efficiency of the whole operation. If she did, she would have to allow considerable credit to Lord Henry who, she considered, carried it off with typical high-handed arrogance—and faultless style. But she was grateful. It was easier to take the comfort and concern for her well-being for granted and simply accept it when more momentous issues were to be faced.

The following morning, after persuading Mrs Stamford with a tact and a remarkable patience, which surprised everyone, that her presence was not essential to the success of the operation, Lord Henry escorted the Marchioness to the chambers of Hoskins and Bennett. Mr Edward Hoskins, a gentleman of advanced years and wide experience, had enjoyed the confidence and management of the legal affairs of the Faringdon family for many years, but his welcome on this chilly morning did not hold much pleasure for his noble employers. The low clouds, Eleanor surmised, accurately reflected the mood of everyone in the dusty, book-lined, wood-panelled room off Fleet Street.

'My lord. My lady.' The lawyer ushered them in with every

consideration and saw to their comfort, pouring a glass of canary for Lord Henry and ratafia for the Marchioness, even though no one had the heart for refreshment. 'What can I say? I could never have believed that such an occasion as this would arise in my lifetime. And certainly not with respect to your family, my lord, so correct and respectable as they have always been in my lengthy experience.'

He took Eleanor's black-gloved hand and pressed it in fatherly concern before taking his position behind his document-strewn desk. Such a lovely lady to be faced with the possibility of so much future heartache! And the Marquis of Burford had always struck him as a most conscientious young man. Mr Hoskins frowned down at the pages before him, hoping that Lord Henry could be relied upon to deal with the situation in a fitting manner. He knew little of the gentleman other than that he had left the country to seek his fortune—but this was sure to be a true test of his character. He glanced up under heavy brows at Lord Henry who stood behind the Marchioness's chair, a hint of the protective in his stance despite the lack of physical connection, noting the stern lines of his handsome face, the implacable will expressed in the cold grey eyes. Mr Hoskins suppressed a shudder. He would not care to make an enemy of this man. He trusted that the absent Sir Edward knew what he was undertaking.

'Sir Edward Baxendale and Miss Baxendale have been to see you, I surmise.' Lord Henry lost no time in broaching the delicate subject, meeting the crux of the matter head on.

'Indeed they have, my lord. Yesterday afternoon. A most personable pair, I might add, in spite of the reason for their appointment. I have heard their story and I have seen the documents. In fact, I have them here in my possession.' He laid his hand on them on his desk, as if with a degree of distaste for their content. 'Sir Edward left them so that I might check their authenticity.'

'And your opinion, sir? No dissimulation, I beg.' Lord Henry cast a quick glance at Eleanor's impassive features. 'I fear that they bear the mark of validity.'

Mr Hoskins noted again the strained but composed features of the Marchioness. She sat perfectly still to hear her fate, but her fingers, closed around the strings of the reticule on her lap, were bone white from the pressure.

'I believe that the documents are legal.' Mr Hoskins stated the matter without inflection. 'The marriage and the birth are recorded, as you are aware. It is simple enough to check the existence of the church and the priest concerned, and thus the signatures—which I am in process of doing. The marriage would appear to have existed.'

'And the witnesses?'

'Sir Edward himself, and Lady Mary Baxendale, their mother, were witnesses of the marriage. Lady Mary is now unfortunately deceased.'

Lord Henry nodded, keeping Eleanor under his close surveillance. 'So tell me, Mr Hoskins, in your legal opinion, where does her ladyship stand?'

Hoskins sighed. It would not be good news. 'There is nothing that I can tell you that you do not already know, my lord. The estate is entailed on the eldest son. A jointure is established for the widow to ensure her comfort for the rest of her life. The Marquis your husband, my lady, made no further will other than to give the trusteeship, if necessary on his death, into the hands of Lord Henry and Lord Nicholas and myself. He would not expect his untimely death at such an early age and so felt no compulsion to outline his wishes in more detail. If Miss Baxendale is proved to be the legal wife of the Marquis, then there is no legal recognition or provision for yourself, my lady, or your son.' He gave her the title, although now so clearly in doubt, through courtesy and compassion, his heart going out to the innocent woman who sat before him as if engraved in stone. 'The recipient of the widow's jointure will be Miss Baxendale,' he concluded, 'the Marchioness of Burford, I should say, not yourself. And the heir to the estate is the legitimate child of that marriage, John.'

'I see.' Eleanor felt as if the walls were closing in on her. She fought to stave off the blackness that threatened to encroach and rob her of all sense. Then, through the mists, she became aware of a warm hand on her shoulder, a firm pressure. The heat spread through the black silk of her spencer to reassure and comfort. As she turned her head to look up, there could be no doubting the depth of understanding in Lord Henry's face as he willed her to be strong. For one moment she covered his hand with her own and struggled to smile in reassurance.

It almost broke his heart.

His voice was harsh as he spoke again to the lawyer. 'Do you truly believe that my brother married Octavia Baxendale some three years ago, sir?'

'I do not like it, my lord. But on the face of it, yes. I am unable to argue against the evidence.'

So there it was. Eleanor covered her face with her hands.

'Forgive me, my lord, my lady. I would never willingly cause you such pain. If there is anything I can do…'

Lord Henry took Eleanor's arm in a firm hold, encouraging her to rise to her feet, then tucked her hand within his arm. She obeyed as if in a trance, all her hopes and dreams for the future destroyed. He fixed Hoskins with a flat stare. 'Will you be so kind as to do one thing for us, sir? Sir Edward claimed that an annual sum was paid to Miss Baxendale from the date of her marriage. A substantial amount, it would seem, to ensure her complicity in keeping the marriage secret. Is there any trace of such a sum being paid from the estate finances? I have asked the agent to look at the estate accounts at Burford Hall. It would be interesting to know if and when any large amounts of money were paid out and apparently unaccounted for.'

'I will certainly do that, my lord. But if there is no evidence of such, it may not prove that they were *not* made, of course.'

'I know. But it is a start and the best we can do.'

They returned home in pensive and uncomfortable silence, in a hackney that Lord Henry hailed outside the lawyer's rooms, to relay the depressing results of their morning's endeavours to Mrs Stamford and Nicholas who awaited their return.

'It is as we feared.' Lord Henry stripped off his greatcoat and strode into the front parlour to pour glasses of port. 'The documents would appear to be legally binding.'

Eleanor handed her spencer, gloves and bonnet to Marcle and

followed, determined to hold herself together. Henry cast one glance in her direction and stalked to her side to take her hand in a firm hold. 'It would be better if you sat before you fall to the floor.' His tone was harsh to cover the depth of his feelings for her. She looked so fragile, the impression enhanced by her black gown. Lost and vulnerable. He suppressed the fury that surged within him as he saw the result of their morning's work and felt the uncontrollable trembling in the hand that, for a brief moment, clung to his. 'Here.' He held out the glass of port. 'Drink this. Don't argue with me, just do it. You have had a most distressing morning, perhaps the worst hour of your life. It is not weakness to admit it and take a little stimulation!'

Eleanor looked up into his face, her eyes betraying her inner fears. She looked stricken—he realised that she must indeed be so, if she was willing to lay her emotions bare before him. All he wished to do was sit beside her and pull her into his arms to shield her from the cruelties of the world. Anything to smooth away the look of helpless desolation.

'Don't give up yet. This is only the first hurdle. We shall come about.'

Tears threatened at his gentle words but she would not, determined to keep her voice calm and composure intact. She sat at the pressure of his hand and obediently took the glass. 'But what hope is there? You heard what Mr Hoskins had to say. Thomas was in all probability wedded to Octavia Baxendale at least a year before I even knew him.'

'I am not convinced, in spite of the evidence to the contrary.' Lord Henry tossed back the port as if he needed it and poured another glass. 'Let us start from the opposite premise. That the claim is false. Consider this. If the whole venture is nothing but a deliberate trickery, a charade, why would they embark on such a risky enterprise in the full view of the *haut ton?* If they fail, and so are unmasked as frauds, the result will be a disaster for them. So what motives would they have to risk all on the turn of a card?'

'Money!' Nicholas stated without hesitation.

'Social consequence?' Eleanor suggested.

'The title!' Mrs Stamford added in flat tones.

'Money would seem to me to be the strongest motivation.' Henry cast himself into the chair opposite his brother. 'I wonder about the financial circumstances of the Baxendales.'

'An easy enough matter to discover, surely?' Nicholas lifted his brows.

'Do you believe,' Eleanor asked, considering a matter that had worried her since the first meeting at Burford Hall, 'that Miss Baxendale is strong enough to have stood against her brother if he wanted her to reveal her marriage to the world? Sir Edward said that she refused to do so when Thomas contracted to marry me, in spite of his persuasion to the contrary. Do you really believe it? She seems so biddable.'

'She might. If she loved my brother enough.' Henry acknowledged the point. 'But she is certainly not made of stern stuff. I think that we should get to know Miss Baxendale a little better. And perhaps without the presence of her more forceful brother. There is a role for you, Eleanor! You will not like it, I dare say, but I think you should further your acquaintance with Octavia.'

'But she is in black gloves.' Mrs Stamford pushed herself to the edge of her seat in horror. 'It is not yet six months since dear Thomas died. It is not fitting that Eleanor start going about in society. What will people say? I cannot condone a plan of action which would result in the Marchioness of Burford being considered *fast*. How can you suggest it?' Her eyes locked with Lord Henry's in accusation. 'I suppose that such casual ways are acceptable in New York...' she sniffed '...but they are not considered respectable in London!'

Henry turned his glittering gaze on Mrs Stamford without compunction. 'I both can and will suggest it. And I will suggest even more *outrageous* action. I think that you, Eleanor, should put off your full mourning and begin to go about a little. There is no hint of scandal yet, but there will be, and without doubt it will take the Polite World by storm. It is too salacious a story to keep quiet.' His lips thinned at the disagreeable prospect. 'We shall soon find that we are living our lives under full public scrutiny and, however unpleasant, I think we must not be seen to be in hiding over this matter. We should go about as normal, make no comment, presume that Eleanor is without question the Marchioness of Burford, and I think that you should try for an intimate relationship with the fair Octavia. If she wishes to confide her troubles, you should be available with a sympathetic ear! I am not asking your daughter to attend a full dress ball!' he informed Eleanor's outraged parent. 'Merely to show herself and the child in public a little and pay some private visits.'

'That should be an interesting development!' For the first time that day, Eleanor managed a faint smile, appreciative of the plan. 'It is better to be active than afraid. I will do it.' Sipping the port, which restored colour to her ashen cheeks, she signalled her agreement. 'We should go about as if nothing were amiss. And I will put off my mourning.' She frowned as her mama prepared to interrupt. 'Better to be *fast* than a pawn at the whim of Sir Edward Baxendale.'

'Good.' Lord Henry had to admit to some relief. And a quiet satisfaction at the success of his scheming, which had effectively removed the stricken look from Eleanor's eyes. Action, as she had observed, would take her mind from the anguish of her situation. Besides, Eleanor's involvement would be all-important to the ultimate success of their campaign. 'And it will give the interested something to consider when the gossips turn their attention to the Faringdon Scandal.'

'What do we say if we are asked why we are not putting up at Faringdon House?' Mrs Stamford enquired, still unwilling to capitulate. 'It will be sure to cause comment.'

'Say that it is no one's affair but our own!' Exasperation cloaked his lordship, a heavy cloud. 'Say that redecoration is being undertaken—if anyone has the temerity to question a Faringdon on so personal an issue. That the noise and dust is too much for a young child. And since I am returned to London and have hired a house for the Season, I have put it at your disposal. Leave the Baxendales to make their own comments on the situation. If we remain calm and confident, the speculators will not know what to believe.'

Which, Eleanor thought, appeared to be his answer to every

difficulty that arose. She could not help but be impressed, and terrified, as she found herself suddenly embroiled in little less than a form of war strategy. She felt a twinge of sympathy for Napoleon when faced with the determination of the Duke of Wellington at the Battle of Waterloo. Lord Henry appeared to have a very similar approach to such matters. Arrogance and a gift for detailed strategy.

'Meanwhile—' Henry had not finished but directed his keen gaze on his brother '—you, Nick, can visit the gentleman's clubs, starting with St James's Street. Find out where, if any, Sir Edward is a member. See if you can discover whether he gambles heavily. And, most particularly, if he is in debt.'

'Thank you, Hal! And how do you suggest that I discover such sensitive information?' Nicholas finished off the rest of the port in his glass and rose to his feet.

'Use your initiative, Nick. I am sure you can encourage the gossips.'

'Very well.' He walked to the door. 'I had better change into something suitable for such esteemed company as the Bow Window Set at White's. *Not* how I would have chosen to spend the day, but I will do my poor best. Perhaps I will look up Kingstone—he usually has his fingers on the pulse and is not beyond a heavy wager himself. And is never at a loss for the *on dit* of the moment.'

'I wish you well. Let us hope that our own situation does not reach his ears any time soon!' Henry grimaced at the prospect as Nicholas raised his hand in acknowledgement of the comment and made his exit with reluctant intent. 'Meanwhile you and I, Eleanor, and you too if you wish it, ma'am…' he glanced towards Mrs Stamford '…are going to pay an afternoon visit on Cousin Judith.'

'Lady Painscastle? What has she to do with this fiasco? The fewer people to know, the better, I would have thought!' Once again, Mrs Stamford frowned her objections.

'You must know Judith well enough to appreciate the advantage of having her as a member of this family,' his lordship replied again with commendable but hard-won patience. 'Her social life is hectic, I remember, and little passes her keen eye or ear, unless she has changed beyond recognition since I saw her last. It seems to me that Octavia must have come out in the spring of 1812. If my memory serves me well, so did Judith. I have no recollection of Octavia at any of the Season's main events, but Judith might. Thomas and I squired her to any number of incredibly tedious parties, balls and soirées when she was intent on fixing her interest with Simon Painscastle. Perhaps she will remember Miss Baxendale making her formal curtsy to society. And, more to the point, if there was any obvious close relationship developing between Thomas and the lady. Judith, I believe, is quite our best source of gossip.'

'An excellent idea.' Mrs Stamford's face brightened as she saw the value of the connection and so allowed a complete volte-face. 'Lady Painscastle is a lively and eminently sensible young woman. She might indeed have noticed something between the pair—which *you* did not.' Thus Mrs Stamford damning the inadequacy of the whole male race.

'Do you agree, my lady?' Henry took the empty glass from Eleanor's hand, noting the return of colour to her face. 'It might be a painful encounter.'

'It might.' She stood and raised her chin. He nodded at the air of determination and the bright sparkle in her eyes. She did not lack for courage, no matter the odds. 'I shall be ready immediately after luncheon.'

Judith Faringdon, now Countess of Painscastle and most eligibly married to her beloved Simon, was in residence in the family home in Grosvenor Square. She had made an excellent match, with love and affection on both sides, and was now enjoying life as a wealthy and fashionable young woman with all the freedom allowed to a married lady. She was a true redhead with green eyes, both characteristics inherited from her mother, and an abundance of energy all, on this occasion, attractively packaged in an afternoon gown of cream and white muslin. With a pretty face and a lively manner, coupled with an appreciation of the fashions that suited her and a wealthy, well-born husband who adored her and pandered to her every whim, she had entrée into the Polite World. Her love of the pleasures of London was immeasurable. As was her ear for gossip.

'Hal! I did not know of your return. You look wonderfully well. Life in the colonies suits you. I cannot imagine its attraction but…' She allowed him to kiss her hand and then opened her arms to clasp him in a warm embrace.

'And Nell. Mrs Stamford. A family party, no less. I did not expect…' She hesitated as she recalled the circumstances. 'I am so sorry, Nell. Forgive me. I did not mean to be so insensitive or unfeeling. Indeed I did not! I too miss Thomas dreadfully—but life must go on, you know.' She rambled on. All good humour and welcome, if a little shallow. All in all, it was difficult not to like Lady Painscastle.

'And who have we here?' She lifted Tom from his mother's arms and spun him round to his obvious delight, tickling his neck until he chuckled. 'What a charmer he will be. Another Faringdon, if I am not mistaken, to break our poor female hearts.' She kissed him enthusiastically. 'Just look at those dark curls and those eyebrows.' She frowned at Hal over the baby's head. 'And have you broken many hearts in America? I expect so.'

He flushed, the faintest of colours on his lean cheeks, but otherwise ignored her comment.

'He has your eyes, dear Nell,' Judith continued. 'How delightful. Perhaps it is time that I pleased my lord and presented him with a son and heir. You almost tempt me to do so!'

Out of which artless comment, it was clear that the Faringdon Scandal had not yet reached the Polite World!

The visitors seated themselves in a cream-and-gold withdrawing-room, stylishly and expensively furnished, tea was served with due ceremony and Tom returned to his mother's lap, where he proceeded to gnaw the carved ivory head of her parasol with serious intensity.

'You all look very grave.' Lady Painscastle disposed her embroidered and flounced skirts with casual grace as she surveyed her family.

'Yes. It is a delicate matter, Judith. And not one that we wish to spread around.' Henry frowned discouragingly at his cousin. 'I believe that you can help us.'

'You can trust me, dear Henry!' She smiled winningly. 'Of course I will help. And I am always discreet.'

'Judith! You are the most incorrigible gossip of my acquaintance.' Lord Henry could not help but smile at his cousin's naïvety.

'But not if it will hurt one of my family.' And however shallow she might be, they knew Judith was right. It made the forthcoming conversation more bearable.

'Think back to your coming-out, Judith,' Henry prompted. 'Four years ago, I think, in the spring of 1812.'

'Yes.' Judith nodded, lifting up her bone china teacup with an elegant hand. 'I have been married to dear Simon for three years now.'

'Can you recall a young girl—about your own age. Octavia Baxendale. Fair hair. Blue eyes. A little shorter than you, perhaps. A neat figure. A quiet and unassuming girl, not one to take the town by storm, but pretty enough. She would have been accompanied by her brother and perhaps her mother. I have no recollection of such a female, but you might.'

'Well, you wouldn't, Hal! Melissa Charlesworth came out in that year. You were besotted, I remember. I doubt you noticed anyone else!'

'Never!' His frown was definitely more pronounced.

'You even went to Almack's, drank tea and lemonade, danced country dances and allowed yourself to be sneered at by the Princess Esterhazy for making a comment about the war or some such taboo subject! You were in love! Until Melissa threw you over—a mere younger son as you were!—and married the Earl of Saltmarshe. She always did have an eye to a fortune, no matter how ugly and old the husband.'

'Never mind that.' He rose to his feet to pace the room with impatience and perhaps a little unease. Eleanor hid a smile in spite of herself. 'What about Octavia Baxendale. Do you have any recollection of her?'

'Well, now. Let me think. Perhaps I do recall… But it is so long ago—and Thomas flirted with any number of ladies. I particularly remember one débutante—but she had curls as black and lustrous as a crow's wing. I believe I envied her, admired her colouring more than my own—foolishly, as Painscastle was quick to reassure me…'

Lord Henry sighed. 'Do try to concentrate Judith. Fair hair, blue eyes…' He looked to the ceiling in despair.

'Well!' She folded her hands and thought, the effort palpable. 'I think I might remember her at some of the occasions. With a brother, perhaps? The name *Octavia* seems familiar… But I am not at all certain. Why do you wish me to remember something so inconsequential?'

'Can you recall—did Thomas flirt with her? He escorted you to enough balls and soirées—he must have come across her if you did.' Henry ignored her demand for some clarification.

'I don't know… Well, yes, perhaps I do remember a fair girl, and perhaps he did. If it is the girl I am thinking of, she had a liking for *pink*. A colour I can never wear.' She bared her teeth as Hal's temper came close to boiling point. 'I know…I am trying, Hal. If it is the girl in question, I remember thinking that he could not be serious about her as a bride—a respectable family only. As Marquis of Burford he could look so much higher than a mere country miss…' She flushed with mortification as she heard her own words, the deep wash of rose clashing remarkably with her auburn colouring as she saw Eleanor blush with discomfort and Mrs Stamford's eyes flash a warning.

'Oh, Nell.' Immediately remorseful, the lady put down her teacup and stretched out a hand to touch Eleanor's cold fingers, 'My tongue runs away with me, as you know. I meant no criticism. Indeed I did not. Anyone could see that you and Thomas were so well suited to each other.'

Henry sighed and tried manfully both to preserve his patience and steer the conversation back into its previous channel. Neither was easy. 'Judith—did it ever occur to you that Thomas *was* more serious about the lady than a mild flirtation?'

'Perhaps. He once rode with a fair lady in the park, I know. And escorted her to supper…. He certainly stood up with a lady of such colouring at Almack's. And I think at my own coming-out ball in Faringdon House. But there could have been any number of fair débutantes. I suppose if it *was* the same lady Thomas must have been taken with her to single her out, mustn't he? Don't *you* remember, Hal?'

'No. Presumably I was still concentrating on Melissa Charlesworth! You are not a deal of help to us, Judith.' Henry set his teeth and continued to probe his cousin's erratic memory. 'Did Thomas go down to Brighton that year?'

'I have no idea.' Judith frowned at the close questioning. 'Why?'

'No matter. What happened to Miss Baxendale after the Season? Did she marry? Did she have another Season?'

Judith shook her head. 'If Octavia is indeed the girl I am thinking of, I believe that she might have left before the end of the Season, before my own engagement to Simon, I understand. Rumour said—I think!—that she had contracted a more than suitable marriage—with money. But more than that I know not. You should talk to my mother. She has an excellent memory. Too good, sometimes, when I wish she might forget some trifling indiscretion from my childhood.' Judith looked from Henry to Eleanor and back again in frustration, green eyes sharp as she scented gossip. 'But why all these questions about someone we do not know and events that happened so long ago? You must tell me! You are keeping me in suspense—which is unforgivable.'

She looked at the faces around her tea table. At the quick meeting of eyes between Lord Henry and Eleanor, Eleanor made the decision.

'It appears,' she informed Judith in a calm voice, 'that Thomas may have been the *suitable match* you spoke of, contracted by Octavia in the spring of 1812. Thomas, it seems, may have married her and kept her in seclusion in the country. And had a son by her.' She hesitated, touching her tongue to dry lips. 'It appears—it is possible that—I am not, and never have been, the Marchioness of Burford.'

Judith's eyes widened in horror.

'And we would be more than grateful if you did not spread that story around town, however tempting it might be to do so!'

Mrs Stamford added with a fierceness not usually encountered over an afternoon tea-drinking.

Judith, eyebrows arched in incredulous disbelief, was reduced, for once, to amazed silence.

Lord Henry trod the stairs late that night.

He was tired. A headache, which he could no longer ignore, however unusual it might be for him to suffer such a trivial affliction, lurked somewhere behind his eyes. A long day with nothing to show for their combined efforts but confirmation of their worst fears. The documents appeared to be legal. Sir Edward was not a member of any of the gentleman's clubs visited by Nicholas and, as far as they knew, did not gamble, whether lightly or heavily. There were the gaming hells next, of course... Henry sighed at the prospect. Nicholas would object, but he would do it with good grace. And Cousin Judith remembered a tender flirtation between Thomas and a pretty fair-haired girl who had retired from society at the end of her first Season with rumours of an advantageous marriage. A young girl whose name she *thought* was Octavia.

He groaned and silently cursed the cruel hand of fate.

It left Eleanor in an unspeakable position, any opportunities for optimism fast disappearing, as mist at the rising of the sun.

What the hell were you doing, Thomas?

Yet, curse as he might, Henry still found it difficult to see his brother in the role of treacherous, machiavellian husband to two wives at one and the same time, with a child by both. The subterfuge just did not fit. Far too complicated and devious for Thomas, far too insensitive to those involved.

Now for himself, Henry mused, well... A grim smile, a mere ghost, crossed his face. It would be more likely, at any event. But even he would draw the line at two wives!

The house settled into silence around him. Nick had gone out to join a party of friends to talk horseflesh and drink gin at Limmers in Conduit Street. Mrs Stamford—who knew? She had sufficient acquaintance in town to provide her with entertainment. Eleanor had retired early, probably worn out through trying to keep a brave face on the fact that she was fast becoming a bigamous wife and her child illegitimate, with no source of support, financial or otherwise. She had used harsher terms, he remembered, in a moment of anguish. *Whore and bastard.* He flinched at the deliberate brutality. It was certainly how the world would see it, and there was nothing he could say to make matters any better for her.

The lights on the first floor were low, one branch of candles left burning. And he was too tired to think any more. Tomorrow he would go to Whitchurch and find the Reverend Julius Broughton. He would verify that cleric's role in the proceedings. It might achieve nothing, but at least he would feel that he was doing *something.* And he would know if the marriage of Thomas with Octavia Baxendale had actually existed.

He yawned. And came to a halt on the landing. Further along on the right a door was ajar. The baby's room. A gentle light spilled out, very low. Probably the nursemaid come to check on her small charge.

Then a soft voice reached him, crooning a lullaby. A low voice, sweet and tender. He was immediately drawn to it and came to stand silently in the half-open doorway.

The child must have been restless. Rather than summon the nursemaid, Eleanor had come herself to comfort him. Of course she would, he acknowledged. The child was her only connection with Thomas, even more of an anchor in these stormy waters.

She sat in a low chair, a single candle on the little table casting its light from behind to rim her figure in gold. Apparently the infant now slept. Eleanor's song had become a gentle humming, her hand on the edge of the crib, rocking gently, her eyes fixed on the sleeping face.

Henry could not take his eyes from her, his thoughts and feelings suspended in that one moment. She had risen from her bed, her hair unpinned from its fashionable style but yet unbraided so that it fell in a glory of waves over her breast. A peignoir lay in soft overlapping layers of cream silk and lace from a high neck to cover her feet. Her face was calm. Her eyes hooded. Her lips curved in a tender smile. A Madonna, indeed.

His heart thudded against his ribs as the scene imprinted itself on his mind. She was so beautiful. And he had lost her to his brother. For the first time in his life Henry cursed the dead Thomas, even knowing that the blame could not in any way be heaped at his brother's feet. He had lost her. And yet for the past two years he had tried to persuade himself that his love for her was dead, destroyed when she had broken her promise to him. Wrong! Totally and utterly wrong! The voice in his mind and his heart would no longer allow him to pretend. His love for Eleanor was as strong as ever. And just as doomed. He must not allow it to be a burden on her—and so must bear it on his own shoulders, his emotions hidden.

A tingle of awareness touched Eleanor's spine and she knew that he was there.

She could pretend that she did not know, of course, conscious of a ripple of embarrassment to be discovered like this. If she kept her face turned towards the crib, he might walk away as silently as he had come. But she felt the compulsion of his eyes, felt her pulse pick up its beat in response. What did it matter that he saw her watching over her child in the dark of the night? After all, there was no one else to care.

She looked up, a slight turn of her head.

Her eyes, deeply violet-blue with love and compassion for her son, looked on his and could not look away, caught in his gaze.

Henry was drawn to her as a moth drawn to its ultimate destruction in the vibrant glow of a candle flame, against all his instincts to keep his distance from this lovely girl—woman, now—who had stolen his heart, and still held it in chains. Walking softly forward, so as not to disturb the child, his eyes never left hers. What compulsion drove him he did not know—and she made no move to stop him, equally trapped in the moment, to bring him to his senses. Placing a hand on the back of the low chair, he bent to allow his fingers to lift to her throat, to caress the graceful curve of her nape beneath her hair. She neither flinched nor resisted. If she had, he promised himself he would leave her. But she remained motionless, perhaps even leaned into his touch when he allowed his palm to brush and then cup her cheek, in the lightest of restraints. So he bent his head, slowly, deliberately, to take her lips with his. Whisper soft, mouth on mouth, encouraged by the small sound of pleasure in her throat. He savoured the sweetness of her breath, her mouth, her surrender to him.

It was a moment of impossible tenderness, recognised by them both, as the babe slept on by their side. Eleanor raised her hand to close her fingers round his wrist, a warm bracelet that held him, gentle yet burning him with its heat. Her breath caught as he deliberately allowed his tongue to trace the outline of her lips. She sighed against his mouth.

'Hal.'

Her perfume, the fine texture of hair and skin, her softness entrapped him, caught in that heart-stopping moment.

Then he eased back to look down into the beautiful face, a depth of emotion in his eyes. He could not have expressed his desires aloud for the world. But he captured her other hand from the side of the crib and lifted it to press his lips to the centre of her palm, marvelling at the softness of it.

'Nell…'

He murmured her name, the only word he had spoken since he had come into the room. A whisper of passion restrained. He ached with hard arousal, desire for her, a powerful need to touch and be touched, pulsing through every cell in his body.

When tears sparkled on her lashes he reached, without thought, to remove them with his lips.

Then he drew back and pushed himself to his full height. What could he say? It was a moment beyond words. So much promise, so much pain between them. So many broken dreams. He gave a little bow, strangely formal. Then turned and left the room as silently as he had come.

Henry's actions—and Eleanor's response—left emotions in turmoil. For both of them.

Chapter Five

On the following morning Lord Henry found himself alone in the sunny breakfast parlour. It was as he expected—and planned; it was still very early, but he intended to be under way to the village of Whitchurch before the rest of the household had risen. With good fortune he would return within the day. It crossed his mind with some force, and had done so more than once during a restless night of knife-edged introspection, that it might be to his advantage if he did not have to make conversation with Eleanor that day. What had driven him to such an unwise gesture towards her? He cursed himself once again for his blind stupidity. Within a few weeks this whole fiasco would be settled one way or another, and he would leave England. He would be out of her life for good—and he would be free to forget her and return to the attractions of Rosalind. But even though he swore at his uncontrolled actions, castigated himself for not keeping his distance, he was being driven to admit that he was not unmoved by Eleanor's plight. Unmoved? He swore again, brows drawn into a black bar. A magnificent understatement! He had loved her once and was bitterly aware that, however inappropriate and insupportable it might be, given their past history, he loved her still. Wanting nothing more than to take her to his bed, to undress her, to touch, to taste and to savour her for the rest of his life. To feel her stretch against him, beneath him, and hear his name on her lips when he roused her beyond thought and beyond sense. It would have taken a man of callous indifference not to respond to her plight of the previous night without tenderness and compassion. And where Eleanor was concerned, Henry was not that man.

So it would be better for everyone if he did not have to exchange polite conversation with her that morning! And doubtless Eleanor too would welcome his absence.

The door opened and there she stood.

They both became very still, Lord Henry with a teacup raised to his lips, Eleanor braced in the doorway. The previous night loomed between them, tension stark.

'Good morning, my lady. I trust you slept well.' Henry rose superbly to the occasion with the first bland comment that came to mind, wincing inwardly at his lack of polish. Then the emotional memories of the previous night were effectively wiped from his mind. With eyes narrowed he surveyed the lady from her head to her feet, momentarily taken aback.

She had taken his advice! And with stunning effect. He had not really expected it, but she had cast off her deep mourning and her black ribbons. The result took his breath, silenced any comment he might have been about to make. His memories of her had been as a débutante, certainly beautiful, but still ingenuously naïve in simple pastel muslins. And then in mourning, the stark black of her high-necked gowns highlighting her glorious hair and porcelain skin, grief adding a fine-drawn maturity to her face. But now he was struck anew by her beauty. Two years had added sophistication, elegance, confidence. An unfathomable grace. He had not realised the true worth of the woman he had lost that night when he had sailed without her. But he realised it now, with a blow to his gut, over the breakfast table with the sunshine pouring through the windows.

She had abandoned her black silk for a walking dress in dove grey spotted muslin, banded with a delicate interweaving of purple and amethyst flowers, the whole completed with a frilled hem. Its sleeves were long and tight with short puffed oversleeves, the neckline high and pleated into a little frilled ruff. It fit to perfection, emphasising her slender figure, the embroidered decoration bringing out the intense colour of her eyes. She glowed in the morning sun, the fragile tints shimmering round her. It might still be mourning, demure and understated, but it complimented her colouring beautifully, her hair falling rich and burnished in a profusion of artless curls from a high knot to her shoulders.

His eyes came slowly back from their appreciation of her transformation, his mouth dry, words beyond him, to study her face. She did not look rested. Her pale skin still lacked colour, her eyes were strained and the shadows still left their delicate imprint. But she looked determined, a challenge in every line of her firm shoulders and the proud carriage of her head. She also looked apprehensive.

How fortunate, she realised, that he could not read her thought as she stood under his unnerving gaze. She had dreaded this meeting, needing all her pride and composure. But she had dressed for impact and raised her chin against any disapproval she might read in his face. She should never have allowed him to touch her. But she had, and had melted beneath the unmistakable tenderness of his touch. A mistake! Which she would not repeat, she promised herself—however great the temptation to do so. She would hide her trepidation behind a mask of fashionable unconcern. Yet she still found it well nigh impossible to lift her eyes to his or accept his critical survey with any degree of ease.

'My lady!' Henry rose to his feet at last, and bowed his head in acknowledgement of her gesture. But he did not approach her. Did not dare if he wished to mask the leap of heat in his blood as he studied her. He cursed again as the fire built and stirred in his loins. 'Allow me to say that you look lovely. And allow me to admit that I did not think that you would do it. What does your mother say?' His eyes narrowed again at the prospect of biting words from that quarter.

'Thank you, my lord. She does not know.' Eleanor still could not meet his eyes, unsure of what she would see in his face. If it was contempt or condemnation for her lack of respect for his brother, she could not bear it. Not after the unbelievable and exquisite cherishing of the previous night. 'I need to ask… I understand the reason for your advice, but I would not wish to show insufficient respect for Thomas. It is hardly more than four months… Do you perhaps consider it improper?' Now she lifted her troubled eyes to his. 'I hope that you would be honest with me. Indeed, I know that you will.'

Henry chose his words carefully to allay her anxieties. He could not take her in his arms as his heart might dictate, so he would use his mind to enfold her with comforting words, to soothe and calm. His face was stern, his voice firm with conviction, willing her to accept and believe. 'Your respect for Thomas can be questioned by no one, Eleanor. Your friends must know your qualities as wife and mother. As for your clothing, it is becoming and befits the situation. All you need is the confidence to carry it off. Yes, people will talk. Of course they will! Let them, until the next scandal raises its head to replace the sordid details of our family difficulties on their lips. We have nothing to hide and we will not allow society to dictate the behaviour of the Faringdons.'

'Even if I am not a Faringdon? It is a matter of some dispute, after all.'

There. She had said it aloud and waited, eyes closed, for his reply.

'There is no doubt in my mind, Eleanor. No matter the weight of evidence, I cannot accept that my brother would make such a terrible mistake with such painful and disastrous consequences for all concerned.'

She sighed and opened her eyes, blinking against the unexpected threat of tears at his firm declaration. 'That is what I needed to hear. I am in your debt, Hal.'

'No. You are not. You are in no one's debt! And besides, the dress is very becoming. You are a beautiful woman, Eleanor. Lift up your head and smile.'

She did just that. The smile might waver a little, but she would hold her own, of that he was certain.

Satisfied with his reply, Eleanor took a seat opposite to his place at the breakfast table and Henry resumed his seat. 'I hoped that I would find you here. I wished to know—what is your next strategy?'

He breathed out slowly. Now they were on even ground again,

without the threat of uncomfortable emotions to stalk and trap them. He could cloak his feelings in practicalities. 'It is my intention to go down to Whitchurch to speak with the Reverend Broughton. I know that Hoskins will be efficient in his investigation, but I would wish to see the village for myself, perhaps speak to some who know the family.' He frowned down at the scattering of crumbs on his empty plate. 'What I will discover I know not. Merely some knowledge of the Baxendale family, I suppose.'

Eleanor leaned forward, fingers linked on the table. 'Would you agree to wait until tomorrow and allow me to accompany you?'

'No.' His reply was unequivocal.

Eleanor was taken aback. 'Then I must go on my own.'

'To Whitchurch? Why should you? It is not a good idea.'

'If you will not drive me, then I will simply hire a carriage and go myself.'

Henry knew when he was being driven into a corner. She was quite capable of doing just that. Her lips were firm, her eyes ablaze with the certainty of her actions and there would be no gainsaying her. Lord Henry's mouth set with displeasure. He retreated but with little grace; the last thing he wanted was to spend the better part of a day in Eleanor's company.

'Very well, if that is what you wish. But, I warn you, I intend to take the curricle and travel fast. I would return within the day. And I will not tolerate your mother with us, so do not even suggest it!'

'You will not have to. There is insufficient room for her in a curricle!' Eleanor was maddeningly matter of fact in dealing with his objection and he suspected a spark of triumph in her eyes before she veiled them. 'Tomorrow it is.'

'Why not today?' he enquired brusquely.

Eleanor rose to pour herself a cup of tea, looking at him over her shoulder. 'This afternoon I intend to pay a visit on Miss Baxendale. I hope to take Judith with me for moral support. She may be able to discuss matters of which I know nothing. Perhaps Octavia will speak more openly if her brother is not present and I would know more of her supposed marriage.' She returned to her seat, her face pensive. 'The most difficult thing for me will be to face the servants at Faringdon House...but I must do it.'

Any ill feelings that Lord Henry might have been harbouring over his change of plan were instantly dispelled by the stark courage of Eleanor's proposed scheme.

'You have all my admiration, Nell.'

'Don't be kind to me or, even worse, show me *pity*, or I shall surely weep,' she snapped immediately. 'I cannot afford to be downtrodden over this. Even though there seems to be so little hope...' Her face was closed, shuttered against his careful scrutiny. She sipped her tea, holding her cup with hands which were not quite steady.

'I would ask a favour from you, Hal.'

Now she looked at him.

'Anything in my power.' He found himself stretching out his hand to her across the table, the lightest of touches on her fingers, a symbol of unity with her. Her reply astounded him, showing the lengths to which she was prepared to go to fight for her good name.

'Will you drive me around Hyde Park this morning? At a time when most of our acquaintance will be there? You said that we should be seen, and I wish to do so. The scandal has to break some time and I believe it will be soon rather than late.' She took a breath. 'I do not know how bad it will be, but I fear it. I cannot allow that fear to dominate my whole life. Will you drive me?' Her eyes pleaded with him, holding his until he would give her an answer. He could not but respond to such anguish, but she misread the brilliant glitter, the firming of the lines around his mouth as he was driven to acknowledge once again his love for her. She drew back a little and looked away. 'If you do not wish to, of course, Nicholas might.'

'You mistake me, my lady.' He kept his voice low. 'I am always at your service.' It was as much as he could say. Then a smile lightened his expression as he saw the possibilities of her plan. 'I will drive you round Hyde Park with great pleasure. And I think that we should go out of our way to make an impression. I will take Thomas's high-perch phaeton, which is sure to draw all eyes. Fine feathers indeed! It is in the stables at Faringdon House with some suitable bloodstock. Will that suit your intention?'

Eleanor shuddered, bringing the equipage to mind. 'If I must. An impression indeed! I...I will not let you or your family down, whatever the reception from the *haut ton.*'

'No matter. I will support you, Nell, whatever the outcome. You should know that.' Standing, he walked round the table, took her hand to urge her to her feet. 'You are not alone in this battle, you know.' He kissed her fingers with grave respect, holding her fingers still within his warm clasp.

'Of course.' Her words might be politely non-committal, but she returned the pressure of his hand, compelled by the instant warmth in the region of her heart.

Henry felt it and was satisfied. 'If *you* have the courage to visit Octavia, then I suppose that tonight *I* must join Nick in the gaming hells of Pall Mall!'

Two hours later, Eleanor presented herself promptly on the front doorstep of their house in Park Lane as Lord Henry manoeuvred the high-perch phaeton to a halt at the curb before her. Eleanor eyed it askance, but was forced to admit the excellence of Henry's scheme. In this carriage they would without doubt draw attention to themselves, as Henry had predicted. The woodwork gleamed glossily. As did the well-groomed coats of the pair of bays with their glittering harness. They pawed the ground with restive impatience, eager to be off. The huge hind wheels and the seat that overhung the front axle had been picked out with elegant simplicity in dark blue. Eleanor chose not to contemplate its height from the ground.

But it would suit their purpose. They wished to be seen and noticed. They could hardly help it.

And Henry himself had risen to the occasion, she was quick to appreciate, in the height of fashion with more care than was his wont. He was now sporting the palest of biscuit pantaloons, highly polished boots, a coat of dark blue superfine, which fit to perfection, and a discreetly striped waistcoat. His neckcloth might not be as extreme as some, but the folds were precise, tied by the hand of a master and secured by a sapphire pin. The whole ensemble was covered by a caped greatcoat, which hung negligently open with casual grace.

Eleanor found herself staring. With his striking good looks, he would draw any woman's eye. What hope was there for her poor heart when faced with his dark splendour? What chance to persuade herself that she did not care and that her heart did not beat faster merely at the sight of his dark hair and arresting features? She would have as much success in persuading herself not to breathe! And it was made even more impossible by knowing that his sometimes hard exterior hid a depth of kindness and understanding. Not to forget the burning kiss to remind her of what they might have meant to each other. She flushed and bit her lip as he reined in and leapt to the ground with fluid agility.

He looked her over critically.

'Excellent! A smile would help.'

And she did. It might be a trifle brittle, it might not quite reach her eyes, but it illuminated her face and would fool those who did not know her or did not choose to look closely enough.

Henry did both and felt his heart stir with compassion and longing.

She had completed her outfit with a close-fitting, highwaisted spencer in black silk. It added the perfect touch of sobriety to the silver grey of her gown. Her grey silk-covered bonnet tied beneath her chin with long ribbons, its brim framing her lovely face, the silk flowers in shades of violet and amethyst, detracting from the severity of the whole. A pair of flat slippers, grey kid gloves, a neat reticule and a silver grey parasol—and she was ready for the ordeal. She had exquisite taste, he acknowledged. Elegance and sobriety, layered in perfect harmony, not full mourning, but quiet and respectful. He could not fault her. And he was struck anew by her beauty as she turned her head to look at him.

He handed Eleanor up into the high carriage, mounted himself and waited as she arranged her skirts and unfurled her parasol.

'Ready?' He closed his hand momentarily over hers, knowing exactly what was going through her head, the pain of the anxieties that gripped her with fierce claws. 'Do we not look splendid?' His smile was wry. 'And highly respectable, of course! Not a whisper of scandal between us!' The groom swung up behind them as Henry took up the reins and the longhandled whip.

Before they could pull away, Nick appeared from the front door to stand beside them on the pavement, dressed to take a turn in Bond Street or stroll through Piccadilly, a quizzical expression on his face as he surveyed his brother.

'I am impressed, Hal.'

'So you should be. I hope the Polite World in Hyde Park will say the same.'

'Can you manage those bays? They can be lively. Perhaps I should offer to drive Eleanor round the park, for her own safety. You must be out of practice. Or do they have such sophistication in the colonies these days?' His lips curled in gentle mockery, hoping to drive away the strained shadows in Eleanor's face.

'I can manage. If you remember, I taught you to drive—to my cost! For your sins, you could find yourself a mount and come and ride with us.'

Henry's expression held a silent message. *A show of force in the face of the gossips would not come amiss. Eleanor would welcome it.*

'Very well. I will join you in the park—so don't crash the carriage before I arrive!'

A superior smile from Henry was the only answer.

'Thank you. You are very kind.' Eleanor's soft murmur told him that she was perfectly aware of his intent. He smiled reassuringly at her, before turning his attention to his horses.

In spite of Nicholas's barbed comments on his brother's expertise, Eleanor found herself in no danger at Henry's hands. He drove carefully through the crowded streets, skilfully avoiding a multitude of carriages and heavy wagons that thronged the centre of the city. He had the horses well in hand. She was left with the freedom to watch and admire his skill, the clever strength of his hands, with their broad palms and long fingers. They looped and wielded the reins and whip with casual and confident ease. She knew the gentleness of their touch for herself. And their power. She turned her face away in dismay.

* * *

Meanwhile, as Nicholas made his way to the stables at Faringdon House to acquire a suitable hack, his thoughts were taken up, not with the complications and, probably, repercussions of the Baxendale claim, but with the teasing matter of Eleanor and his brother. There was some past history here. The more he watched them together, the more he was certain of it. And it had left a bitter residue. He tightened his lips as he remembered their first meeting in the withdrawing-room at Burford Hall. The tension in the atmosphere. The crackle of shock, of controlled hostility, particularly from his brother. Nicholas had decided, although he did not understand it, that it was simply a case of instant dislike, but now he was not so sure. Hal was so caring of Eleanor. So concerned. He had altered all his plans, transported them all to London and was intent on waging an all-out battle campaign. Yes, to protect the family name and Thomas's integrity, of course. Hal could be expected to do just that. But there was a far more personal involvement here. Nicholas saddled up his hack, deciding that he would be prepared to wager five hundred guineas that Hal's feelings for Eleanor were not those of a brother towards a sister. As for Eleanor, it was difficult to tell. Who could ever read a woman's mind with any degree of accuracy! With a shrug, he pulled on his gloves, looped his grey's reins and set himself to join the fray in Hyde Park.

Some ten minutes later Lord Henry Faringdon and the Marchioness of Burford turned into the formal gates of Hyde Park near Apsley House, to be immediately swallowed up by a constant promenade of those of the fashionable world who wished to see and be seen. Carriages, riders, saunterers, turned out in the height of fashion, ready to hail acquaintances, issue and accept invitations, chatter and gossip. Eleanor squared her shoulders and set to face the unknown beast in its den. Her smile was securely pinned in place, her parasol positioned to a nicety as she looked around her with commendable interest and confidence, not afraid to meet anyone's eye or raise her hand in greeting.

It did not take long.

Veiled looks. Whispered comments behind gloved hands or hidden by the little feather muffs that had become so fashionable. Quick speculative glances from bright eyes.

'They know!'

'Yes. It had to happen.' Henry, too, was aware. 'But *we* are not concerned with trivial and empty gossip. We know the truth. You are the Marchioness of Burford.' He smiled at an acquaintance and nodded his head as he looped the reins to pass a curricle. 'Your son is the Marquis of Burford. Don't forget it.' He inclined his head with superbly arrogant condescension toward an elderly Dowager who raised her lorgnette in their direction.

The Marchioness promptly followed suit. She took a deep breath and set herself to follow instruction as Nick joined them on a lively grey hack.

'I see they're tattling.'

Which brutal words, Eleanor decided later, summed up the experience of the next hour.

It proved to be an education. Few people were secure enough in their knowledge to risk an outright snub to the well-born Faringdon brothers and their fair companion, no matter their doubts over the lady's present position.

The Princess Lieven, handsome wife of the Russian ambassador, did, of course. As her barouche drove past, she stared straight ahead, eyes cold, mouth unmoving, the epitome of cold disapproval of the English in general and the Faringdons in particular. The Faringdon phaeton might as well have been invisible. There was no recognition of a lady with whom the Princess had taken tea or exchanged cool pleasantries at Almack's. What would you expect from the most feared patroness of Almack's, so fixated with what was seemly and proper and good *ton*, Eleanor thought, her heart sinking.

'A disagreeable woman with an acid tongue!' Henry broke into her thoughts with a more forthright observation and lifted her spirits. 'All self-consequence and pride with nothing but contempt for those around her.'

'No more vouchers from Almack's from that quarter!' Nick, riding beside them, smiled wryly at the calculated snub.

'Thank God! A blessing in disguise!'

Eleanor laughed at Henry's irreverence and had to admit the truth of it. But it hurt.

Mostly the pleasure-seekers in Hyde Park were unsure. They were quite prepared to smile, wave or stop for a brief exchange of words. But eyes were uneasy. Glances interested, assessing the weight of evidence—or lack of it—that might suggest that the Marchioness of Burford was an impostor. And her infant son... Well! Knowing eyes slid away from too close a contact. Yet the Faringdons still received an invitation to a quiet evening party, from no less a personage than the Countess of Sefton. Just a small gathering. Perfectly proper for their present situation, with the loss of dear Thomas. Isabella Sefton's eyes were full of sympathy, her soft tones saying what her words could not. But the fact that she had gone to the lengths to instruct her coach-man to rein in so that she could speak to them was balm to Eleanor's soul. Such kindness from one of the patronesses of Almack's threatened her composure.

They met Cousin Judith being escorted by the Earl of Pain-scastle in a smart barouche. The couple made a point of stopping to engage in animated conversation. Eleanor intercepted an eloquent glance between Henry and the lady, immediately alerting her suspicions. Henry had arranged the very public assignation, intent on leaving nothing to chance. A show of family unity and support could do nothing but good.

When the gentlemen fell to discussing horseflesh, Eleanor took the opportunity for a quiet word with Judith across the two carriages.

'It is my intention to pay an afternoon call on Octavia—I would be more than grateful if you could accompany me.'

'Octavia?' Judith's face lit up with sly enthusiasm. 'Of course I will come. I would not miss it for the world. What do we talk about?'

'Herself. Thomas.' Eleanor shrugged a little helplessly. 'Anything that might help me to understand.'

'Anything that might brand her as a liar?'

'Yes.' Eleanor sighed at the outspoken truth. 'That is what I could hope for.'

'I will definitely accompany you.' The Countess of Pains-castle opened her frivolous lace parasol with a definite snap. 'I will collect you in the barouche at three o'clock!'

They drove, waved, exchanged polite greetings under the intense scrutiny of the Polite World for more than an hour.

'Take me home, Hal. I have played out this role for long enough.' Eleanor furled her parasol with weary distaste.

'You were magnificent. You should feel nothing but pride.' Henry's quick glance at Eleanor confirmed his suspicion that the morning had begun to take its toll. If she would admit to it, a headache had begun to build behind her eyes from the strain of smiling and denying the effect of sharp, critical glances.

He would take her home. He would have liked nothing better than to take her away from London, from the whole sorry mess. To remove the hurt and the humiliation. But he could not. They must face it and defeat it if they were to restore Eleanor to her rightful place in society—and in her own eyes, a matter of even greater importance. Her spirit had been superb, carrying off the morning's exercise in full public gaze with considerable panache, but the threat of society's condemnation loomed on the horizon, as threatening as a thunder cloud.

They turned out of the gates, once more below the imposing façade of Apsley House.

'You did not stop to speak to Melissa Charlesworth,' Eleanor noted as a landaulet bearing the lady, now the Countess of Salt-marshe and once the object of Henry's gallantry, passed them with no change in speed.

'I did not see her.' His voice was surprisingly harsh.

Eleanor's brows arched. 'No?'

'No. She is not important.'

With which caustic comment Eleanor had to be content.

Eleanor and Judith arrived, as arranged, at Faringdon House to pay an afternoon call on Octavia Baxendale. The door was opened by Eaton, the Faringdon butler, momentarily lost for words when faced with the mistress of the house come as a visitor on a social call.

'My lady…' he stammered. 'It is not fitting that you should remain standing on your own doorstep…'

Before embarrassment could fall and smother both parties, Judith took the matter in hand, manipulating the situation in a high-handed and confident manner worthy of her mama, Lady Beatrice Faringdon, a lady of considerable presence and force of character, indicating that the Marchioness was staying with Lord Henry who had hired a town house in Park Lane, but only until he returned to America later in the month.

'It is more convenient, you understand!' But for whom and for what purpose the Countess of Painscastle made no attempt to explain.

And how was Eaton? As well as ever? And was Sir Edward Baxendale at home? No? How unfortunate… But perhaps Miss Baxendale was receiving visitors? She would no doubt welcome some company, knowing so few people in town! Perhaps Eaton could discover if…

Eleanor caught Judith's eye in deep gratitude—and then they were being shown into the familiar red-and-gold-striped withdrawing-room where Miss Baxendale sat alone beside the fireplace, a piece of needlework lying abandoned on the table beside her. The lady sprang to her feet as Eaton introduced the guests with a flourish. He did not know the full background to this development, and although common gossip was rife…he would dearly have loved to listen at the door, except that it was below his dignity. A pleasant enough young lady, Miss Baxendale, but not to compare with the Marchioness, of course. But the word in the town suggested deep doings. He shook his head as he departed for the kitchens to organise tea and inform the members of the servants' hall that *things were afoot* upstairs.

'Edward is not at home I am afraid.' Octavia looked rather nervously from one lady to the other. 'But if you would care to sit. And take some tea?'

The faint look of unease that hung about her black-gowned

figure suggested that she would rather they did not, but Eleanor came forward in friendly mode with hand outstretched and a smile on her face. There was nothing for Octavia to do but participate in the gentle social occasion with the lady whose social position, it appeared, she had every intention of appropriating for herself.

'We have come to see you, Miss Baxendale, to find how you are settling in,' Eleanor explained. 'I trust that we are not disturbing you. And my cousin Judith has come, with whom you might be acquainted.'

Octavia looked at the lively redhead as they made a polite curtsy. 'Perhaps… You were Miss Faringdon, were you not? And now the Countess of Painscastle? Pray take a seat.'

They did so.

'How uncomfortable this is…' Octavia picked up her embroidery and promptly put it down again, lost for words, unable to raise her eyes above her restless hands.

'But it will not stop us drinking tea together and having a cosy exchange of news.' Eleanor tried to put the lady at her ease, not for the first time wondering how Thomas could have possibly married this pretty but insipid creature.

'We came out in the same Season, Miss Baxendale.' Judith smiled encouragingly. 'I believe that we met at any number of balls and soirées.'

'Yes. I met so many people. But I think…I am sure that I remember you. I came to your coming-out ball in this very house. My aunt and uncle—and my brother, of course—chaperoned me. I remember thinking what a beautiful house it was. I never thought that I should be living here…' With which ingenuous comment she flushed and turned her head with relief when Eaton and an interested footman brought in the tea.

The ceremony was performed with nervous competence by Miss Baxendale, the tea was served, and the ladies chatted about a range of inconsequences of fashion and the events offered by London to ladies with a degree of leisure and affluence. Then Judith returned to her reminiscing over the glories of her Seasonal debut, Octavia agreeing and nodding but adding few of her own impressions.

'And how are you spending your time in London now?' Judith tried for another approach as the conversation dried.

'Sir Edward has been very busy,' Octavia explained. 'I have rarely been out.'

'And of course, you are still in mourning.' Eleanor sympathised with a sad smile, eyes keen and watchful.

'Why, yes…it would not be seemly for me to go about in public to any great degree. I see that you, my lady, have laid aside your black gloves.' She took in the glory of silver grey with some surprise.

'Indeed I have.' Eleanor did not elaborate. 'Have you perhaps driven in the park yet, Miss Baxendale? The days have been very pleasant. And I am sure Sir Edward would drive you to take the air. It would be quite acceptable for you in your situation.'

'No. I have not been beyond the garden.'

'Do you enjoy music or painting? To help to pass the time a little when your brother is from home?' Judith arched her brows.

'No. I do a little embroidery, as you see.'

'Perhaps you miss your garden in the country. Where is it that you lived?'

'In Whitchurch. And, yes, I miss it so much. The roses will just be coming into bloom. I shall not be there to tend them and wish I was…' It was the first animation that Octavia Baxendale had shown since her guests had arrived, her whole countenance blooming as did her roses, but only to be stemmed as if she feared an indiscretion. 'But, of course, it is necessary for me to be here.'

'You must miss it indeed. Now I have no interest at all in gardens, but I understand that it can be a great solace in times of grief.' Judith put down her teacup and leaned across the little table to pat Octavia's hand. 'Eleanor has been telling me about your little son. What a splendid boy he is. Could we perhaps see him? My lord and I are hoping for a child very soon…' She lowered her lashes in coy anticipation.

Eleanor hid a smile. Cousin Judith had a remarkable range of skills of which she had been unaware until now.

'Of course.' Octavia appeared a little surprised that her guests would wish to see her son, but rose to her feet to pull the bell hang beside the fireplace.

'Would you ask Sarah to bring the child down?' The footman bowed and departed.

Within minutes the door opened. In came the young woman whom Eleanor had last seen in Burford Hall. Fair and neat with a ladylike composure. Fair enough, perhaps, to be one of the family. A dependent of good birth, Eleanor decided, but most likely fallen on hard times, now holding the hand of the child, John. John Faringdon, if the documents were correct.

'This is Sarah,' Octavia said, confirming Eleanor's impression. 'She has been my companion and now acts as nurse to John.' The lady curtsied and released the little boy, who immediately ran to show his mama a wooden boat that he had clasped in his hand. Miss Baxendale patted his head. John thrust the precious possession into her hands, announcing 'Boat!' with a disarming smile.

'What a beautiful child.' Judith held out her hands. 'Come here, John. Let me see your boat.'

The child, aware of the possibility of a wider audience, walked shyly to Judith and then gurgled with shocked pleasure when she snatched him up and sat him on her knee. 'What a handsome boat. And so are you very handsome. All those golden curls and such blue eyes.' She pinched the end of his nose to make him laugh.

'He is a good child.' Octavia nodded and smiled as Judith stood him back on his feet when he struggled for freedom and restored his boat to his grasp. With a crow John launched himself back towards Sarah where she had remained beside the door, but, with uncoordinated enthusiasm, fell on the wide expanse of deep turkey carpet. For a second he crouched motionless. Then tears came to his eyes and a sob to his chest.

'There, now,' Octavia said. 'You are not very hurt.' Sarah swooped, picked up the child, kissing his cheek, smoothing away his tears with her hand, crooning to him in a soft voice.

'Is he well?' Octavia watched the little scene with a graceful turn of her head. So did Eleanor and Judith.

'John took no hurt, ma'am.'

'Perhaps you could take him back to the nursery, Sarah. He tends to get a little excited in company' she explained to the visitors. 'It is not good for a child.'

With a curtsy to the assembled company, Sarah walked to the door, holding the boy close, and left.

What else should they talk about? Judith tried fashions and the opening of a number of new modistes where the most ravishing hats and gowns could be purchased, but although Octavia was pleasant and smiling, she had little to say and shared little interest in what might or might not be considered *de rigueur*.

'I believe that it is time we left.' In desperation Eleanor was about to rise to her feet. 'My own son will be missing me by now, I expect.' Then the door opened to admit Sir Edward Baxendale. He greeted his guests with great charm and a warm smile, sat with them and accepted a hand-painted porcelain cup of tea from his sister. The talk encompassed the weather and Judith's new barouche, which awaited them at the door, but it was noticed that Octavia said no more.

'Well?' Eleanor and Judith were once again ensconced in the comfort of Judith's barouche after what could only be described as a frustrating and disappointing afternoon.

'That child is no Faringdon!' Judith pulled on her gloves with conviction.

'But he is very fair like his mother.'

'Faringdons breed true!' Judith insisted. 'Look at your own son. He might have your eyes, but his father's hair, his nose and mouth are very pronounced. There is no denying his parentage. I swear there is no trace of Thomas in that child!'

Eleanor flushed and hesitated at Judith's observations. 'But that is not proof. *You* inherited your mother's red hair and green eyes rather than your father's features.'

'Very true. But I have the Faringdon nose. And eyebrows. There is no mistaking them. The golden-haired child *we* have just seen bears no resemblance at all.'

'No. Perhaps not.' It had to be admitted. 'She is no doting mother, is she?' Eleanor commented. 'That surprised me a little.'

'Ha! Just because you are!' Judith smiled in understanding. 'We are not all born to lavish unbounded love and affection on our offspring. He is certainly a healthy child and well cared for.'

'I suppose.' Eleanor frowned at her recollection of the child's tears. *She* would not have been able to ignore them—to allow his nurse to lift and comfort him! 'I presume that Octavia's reminiscences of her coming-out were correct?'

'Yes…' Judith wrinkled her nose '…but she does not have much to say, does she?'

'No. And even less when Sir Edward arrived home.'

They were silent in thoughtful communion as the barouche made its steady way towards Park Lane.

'You know…' Judith ventured, brow furrowed in thought, 'Simon would make himself scarce if he knew a party of ladies were gossiping in his withdrawing-room. Wouldn't Thomas have done the same?'

'Why, yes…I hadn't thought. Thomas would have gone to the stables until they had all gone! Sir Edward joined us straight away. Why do you think that was?'

Green eyes met amethyst, their thoughts clear between them.

'But it does not add up to much, does it?' Eleanor queried. 'Merely that Sir Edward would prefer his sister not to be alone with visitors.'

'Or is it that he did not wish Octavia be alone with *you!*' responded Judith.

There was no answer to it.

The two ladies prepared to part company on Eleanor's doorstep. Judith leaned down from her carriage to where Eleanor stood on the pavement and clasped her hand in firm support.

'Have we proved anything?' Judith asked.

'No.'

'Except that Octavia was definitely not Thomas's usual flirt!' Judith tightened her hold to enforce her point. 'It is very difficult to believe, after spending such a tedious half-hour in her company, that he fell in love with her and married her. Whereas I can quite believe that he loved and married you, dear Nell!'

Eleanor took a breath. 'Sir Edward said that—'

'Tell me, Nell.'

'When they first came to Burford Hall—when they told us of the whole dreadful complication—Sir Edward said that Thomas forced Octavia to keep their marriage secret because of her lack of rank. That his family would disapprove.' A line deepened between her fine brows as her mind worried at the problem. 'But *my* birth, Judith, is no better than Octavia's, and I know that the Faringdons would never have chosen someone of so little consequence as myself for Thomas's bride, however supportive you and Aunt Beatrice might be now that we are faced with this scandal. Yet Thomas followed his own wishes in the face of family opposition and married me with as much public display as he could achieve.' She smiled a little sadly as she remembered the festivity and ceremonial of her marriage. 'All I am trying to say is that social standing does not seem to me to be a good enough reason for Thomas to hide Octavia away in the country—if he truly loved her and wished to marry her.'

Judith had flushed uncomfortably at her companion's devastatingly accurate reading of family opinion on her marriage to Thomas, but patted Eleanor's hand, for once all the careless flippancy quite gone from her face. 'Of course Thomas never married Octavia, dearest Nell. You must never allow yourself to think that. And as for your lack of rank—all I can say is that marrying you was one of the best decisions Thomas made in his whole life.'

'Thank you, Judith.' A faint smile touched Eleanor's pale lips. 'At least that is something for me to hold on to!'

In the entrance hall Eleanor's path crossed that of Henry and Nicholas as the two gentlemen prepared to leave the house and look in at Gentleman Jackson's Boxing Academy in New Bond Street before repairing to Brooks's for a hand or two of whist.

'Any fortune with your visit to the fair Octavia?'

'None. But tell me. If I were entertaining a group of ladies to tea and you arrived home, what would you do?'

'Head for the library and take a glass of port until they have gone.' Henry's response took no thought.

Neither did Nicholas's. 'Turn around and go back out to the stables.'

'Thank you. I would expect as much.' Eleanor nodded her head and proceeded to climb the stairs.

'Did we say the right thing?' Nicholas asked.

'I have no idea. Women can be very uncommunicative—and devious! But I am sure that Eleanor will let us know in her own good time. And since we have no library here in this house…' Henry turned on his heel towards the door of the morning room '…I think I need a glass of port before we depart!'

Later that evening Henry and Nicholas prepared to visit some of the discreet gaming establishments that opened their doors to those who had bottomless pockets and sought more excitement than the play offered at Brooks's and White's. There were any number of them with unmarked doors, opened by black-clad individuals who were careful whom they admitted. Some were more legitimate than others, some more honest, but the stakes were high and the play keen in them all. Some were the haunts of card-sharps, quick to lure young men newly arrived in London into the dubious delights of hazard and macao, where disgrace and ruin waited for the unwary flat. And if *point non Plus* was reached, it was always possible to patronise the fashionable establishment of Messieurs Howard and Gibbs, who were more than willing to lend at extortionate rates of interest. It might be that Sir Edward passed his evenings in such company. It might be that he had lost heavily and so was now in debt, sufficient that he would be prepared to risk an outrageous plan to get his hands on a vast fortune. It might provide them with a reason why he should put forward such a preposterous claim of marriage on behalf of his sister.

It proved to be a long evening.

By the end of it, after numerous hands of whist, reacquaintance with French hazard and roulette and too many glasses of inferior brandy, they had nothing to show for it other than lighter pockets and the lurking prospect of a hangover.

Sir Edward Baxendale did not spend his evenings or his money in any of the gaming hells they visited.

'So what does Sir Edward do with his time when he is in London?'

They strolled back to Park Lane in the early hours of the morning.

'Horses?' Nick suggested. 'But how we are to discover if he squanders his money on the Turf, I know not. I suppose we could look in at Tattersalls and see if he is known for betting on the horses. We do not know even if he is in debt.'

'No.' Henry fought off the looming sense of depression at the futility of the evening and the prospect of the long journey on the following day.

'Do you think he has a mistress?' Nicholas asked.

'To demand vast sums of money and diamond necklaces? A possibility.' Henry grinned at the prospect. 'Mistresses can be very expensive.'

'The voice of experience.' Nicholas returned the grin. 'And how would we discover that?'

'Have him followed, I expect!'

'That I will not do!'

'Go and talk to Hoskins tomorrow. Suggest to him that he make discreet enquiries with Howard and Gibbs—unless you care to? No, I thought not.' He laughed as he saw the expression on Nick's face They had arrived on the steps to their front door. 'But if Baxendale is short of the readies, and does not wish to advertise the matter, a moneylender would be his first port of call. Hoskins will know how to go about it, I expect.' He thought for a moment before opening the door, all humour drained in the dark shadows. 'But you might visit the other gaming houses. Meanwhile I will see what the Reverend Broughton has to say about our elusive gentleman.' He hesitated, but only for a moment. 'I don't suppose you would consider visiting Aunt Beatrice to discover her thoughts on the Baxendales four years ago. Judith reminded me that she has a formidable memory.'

'No.'

'Mmm. Then I will suggest that Mrs Stamford pay a morning call. They can enjoy a comfortable dissection of the manners and morals of the younger generation—and perhaps Aunt Beatrice will remember something of import.'

Chapter Six

Henry leaped down from the curricle, winced at the headache, cursed all gaming hells, and walked back into the entrance hall as Eleanor emerged from the breakfast parlour on the following morning. She had dressed in a smart travelling costume of deep blue, the fine wool double-breasted coat with its long tight sleeves and high waist already buttoned. She was in the act of arranging the wide collar so that it draped elegantly into a cape effect. If his lordship noticed that she wore a particular jewel on her breast, whether deliberately to provoke or through custom, he chose to make no comment.

'I am ready to leave.'

'Are you sure this is a good idea?' He frowned at her as she tied the bow of her neat straw bonnet beneath her chin to charming effect.

'Yes. There is no need to scowl at me, my lord. We have already had this conversation and come to an agreement.'

'I do not remember actually *agreeing* to anything—simply bowing to a stronger force when you threatened to go on your own.' The scowl did not lessen. 'I hope that you realise that we may learn nothing. I could see the Reverend Broughton myself and be back here within the day…'

She shook her head. 'You do not understand. I want to see the village…and hear what he has to say.'

'Do you not trust me to do the right thing?' The demand was brusque, Henry's mouth set in displeasure.

Did she? She looked at him consideringly, head a little on one side. All she knew for certain was that she must not rely on anyone, certainly not on Hal. She had trusted Thomas, had accepted his offer of marriage—which was more than she could ever have dreamed of and for which she would always be grateful to the depths of her soul—but look where that had got her. She must look to her own inner strength to weather this storm.

She turned her back on his lordship to pick up her tan leather gloves, thus evading the answer—which he was quick to notice with regret and a degree of hurt that jolted him. She did not trust him, not even to do all in his power to restore her good name.

'I simply need to go there,' was all that she would say.

The weather was set fair for travel. They made good time in the curricle on the main roads as they negotiated their way out of the growing sprawl of London. There was little conversation between them. Eleanor was too tense and could find nothing to say. Henry concentrated on his horses. When they took to the country lanes their progress was slower, but the pair of greys were excellent animals with strength and stamina and well up to the task. Henry drove them with patient skill to conserve their energies.

Eventually as the sun rose to the height of noon, they drove into the village of Whitchurch. They could see the cluster of stone houses nestling around a squat Norman church over to their left, calm and peaceful in the growing warmth, hardly the place where sordid schemes were in hand. Before reaching the village street, to their right, they drew level with a pretty stone manor house and Henry reined the greys to a walk. Jacobean in construction, behind its ornamental gates and stone wall with well-tended gardens on either side of the gravelled walk leaning up to the main entrance, it made an appealing picture. Behind the house were glimpses of a walled garden and an orchard with a rose-covered pergola leading to a sweep of open parkland.

Lord Henry halted the curricle before the wrought-iron gates.

'What do you think?' Eleanor sat and looked at the house where her husband might have spent time of which she knew nothing.

'It could be. An attractive little estate.' He studied the mellow stonework with a critical and knowledgeable eye. 'Well cared for. Prosperous enough.' A gardener was engaged in clipping a neat box hedge. 'There is someone who can furnish us with a little information.' Henry hailed him. 'Tell me. Does Sir Edward Baxendale live here?'

The gardener, a man of advanced years, opened the gate to come and stand beside the curricle, pulling off his hat and squinting up at his lordship.

'Aye, y'r honour. But not at home—none of the family is. In London, so they says.'

'And his sister?'

'Gone with him, I expect. There's no one 'ere at any event—and not likely to be for the near future, so they says.'

'My thanks.' Henry tossed him a coin and watched him amble back to his box clipping. They sat for a moment and took stock.

'It does not suggest an immediate need for money, does it?'

Eleanor shook her head. 'Do you suppose…?' She hesitated, a deep groove forming between her brows. 'Do you think that Thomas came here to visit Octavia? Did he walk in this garden with her? Beneath those roses? Or sit with her in the arbour in the dusk of a summer's night? Octavia is very fond of gardens…'

'Enough, Eleanor. You must not torture yourself like this! Did I not warn you that it would have been better for you not to come here?' His voice was harsh and when she glanced up in some surprise, she saw no softness in his face. 'What is the point,' he continued, ignoring her distress, 'of *perhaps* and *what if?* It will only lower your spirits and drain your courage. It may be that Thomas did all of those things.' He looked away from the pain that filled her beautiful eyes and swore silently. 'But we still do not know the truth of it.'

She looked away from him and swallowed against the knot of fear and desolation in her throat, unable to find an adequate response. She had not expected such sharpness from him and yet had to admit that his words were justified. He had indeed warned her.

'So what do we do first?' Her voice was admirably controlled.

'We find the inn. It is after noon and you need food. And it might be to our advantage to talk with mine host before we tackle the servant of God.'

They left the curricle and horses in the charge of the ostler at the Red Lion Inn, which overlooked the village green. They were shown into a dark, dusty parlour where the innkeeper fussed over having the gentry call at his establishment. Not many people travelled through the village, the main post road passing to the east as it did. He could not remember the last time that a lady and gentleman of Quality made use of his inn, other than the people at the Great House, of course. But he hoped they would not find the Red Lion wanting. Certainly he could provide refreshment for his lordship and the lady. If they would care to be seated. He whisked ineffectually with a grubby cloth at the dust on table and chairs as his wife bustled in with bread, meat and cheese and a jug of local ale.

Lord Henry pulled out a chair for Eleanor to sit at the table and silently frowned at her so that she began to eat, or at least crumble a piece of bread on her plate.

'You are too pale. And I wager you did not break your fast before we left.' He took a seat opposite, cut a wedge of cheese and added it to the crumbs on her plate, ignoring her objections. 'I would prefer to deliver you back to your son in one piece and in good health.' She had lost weight, he thought. Of course she would in the circumstances, food would be her last consideration, but he had to try to do something to help her. When she had looked at the comfortable manor house and the pretty gardens, when she had envisioned Thomas living out a dream there with another woman, it had taken all his will-power not to drag her into his arms and blot out the cruel vision with his own kisses. He tightened his lips in a wave of disgust. So what had he done? Only snarled at her and increased the pain by his vicious words. He lifted his shoulders a little, discomfited by the thought that his command of his emotions when dealing with Eleanor was not as firm as he would like.

He took a mouthful of ale and then, tankard in hand, engaged the hovering landlord, who had returned to the room with a platter of fruit, in casual conversation.

'We had hoped to visit an acquaintance of ours in the village. Sir Edward Baxendale. We understand that he is from home.'

'Aye, my lord.'

'We do not know him very well. Have his family lived here long?'

'Generations of them, my lord. There's always been a Baxendale in Whitchurch, at the Great House.' Mine host, to Lord Henry's relief, was not reluctant to demonstrate his local knowledge and did not object to their interest in the local gentry.

'Do you see much of the family?'

'Quite a bit. With the hunting. And church. And the ladies walk in the village.'

'Are they well thought of locally?'

'Aye, my lord. Sir Edward's open-handed enough and a fair lord of the manor.'

'I am more acquainted with his sister,' Eleanor prompted, hoping for enlightenment on Octavia.

'Aye. Poor girl.' The innkeeper shook his head in ready sympathy. 'Not that we see much of her, o' course. But it can't be easy for her.'

'Oh?' Eleanor looked up enquiringly, hoping to encourage a more detailed comment.

Mine host nodded. 'What with a baby—growing up he is now—and a husband not long dead. Poor girl. And so pretty. But Sir Edward will ensure that she lacks for nothing—there'll always be a roof over her head. He's always been caring of his family.'

'Of course.' Eleanor smiled and nodded despite the tight band around her heart. 'Did you…did you ever meet the lady's husband before he died?'

'Don't know that I did.' The innkeeper scratched his head. 'Away from home a lot, as I remember, but the lady had made her home here with her brother.'

'Has she…has she gone to London with Sir Edward now?'

'Aye, ma'am. All of them. Saw them myself. And the baby as well. Not to mention the mountain of luggage. Seems like they intend to stay for the Season and the Great House all shut up. Pity you missed them.'

As the innkeeper prepared to return to the public room and leave his guests to eat their luncheon in peace, Lord Henry stopped him.

'One more matter, sir, if you would be so kind. The Reverend Julius Broughton—is he vicar here?'

'Aye, my lord. He is. If you wish to speak with him, the vicarage is the house next to the church, set back behind the stand of elms. But you'll likely find him in the church. They're burying old Sam Potter from down by the forge. So the Reverend Broughton will be doing the Lord's work today at least—you can't turn your back on a funeral if the body's coffined and waiting at the church door! He'll be there—at least for today.'

An interesting comment, Henry thought, not sure what to make of it. Or the slight undercurrent in mine host's voice. Was it dislike? Contempt?

'Do you know the Reverend well?'

'Some.' The innkeeper's smile was sly as he turned for the door. 'Some would say more than an innkeeper should! Likes his ale does the Reverend, and fine brandy. And he has a mind to other things many would say as he should not, being a man of the cloth. Some days he's in the Red Lion more than he's in the church! Not to mention his comforts at home!'

On which he left them.

With Eleanor's hand drawn through his arm, held firmly, Lord Henry stepped out of the Red Lion and strolled down the village street in the direction of the church. The village itself was small, not much more than a score of stone cottages at most, the village street merely hard-packed earth with grassy verges, but the church was impressive with solid walls and zigzag carving on the round-headed arches of door and window. When they came to the gabled lych-gate into the churchyard, they discovered that the innkeeper had been accurate in his information. A funeral was in progress with a small knot of mourners in the far corner of the churchyard where the coffin was being lowered into a grave. They could make out the black and white vestments of the Reverend Julius Broughton amongst them, his white surplice and ministerial bands fluttering in the light breeze.

'We must wait on Samuel Potter for the final time, it seems.' Henry led Eleanor to a sun-warmed seat beside the church door to wait. It was a tranquil spot, sunlit and restful, only the distant murmur of voices to disturb the silence and the nearer chirp of sparrows which were nesting in the roof above their heads. A tranquil place indeed. But one, Eleanor feared, where she might discover the indisputable evidence that she was not Thomas's wife, never had been. In this church Thomas could have been joined with Octavia Baxendale in the sight of God. His son named within those sun-warmed arches. She bit down on the panic that swelled beneath her breast bone. Her life would be shattered beyond redemption.

At last the mourners departed.

'Sam Potter returned to his Maker.' Henry took one of her hands in his, noting her calm outward composure. Perhaps too calm. 'Are you well enough to face the Reverend? I will speak to him alone if you prefer it.' On impulse he pressed his lips to her fingers. 'I do not doubt your courage. I never could. You have nothing to prove to me, Nell.'

'I know. And I know that you would take on this burden.' She smiled her thanks, but rose to her feet, smoothing the skirts of her coat with nervous hands as the clerical figure approached them along the path. 'We will see him together. He cannot tell us anything worse than the knowledge which we already have.'

Introductions were made, the cleric expressing polite interest. Henry, after a glance at Eleanor, opened the point at issue.

'We wish to speak with you, sir, concerning a marriage and a birth in this parish. It concerns a member of our own family.'

Julius Broughton raised his brows at the request, but smiled his compliance. 'Very well. Perhaps you would come to the vicarage where we can sit in comfort and I will see if I can help you.' No hint of unease here.

They followed him to the spacious vicarage, built in the previous century and tucked away behind the elms, to be shown into a library at the front of the house, overlooking the churchyard and the church itself. A pleasant room. Wood panelled, lined with books, a fire offering welcome from the hearth, the retreat of an educated and scholarly man. It was also spotlessly clean, the furniture polished with the books properly on their shelves and the papers on the desk in neat order. It gave the impression of care and order and efficiency, suitable to a conscientious man of the cloth.

The appearance of the man who faced Henry and Eleanor also confirmed this impression. Shorter than Henry, he had a spare figure, fair hair with a touch of bronze when the sun caught it, and pale blue eyes. His narrow face was also that of a scholar with fine, aesthetic features. He had an easy smile that made them welcome as he offered refreshments. Yet Eleanor felt uneasy in his company. She thought there was a slyness in his gaze, which did not sit and linger on anything for long. And his lips, which smiled so readily, were too thin.

The priest rang the bell beside the fireplace and the door was immediately opened by a young girl, as if she had been close at hand and awaiting the summons.

'Molly.' Julius Broughton addressed the girl. 'We have, as you see, visitors. Be so good as to bring brandy for his lordship and ratafia for the lady.'

She bobbed a curtsy, casting a sharp eye over the guests. A village girl, Henry presumed by her simply cut blouse and skirt, very pretty with dark curls under her white cap and attractive curves not in any way disguised by the white apron that enveloped her. Her smile revealed a dimple and she was not averse to a flirtatious glance from beneath long dark lashes. She had an air of smugness and her smile a hint of sly. Henry would wager that Mistress Molly was a most competent housekeeper, if surprisingly young for the position. He suppressed a sardonic gleam as he found himself remembering the innkeeper's enigmatic comments on their priest's interests. They were not difficult to understand,

The refreshments were dispensed, with graceful skill and

concern for their comfort, and then as Molly departed with a final swing of shapely hips the visitors were free to turn to business.

'We are looking for information, sir,' Henry repeated, wondering fleetingly if Mistress Molly was listening at the door.

'So I understand.' The Reverend indicated that they should make themselves comfortable in the charming room. 'I will try to help. Is it something that occurred within my holding of the living here?'

'Yes. The first event less than four years ago.' From his pocket, Henry took a number of gold coins, which he placed, without a word, on the desk beside him.

The Reverend's eyes fixed on them for more than a second, a flush mantling his cheeks. He pressed his lips together. It was, Henry knew, a gamble, based purely on first impressions. It crossed his mind that the priest could see it as an insult to his pride and standing in the community, and so refuse all co-operation with sharp words. Justifiably so if he were an honest man. But he did not. He answered, his eyes still on the money being offered so blatantly, 'Of course, my lord. As I said, I will do what I can.'

Lord Henry had read his man well.

'A marriage. At which you officiated. Between Octavia Baxendale and one Thomas Faringdon. Can you remember such a marriage?'

'Dear Octavia.' The clergyman took his seat behind his desk, resting his hands before him on the polished oak, fingers spread. His lips curled in a smile—or perhaps it was not. 'She is well known to me. A most beautiful girl. Indeed I officiated at her marriage. I remember it. A handsome couple.'

'Were you aware,' Henry asked carefully, 'that the groom was the Marquis of Burford?'

'No, I was not. Before God, a man's title has no relevance. And the law merely requires his name. You hinted, sir, that the matter concerned a member of your family.'

'I did. Thomas Faringdon was my brother.'

'Was he now?' A strange little smile again flirted with the cleric's lips. 'Now I begin to understand. Can I help you further in your search for truth, my lord?'

Henry frowned, but continued. 'I understand that Lady Mary Baxendale, who was a witness to the marriage, has since died.'

'She has. She is buried in the Baxendale tomb here in the crypt. I myself conducted the service.'

And Sir Edward Baxendale. He, too, was present at the marriage ceremony?'

'He was present.' Julius Broughton bowed his head in acknowledgement. Eleanor's brows arched a little. Was it her imagination, or were those clerical fingers suddenly clenched together?

But the Reverend was in no manner disturbed by the questions. His voice remained calm and assured. 'Why do you ask? There was nothing illegal or unseemly about the marriage of Octavia. I have known her, as I said, for many years.'

'And the birth of her son?'

Now there was the slightest hesitation, but the answer was forthright enough.

'You must mean John. I certainly baptised the child John in this church. He will be about two years old now, I surmise.'

'Yes.'

'And the image of his mother! I am sure she is very proud of him. He must be a great solace to her in her time of grief.'

Henry glanced again at Eleanor who shook her head. It was difficult to see where the conversation was leading.

'I presume that you know the Baxendale family well.'

'Indeed I do. You must know that the living here is in their gift. I have every reason to be grateful to Sir Edward for his Christian charity.' The lips that smiled at them were now drawn tight against his teeth. 'He has assured me of his continued benevolence, to the parish and to myself. I have always found him to be a man of his word.'

'If you will forgive me, sir, I hesitate to push the point but— this is a difficult question to ask—have you ever found reason not to trust Sir Edward? To question his honesty?'

'A strange question, if I may say so, my lord.' The Reverend continued to smile, but there was no humour in his pale eyes. 'Let me answer it like this. Octavia is as dear to me as any member of my own family. And I know nothing of Sir Edward that would make me question his integrity. Does that suffice, my lord?'

'Yes.' Henry stood and inclined his head. 'I must thank you for your time and patience, sir.'

They left the room, leaving the little pile of coins on the edge of the desk, glinting brightly and enticingly in the sun.

'I do not like him. I don't know why, but I would not trust him, clergyman or no.' Eleanor spoke her doubts as soon as they were out of sight and sound of the vicarage. 'He smiled like a snake.'

'I have never seen a snake smile, but I take your point. A wily character, I make no doubt. But equally without doubt, he confirms all we knew and feared.' Henry's expression was bleak as he replayed the conversation in his mind. 'Thomas married Octavia. And a son, John, was born.'

Eleanor could make no reply. After all, it was the truth.

The sun still shone. The sparrows still chirruped in the churchyard. And Eleanor's life, as she had feared, lay in pieces at her feet.

During their brief interview the heavy rain-clouds had begun to gather on the horizon and the evening drew close. Seeing the threat of poor travelling weather, Henry made a decision.

'We stay here tonight. I have no mind to be drenched before we arrive home. Let us see if the Red Lion can provide us with some suitable accommodation.'

The landlord at the Red Lion, by the name Jem Abbott, welcomed the return of the lord and lady to his inn with a greedy eye to their generosity. Yes, he could provide them with accommodation. Perhaps not what they would be used to, but comfortable enough. There was a private parlour they could make use of and an adjoining bedroom. Would that be sufficient for their needs? They would not be disturbed. He surveyed them with mild interest. There did not appear to be the stuff of scandal here, but you never knew with the Quality. A law unto themselves, they were! No matter how confident and assured his lordship might be in the settling of his affairs, no matter how elegant and composed the lady. Whether the lady was his lordship's wife was open to debate. But it was none of their concern, as Jem Abbott informed his critical wife, if his lordship had brought his mistress to their establishment. As long as their guests were prepared to pay with hard coin, who were they to judge!

So the landlord set himself to please. His wife could serve an adequate meal for them in the parlour—in an hour, if that would suit. They did not keep late hours in the country. If they would care to sit in the downstairs parlour until all was in readiness? And perhaps some refreshment for the lady, who looked a little tired after her long day? Lord Henry accepted. It was now far too late to return to London, having waited on the affairs of Sam Potter. And the burden of the Reverend Broughton's information pressed heavily on Eleanor.

They were soon ensconced in the promised private parlour, dusted more adequately than the public room, probably by the lady of the house. A fire warmed the room which was low beamed and whitewashed, provided with an array of old country-made furniture, which had seen better days but was not uncomfortable. Mrs Abbott was able to produce a raised game pie and a roasted chicken with various side dishes, more than sufficient for their needs, as promised, and a platter of fruits stored from the previous season.

'I hope it will be acceptable.' Mrs Abbot added logs to the fire, then, stopping to wipe her grimy hands on her apron, 'Not expecting your honour and the lady,' she apologised. And won Eleanor's heart by producing a dish of tea, albeit somewhat bitter, as well as the jug of ale. She smiled and thanked their hostess with real warmth. They would do very well.

Eleanor shed her coat and bonnet, determined to do justice to the simple meal provided for them and to banish the depressing outcome of their conversation with the priest until later. But there was no hope of her achieving either. In the event she picked at her food and Henry did not have the heart to remonstrate with her. Even so, by the time she had tried the pie and sampled the chicken, the food and the warmth from the fire had returned colour to her cheeks and her eyes were less bleak.

Henry disappeared through the door that led downstairs to the public rooms, returning with a dusty decanter of port. Without comment he poured two glasses and sat, beginning to pare one of the wizened pippins from the dish. He quartered it neatly and pushed the pieces to Eleanor. She thanked him with a smile and ate.

'Tell me about your life in America,' she asked suddenly, deliberately breaking the silence, pushing her chair back from the table. 'What is it like? What are you doing with your life there? Is it what you could have wished for?'

And so he told her. Watching her eat the sweet apple. Not so much to tell her about the momentous changes in his life since leaving England, but to distract her mind from the developments of the day.

'I live in New York. I rent rooms there, but it is in my mind to build a house for myself in the future. It is a thriving place and growing by the day. There is money there and it hums with energy. It is difficult to imagine unless you have experienced it for yourself.' He frowned down at the rings of apple peel as he let his mind return to his new life. 'One day New York will be as elegant as London. There are new people arriving every day. Different languages. Different customs. It has an excitement that stirs the blood.'

'Are you making your fortune—as you planned?'

'I am trying hard.' His face was lit by a sudden sardonic smile as a thought struck home. 'Your mother would sniff in disgust. I have become engaged in *trade!* She would certainly not approve! But there is money to be made, businesses to invest in, and I intend to make my mark. I would be a fool not to. Birth is less important than energy and initiative. I like it. It is novel to be addressed as Mr Faringdon.'

'So you will be a big name there?' She smiled a little at the subtle tension that gripped him, the shimmering ambition that she had not seen since he had left her two years ago.

'With good fortune.' His eyes now held hers, alive with subdued excitement. 'I am in partnership with Nathaniel Bridges—Faringdon and Bridges, no less. He is another young man of ambition and useful contacts—and a little capital, which he is willing to sink into the business, like myself. Now that the war with England is over our trade will expand. The treaty was made just before I landed, and it made expansion possible. This year we have a tariff to protect our own manufactures from foreign imports. We aim at self-sufficiency, which can be nothing but good for those prepared to invest in the future.'

She noted his casual identification with the new world, even if he did not. There was no doubt that he would return to New York when the inheritance was settled one way or the other. London, even Burford Hall, held nothing for him now except for memories of the past. She tensed against the pain around the edges of her heart when she acknowledged that he would leave again. Not that it should matter to her, of course. She turned her face away so that she could not see Henry's burning desire to be gone from England, away from her and the hideous complications left by his brother.

'Roads and canals are being developed,' he continued, unaware of her disquiet. 'And we are looking to develop trade routes further with Iberia and southern Europe. There is certainly a demand for wheat and we can produce it in huge quantities.'

'So you are making money, it seems.' She brought her thoughts back into line.

'It seems very possible—and we only pay a quarter of taxes compared to English tax payers. So it will leave us with more money to plough back into the business and into a comfortable lifestyle. But not yet! We are ploughing all our profits back until the company is more secure so there is little money to spare. Hence the rented rooms over a shop.'

'And when there is money to spend? What will you do then?'

'I intend to build a large house as befits my new status as successful entrepreneur and businessman!' Henry stretched back in his chair as he envisioned the future. 'There is plenty of timber and prime sites to be had. The Commissioners in New York have drawn up plans to rebuild the city on impressive lines. Nothing like London, all congestion with narrow streets and winding roads and dark alleys. It will be very splendid with wide avenues crossing each other into a grid. If fortune smiles on us—and a little business acumen—Faringdon and Bridges will be part of it.'

Eleanor watched him as he spoke, assessing the new Hal compared with the one she had known. All the old enthusiasm was still there, but now tempered with experience and knowledge and an edge to his maturity that had been missing when he was still enjoying a life of moneyed leisure in London. His eyes glowed, dark and vibrant, as he outlined the plans of Faringdon and Bridges, probably forgetting to whom he spoke. Her smile was a little sad as she realised that he might have been addressing Nicholas or the unknown Nathaniel Bridges. She had no doubt, no doubt at all, that he would be successful.

'We think we might invest in our own shipping.' His thoughts drifted through the endless possibilities for men with money and the willingness to take a calculated risk. 'And then there is the prospect of the opening up of the west. A lot of migration is under way and new states being added every year. And where people settle, they need goods and commodities. So much opportunity for those prepared to supply them… Forgive me.' His lips twisted in a grimace. 'I did not intend to bore you for so long. If you are unwise enough to ask, I am afraid that you pay the penalty.' The curl of his lips was apologetic.

'You did not. I would not have asked if I was not interested.' Eleanor looked at him consideringly. 'Will you marry?' Why she had felt the need to ask so personal a question, she did not know, but waited for his reply.

Henry regarded her with a quizzical look. 'Do you mean have I a lady in mind? No, I do not. But one day I shall marry.'

'Do you have a mistress?'

'Yes.' His brows arched at her question, perhaps a little amused at her directness.

'Is she pretty?'

'Rosalind. Yes. She has dark hair and green eyes.'

So now she knew. Eleanor reprimanded herself for initiating the subject. All she had achieved was a sore heart and a leap of jealousy that sank its claws into her flesh, even though she knew that she had no right or claim on him. But she envied the unknown but pretty Rosalind, with her dark hair and green eyes, with all her heart. He had smiled when he spoke her name. There would be no weight of guilt or betrayal from the past to hinder their love. Eleanor immediately knew that there was a harsh lesson here for her that she would do well to learn and act on without delay. Hal was not for her, and never could be.

She fell into silence, brooding a little, unaware of his watching her.

'What are you thinking?'

She blinked and withdrew her gaze from the flames, brought back to the present. Her eyes were suddenly clear and cold as she pushed herself upright in her chair, spine braced against its curved back. Her voice was equally cool and measured.

'Why, I was thinking about what I must do now. It is perfectly clear to me that my marriage did not exist. I can no longer deny it, even to myself. We have heard nothing today to undermine Sir Edward's written evidence and I must accept it.' She took a visible deep breath. 'I need to consider my future—I can put it off no longer.' Spreading her fingers, palm downwards, before her on the table, she contemplated them with a little frown. Then, without comment, she slid a gold ring set with a hoop of diamonds and sapphires from her finger and placed it carefully, deliberately, in front of her on the table between the empty plates and glasses. The sapphires gleamed balefully at their rejection, the diamonds glinted. She could not take her eyes from them, shocked at what she had just done, but she spoke firmly as if compelled by an unseen force. 'I need to make some decisions and act on them. And I may as well start now! It would seem that I have no right to wear that ring. Thomas gave it to me on the day that we were wed. I know that it is one of the Faringdon jewels and that your mother wore it as a bride.' She touched it with one finger, almost a caress, before drawing her hands away into her lap, fearing that in a moment of weakness she might snatch up the ring and replace it on her finger. 'I cannot wear it.' Her eyes, glassy with unshed tears, were no less bright than the stones that she had just discarded amongst the debris of the meal.

Her action stunned him. And painted for him, more clearly than words could have done, the quagmire that the future would hold for her. He opened his mouth to deny her words, to say anything that would restore a fragment of hope, but could not. He would allow her to speak her mind before offering any advice, before putting forward his own suggestions.

'So what will you do, Eleanor, if matters stand as Baxendale would have us believe?'

'I do not know.' A hint of panic nibbled at her determination to be strong-willed and positive, to take her future into her own hands. 'I do not as yet know where I will go.'

'Your family home, perhaps?' It was not a plan that would seem to hold much attraction, for any number of reasons.

'Yes. I can return to the village where I was born. My mother still has the house there, so there will always be a roof over our heads and we shall not starve.' She shivered a little as if a draught had suddenly crept into the room. 'I don't think I can do that.' Her courage wavered a little. 'Everyone in the village has known me since I was a child—they would know about my present…situation. What would I call myself? Miss Stamford? With a child, but with no claim on its father? And not even the right to call myself a widow?' She laughed, but there was a sharp edge to it, and her eyes were desolate. 'I cannot contemplate it. I will have to accept talk, of course, but not intimate knowledge from everyone I meet. It would be too humiliating, day after day.'

He remained silent, but filled her glass again and pushed it across the table. Her fingers toyed nervously with the stem as she allowed her thoughts free rein.

'Are you aware,' Henry enquired finally, when the silence stretched uncomfortably, her thoughts apparently bringing no joy, 'that Sir Edward has made the suggestion to Hoskins that the estate pay you a small pension?' How would she react to that? he wondered.

'No!' Her head snapped up, her eyes sparkling with quick temper. 'The thought of such charity appals me!'

'Are you in a position to refuse? For your son, if not for you?' He kept his voice deliberately gentle. 'You married Thomas in good faith. I suggest that the estate owes you enough and more to allow you and the child to live in comfort. Don't reject it out of hand, I beg of you.'

'No!' He watched her struggle for control, but then she sighed, and although she kept her head high in defiance against the agonies that the fates had flung in her path, her answer was bitter and plumbed the depths of despair. 'Your are right, of course. How could you not be? For my son's sake I must realise that I have no right to refuse. I must accept Edward's...*kindness!*'

'Can I tell you what I think?' Unable to remain seated, unable to bear her pain without sheltering her in his arms, Hal rose to his feet to stand beside the fireplace. 'I don't think you should shut yourself away in the depths of the country. It would be a terrible mistake. You are young. Very beautiful. There is no reason why you should not attract a husband and marry again. And find contentment, even happiness.'

She was silent, eyes wide as they connected with his.

'You look as if you had never contemplated the possibility!'

'No. How could you expect it? My situation would hardly attract a husband. No man would want his wife to be the subject of gossip and speculation. And without a dowry, not to mention an illegitimate child into the bargain.' She hesitated a moment. 'Apart from the fact that my experience of marriage would not encourage me to repeat it. I think not!'

Henry remained motionless, elbow resting against the heavy oak mantel, face set, no hint of the direction of his thoughts. Then, 'I would marry you, Eleanor.' He ignored her sharp intake of breath, as much surprised as she. 'I would protect your reputation from the world's censure with my name.' He stepped across to her, reached down to still her restless fingers with his own. 'Consider the advantages before you refuse.'

As he watched her reaction, one of utter amazement, he was forced to admit to his own astonishment at his words, which had come unplanned, unbidden, but at the same moment knowing in his heart that he wanted it more than anything—to protect and shield her from his brother's disastrous and ill-chosen course of action. But he was by no means certain of her response to his offer, and could have wished it unsaid as he saw the reaction sweep over her.

Eleanor flinched as if she had been struck, a sharp open-handed slap, her face becoming ashen as blood drained from beneath her fair skin. Her hands flexed under his. When she could find words to speak around the confusion of horror and intense longing in her mind, it was the horror and bone-deep humiliation that emerged to the surface, to colour her answer.

'Do you really think that I would leap at the prospect of marriage to you, Hal? After your deliberate and callous rejection of me?' Her voice was low, a bare whisper, but laced through with deadly venom.

'Why not?' Her refusal did not surprise him to any degree—but the tone of it hurt. 'I did not reject you…' What use going over this old ground? 'Surely we can deal well enough together, given the present circumstances. I can offer you security and respect, a comfortable life for you and your son.'

But not your love! 'Two years ago you did not want me.' She held up her hand, palm outward toward him, as he would have refuted this accusation once more. 'So why change your mind now? How dare you offer me pity!'

'I would never offer you pity, Nell.'

'No? It is the only reason I can think of, why you would offer me marriage now! Or do you think that our night here together might compromise my reputation? It may have escaped your notice, Hal, but I have no reputation.' The bitter irony lay heavily between them. 'You owe me nothing! I suppose I should thank you for making the grand gesture so selflessly, in spite of your attachment to Rosalind. You should feel proud of that. But you will doubtless be relieved to know I refuse your offer! There is no need to make the ultimate sacrifice for me.' Pushing back her chair, she stood, her eyes now level with his and full of contempt.

'Think what you wish, Nell. But don't be so quick to misjudge me.' There was a hint of temper in his voice, brows snapped together. 'I would give you and the child—Thomas's son—some security, some respectability—some recompense for the loss of all you had hoped for, if you wish. There could be worse scenarios, as you yourself admitted.'

'I don't doubt it! I could live in the gutter with the dispossessed of London!' He was taken aback by the sneer. The débutante he had known did not sneer. 'But to live in gratitude for *your* sacrifice for the rest of my life? For my son and myself to be dependent on *your* charity? I will not. Rather Edward's than yours!'

Tell her you love her, you fool. She is hurt and despairing and without hope. Of course she will refuse your offer! Take her in your arms and kiss that soft, sad mouth. Tell her that she holds your heart in her hands, and always will. And that Rosalind means nothing to you.

But in the face of such contempt he could not. He sighed, lips pressed together into a harsh line.

'Go to bed, Eleanor. Perhaps we have both said too much this night.' He turned away, so did not see her blink back the tears before she turned to the door.

Well done! You handled that magnificently!

Henry flung himself back into the chair with a curse, disgust riding him hard. He had been given a chance to make her life easier, with care and consideration, with compassion. Perhaps even at some time in the future to win her love. Instead she was under an indestructible impression that he had made his move through pity. The barrier that she had built between them in the last half-hour was formidable indeed. And to be honest, he could not blame her. He had, unwittingly, helped her to heap stone upon stone between them.

He swore again and reached for the decanter of port to refill his glass.

And, even worse, she would in all probability refuse out of hand *any* help offered by him now.

Subtlety? Finesse in his dealings with women? Ha! He did not know the meaning of the words! Instead he had ridden rough-shod over her feelings and sensibilities. To offer her marriage in such a situation had been crass in the extreme. But what man of honour could remain unmoved before so courageous and so lovely a woman in distress?

And he loved her.

He had tried to build her trust and, he thought, with some success. She had begun to relax a little in his company. He remembered her listening to his plans not an hour before, a smile on her face, a certain contentment in her eyes. Now all destroyed. He had hurt her pride—and she would feel that pride was all she had left. She was so sad and he had simply made it worse.

He drank the port, struck anew by the knowledge that, although she had now rejected his offer of marriage twice, he could still want her. And it had nothing whatsoever to do with pity!

What had she said to him? Hurtful things. Terrible things. She had meant none of them, but they could not be unsaid and now he would never forgive her. Eyes closed, she leaned with her back against the bedroom door, permitting the longing in her heart to sweep through her. What better future could she envisage than to allow him to take all her troubles on to his strong shoulders and let him stand protection against the world and its condemnation. And Tom. Her son would grow up with no slur on his name. As he should, as was his right.

And perhaps, one day, Hal might even return the love that burned so brightly and hopelessly through her veins.

The tears that she had battled against claimed victory at last. She removed her dress with fingers suddenly numb, her shoes, to stand in the centre of the room, in her chemise, hands by her sides, and weep helplessly, heartbrokenly for all that was lost.

Because she truly did not know what to do and Hal had offered her her dreams, to hold in the palms of her hand. And by the manner of her refusal, she had alienated him irrevocably. She knew that he did not want her, so she had refused his offer. Of course she had, as any woman of integrity must—but her pride was obliterated by bitter tears.

In the parlour, Henry rescued the sapphires and diamonds in their golden setting from the table. He held the family jewel in his hand as if it might give an answer to his problems, and then, with a shake of his head, slipped it into his pocket, to return it to her on a less emotional occasion. A thought struck him, chilling him to the marrow in his bones. He had offered Eleanor marriage carelessly and without consideration, acting without any thought other than his own desires, other than the simple expediency of rescuing her from her worst fears.

But it could not be.

The law recognised Eleanor's affinity to him only as his brother's wife and so in its wisdom frowned on any closer association between them. Certainly not marriage.

Eleanor had not realised it. Nor had he in the heat of the moment.

Marriage, with the possibility of further scandal attached to Eleanor's name, was no answer at all. The realisation stuck him with the force of cold steel.

The minutes ticked past in the Red Lion in the village of Whitchurch. Henry continued to sit by the fire, booted feet propped on an iron fire-dog, contemplating an uncomfortable and sleepless night, probably on the oak settle, when a faint sound from beyond the door to the bedroom brought him out of a morass of far from pleasant thoughts.

He sat up. And knew without any doubt.

Oh God, no! He rubbed his hands over his face, dragged his fingers through his hair and pushed himself to his feet.

The coward in him told him to ignore it. Eleanor would soon be exhausted and would fall asleep without any intervention from him. Any attempt to comfort her would solve nothing for either of them and might make the situation even worse with impossible legal complications that he did not feel up to explaining to her just at that moment. He bared his teeth in a grimace at the prospect of holding her in his arms and remaining unmoved by her softness and her beauty. *No! Don't even think about it!*

But he could not ignore it, of course he could not. Especially when he had in some sense been the cause of her emotional state of mind. His mouth curled sardonically. He had not expected that an offer of marriage would reduce any woman to a fit of hysterics! Rosalind, he thought, would leap at the chance.

With a sigh he walked to the door where he hesitated, listened, head bent. And then, without knocking, before he could change his mind, opened the door and went in.

She stood on the rag rug in the centre of the floor in her chemise, her feet bare. She was shivering with emotion and cold, but had been unable to make the decision to get into bed. And she wept, sobs that shook her whole body, tears streaming down her face. She made no effort to hide them or her tear-ravaged face from him, even if she were aware of his presence. He was not certain. She was beyond awareness, lost in a wilderness of insecurity and grief.

'Nell.' He felt his heart turn over in compassion, touched beyond measure by her wretchedness against which she had no defence. Courage she might have, but not the will to fight this deluge of pain. 'This is no good.' He stepped quietly to her. 'You will make yourself ill if you weep in this way.'

'Go away!' She choked out the words and now covered her face with her hands. 'I don't want you!'

'I will not.'

Without hesitation, he folded his arms around her, as any man must, and pulled her close, using one hand to press her head to his shoulder. She resisted, as he knew she would, standing rigidly against him, refusing to accept his comfort. But he persisted, until suddenly on a sob she melted and clung to him, turning her face against the base of his throat. Too sad to be embarrassed or to refuse the warmth offered by the one man who had possession of her heart and whose offer she had discarded with wounding and unforgivable words.

Henry stroked her hair, removing the pins that secured her curls as he did so, allowing it to tumble over his hands in a heavy fall of silk. He murmured and crooned, foolish words that promised the impossible, the unattainable, and yet soothed by their mere sound. He kissed her temples, the lightest of kisses, and let her cry, his cheek resting against her hair. She would have fallen at his feet if he had not held her.

'My love. My dear love. I will not leave you. I could not leave you to grieve alone. I will love and care for you, whatever the future brings.'

Momentarily horrified at hearing himself speak such sentiments aloud, he could not regret it, but fervently hoped that she would not remember when she awoke.

Gradually her breathing quietened, so that he was able to stoop and lift her high against his heart, carrying her to the bed where he placed her, sitting beside her to rock her in his arms until utter exhaustion claimed her and her lashes closed on her tear-stained cheeks. Only then did he turn back the covers, place her against the bank of pillows and tuck her in. He would not look at her. His instinct told him to leave, to go whilst he could still resist the lure of her fragile femininity and her need for comfort. But she held on to his hand, even in sleep, and it would be cruelty indeed to reject her now.

So be it.

He eased into a chair by the bed and let her be comforted by his presence, watching her now-sleeping face. Even when her fingers finally relaxed he still remained, unwilling to leave her for fear that she would wake alone in the dark and be unable to deal with the torment in her mind.

Eleanor…

Images flooded back into his mind from that night two years ago, that night that had haunted him every hour of every day since, no matter how hard he had tried to banish the painful and yet glorious memory. Images that swamped him with their clarity and intensity. He would like nothing better than to strip away the fine linen and lace chemise, to feast his eyes on the creamy white perfection of her exposed body. As he had in the summer house beneath the rose pergola, in the garden of Faringdon House. Escaping her chaperon, they had been intoxicated by the sense of freedom as he had pushed her gently back on the cushions. He had seduced her with tales of America and their new life there together. And with his kisses, the touch of his hands that awakened her innocent emotions, setting her blood on fire. She was virgin, of course, but as caught up in the silver enchantment of the moonlight, as he had been. He should have known better than to take advantage of her, he now admitted in that shadowy room in Whitchurch, but that night he had given in to youth and impulse and an overriding need to bury himself within her soft and tantalising heat. The scent of honeysuckle and jasmine invading the senses, robbing him of all integrity and responsibility towards her. And yet she had willingly given him the greatest gift she could, clinging to him as he took her with less than subtle skill. He smiled bitterly. He knew more about women now. He might not be much older in years, but was vastly more experienced in the arts of seduction. Now he knew how to awaken passion, how to pleasure and delight. He must have hurt her in that moon-kissed garden, but she had wrapped her arms around him, vowing her everlasting love.

What had gone wrong? Why had she not joined him when he had sailed for America? He could not believe that on that one night, drunk on shared passion, she had not loved him to the exclusion of all else. And yet she had rejected him. Wilfully ignored, presumably destroyed, the letter that he had sent, which he *knew* she had received, and thus turned her back on his offer to share his life with her. And even if he had not been so very certain of this letter, diligently delivered by his groom, there was the one further note that he had hurriedly penned on his arrival in New York. She had also failed to respond to that plea for an explanation. She might deny their existence, but the evidence weighed heavily against her. It would have been far better if she had told him bluntly that she had simply changed her mind. It would have sliced at his heart, but anything would have been kinder than the cruel edge of indifferent silence.

He breathed deep to still the beating of his heart, the pumping of his blood to his loins. Because, in spite of everything in their past, in spite of all her apparent duplicity, he could not get her out of his mind, much less out of his blood where desire still surged. He wanted her. Now. To show her again the splendour of passion that could be awakened between a man and a woman. To bury himself deep within her hot, velvet-soft body, so that she could forget everything but the two of them. To drive her beyond control so that she could forget uncertainty and grief. To claim her as his own, bodies joined, slick with desire. To own her and possess her, the one woman he desired. He wanted all of that now!

But he could not. And deliberately eased the unwitting tightening of his fingers around her hand. She was his brother's widow. With a fatherless child, a reputation under attack and complications on all sides. He must not allow himself to forget it, no matter the temptation to sweep it all aside and cover her body with his own, crushing her to the bed so that she cried out his name in the dark. She needed comfort and support. He would try to think as a gentleman, remember his duty towards her as a trustee of the Faringdon estate, and give her what she needed most. But, by God, he had given himself a hard task!

He looked at her, drawing on his memory and imagination. Tormenting himself but unable to fight the bittersweet longing. Long, slender legs that she had wrapped around him. High firm breasts, her nipples hardening under the onslaught of his lips. Shadowed secrets waiting to be discovered. He had not forgotten and wanted nothing more but to rediscover them again.

'I will care for you,' he murmured on a sigh of frustration, softly so as not to wake her. 'I will not let the world condemn you for some mischance that is no fault of yours. I will look after you, whether you wish it or no.'

Quite what he intended to do, he was unsure, but it was a solemn and binding vow, even though she slept on, unaware of it.

Eleanor awoke at some time in the night, disorientated and in discomfort from her long bout of tears. But even though her head ached, her first conscious thought was one of simple pleasure, that Hal had not left her. He was asleep in the chair beside her, head pillowed on one arm, resting on the edge of the bed. His other hand was still covering hers, even though lax in sleep. His face was turned away, hidden from her. She would have liked to touch his hair, the dark, vibrant strength of it where it curled onto his neck, but feared to wake him, nor did she wish to lose contact with his hand on hers. He had stayed with her, even though his stiff, cold muscles would be a matter for regret in the morning. But she would not reject his decision. Simply his presence comforted her. Thomas had been her friend, but Hal was the love of her life. She fell asleep again, holding the thought, as she held his hand, against the onslaught of disturbing dreams.

When Eleanor awoke again the next morning, with light creeping through the heavy swags, he had gone and the place where his head had rested was cold. She felt an instant chill of regret. He might comfort her, he might watch over her as she slept, but he had felt no desire to repeat the experience of two years before in the gardens of Faringdon House. An experience which she *would not* remember! Even after two years she flushed as the memories pushed their insidious tendrils into her thoughts, just as the wisteria invaded the balustraded terrace at Burford Hall. She could not imagine how she could have been so unmaidenly. A chaste kiss, perhaps, but she had allowed Hal far more intimacies. The flush deepened to flaming rose as she recalled the episode in the summer house with a ridiculous mix of horror and intense delight. He had handled her with such care, mindful of her innocence. Loved her, cherished her, left her in no doubt of his tender feelings towards her, except that they had apparently not been sufficiently strong to outlive the night! Perhaps he had been disgusted by her lack of skill, her lamentable lack of knowledge, the still unformed curves of a young girl. He had certainly discovered no desire to develop their relationship further! She had not seen him again until he had bowed before her in the withdrawing-room at Burford Hall. No matter the soft words and beguiling images he had painted of their future together, his promises had been empty indeed, proof that no man could be trusted!

Turning back the bed covers with a little huff of disgust at her wayward thoughts, she noticed, and remembered—and understood, with a sinking heart. Her ring. She had removed it in despair, leaving it on the table in the parlour, but now it was back on her finger. She twisted it so that the morning sun glinted on the edges and the tiny jewels. Hal must have restored it while she slept. She could not but admire his loyalty to his brother's name, even when she herself had despaired and denied the legality of her own marriage. But she also understood very clearly and knew that it would be wise of her not to forget. For the ring was a symbol of her union with Thomas, and Henry had replaced it where he considered it belonged. That simple action should tell her more plainly than any words that Henry saw her as his brother's widow, and nothing more in his life.

Chapter Seven

The gathering of the Faringdon family in the morning room of the house in Park Lane on the following afternoon, when Henry and Eleanor had arrived back in London, could not be described to be in a spirit of optimism or even qualified hope. They brooded over their lack of progress.

The visit to the village of Whitchurch had achieved nothing to their advantage, Henry reported. The Reverend Broughton might not be the most likeable of characters, with a shadow thrown over his morals and behaviour as a clergyman, but there was no reason to disbelieve him in the matter of the marriage of Thomas and Octavia. He had confirmed the events of marriage and birth. The documents appeared to be genuine. Sir Edward Baxendale was well known with a good reputation, and the existence of a sister with a recently deceased husband and a young baby was common knowledge. Eleanor said nothing, merely a silent witness to their failure to unearth any incriminating evidence.

The only outcome of the visit, in Mrs Stamford's unexpressed opinion, was a certain intangible tension in her daughter. As now, she thought, glancing across at her. Eleanor might have been alone in the room, with eyes unfocused as if her thoughts were far away, turning the ring on her finger round and round with terrible monotony. And there was a distinct unease between Eleanor and Lord Henry, for which Mrs Stamford was not sorry. Too much intimacy would certainly be unwise. But Mrs Stamford was wise enough to remain silent about the night they had been forced to spend in the Red Lion in Whitchurch. Given the circumstances, and her memory of the previous occasion of confrontation when she had quite clearly lost the battle of wills, she did not feel up to taking on Lord Henry on such a personal matter. Even if she was the Marchioness's mama.

London, likewise, had provided no scandal. Kingstone knew nothing of any interest about the parties. As far as Nicholas knew, Sir Edward was an exemplary character with no interest in gambling, horses or loose women.

Mrs Stamford frowned at his comment.

'For whatever reason, Baxendale does not appear to have arrived at *point non plus*. He has no interest in the turf. He does not own a racehorse. He is not known at Tattersall's. He does not frequent gambling dens. He does not keep a mistress. Nor does he visit opera dancers!' Nicholas deliberately expanded on the subject, his lips curled with mischief as Mrs Stamford stiffened and sniffed her disapproval. 'Sir Edward is a veritable pillar of society.'

'So I must accept the situation.' Eleanor had earlier returned from an emotional visit to her son in the nursery and, after holding him in her arms, watching his sturdy limbs as he pulled himself upright against his crib, she could not deny her duty to the child. 'I must take the offer of an annuity from Sir Edward—and thank him for his generosity!—and find somewhere for myself and Tom to live. Perhaps we should return to our house in Leavening, Mama.'

'No. It is too soon—' Henry immediately turned his head, intent on halting such a scheme, but Mrs Stamford interrupted, very much of the same mind.

'No, Eleanor. We should not. I went to see Lady Beatrice yesterday. Perhaps you had forgotten my errand in that direction. I swore her to secrecy, of course. I found her a most well-informed lady—not as flighty as her daughter. We had quite a detailed conversation and exchange of views.'

Henry avoided Nicholas's eye.

'I think you should not be in too much of a hurry to accept Sir Edward's offer, Eleanor. For once I am in total agreement with Lord Henry.' She smiled thinly at him. 'It is true that Lady Beatrice remembers a fair girl with whom Thomas was much taken. And she thought there was a brother with her on some of the social occasions. But she is not sure, and is not convinced that the name Baxendale rings true. She claimed to know no Baxendales. But she had to admit that she is better at faces than names—after all, it was four years ago.'

She looked round the circle of faces.

'I do not know if that helps us or not.' Nicholas rubbed his chin. 'I suppose that it is the only hint of doubt we have in an otherwise cast-iron case.' He looked to Henry. 'What do you suggest, Hal? Arrange a meeting between Sir Edward and Aunt Beatrice? Now that is an occasion which I would not want to miss.'

Henry frowned at him for a moment, considering the possibilities. Then: 'Very well. This is what we will do. We will entertain. A small party—we have sufficient rooms here. Very select—mostly family. Cards, music, refreshments—you know the sort of thing. Eleanor will be hostess.' He looked towards her, brows arched, not totally convinced that she would comply.

'Yes. Of course, if that is what you wish.'

'I do.' He smiled at her, an unusually tender smile, which was not lost on the audience. 'Don't despair, Nell. We still have all to win—but we will not wave the flag of surrender quite yet. And a family party will be quite the thing, in spite of Thomas's death. You need have no concern about that.'

She returned the smile, although a little sad, unable to resist such comfort. 'Thank you, Hal. I shall never forget your kindness, whatever the outcome.' As she looked down at the sapphires on her hand, they both knew that her thoughts were far from that room in Park Lane.

'And we will invite the Baxendales.' Nicholas picked up on Hal's suggestion to deflect attention from the pair, aware of Mrs Stamford beside him, rustling in displeasure at the unexpected intimacy. He would give a pony to know exactly what had happened between them in Whitchurch. He must make certain to ask Hal.

'We will stress that it is a family occasion. They will hardly be able to refuse since they are intending to fill their own niche in the Faringdon family tree. It will make for an interesting evening!'

'And I must be certain to invite Aunt Beatrice?' Eleanor asked quickly appreciating the plan.

'Exactly!' Henry rose to his feet and strode towards the door. 'We will try every means we have to flush the bird from the covert. Even if it means spending an evening in Lady Beatrice's overbearing company!'

'Will you escort me to the theatre? Tonight, my lord?'

Eleanor confronted Lord Henry in the breakfast parlour two days later and made her request without preamble or explanation, even before she had closed the door behind her. She had positively erupted into the room in a flurry of muslin skirts.

'Well, I…' His lordship looked up from his perusal of the *Morning Post,* suitably taken aback.

'I realise that you might have other plans—and I would not normally ask that you put yourself out, particularly at such short notice—but I find that it is vitally important.' The words tripped off her tongue, indicative of strong emotion. She came to stand before him, determined to have his attention. Lord Henry promptly put down the paper to watch her warily, aware of the high colour slashed along her cheekbones. Now what was afoot?

Since their return from Whitchurch the strain between them had lessened a little, submerged under a cool sensible acceptance of the need to unite in their resistance to the Baxendales' claims. Although they were successful in keeping a distance, awareness of each other remained, a tangible thing. And so Henry was wary of Eleanor's request.

'Why?' He hoped the suspicion did not sound in his voice.

'We have not been invited—*I* have not been invited—to the Carstairs's Drum this evening, when we know that all the world and his wife will be present. I would not even have known of it, if it had not been for Beatrice asking if she would see us there.' Eleanor flung away from him to pace to the window, and back again. 'How long has Marianne Carstairs been closely acquainted with this family? For ever, I shouldn't wonder. She certainly counted your mama as one of her closest friends. And,' she interrupted, brows drawn together in an uncompromising line, as Henry opened his mouth to reply, 'don't tell me that they are being considerate for my state of mourning. I have been out and about so often recently that no one in town would be under any illusion about my present circumstances.' Eleanor sat herself in one of the straight-backed chairs with a flounce of indignation. 'It is a deliberate snub. I will not stand for it from a family I considered friends. So I wish to go to the theatre.'

'Perhaps the invitation has been mislaid?' Henry tried for a mild reply, to calm the seething lady before him.

Her stare of withering disbelief was answer enough.

'No. Of course, you are right.' Henry mentally postponed his evening, which had promised a leisurely hand of cards at Brooks's and a convivial drink with old friends. He managed not to sigh. 'So, what do you wish?'

'I wish to be seen at Drury Lane. I will not sit and hide at home when every other person of consequence in London is making merry!'

'Shakespeare?' His lordship mentally winced.

'By no means.' Eleanor was forced to smile at his reluctance. 'The Bard is distinctly out of fashion since you left these shores. Mr Elliston, who has taken on the management of Drury Lane, has decided that a more popular entertainment is more the thing—and will bring in more money to his pockets! So it is likely to be *The Beggar's Opera* rather than *King Lear.* Not as erudite, but more economically attractive, you understand.'

'Then I will escort you,' Henry agreed, amused at Eleanor's quick assessment.

'I can even promise you any number of opera dancers who will doubtless cast out lures to you. Your evening might not be wasted!'

He ignored her caustic comments, appreciative of her disordered spirits. 'And to escort so attractive a lady as yourself. It will be my greatest pleasure. How can I refuse?'

'How indeed.' Her brows rose.

'Ah—are we to be chaperoned to this seductive event?'

'Of course. It is not my intention to be seen alone with you at such a performance—to replace one scandal with another. My mother will accompany us. We shall all enjoy every minute of it!'

Thus a private box was procured at Drury Lane.

Eleanor made an appearance, spectacular in a new gown, guaranteed to catch every eye. The Italian silk and lace shimmered in the candlelight, its intense violet hue iridescent and sumptuous. A jewelled aigrette held a discreet spray of egret feathers in her hair. A rope of amethysts wound its shining path around her slender throat. She had even made judicious use of cosmetics to disguise the ravages of strain and sleeplessness. A little Olympian Dew to bring a sparkle to her eyes, the veriest hint of Liquid Bloom of Roses to enhance the soft colour in her cheeks. Her appearance at the theatre, Henry realised, was to be a deliberate challenge, a throwing down of the family gauntlet to all those who would dare to question the Marchioness's presence in London society. She looked magnificent, as had been her intention.

Henry dared make no comment, resorting instead to discretion, knowing that any compliment would have received a short reply. There was fire and temper in her eyes this night. So he merely bowed as he handed her and her watchful mama into the town carriage, quelling the desire with stern intent, desire that had run hot through his blood when faced with the glory of her appearance and her enforced proximity.

It was a tension-filled evening: more than one lorgnette levelled in their direction; more than one cold shoulder turned as Lord Henry ushered the two ladies with consummate ease through the crowded lobby; more than one half-heard whisper. But Mrs Stamford, well rehearsed by her daughter in her role for the evening, acted her part with undisturbed composure and dignity, set to ignore any unpleasantness as if it were beneath her notice. Eleanor was at her superb best. She bowed, smiled, conversed, sipped champagne—not everyone was at the Carstairs's

Drum!—gave her full attention to the performance as if nothing troubled her thoughts beyond the colour and style of the gown that she would wear on the following day. And she stared down those whose gaze she considered too insolent to be tolerated. She watched the remarkable Vestris in the role of Macheath, shapely legs scandalously clad in masculine breeches, with due admiration. She frowned at the courtesans who paraded in the lobby and sent flirtatious glances at her escort—how dared they!—and frowned equally at her escort, who was not averse to returning the smiles. And she engaged Henry in trivial and lively conversation to keep from dwelling on the critical stares of the Dowagers in their boxes.

Mrs Stamford found need to comment on young women—no lady here!—who *cavorted* on stage in male attire. She could not imagine why anyone of breeding and sensitivity would prefer such a performance to a production of *King Lear* with Edmund Kean—so talented as he was. The Darling of London indeed! Vestris was in Mrs Stamford's considered opinion no better than she should be! What was the world coming to! Eleanor turned a deaf ear.

Henry watched the performance with an amused smile and appreciative eye.

'I trust you are enjoying yourself, my lord?' Eleanor wielded her fan with considerable energy and expertise. Her mama was momentarily and safely occupied in conversation with a passing acquaintance.

'I am.' He slanted a glance at her lovely face.

'And you approve of Vestris?'

'Miss Lucy Bartolozzo? Definitely an asset to the production. It is everything you promised me. And the company of a beautiful woman, of course. You outshine everyone here, even the ladies of the lobby.' His smile was fast and devastating. Dangerous, Eleanor decided, lowering her lashes to hide her confusion at his compliment.

'Thank you, my lord.' Her lips curved in a genuine smile, despite her best intentions to remain censorious on the subject of the courtesans. 'Such a compliment lifts my spirits inordinately.'

'Is it possible that you are flirting with me, madam?'

'Certainly not!'

Henry laughed aloud, drawing more than one pair of eyes towards their box.

'Hush! I would not willingly give the town tabbies anything other to talk about! I was merely expressing my heartfelt gratitude.' Eleanor looked away, more than aware that her cheeks were burning.

'You must not, you know.' Henry covered her hand for a moment with his own, his voice very gentle. 'You are doing very well, Eleanor. It is not necessary to take the town by storm.'

'No? I think that perhaps it is. Smile, Hal.' Her own was brittle, but she held her head high. Once again, he could not but admire her spirit. 'The town is watching us. I will enjoy this evening if it is the death of me!'

At last the never-ending evening drew to a close. At last! Henry helped the ladies from their carriage and into the entrance hall in Park Lane.

'Satisfied?' he asked, with a quizzical glance.

'Yes.' Eleanor raised her chin, still vibrating with energy.

'Something you would wish to repeat?'

'No.' She could not lie. 'Not in the foreseeable future. If you wish to renew your acquaintance with Vestris, it will be without my company. But you have my gratitude, Hal. I felt a need to…to make a grand gesture and be noticed. I do not regret it.'

Mrs Stamford halted on the bottom step before retiring to bed, turning to look at his lordship over her shoulder. 'I have to thank you, Henry. For your unfailing support of my daughter. It should not go unsaid.' She spoke as if the words were wrung from her against her better judgement.

'My pleasure, ma'am.' Henry bowed, hiding his initial amazement.

'Not the easiest of evenings,' the lady continued, arranging her embroidered Kashmir stole more elegantly round her shoulders. 'And I am sure that you would have preferred to spend your time in other amusements.'

'Not when the comfort of her ladyship is a priority.'

'No. I realise that you have Eleanor's best interests at heart. I have not given you sufficient credit for that in the past, have I?' She gave him a considering look 'Perhaps I—' She broke off, redefining her thoughts. 'But no matter.'

She turned on her heel to precede them up the stairs.

Eleanor's eyes met Hal's in lively astonishment.

'Now that must be a first,' he murmured, when Mrs Stamford was out of hearing. 'Your mama's approval is a state that I had never hoped to achieve.'

'I advise you to treasure it,' was Eleanor's dry reply. 'In all probability it will never happen again.'

Before the Faringdon family could embark on their own social event, they were committed, the following evening, to the small soirée at the elegant London home of the Earl and Countess of Sefton.

'I would rather not go,' Eleanor stated, with every intention of following her statement with action, making a graceful withdrawal from the invitation. Taking the air in Hyde Park was one thing. So was an intimate family gathering. Even a private visit to the theatre. But appearing in public at so splendid an occasion, with the *haut ton* present, when she would draw the attention of, and need to converse with, any number of people without means of escape, was quite another matter.

'If you will take my advice…' Henry leaned heavily on the words, but with a bland expression '…you will present yourself with all the consequence you can muster as Marchioness of Burford and carry it off with the utmost assurance. I suggest you wear the diamond set, complete with tiara.'

'But I don't like the diamond set.' Eleanor was momentarily distracted. 'It is far too heavy, and the setting is very clumsy— it makes me feel like a Dowager of advanced years. And the stones need cleaning.'

'You *are* a Dowager—so wear it.' She silently dared him to mention her age, the glint of a challenge in her eyes. His lips twitched a little, but he desisted. 'If you are carrying a fortune of badly cut diamonds on your person, personally designed by my grandmother, no one will dare treat you with anything less than supreme respect!'

'But not the tiara!' She might be prepared to compromise, but only to a degree.

'Definitely the tiara!.'

'It is not my choice of an evening's entertainment either.' Nicholas also would gladly have cried off. 'Readings from somebody's recent masterpiece. One of Lady Sefton's protégés, I expect. A poet? Have mercy, Hal.'

But Henry took Nicholas aside when Eleanor had left the room with more than a suspicion of a revolt in her step. 'You should attend with the rest of us, Nick. It might not be the easiest of evenings for her—we cannot know—and Eleanor needs all our support if any of Lady Sefton's acquaintances takes it into her head to play the *grande dame* and turn the shoulder. Besides, it will be good to see the Faringdons out in force.' His lips curved a little as he anticipated his brother's reply. 'It is not necessary for you to stay for the whole evening. I give you permission to leave before the poet takes centre stage!'

'Very well.' Nicholas laughed. 'Whilst you, for your sins, can stay to the bitter end, to wallow in sentimentality and bad verse. Tell me, Hal. You seem to have come to some accord with Nell.'

'Do I?'

'Yes. Since your visit to Whitchurch.'

'Perhaps.'

'And you intend to tell me nothing.' Had Nick really expected his brother's confidence on this issue?

'Something like that.' There was nothing to be learned from the bland reply.

'Treat her gently, Hal.' Nicholas was suddenly serious. 'She has had an unenviable time since Thomas's death. And now all this…'

'I have every intention of doing so.' Nicholas flinched a little at Henry's fierce response. 'Do you consider me to be so insensitive?'

'Of course not.' Nick decided to take a step on forbidden ground. 'It's just that—you will be leaving soon—and…' He found it difficult to continue under his brother's intense stare, but then Henry shrugged and allowed himself a smile.

'I know. Don't worry, Nick. I will treat her gently.'

'Don't break her heart, Hal. She is very vulnerable.'

'I am aware.' An icy reply. There was no chance. No chance at all of that.

Nick changed the subject with ease when it became clear that his brother would say no more. 'I have discovered that you have a pronounced aptitude for management, Hal. I did not realise it—and must beware in future.'

'I can only hope it pays off.' But doubts crowded in. And not least that he was finding it increasingly difficult to disguise his emotions in his dealings with Nell. If Nick had his suspicions, he must be more circumspect. After all, who knew better than he just how very vulnerable she was? No, whatever was to come in the future, he must heed Nick's warning and ensure that her heart remain intact.

Eleanor chose to wear a stylish evening gown of amethyst silk. She knew it was beautiful and could not but enjoy the sensation of restrained good taste in the silk shell with its muslin overskirt, patterned with tiny flowers, falling in soft folds. The low scoop of the neckline served as a frame for the diamond necklace and she clipped matching bracelets over her long gloves. She even pinned the heavy ring brooch to the lace on the bodice. But wear the tiara she would not, the corners of her mouth lifting a little as she contemplated Henry's probable reaction. A lavender fan with silver sticks completed the ensemble. At the same time she cloaked herself in a veil of calm confidence, determined to smile and find enjoyment in the occasion since her family were so equally determined to support her. There would also be friends there, kind and supportive, as well as Lady Sefton's warm compassion. Nothing to fear, nothing to make her heart beat in her breast like a trapped bird.

They gathered in the front parlour, Henry and Nicholas splendid and austere in black satin evening coats and breeches, white linen and subdued waistcoats. The Countess of Sefton might promise a small soirée, but they knew her of old.

Eleanor thought that they looked stunning together. Tall, broad shouldered, lean and well muscled, their physical power and attraction enhanced rather than disguised by the formal clothing, she knew that they would take every eye in the room. They looked, she decided, dark and smooth and dangerous. How could she be nervous? They were quite magnificent.

Quietly elegant in deep blue brocade with a heavy lace overslip, Mrs Stamford ran a critical eye over her daughter. 'Very nice,' she admitted. 'Although, I have to agree, I have rarely seen so ugly a setting for fine stones. And so old-fashioned. What can your grandmama have been thinking of?' She frowned at Lord Henry as if he were in some indefinable way to blame for his grandmother's taste for the heavy and vulgarly ostentatious.

'Impressive!' was Henry's only comment as Eleanor innocently arranged an embroidered stole around her shoulders, refusing to meet his eye. His brows arched at the lack of the tiara and knew that she was waiting. So he said nothing. But privately thought that she would outshine every lady present that evening. Her eyes glowed, reflecting the tint of her gown and her nerves gave her cheeks a delicate colour, with or without the careful and subtle application of cosmetics. She was lovely. He raised her fingers to his lips and bowed his silent appreciation, since he was in a position to do no other.

Lady Sefton's town house in Berkeley Square, large, palatial and expensively furnished, and at the best of fashionable addresses, had been sumptuously decorated for the occasion with banks of flowers and silk swags. And as expected, the cream of society was present to hear the lady's fledgling poet.

The Earl and Countess welcomed the Faringdon party, the Countess with a warm handclasp and particularly understanding smile for Eleanor. 'Relax here tonight, my dear, and enjoy the company. I am well aware of what is being said. But you must not be embarrassed…' She tightened her hold in warm affection and leaned closer for a private word. 'I knew Thomas well. An estimable young man, of great integrity. As are all the Faringdons.' She cast an admiring glance to where the gentlemen were still in conversation with her husband. 'So attractive… My guests will respect your position, of course. I think you need fear no ill will here tonight.'

'You are very kind.' Eleanor felt her colour deepen as emotion welled. 'It has not been the easiest of weeks.'

'No. But you are here to enjoy the evening. A little conversation. Some music. A poetry reading, no less, by a remarkable young man. And here—' she beckoned a passing footman '—a glass of champagne. Permit me to tell you, dear Eleanor, your gown is quite beautiful. You must be sure to tell me who made it for you—later, when we have a little time.'

Eleanor felt a gentle warmth creep through her iced veins with the bubbles of the champagne, bringing her alive again. How valuable good friends were. She need not have been so concerned. Across the room she could see Lady Beatrice Faringdon, as well as the Earl and Countess of Painscastle. She wondered idly if Henry had once again exerted some influence on this show of support. He must certainly have bribed Nick to guarantee his reluctant presence.

'You must find your family most supportive.' Lady Sefton picked up Eleanor's thoughts before she moved away to greet more guests.

'I do indeed.'

'And I am interested to note a predatory look in Lord Henry's eye for anyone he suspects of showing you less than good manners.'

'Do you?' Eleanor looked across the room to Henry in some confusion.

'Of course. He is most attentive. And so very handsome. I am quite jealous.' She tapped Eleanor's wrist playfully with a pretty ivory-sticked fan and laughed. 'Perhaps you should try to persuade him to remain in London. There are so few *very* attractive men in comparison. And certainly none, I suggest, in the marriage market!' On a little laugh, seeing Eleanor's deepening colour, Lady Sefton made her departure.

Does she suspect me of flirting with Henry? With my husband dead little more than four months? Eleanor was horrified as she turned to look to where Henry was in conversation with his aunt,

Lady Beatrice Faringdon, a stout Dowager of considerable presence in sumptuous maroon satin and nodding ostrich feathers. Formidable indeed, as her mother had intimated. Then his lordship looked up as if he sensed her questioning gaze on him and, unsmiling, very grave, raised a hand in tacit recognition before bending an ear back to the Dowager, who was holding forth on some subject. *Yes. He is attractive. And he cares. No matter what was between us in the past, he cares. Whatever happens, I am not alone in this.*

And Nick watched the silent exchange. And understood. The flash of recognition, the almost intimate connection between them. Hal might as well have kissed her! The fierce heat, the intense possession in Hal's eyes were unmistakable. He had set himself up as Nell's protector, but there was far more involved here than family support in a potentially stressful situation. Just as there was no mistaking the delicate flush on Nell's cheeks as she turned away. They might deny it, as he was sure they would. They might succeed in hiding it from the fashionable world, as was doubtless their intent, but Nick could read the love between them as clearly as if they had shouted it from the rooftops. He swallowed against the dismay as he contemplated the terrible uncertainty of the future.

With a lighter heart, unaware of Nick's concern, Eleanor turned her thoughts back to the pleasures of the evening. Behind her a familiar voice took her attention and she soon found herself deep in conversation about the prevailing fashion for silk-edged bonnets with Cousin Judith and Miss Hestlerton, a pretty girl related to the Seftons and in her first Season. Perhaps the polite world was not so quick to judge after all.

But her renewed confidence was to be short lived. Lady Sefton requested in her gentle voice that her guests take a seat to listen to a poem, an 'Ode to Love and Romance', which was to be read by its author, a young man very much in the Byronic mode with ruffled dark locks and pale features.

There was some manoeuvring and much comment in the salon as guests took their places or attempted to withdraw to a little side salon, which had been set aside for those whose taste ran to a hand of whist.

'Eleanor.' Judith drew her notice with a hand on her arm. 'Can I introduce you to Lady Firth? I am not sure that you are acquainted. She has been out of town for some months with her husband who is a keen traveller.'

Before them stood a thin, fair lady of her mother's generation. Eleanor noticed that she had the coldest grey eyes. And for the first time there was no polite or welcoming smile, no exchange of light talk, nothing but contempt, barely concealed.

The thought flitted across Eleanor's mind. Lady Firth. No, she did not know the lady, but she knew of her. An associate of the Princess Lieven, which would explain much. The lady looked at Eleanor with a frown. She raised a pearl-handled lorgnette, with thin-lipped superiority. There was a world of distaste imprinted on her haughty features and in her gesture as she raked Eleanor from head to foot with condemnation in her eyes.

'No, my dear.' Lady Firth addressed herself to Judith. 'I do not think that I wish to be introduced to this person.' Her smile could have cut through glass, all edges sharp. 'I believe that she is here under false pretences and has no right to the title that she claims as hers through marriage. Lady Sefton really should have chosen with more discrimination for her guest list—but I suppose it is difficult to believe the depths to which some people will descend to be noticed.' The lady's voice had an unfortunate carrying quality that drifted across the elegant room, slicing through the conversations. Heads turned in their direction. Silence fell. All attention was drawn away from the budding poet.

Judith rose to the occasion without hesitation, eyes fierce, her red curls aflame with indignation. 'I am certain, Lady Firth, that it is no such thing. The Marchioness of Burford is my dear cousin and worthy of all respect.'

Eleanor drew herself together, all dignity and pride and glittering diamonds. She had expected to be overwhelmed with shame, but it was anger that surged through her veins in a veritable tidal wave. She would not bow her head before idle gossip and common innuendo. How dare this woman snub her in so public a manner! How dare she presume intimate knowledge on so delicate and private a matter! If Judith's eyes sparkled with indignation, Eleanor's flashed fury, entirely at odds with their beautiful, soft-violet hue. 'It is no matter, Judith. Do not allow yourself to be disturbed.' She bent her cold regard on the lady with a curl of derision to her soft mouth, spine held rigid. 'If Lady Firth is sufficiently ill mannered as to discuss my private affairs in Lady Sefton's salon, she does not deserve any word of explanation or apology from our lips. If she chooses not to recognise me, then—'

A cold voice, frigid and lethal as the wind from arctic snows, interrupted and finished the sentiment, '—then it is her loss.' A strong arm was placed beneath Eleanor's and a long-fingered hand closed around her wrist in a firm embrace. At the same time she was aware of Nicholas, unusually stern and forbidding, standing to her other side.

'Forgive me, Lady Firth.' Lord Henry bowed with impeccable grace and deliberate intent. 'Considering your ill-bred comment, it is not suitable that my sister remain in your presence. Come, Eleanor. You should not remain with one who listens to scurrilous gossip from the gutters and would give credence to it.' The silence in the room increased, positively crackling with tension as ears strained to grasp Henry Faringdon's words. He bowed again. 'Since the Countess of Sefton has made us welcome here tonight in her home, may I suggest that your own presence, Lady Firth, is suspect indeed if you would choose to be discourteous to one of her guests.' He turned his back on the astonished lady with deliberate and graceful arrogance and led Eleanor away towards a chair beside Lady Beatrice.

'An excellent response, my dear Eleanor,' he murmured through gritted teeth. 'There is no need for you to feel in any way discomfited by such ill manners. Just think of what is due to the fortune in stones around your pretty neck!'

'Of course.' And she smiled, a little startled at his barely repressed temper. 'Thank you for rescuing me, Hal.'

'I do not deserve your thanks! You should not have had to suffer such crude indignities. Permit me to say that you handled the whole affair magnificently. You have my total admiration, my lady.'

Eleanor made no reply, unless it might be the hot colour in

her cheeks, unwilling to exacerbate the rigid tension in the muscles and tendons of Henry's arm beneath her hand, masked by the softness of the satin. Conversation flowed on around them. Everyone keen to gloss over the slight to one of their number— for the moment at least. She took her seat beside Aunt Beatrice, who patted her hand whilst scowling at the distant figure and flushed face of Lady Firth. For the rest of the evening, Eleanor rose to the occasion superbly, with grace and assurance and humour, a residue of anger sending ripples of energy and exhilaration through her bloodstream. No one watching her would know the fear that lurked below the surface. But Lord Henry saw and understood.

'I know that you do not want my gratitude, but indeed, Hal, I—'

'I did nothing.' Henry interrupted, more than a little curt. 'You seemed to be perfectly capable of conducting your own affairs. Your demeanour and response to Lady Firth were both incomparable, sufficient to quell the most arrogant comment. A positive rout, I would wager, without any real need for intervention on my part.'

'Why will you not accept my thanks?' He saw hurt and confusion in her face, which strengthened his resolve further. He knew without doubt that this was the wrong time and certainly the wrong place for an intimate exchange of views between them. He had delivered Eleanor home to Park Lane and would now make himself scarce, for both their sakes. It would be too easy for emotions to run high.

'Any man of honour would have acted as I did.' His reply was thus even more brusque.

'Yet you have in the past accused me of treachery and betrayal. If true, if you truly believed me capable of such things, then you have no duty or demands of honour towards me. Yet you came to my defence with devastating effect and in full public gaze. I cannot let such kindness go unacknowledged.'

They stood facing each other, rigidly polite, uncomfortably distant, hostility sparkling between them as bright as Eleanor's hated diamonds, on the landing of the first floor of the Park Lane town house. Lord Henry had escorted Eleanor home from the Seftons' soirée with the intention of going on to relax over a hand of cards and a glass of brandy at Brooks's. The night, although it had been fraught with dangers both personal and public, was not too far advanced. The last thing Henry had wanted tonight was this confrontation with Eleanor where, against all his best intentions, all his determination to keep a circumspect distance between them, his self-control might be stretched to the limit— and beyond. But he must play out the present scene before he could leave her with formal courtesy and cool respect. Neither of which sentiments was responsible for the vicious and aching need that held him in an iron grasp. He wanted her, in his arms, in his bed.

'So I should leave one who bears my family name to be ripped at before the avid gaze of the polite world by the likes of Dorothea Firth?' Ice coated Eleanor's veins as she listened to Lord Henry's aloof assessment of the event. 'It was merely a matter of family honour, nothing more and nothing less. As I said, it does not require your gratitude. Nicholas would have done the same if he had been nearer to you.'

'Why are you so cold towards me?' Eleanor shook her head in a little movement of denial, unable to comprehend the chill that emanated from his lordship to settle around her. 'I find your attitude incomprehensible. You would condemn me, reject me in one breath and yet come to my rescue with the next. One moment you are caring and protective, the next your tone would freeze me to the marrow. You escorted me to Whitchurch and held me when it all became too much to bear and I wept in your arms. You have stood between me and society's condemnation here in London. But now…I do not understand. What have I done to earn your displeasure?'

She stood before him, tall and straight, yet intensely vulnerable. Challenging him. Demanding an answer. Yet it would be so easy to hurt her. Lord Henry groaned inwardly with frustration, a quick brush of temper. Why could she not simply retire to bed and allow the stresses of the night to calm before they must, by necessity, meet again over the breakfast table? He did not know what drove her. He only knew that desire and need had begun to simmer in his blood when he saw the proud light in her eyes, the indomitable spirit. Through narrowed eyes, he took in her flawless complexion, glowing in the soft light from the branch of candles at his right hand. Her soft lips, eminently kissable. The curve of her breast, enhanced by the low neckline of her gown and the glitter of precious stones. By God, he wanted her! He clenched his hands into fists and breathed carefully.

Eleanor stared at him, unable to interpret his stern expression, trying to clear her brain from the mist that engulfed it. Some unknown force seemed to be pushing her tonight. There was no need for this conversation, confrontation even. She should, if she were sensible, turn on her heel and leave him, ignore his ill temper, whatever the cause. She had played her role, held her head high through the whole nerve-wrenching proceedings, thanked him for his supreme moment of chivalry. And surely that was enough. But he stood there in the silent shadowed space where tension all but crackled around them. All dark power and male magnetism. And something kept her from sensible retreat. A need to provoke, she admitted to herself in that moment, honesty demanding that she see her motives for what they were. A need to strip away the polite exterior, the bland response. To discover what really lurked behind his cool, sophisticated, superbly governed outer defences. To see if this man before her bore any resemblance to the Hal she had known two years before, when she remembered his spirit and energy, his unquenchable thirst for a life of excitement and achievement that would cause his pulse to beat and his blood to run hot. When she remembered the heat in his eyes when he looked at her.

But did she know what she was doing? Unlikely, she decided, with a quick wash of panic that brushed the skin along her arms. It was like teasing a fireside cat, all fur and soft paws, only to discover a panther, sleekly elegant, but hiding lethal intent and deadly claws.

Emotion arced between them on that upper landing, unbidden, undesired and as yet unacknowledged. Created by their close proximity, the high, tension-filled emotions of the evening and their own past history. Alone, separate from time and space, they faced each other. Only themselves, so it seemed to be, in the silent, shadowed house. Caught, entangled in a fine web of silken strands, magical and unbreakable, which drew them together and bound them for ever whether they wished for it or not.

And they did. Albeit unacknowledged. The desire was there, unspoken, in their eyes, in the tingling awareness of their bodies, one for the other.

Henry was the first to speak, to break the spell.

'Eleanor…' He grasped at sense, control, honour, all of which seemed to be sliding inexorably beyond his reach. 'I must go.' He took a step back from her.

'Hal—' Stretching out her hand, that one word and the plea in her voice proved to be all that was needed to bring him to a halt. Was she really so wanton? The possibility astonished her, as did the answer in her mind. It did not seem to matter any more. Only this moment mattered. 'Ah, Hal—don't go. Don't leave me.'

'What do you ask of me, lady?' A hint of desperation crept into his voice.

'I don't know.' And indeed she did not. A suspicion of a tear escaped from the amethyst depths onto her lashes, as bright as any diamond, a rival to the brilliance of the fortune which clasped her throat.

It was his undoing. He answered the demand in his body rather than the sane advice of his mind, now completely overthrown. 'I know only one thing, Eleanor. I want you. I do not know if this is good or ill. Wise or unwise. But I can no longer deny it. I wanted you then—two long years ago. And I want you now—the feelings are no different.'

Before she could regret her ungoverned and blatant invitation, he took one stride towards her, grasped her wrist and stalked the length of the corridor, pulling her with him, deaf and blind to any resistance. Except that there was no resistance, which merely enhanced his desire for an ultimate fulfilment of this shattering revelation. Determined on privacy, he opened the door to his own room, pulled her through and closed it behind them. Locked it behind them. Then simply stood and looked down into her eyes, wide with anticipation, her lips parted, her breathing shallow.

'Tell me that you do not want this,' he demanded, 'and I will open the door and let you go free. But tell me now before it is too late.'

'You know that I cannot.' Her voice might be soft, but her reply was immediate. Her eyes never faltered.

'Have you then become a temptress, my lady?' She could not read the expression on his face, the edge in his words.

'No. Or perhaps yes.' She would not lie, caught in the force-field of his power. 'I am not the naïve innocent that I was, no longer a green girl with no knowledge or acceptance of the desires of my own heart. And I remember you, Hal. I remember what it was like to lie in your arms. I remember only too well. So, yes, I want you. I would be a fool to deny it.'

He could wait no longer but pulled her close, destroying the distance between them. Her body was held hard against his, that she would feel the strength and urgency of his desire for her. His mouth met hers, hot, feverish, her lips parting beneath his in willing submission as his tongue sought out the inner softness of her lips. Yet it was no submission. There was no force here. Her response was as heated as his, meeting fire with fire, as demanding and overwhelming as the need that surged through his own blood.

Now, although he released her to stand alone, he gave her no chance to retreat. They were beyond that. With clever fingers he dealt with the intricacies of her gown, removing it with all due care to her and the delicate fabric that she wore, all the while subjugating the force that drove him to tear and ravage, to permit the sensation of his hands against her skin. Her silk stockings were unrolled to reveal elegant calves and high-arched feet, as soft and smooth as their delicate covering. The diamonds were unpinned and unclasped to be discarded at her feet as so much dross. Until she stood before him in her chemise, her feet bare, her face naked and vulnerable before his searching gaze.

'I had forgotten how very beautiful you are.'

With neither reply nor response to the stunned amazement in

his voice, Eleanor bent her head and began to unfasten the ribbons to remove her own chemise. She would not allow him this final intimacy, but would accomplish it herself. The gesture stripped him to the bone. Took his breath—and even more, when the silk and lace folds slithered unhindered down her limbs to lie on the floor.

'I had indeed forgotten. I have longed to see you. How could I possibly forget such perfection?' He simply looked at her, could not take his eyes from her, transfixed for the moment by the magnitude of the gift she was offering him with such deliberate concentration. If she had been vulnerable before, now she was at his mercy, yet she met his gaze with her own, a challenge still in her raised head. He allowed himself the ultimate pleasure of his eyes lingering on every curve and dip of her body. Feminine with high breasts, the soft swell of hip and thigh from her slim waist, she had indeed matured into a beautiful woman from the shy débutante of the moon-shadowed summer house. Flickering light from the single candle on the nightstand illuminated and cast shadows as it would, to entrance and invite his touch. She simply stood, arms loosely by her side, and let him look his fill.

And he knew that it could not be enough. It pleased him that when he finally stretched out his hand she did not flinch from his touch or withdraw into shy embarrassment. Yet he did not touch her yet, still intent on savouring the moment to come, but removed the pins from her hair, one by one, until the lustrous glory of it cascaded into his hands and over her breasts in a shining fall. Until his own needs allowed him to hesitate no longer.

Then, stripping off his own clothes, leaving the single candle burning, he came to her. Without further thought of the sense of his actions, he lifted her high in his arms and tumbled her onto the bed. To join her there, flesh against flesh at last. 'Why can I not rid my dreams of you? You haunt me so.' A touch of anger here as he framed her face with his hands. 'I feel the touch of your hands on my skin, your lips on mine—both waking and sleeping. I can't get you out of my mind.' He crushed his mouth to hers, holding her as he wished, angling his head to take her lips more completely.

'I have dreamed of this moment through so many nights.' He rolled with her, pinning her body beneath him with his weight, braceleting her wrists with strong fingers to stretch her arms above her head. Even though his dominance might underline her vulnerability to him, Eleanor accepted it with a low purr of pleasure in her throat, secure in the knowledge that he would never be capable of hurting her. Only to drive her to the sharp edge of desire—and then over into dark delight.

Tracing a burning path with his mouth, Henry claimed her from her lips to slender throat, to satin shoulder, intoxicated by the heavy pulse that throbbed beneath her skin. He could not get enough of her, nor she of him. Here were no soft moments of tender reminiscence. No gentle interludes full of earlier memories. Only an onslaught of lips and hands to touch, to caress, to excite. Her wrists released, Eleanor was free to explore the man she remembered, as he explored her, hands stroking and moulding the taut muscles of his chest and arms, the flat planes of waist and hip and thigh. Ravaged bedcovers were pushed aside, as tangled and tumultuous as their emotions. Candlelight gleamed on sweat-streaked limbs that entwined, stretched, slid and clung luxuriously one against the other.

Relentlessly, refusing to let her rest, he brought her to the peak of arousal when her body shivered under his hands regardless of the heat. And raised his head as he felt the beginning of her response. Looked into her face.

'Look at me.' It was a demand from which she found no retreat, as she could find no escape from the glorious heat spreading from between her thighs, flushing her skin a delicate rose. 'Open your eyes, Eleanor. Know who owns you, who possesses you this night. You are mine. I took your innocence—now I claim you again. You will never forget me.'

'I cannot forget you.' Her admission was wrung from her on a sharp intake of break as his teeth closed around one taut nipple, driving her near to insanity.

'You torment me,' he murmured against the hollow between her breasts where he planted flesh-searing kisses. 'But I will not suffer alone. I will make you want me tonight.' Hands slid, held, fingers drifting over the gentle swell of her belly to search out the ultimate softness between her thighs. She arched her body on a cry at the intrusion, but in welcome. As urgent, as aroused as he. Hot and wet, she opened for him.

Oh God, he wanted her, must have her.

'Want me, Eleanor. Tell me that you want me.' Past and future held no meaning, only this one moment together in the flickering candle-flame. Perhaps the only moment they would ever have. A moment that should never have been theirs to claim. His conscience damned him for it, but he ruthlessly closed his mind against it, unable to see past the fierce call of his heart and body.

'I do. I want you.' Her reply, the rise and fall of her breasts on ragged breathing, destroyed any conscience which he might have held to. As did the immediate response of her body to his.

As she had given him her virginal innocence, now Eleanor gave him her maturity cloaked in fire and inner knowledge. Touched him, stroked him, set him ablaze with her fine but confident fingers, closed her hand around him, revelling in his groan of shock, of desire. Tomorrow was soon enough for regrets. Tonight she would relive all her hopes and dreams. She burned for him. Flames coursed through her as she enticed him, lured him, the very temptress he had called her. She had dreamed of a night such as this for so long, long nights when it had seemed such an impossibility and she had awoken with tears on her face. Now reality made it true and she would not hold back from him. Moulding herself against him, marvelling at his strength, his muscled power, his weight as he lowered his body to hers, the heat of his erection against her thigh, she laughed softly as she covered his face with kisses. Ah, yes. Henry wanted her as much as she wanted him. It was no time for maidenly blushes or shy hesitancy on her part.

On a breath, unable to delay further, Henry slid into her, lifting her hips to take her to the hilt. On a gasp of stunned amazement and delight she surrounded him in impossible softness, impossible tightness.

A sigh of completion united them. They remained suddenly frozen in time, all frantic demands stilled without words, lost in each other, held fast in each other's eyes, their bodies joined in this most intimate of joining. Taking his weight on his arms, he pressed her hands to the bed, linking his fingers with hers in perfect union, palm against palm.

'Yes, Eleanor.' He answered the question in her eyes, his voice harsh with emotion. 'You know you are mine.'

Only then did he began to move, slowly, deliberately, withdrawing and then reclaiming, watching her every expression as he filled her, stretched her, made her whole body shudder beneath his. It was his intention to keep the pace, to draw out the intense pleasure, but the fire was too great. Caught up in it, its urgency consumed him, the needs of his body overturning the planned campaign. More forceful, more demanding, hips flexed, thrust after thrust, he destroyed them both, carrying her with him to the end. He had no choice but to allow his body to rule.

Without control, Eleanor arched her hips for him, to take him deeper if that were possible. Heat built within her again, low and liquid and throbbing once more in her belly and she rejoiced in it.

'Say my name!' he groaned through gritted teeth as he still clung to the knife-edge of control. 'Say it.'

'Hal. Oh, Hal.' Her body convulsed in heat and light as a meteor shower erupted in golden spangles through her blood.

His control was at an end. Hal followed her into the darkness, losing himself in her, whispering her name as he buried his face in her hair.

Afterwards, when she would have curled into him, content to drift in a soft cloud of fulfilment, in his warmth and comforting presence, Henry exerted all his will-power to fight against the desperate temptation to allow it. Instead he left her warmth, shrugged into his gown to wrap her in a sheet and carry her back to her own room. It would be better so. To spend the night with her would be too painful. It was all too difficult. He should never have allowed such sweet but cruel-edged temptation to overcome him. Where was his much-vaunted control now? He steeled himself against the weight of her head on his shoulder as he carried her and the perfume of her hair that invaded his senses, aware once more of the response in his loins. It would be so very easy to give in and simply love her. To allow her to sleep in his arms, to give himself the pleasure of kissing her awake and taking her once more when dawn lightened the shadows of the bed.

'Forgive me if I have done wrong, Nell. You were far too enticing tonight.' He whispered the words as he relinquished his burden and she slept in her own bed, hair tumbled in a ruffle of curls onto her pillow. 'I could wish that you had repulsed me—but the fault is undeniably mine. And how can I regret it?' He gently touched a curl before withdrawing his hand as if it burned his flesh to the bone. 'You are beautiful and desirable and I regret the events that separated us to the depths of my soul.'

Dousing the candle, he left her.

Only when he had returned to his own room, to spend a sleepless and restless night, did the thought come to him. Not one word of love had been spoken between them during the whole of their intimate coming together. Only of raw hunger and longing. It had been simply a moment of blazing need and desire for each other, a passion that had carried them along in its torrent as leaves in a fast-flowing stream, leaving them shaken and exhausted by the intensity of feelings at the end. But of love—not one word.

Perhaps because there was no love between them. That was the easiest conclusion to reach, the voice of cold sense and caution warned him. Perhaps the basic hunger of a virile man for a beautiful woman had now been assuaged. Perhaps the burning need to touch her, to possess her, had been cauterised by that one moment of brilliant, diamond-bright madness.

Perhaps. But he could not believe it.

Yet it would be better if that were so. Too many shadows surrounded them. The past with its weight of guilt and denial. Thomas, who had willingly taken her as his wife, a role that Eleanor had equally willingly accepted. And, not least, the pathway forward, which was too indistinct and uncertain to decipher. He should pray that this shimmering need had indeed been burned out in that final moment of glory.

But he had worshipped her with every movement of his body,

every caress. Shown her consideration even within the towering demands of his passion. Never pushed her beyond what she was prepared to give to him. And she had given him everything with a generosity beyond measure.

All he wanted was to take her into his arms and repeat it.

And what he could possibly say to her when they came face to face on the following day, he could not envisage.

Little wonder that sleep evaded him.

The house in Park Lane began to hum with unusual bustle at the prospect of a small evening party for members of the Faringdon family and a select number of close friends. Mrs Stamford, in her element at having been given *carte blanche* by Lord Henry, took it upon herself to organise a tasteful, even cosy, evening with the hint of expensive sophistication. Eleanor too found her thoughts given new direction, away from the looming catastrophe of her social status, but her activities did nothing to redirect her mind from thoughts of her outrageous behaviour on the night of the Sefton soirée. She could blame it all on Henry, of course, who had lured her into such a provocative response. Had she actually removed her own chemise? She closed her eyes against the vibrant recall, but her blood heated at the image of his fierce eyes on her exposed body. But honesty forced her to acknowledge her own very willing complicity. He would have left her if she had allowed it, had resisted him to any degree. And she had done neither. Rather, she had flung herself into his arms. She closed her eyes in delicious sensation, ignoring the lists of guests beneath her hand as she sat at the elegant little desk in the blue parlour. He had fired her blood and she had stepped into his embrace and into his bed without hesitation. And she very much feared that she could be lured again.

What must he think of her, of her wanton behaviour? She had no idea. And it had to be admitted, as she sat contemplating the sunbeams stealing across the paper before her, she did not seem to care. All that mattered was the image of his intense loving, the desire that had burned in his eyes and in the heat of his restless mouth. It had swept her beyond thought and conscience. He had wanted her and given in to the temptation. She hugged that thought close as she realised that she had discovered within herself the power to drive him beyond control. She held her breath at *that* thought, releasing it slowly as she also discovered an overwhelming desire to repeat the experience. It was, she acknowledged, a morning for unsettling revelation.

But he had uttered no word of love. Not once, in all the other words he had whispered in the dark expanse of his bed. But then, neither had she. Surely he must have some affection for her. The line between her brows deepened, as she once again demanded honesty from herself. But it was not affection she wanted from him. It was a blaze of love and passion to sweep all before it. Perhaps men were capable of such physical desire without the need for love and she must accept it. But she loved him—and knew it beyond doubt.

Her fair skin shivered at the thought and became suffused with colour. Yes, she loved him, but that did not mean that she wished every glorious detail to be imprinted on her memory every waking moment of every day! Or in her restless dreams. She huffed out her breath in frustration as she focused on the list on the desk, seeing Hal's name written again and again in the margin. With an unladylike hiss, she tore the page in two, consigned it to the flames, and began another. Then, she admonished herself, she must turn her mind to the far more important matter of staff to serve the food and wine to so many guests.

Although she would have preferred to take herself to the opposite ends of the house, even the attics, Eleanor found need to run Henry to ground in the small morning room which he had taken over as office, in lieu of a library in their rented home, and a masculine haven to escape the women of the household.

'I need to know about staff, my lord. Do we hire more footmen? Do I leave it to Marcle to decide what is necessary?' She kept her distance, remaining with her back against the closed door. She looked anywhere but at his face.

'Yes. You need not concern yourself. I have already spoken to him and, unless your mama decides to serve a seven-course banquet, God help us, we should cope more than adequately.'

'Very well.' She was well aware that Henry had hardly looked up from the table at which he was sitting. Which was perfectly acceptable as far as she was concerned! She would have left with a swirl of muslin skirts, but noticed a pile of letters spread before him, some distinctly travel-worn, through which he was steadily wading. They clearly took all his attention. It pricked her conscience and it enticed her to stay, to approach.

'Mr Bridges?' she enquired, remembering his enthusiasm when discussing his new partner and their fledgling company.

'Yes.' He smiled and answered abstractedly. 'I seem to have received a lot of correspondence, all in one batch. The post is still haphazard.' He discarded the top sheet and went on to break the seals on the next. 'A matter of new investments that we hope to take up. Nat has a mind to put some money into a new textile town in Massachusetts. He sees it becoming a second Manchester. And he could just be right. Power looms will make all the difference and there is plenty of water to drive them…' He gave his attention back to the letter under his hand.

She looked at his bent head. Tried not to think of the smooth texture as she had curled her fingers into his hair. Or allowed her lips to trace those elegant cheekbones. And she could not possibly look at his hands without reliving their demanding caresses on her own body. A little shiver feathered across her skin and she silently damned him for reawakening such heady desires.

And then she looked once more at the piles of correspondence, noting Henry's preoccupation with the advice of the absent Mr Bridges. It was all the proof she needed, as if she needed further confirmation, that he would go as soon as he could. The reinforcement of the knowledge destroyed all her remembered pleasure and her present composure in one fatal blow. Her heart ached in anticipation of the loss.

'I think you should return to New York,' she found herself saying brusquely, even though her soul shrieked its denial.

Henry now looked up, attention definitely captured by the harsh edge rarely heard in Eleanor's voice.

'Your business cannot wait for ever. Mr Bridges must feel the need of your presence.'

'Perhaps.' He had not expected this from her. The strain was showing this morning in her colourless skin and the shadows beneath her lids. Even her eyes had lost their sparkle. He realised that she was near breaking point and felt helpless to do anything constructive to alleviate it. Thus his answer was carefully worded. 'But Nat is quite capable of holding the fort for a little while longer. This is merely informing me of decisions he has made in my absence—and I would have done no different. My business is in good hands.'

'What use is there for you to remain here?' She was cold, so cold. 'There is no guarantee that our little event on Saturday night will produce anything of value. You cannot alter the demands of the law if Sir Edward's claims are genuine.'

'No.' Henry now rose to his feet, sensing her distress, intent on taking her hands to offer comfort. 'I trust the Baxendales have replied that they will honour us with their presence on Saturday?'

'Oh, yes. I doubt they could resist being introduced to the family, as you planned. But what will Aunt Beatrice remember? Perhaps nothing. It is a wild goose chase.' Eleanor took a step back.

He shrugged, allowing her to retreat against his better judgement, unwilling to damage the brittle shell which was holding her together. All she said was perfectly true.

'Go back, Hal.' Eleanor turned away and walked to the door.

'Nell.' His voice stopped her. 'I cannot go back. Not yet.'

She stood silently. He had heard the desolation in her voice—she had not been able to prevent it.

'Do you really wish me to do so?' he asked gently.

Now there was an impossible question. 'Yes. I think you should go.' How cold her voice sounded in her own ears. What would he think of her now?

'Nell…'

'No, of course I do not wish you to go! You must know that. But it might be better if you did.' The words, the stark truth, were wrung from her.

'Better for whom, Nell?'

But she closed the door behind her without reply.

Hal was left, hearing the echo of the sharp click as the barrier closed between them. The need to give comfort to her was so great it frightened him, as did the yawning abyss between them. Although he had to accept, with more than a little disgust, that comfort had not been uppermost in his mind when he had all but dragged her to his room. Possession. Need. The control that he had spent years in perfecting had snapped in that one moment when she had raised her eyes to his, had begged him to stay, begged him both with and without words, but none the less with transparent longing. And she had allowed herself to be drawn along, as a leaf in a whirlwind, answering his every demand.

His mind once more stumbled over the fact that he had not told her that he loved her. And perhaps it had been deliberate. And certainly sensible—probably the only commendable part of his behaviour towards her that night. To burden her with his love, against her wishes, would be cruel and insensitive. He hoped, in the inner recesses of his mind, that she would know that she held his heart in her keeping. Remembering her final words, he doubted it, and perhaps it was for the best. He would do all in his power to rescue her from the scandal created by Sir Edward Baxendale and then would indeed return to America for good.

By nine o'clock on Saturday evening, the rooms in Park Lane, perfectly arranged to Mrs Stamford's exacting standards, were soon flatteringly full. Not as elegant as Lady Sefton's soirée, of course. No music had been provided. No poet—thank God! But conversation, cards for those who wished it and an extensive supper, all hosted by Lord Henry at his most urbane and the Marchioness of Burford in softest dove grey, but without the Faringdon diamonds.

Sir Edward and Miss Octavia Baxendale had duly arrived, two of the earlier guests. Octavia was swathed from high neck to ankle in black, as severe and unflattering as ever to her slight figure and pale colouring, and seemingly reluctant to attend any social occasion, but she had smiled prettily and thanked Eleanor for the considerate invitation. She hoped that attention would not be drawn to them. They were simply friends of the family. Eleanor smiled reassuringly, but sardonically. Had Octavia given no thought as to why they should be putting up at Faringdon House when the Marchioness and the rest of the close family were living in Park Lane? Surely she could not be so naïve as to think that there would be no speculation or innuendo? Heaven only knew what people made of it! But Octavia appeared oblivious to the speculation and interested glances.

What did she and Octavia find to talk about as she led the lady to a seat and found some refreshment for her? Afterward Eleanor could not remember. Octavia was decidedly dull, with no opinion of interest to offer on even the most frivolous of topics, once the condition of her rose garden and neglected flower borders had been thoroughly discussed.

Eleanor delivered her with some relief into the safe keeping of Aunt Beatrice and found herself drawn into a few unsettling words with Sir Edward. It was an embarrassing, anger-provoking conversation, despite being quite private. Even though she was aware of Henry's hawk-like eyes on her in case he sensed her distress. She was angry, she thought, on any number of occasions recently, but put on her best sociable manner as hostess.

Sir Edward was as kind and compassionate, as sensitive to her situation as he had been throughout the painful developments. His fair countenance, with all the gravity of deep concern, should have comforted her. It did not. She took a step back when he would have touched her hand in sympathy. She found herself being complimented on her appearance and her fortitude under adverse conditions, which promptly set her teeth on edge. Henry might do so—but not Sir Edward. And her courage was remarkable in holding a social occasion—however informal—when the whole town was so obviously talking and smiling in derision behind its collective and judgmental hand. Eleanor held her breath until the urge to express her true sentiments in less than flattering terms had calmed.

Sir Edward bent his kind and understanding smile on her. 'I believe that Hoskins will have confirmed the legality of all documents by next week, my dear lady.' *How dare you address me with such familiarity! I am not your dear lady and never will be!* 'I have discussed the ultimate outcome with him, of course.'

How dare you!

'We must end this unsatisfactory situation soon. For your sake and for my dear sister's. To postpone the final settlement would be unwise.'

How dare you choose my social event for such a sensitive matter!

How dare you and your sister even exist!

'You are too considerate, sir.' Eleanor's clenched jaw ached.

'I have instructed Hoskins to offer an annuity for yourself and the unfortunate child. Will you take it?'

'I am considering it.' She marvelled at her even tones. At the smile which remained in place.

'There will be scandal, but it is unavoidable. My sister must take on her rightful title. She is very keen to be settled, as you might imagine.'

'Of course.' She continued to smile. She knew that Henry would bear down on them if she appeared in any way distressed—but her eyes were empty of emotion rather than unladylike, and rigidly contained, fury.

'And we must then discuss your moving to your own accommodation, of course. I believe that Octavia would wish to take up residence as soon as possible at Burford Hall. Life in town does not suit her. She enjoys country air.'

'I will inform Hoskins of my arrangements, Sir Edward. They are all in hand.' *But I will not discuss them with you!*

Still keeping a tight hold on the anger that seemed to be directed equally at Sir Edward, at Thomas and at fate in general, Eleanor moved through the rest of the evening like a child's puppet, automatically fulfilling her role. It seemed to be a success. She was complimented more times than she could count. She did not care.

After supper, at which she ate nothing but an asparagus tartlet without even tasting its succulent and delicate flavour, Eleanor made it her policy to find her aunt by marriage in a quiet corner where they would be undisturbed. Lady Beatrice had been able to watch and speak with Sir Edward and Miss Baxendale for a whole evening. She must have some recollection of any past meeting, if any such meeting had occurred. Eleanor had to know. Had Thomas cared for Octavia? Enough to have married her against family opinion and have a child by her? One more tiny nail in the coffin that was threatening to enclose her entire life. As cold as death itself, Eleanor faced the lady. Sensing her purpose from across the room, and not wishing her to be alone when his aunt delivered in typically forthright manner any bad news, Henry moved, silent as a ghost, to appear at her shoulder, to take up the initiative.

'Well, Aunt. You said you remembered Thomas flirting with a fair girl. You have had the opportunity to see the lady and her brother. Do you remember her?'

'Oh, yes.' The Dowager, remarkable in puce satin and lace with garnets, which did nothing to compliment her fading red hair, turned her critical gaze on the innocent object of their discussion. 'I remember her. She was a pretty little thing. Still is, of course but a trifle pale—understandable in the circumstances, whatever the truth of the matter. Thomas certainly had a *tendre* for her. Showed her a great deal of attention, in fact. Dancing with her on more than one occasion…more than I thought was appropriate. It does not do to raise pretensions and it was clear that the girl saw the glitter of a title within her reach. Judith was perfectly right. Thomas and the girl were infatuated—such a very unfortunate emotion, don't you think.'

'Oh.' Eleanor forced her mind to hold the dreaded words.

'I actually warned him off on one occasion—the child was far too provincial for my taste. Not suited to be Marchioness of Burford. Not like you, my dear.' She patted Eleanor's unresponsive hand with superior condescension. 'You have a touch of class, as I was quick to tell Thomas when some of the family expressed their disappointment at his choice of bride.' Realising what she had said, she coughed and spread her fan. 'Your paternal uncle is, after all, a baronet. Most acceptable, my dear. But that is all in the past.'

'So it is true…' Eleanor sighed '…Thomas did marry Octavia.' Henry took Eleanor's cold hand into his keeping and refused to let her pull away. At that moment he did not care who might see or pass judgement.

He simply needed to touch her.

'It may well be. He certainly did not take my advice, if rumours do indeed run true.'

Eleanor looked up at Henry, eyes over-bright. 'It is hopeless, then, as we thought.' But she tried to keep the smile. She would not weep. She would not shout her despair to the world. 'At least we know—it is better perhaps than all the uncertainty. False hope is almost impossible to live with.'

'There is one thing.' Aunt Beatrice reclaimed their attention with narrowed eyes. 'I do not quite recollect her name—Octavia, certainly—but I did not think that it was Baxendale.'

Henry sighed. What use to dredge up any more hope on such a flimsy point of order? He did not think Eleanor could take much more. 'It was a long time ago, ma'am. Even your prodigious memory might play tricks. I cannot think that it is strong enough to cast doubt on the whole question of the legality of their claim. We have to accept that Octavia is Thomas's legitimate widow.'

'Now don't be hasty, young man. Just like your father! Too impatient for your own good.' Lady Beatrice fixed him with a withering glance which he remembered uncomfortably from his youth, and she drew her stout figure up to its full height before delivering her final opinion. 'About the name. As I said, Baxendale I am not at all sure about. But there is one thing I can state for certain. And my memory is excellent when remembering faces! That man, Sir Edward Baxendale, is not Octavia's brother! He is without doubt *not* the young man who was introduced to me as her brother four years ago.'

'Are you sure?' Henry frowned. Whatever they had hoped for, this was most unexpected.

'Sure! Of course I am! I would wager my emeralds on it.'

'But she may have more than one brother.' Eleanor refused to believe that at the eleventh hour there might be the slightest chink of light, of hope, in the dark walls which hemmed her in. 'You may have met—'

'Don't be foolish, my girl. That is not the man who squired Octavia to parties in her London Season.'

'And I distinctly remember the occasion when Sir Edward said that he had been with Octavia when she had made her curtsy to the polite world!' Henry allowed the fact to filter slowly through his brain with all its possibilities. 'Why are you so sure, ma'am?'

'I remember the brother very well—because I took him in instant dislike. Octavia was charming enough, but no family would wish to acquire her brother around the dining table, take my word for it. He had the appearance of a gentleman and the manners were well-bred enough—but there was an unpleasantness about him. You would not trust him with a purseful of gold. Or with the reputation of any pretty young woman—he had quite an eye for them, I am afraid. Or so my husband informed me. I understand he frequented some of the more unsavoury gaming establishments in town. Also I was led to understand that he had an arrangement with a lower class of woman—if you take my meaning. Not that *you* would be acquainted with any such shady dealings of course, Henry.' She dared Henry to contradict her, but he recognised the glint of humour in her face.

'Definitely not, Aunt. Can you describe him—the gentleman introduced as Octavia's brother?'

'Rather like Octavia, I suppose. Taller than Sir Edward. Slighter. A thin face. Hair not quite as fair, perhaps. And cunning eyes, my boy. Not quite the thing at all.' Lady Beatrice furrowed her brow. 'I cannot remember his name—I wish I could. Thomas did not like him either,' she added inconsequentially.

'It is not much to go on, but perhaps enough.' Henry gripped his aunt's hand in gratitude. 'It may be that the whole family will owe you their thanks tonight for your part in overturning this cruel and malevolent plot.'

'Family is important, Henry, as you very well know! It delights me that you are giving your support to Eleanor in a time of trial. Why you should wish to take yourself off to some God-forsaken wasteland on the far side of the world, I shall never know. Much better to settle here, take my word for it!' Lady Beatrice, her mission completed, prepared to return to a cosy chat with one of her intimates. 'But there is one thing I think you should do.'

'And that is?'

'Come, my boy! Use your wits! Ask Octavia how many brothers she has, of course.'

They held a post-mortem in the early hours of the morning when the guests had gone, Aunt Beatrice's words heavy in their minds. Hope, so long dashed, began to run high, despite the essentially trivial nature of the information, and no one thought to claim exhaustion after so successful an evening.

'So who is Sir Edward, if not Octavia's brother?'

'I see you like to start with the easy questions, Nick!' Henry stretched out in a chair beside the settee on which Eleanor and her mama had taken up positions, his hands linked behind his head, ankles crossed. 'We do not know the answer to that one!'

'So what *do* we know?' Mrs Stamford demanded clarification. 'That her name was probably not Baxendale when Thomas met her. And Sir Edward is not her brother. Does it help us at all?' Doubts still drew a sharp line between the lady's delicate brows.

'Octavia only has one brother,' Eleanor put in quietly. 'I asked her about her family, a casual query you understand, over a glass of wine. She said that Edward was the only family she had remaining alive. Her parents are dead and she had no sisters. She offered the information that she and her brother are, and always have been, very close.'

'So we will work on the premise that Beatrice is correct.' Henry frowned down at his highly polished boots.

'But the innkeeper at the Red Lion—' Eleanor turned towards Henry, impatient with her memories of their visit to Whitchurch '—he said Sir Edward had a sister who had a young child. And that the sister's husband had recently died. A husband who rarely visited the Great House. Would he deliberately mislead us? I cannot see it.'

'No. I do not think he lied.' Henry found his mind working furiously with the scant evidence they had. 'He would have no reason to do so—he did not know the reason for our visit.'

'And they knew Sir Edward—both the landlord and the gardener,' Eleanor reminded him again. 'There was no dispute over his name or his living in the Great House.'

'There was in all probability no reason to do so. He most likely *is* Sir Edward Baxendale and I am certain that he does live in Whitchurch. So consider. If you are going to set up a fraudulent claim to a valuable inheritance, surely it must be safer to use as much truth as possible. The more truth, the less chance for the lies to be suspected and detected. It is *Octavia's* name which is in question after all, not Sir Edward's. And the identity of her brother—although how he fits into the puzzle I know not.'

'But Sir Edward has a sister with a baby,' Eleanor persisted.

'Yes. I don't dispute it. But not Octavia.'

'I still don't know where that leaves us.' Mrs Stamford lifted her hands and let them fall into her lap in frustration. She clearly spoke for them all.

'Tell me, Eleanor.' Henry now sat up and fixed the lady with a compelling stare. It appeared that he had come to some conclusions. 'When you first saw the child John, what was your first thought?'

'After I had recovered from the shock?' She laughed a little. For the first time in days it seemed that a weight had been lifted from her mind. They still knew so little, yet there was a distinct crumbling in the edifice built up by Sir Edward. He had lied. And how many lies he had been prepared to tell they had yet to discover. She must hold on to the fact that Thomas's marriage to Octavia was all a sham. And they would prove it! 'I shall never forget those first revelations!' she admitted. 'I suppose I thought that the boy looked nothing like Thomas. And later Judith said—'

'Judith said that Faringdons always breed true.' Mrs Stamford smiled, the slightest touch of triumph as she followed the line of thought. 'Look at dear baby Tom, the image of his father. And Judith is so like her father, apart from that unfortunate red hair which she inherited from Beatrice. But John looks like Octavia. Or even Sir Edward. Both very fair with blue eyes and fair complexions.'

'What are you thinking? Who is the child's father, if not Thomas?' Eleanor's face was suddenly flushed with a delicate colour.

'I don't know yet.' Henry lifted his shoulders and let them fall, but there was the fire of battle in his eyes. 'Who would know more about this?'

'But look, Hal.' Listening to the unfolding suppositions, sympathising with the need to destroy Sir Edward's case, Nick could still see one major sticking point. 'You have forgotten the documents. The marriage and baptism. All legal, signed and sealed, with witnesses. Guaranteed by Church and State. Can we argue round that? I don't see it. We can destroy Baxendale's credibility, but can we discount the documents in Hoskins' possession? He certainly believes them to be above question.'

'One witness of the marriage is dead.' Eleanor reminded him. 'Octavia's mother. It is very convenient, I suppose.'

'And do you remember the identity of the other?' asked Henry. 'It was Sir Edward. Even more convenient!'

'So was the priest also lying? Witnessing something that never happened? Forging documents? Is that what you are suggesting?' Mrs Stamford looked suitably shocked. 'A man of the cloth, too! What a terrible muddle this all is.'

'We need someone who can tell us more about the Baxendale family.' Nicholas returned to his brother's previous question. 'Someone who will know about relationships, scandals, whatever, and be prepared to talk to us.'

'That's easy!' Henry pushed himself to his feet to pour a glass of brandy, offering it to his brother. 'Servants. They always know more about the family than the family members themselves. If you ever wish to know anything about the Faringdons, for the past two generations at least, ask Marcle. Don't ever be under the misapprehension that you have any secrets, Nick!'

'There is only the nursemaid here with them in London. Sarah, I think.' Eleanor looked at her mama for corroboration.

'Perfect! Eleanor…would you care to pay a visit to Faringdon House again tomorrow?' Henry poured brandy for himself. 'On the pretext of enquiring after Octavia's health after her social introduction? And see if you can find an occasion to speak with Sarah.'

'But what on earth do I ask?' she demanded, startled at the

role suddenly thrust at her. 'Are your employers perhaps charlatans? Do they lie and cheat and—?'

'I will go with you.' Mrs Stamford rose to her feet. 'Come, my dear. It is late. We will think of something. And if words do not get the right results, gold might! In my experience, money will open a multitude of doors.'

'Well, Mama…' Eleanor failed to hide her surprise '…I shall certainly not refuse your offer. We will be able to enjoy another exciting conversation with Octavia about the state of her roses! If you will accompany me, it may give us the opportunity to distract her so that one of us can talk to the child and Sarah. I shall take Tom with me. What a cosy family party we shall make, to be sure!'

'Have faith, Eleanor. It seems that we have a mystery on our hands at last, rather than an open-and-shut case.' Henry walked with habitual grace to open the door for the departing ladies, bowing them out. 'And brother Thomas is beginning to look like an innocent pawn in an intricate and dangerous game of chance. More innocent by the hour.'

The ladies went to bed, deep in discussing tactics for the morrow. Hal and Nick sat on in the parlour, Hal deep in thought, a bottle of brandy between them.

'What is it?' Nicholas asked at last—his brother had spent the past ten minutes saying nothing, but staring into the fire.

'I have been thinking.'

'Never!'

Now he looked up, lips curving a little. 'The documents presented by Sir Edward. They must be false. And Aunt Beatrice's description of Octavia's brother…'

'So?'

'Little brother.' Henry smiled in gentle malice. 'Would you care for another tour of the gentleman's clubs and gaming establishments of London? And perhaps another informative conversation with Kingstone?'

'No. I would not!'

'I think this one may pay off. Just a hunch but… Say nothing to Eleanor. It would not do to raise her hopes until we have more concrete evidence than Beatrice's ramblings. Our aunt has more faith in her memory than I have. But I think…I just think that we may have been looking for the wrong person!'

Chapter Eight

At eleven o'clock on the following morning, Mrs Alicia Stamford, as promised, accompanied by the Marchioness of Burford and the infant Marquis, all suitably dressed for an informal morning visit, took the barouche to cover the short distance to Faringdon House in style.

'We must devise some means to encourage Octavia to bring the nursemaid and the child into the room. I doubt it will be too difficult.' Mrs Stamford settled herself in the carriage in a decided manner and unfurled her parasol. 'Since you have the baby with you, it would be natural to wish to praise and admire.' She removed the tassel of her embroidered reticule from Tom's inquisitive fingers with firm and well-practised skill. '*I* will engage Octavia in conversation. *You* may talk with Sarah about the family.'

'Thank you, Mama!' Eleanor's smile was wry. 'I am not sure who has drawn the short straw.' She distracted Tom from eating the fingers of her new kid gloves. 'I hope that she is of a confiding nature!'

As it happened, there was no need for devious plotting on the part of the two ladies. The morning was warm and sunny. There, in the private garden with its ornamental railing in the centre of Grosvenor Square, they spied Octavia Baxendale, her nursemaid and her son taking advantage of the mild temperature. Octavia sat comfortably beneath a tree, a little apart, a book open on her lap. On the grass some distance before her sat Sarah with the child John. High voices and excited shouts gave evidence that other families from the Square, both children and nursemaids, were enjoying the fine morning with childhood games.

'Fortune smiles on us so far.' Mrs Stamford gave her hand to their coachman and descended, all regal dignity, to take this crucial meeting with Octavia Baxendale under her control.

The ladies exchanged greetings. Enquired after their respective health. They had come, Mrs Stamford explained, to ask after the welfare of *Miss Baxendale* after the demands of the previous evening and her meeting the Faringdon family *en masse*. A most successful *at home,* was it not, as acknowledged by all. Lady Beatrice Faringdon had particularly commented on her enjoyment at renewing her acquaintance with Miss Baxendale. She clearly remembered their previous meetings very well, when Octavia had first made her curtsy, in spite of the passage of time. And had Sir Edward found it an amusing experience? Mrs Stamford had noticed that he played a skilful hand of whist.

Eleanor hid a smile and simply allowed her mother to continue unchecked. Octavia expressed no surprise, no recognition of, or response to, Mrs Stamford's subtle comments and answered in her usual calm manner. She smiled. Her eyes rested on her visitors with guileless acceptance. She was very well. No, she had not found it unduly stressful. Yes, she had enjoyed the evening, particularly her conversation with Lady Beatrice, who reminded her a little of her mother. So pleasant to have such a large family. Edward had said what an agreeable evening it had been. All so elegant and comfortable, as they had expected, of course.

Eleanor sighed inwardly and did not envy her mother her self-imposed task of bringing Octavia out of herself.

But Mrs Stamford sat beside Octavia, all determination, arranged her skirts and her parasol and set herself to entertain and elicit information. They discussed the care and design of gardens—of which Eleanor's masterful mama had limited knowledge, but yet approved as an interest worthy of a lady; and Byron's latest offerings of *Parisina* and *The Siege of Corinth,* both offered in the same volume—which she had never read but willingly condemned, as she did with equal fervency the infamous author for his scandalously wild life and lack of gentility, despite his elevated birth. There was no accounting for such aberrations in even the most well-born of families, she declaimed with a sharp glance at Octavia.

But Octavia had little to add beyond another smile and an inclination of her head. Nor did she claim acquaintance with the works of Lord Byron. Mrs Stamford quickly came to the conclusion that she had never spent so tedious a morning. Miss Baxendale might be a pretty girl with acceptable manners—no fault to be found in *her* upbringing, for sure—but she had absolutely nothing to say for herself. How Thomas could have married her, she would never understand! But then, she caught herself on the thought, she had to hold on to the conviction that he had never done so.

Meanwhile Eleanor, to the detriment of her figured muslin gown—but it was in a good cause, after all—sat on the grass with Sarah and the two children. Tom was intrigued, too young to enjoy the company of another infant, but content to crawl and to try to eat the daisy heads, which were opening in the sunshine. John ran about on sturdy legs, throwing a ball to Sarah when she encouraged him, but lured by the cries of the other children in the garden. Sarah allowed him to approach their game when the temptation grew too great to withstand, but kept a sharp eye on him. Octavia seemed unconcerned, deep in a discussion with Mrs Stamford of the value of auriculas for spring planting.

Here was Eleanor's chance.

Naturally enough, Eleanor tried to encourage Sarah to talk about children. Their ailments. Their diet. The needs of a tearful, teething baby and how to encourage an excitable child to sleep. It should have been easy, but Eleanor found it hard work. Sarah was, for the most part, monosyllabic. Not shy, Eleanor decided, so much as intensely reserved, although clearly knowledgeable about the range of subjects that they covered. She unobtrusively took stock of the young woman sitting on the grass. *Neat,* was the word that sprang to mind. Hair drawn severely back into a knot at the nape of her neck with no curls allowed to flatter her face. Carefully dressed, without decoration of any degree, but in good quality clothes. Fair skin, blue eyes. As they talked she relaxed a little and was more willing to develop her answers to Eleanor's gentle enquiries. Her voice low and well modulated, her speech evidence of a thorough education. And there was a certain confidence about her as she sat with the sunshine dappling her hair and features, shining through the leaves of the elms above them. Her eyes were reluctant to meet Eleanor's at first, but gradually did so as she forgot her restraints in conversation with the Marchioness of Burford. Her hands, loosely folded in her lap, were long fingered and fine with none of the roughness that might be expected in a domestic servant.

Eleanor was puzzled. And then realised that there was no need. Here in all probability was a young woman from a good family, fallen on hard times, and forced to take service as companion or governess with an established family. It was a frequent occurrence, after all. She had Eleanor's sympathy.

Having wrung every possible detail from the topic of children, Eleanor attempted to extend the conversation. To the matter of the Baxendales. How loyal would the nursemaid be in the face of pertinent questions? There was no way for Eleanor to know until she tried.

Did she enjoy town life? Would she rather be back at home in the village of Whitchurch? Did she find it very secluded there or did the Baxendales have a vast acquaintance who might visit the Great House with children for John to play with?

Sarah rapidly took refuge in monosyllables again, eyes downcast. Eleanor was getting nowhere, but persisted.

Did Sarah remember when Octavia came out? Was she in the family employ? How long had she been with the family? Miss Baxendale had said that Sarah was once her companion before taking over the care of the child. She must have enjoyed being in such a close relationship with her employer.

The Marchioness gritted her teeth. With no encouragement from Sarah, it was fast giving the appearance of a cross-examination. So Eleanor gave up. If they were to learn anything about the Baxendale family, it would not be from this girl who sat so still and composed and *distant* beside her. And was intent on saying nothing but yes or no! But why did she get the impression that there was far more below the controlled surface, something that troubled the girl, her eyes strained, her lips pulled tight and thin in her otherwise serene face? It occurred to Eleanor that there was an indefinable sadness about the young woman, but there would be no confidences exchanged here, even without the social divide of Marchioness and servant.

They were suddenly interrupted by a squabble and sharp voices between the knot of children in the centre of the garden. Who should hold the lead of a lively brown terrier owned by one of the families? The result was much shouting and pushing. As the youngest and smallest, John came off worst. There was a howl, not of pain but frustration, when the children abandoned him to race off with the dog to their own nurse across the garden. John howled louder, tears of temper sparkling in his blue eyes when he could not keep up with their longer legs.

Eleanor watched the outcome, her interest caught.

Octavia did not divert for one moment from her discussion of herbs suitable for a kitchen garden, despite her son's loud expression of fury. Sarah immediately, without excuse or apology, leapt to her feet and abandoned the Marchioness. All her composure was gone in that moment of animation. She swooped on the child with expressions of concern, picked him up, wiped the tears away and promised a treat for little boys who were good and did not cry. The child's tears instantly receded, replaced by a bright smile of anticipation. Sarah nuzzled his neck, kissed his damp cheeks, John returning her embrace enthusiastically and beginning to giggle when she tickled him.

Eleanor's gaze became suddenly intent. Then she dropped her focus to her own child, who was attempting to crawl into her lap, taking in his dark hair and the promise of the striking Faringdon features. The differences were remarkable—there could be no denying it. So she stood, determined to seize the moment, smoothed down her skirts and approached the nursemaid who had set the child on his feet again, straightening his collar with loving fingers.

'Sarah. Tell me…who is the father of this child?' Eleanor bent to stretch out her hand, to touch the silky fair curls, to cup the soft curve of his cheek.

There was a flash of panic as the laughter in the nursemaid's eyes vanished. Sarah cast a glance towards Octavia, who remained unaware of any development. Then she gathered John up again into her arms, held close despite his sudden squawk of protest, as if she would shield him from some unseen physical attack.

'Sarah. I mean you no harm. Indeed…' Eleanor would have taken her hand, but Sarah stepped back out of reach.

'Excuse me, my lady. I must take him inside. He will be hungry…'

She fled, almost at a run, with a mumbled apology to Octavia in passing, and vanished through the doors of Faringdon House.

Eleanor picked up Tom, smoothing his hair reflectively. Sarah was afraid.

'I have spent so dull a morning! You cannot imagine.' The ladies were once more seated in the barouche, Mrs Stamford holding forth. 'She appears to know little and will say even less! Her head is stuffed with nothing but pergolas and French marigolds!'

'Sarah was even less communicative,' Eleanor admitted. 'I found out nothing other than an old wives' cure for an infant colic, which I would certainly never try on any child of mine! A poultice of common groundsel, applied to the stomach of the poor little mite—I shudder at the thought. But Sarah swears by it.'

'Which does not mean there is nothing to find out, of course.' Alicia Stamford turned her severe stare on her daughter, choosing to ignore the diversion into country remedies. 'Surely you could persuade her to drop some gossip about her employer?'

'No! I could not! What do you suggest? There is no point in scowling at me, Mama. Short of asking her if *Baxendale* is her mistress's real name, I could see no way of doing so.' She turned her face away, holding her son close for a long moment. 'But one thing is certain. There is some secret there that surrounds the child. And Sarah is not at ease.'

* * *

'Hal! You were right! I have found it!'

Nicholas erupted into Henry's bedchamber as the latter was putting finishing touches to his cravat.

'Come in, Nick!' His lordship continued to concentrate on his image in the mirror. He was no dandy, as he would be the first to admit, and was very ready to dispense with the services of a valet, but he knew that it was important to keep up some standards in London.

'A Waterfall, unless I am much mistaken.' Nicholas laughed and flung himself into a chair by the window to watch the operation. He was still in shirt sleeves and, although the morning was somewhat advanced, gave the appearance of not being long from his own bed.

'I like the coat—very Weston—and the sartorial elegance of the cravat is amazing for someone wedded to the undeveloped backwoods and social equalities of the New World. A pink of the *ton,* no less.' Nicholas smiled in friendly mockery. 'But that's not important! I would have come last night—this morning…it was only a few hours ago—but I presumed you would be asleep.'

'I was.' Their eyes met in the mirror. 'And don't sneer too loudly, little brother. New York may not yet be a centre of *sartorial elegance* as you put it, but neither it is the backwoods of anywhere. I can still cut a pretty figure.'

'So I see. And do the ladies of New York appreciate this jewel in their midst?'

'Rosalind has no complaints.'

'Ah. Rosalind. Is she a serious matter or in the form of entertainment?' There was more than a casual question in the voice that caused Henry to glance across from his task.

'None of your business, Nick.' Henry took a final glance at his reflection.

'Of course not.' He shrugged and grinned with easy acceptance of the rebuff from his brother. They knew each other very well. 'I only wondered if you had marriage in mind—to set up your own dynasty to inherit the vast fortune you are intent on making.'

'You will be the first to know when I do,' was the only dry comment he received in reply. 'Do I presume from your good humour that your efforts in the dens of iniquity paid off?'

'More than you could ever guess.' Nick settled himself more comfortably, one leg hooked over the arm of the chair, to regale his brother with the details. 'I managed to run him to ground. Our sly fox is a frequenter of White's, would you believe. And also the new establishment in Pall Mall—Whittaker's, I think. The place where the major-domo looks you up and down as if you might be up to no good and about to steal the silver.'

'So.' Henry anchored his cravat with a sapphire pin, smiling down at his brother's face, flushed with triumph. 'We have tracked him to earth.' His smile was not pleasant as he thought of the effect on Nell over the past weeks of fraudulent scheming. 'So what has our friend been doing recently?'

'He is not a frequent visitor to the clubs, but then puts in an appearance for a few nights in one week—as you would expect—when he escapes from his duties. He plays deep. *Vingt-et-un* is his poison. It does not need much skill—just a steady nerve, and our friend, it would seem, has neither. So he is in debt, I gather, to Spalding to the tune of 2,000 guineas. And perhaps to Robert Mallory—you remember him? You once bought a hunter from him—but I am not certain. But he owes something near to 5,000 guineas all told.'

'And where would he find money like that to pay off the debt?'

'Exactly. Shall I tell you more? I had a very busy night.'

'Please do.' Henry's eyes gleamed at the prospect of progress at last.

'It gets better. When I mentioned the name to Kingstone, he was an amazing source of information. It cost me a bottle of brandy, but it was well worth it. There was a scandal recently. We did not hear of it because I was at Burford and you were in New York. It involved a new young actress called Elizabeth Weldon. She was taken up by an admirer and had a child. Both actress and child were found dead in her lodging, their cause of death uncertain. Rumour connected our quarry's name with the girl, but there was no proof and his status would speak against it so the case was not pursued. But even so, Kingstone tells me that he is not liked. Hers was not the only name he has been linked with. It would seem that his appetite for pretty young girls is…shall we say, extreme.'

'Better and better.' Hal thought for a moment, toying with a silver-backed hairbrush. 'What you say does not surprise me. Aunt Beatrice hinted as much. He has a very attractive young housekeeper, I remember, with a pronounced invitation in her smile. Our esteemed aunt would definitely not approve.'

'Yes. Well, it would fit with the rest of the picture. And I only had to spend one night to get the information! Oh, and by the by, he drinks—to excess. Another reason for his being a poor gambler. Kingstone says that he has been asked to leave more than one club. His behaviour must have been vulgar indeed.'

'I am indebted to you, Nick.' Henry put down the brush and shrugged into the dark superfine coat which had attracted Nick's admiration. 'I think another visit to Whitchurch is called for. Tedious, but it will be worth it. Do you care to join me? This time Eleanor will be remaining in London, if I have to lock her in her room.'

'I will go to Whitchurch with you willingly. But restrain Eleanor? I will not volunteer to help—on your own head be it. Besides, she would forgive you quicker than she would forgive me.' Nick watched his brother closely, to see his response.

'I doubt it. The lady has not hidden the fact that she has a low opinion of both my involvement and my motives in staying to unravel this unholy mess!'

'Then you should not doubt it! The problem is, Hal, that you do not see what is under your nose where Nell is concerned. I thought you did not like each other at first. I admit I was wrong. Totally wrong. I am still not quite sure what drives both of you— or perhaps I am. In fact, I am convinced! But I know that you would not thank me for my opinions or advice.' With which set of blindingly enigmatic statements, Nicholas rose to his feet and made to depart.

Then Marcle knocked at the door and entered with a silver salver bearing a note.

'From Lady Beatrice, my lord.'

Henry sighed and frowned. 'Now what.'

He broke the seal, unfolded the single page and read the brief note of a few lines. And then re-read it.

'Well?'

He passed it on to his brother. 'I think that we have just discovered our pot of gold.'

My dear Henry,

I remember the name. It came to me at some inconvenient hour in the dead of night when I could not sleep, as is ever the case. Perhaps it came from seeing the girl and speaking with her at your evening on Saturday. Her name is—or certainly was—Octavia Broughton.

I hope this information is to your advantage. I would hate to see the title fall into the wrong hands.

Your loving aunt,

Beatrice

'God Bless you, Beatrice!' Henry took back the note and stowed it carefully in his pocket.

'And the Devil take the Reverend Julius Broughton, Octavia's loving and expensive brother!' Nick added with some venom. 'When do we set out for Whitchurch?'

After Nicholas's departure, Lord Henry added a gold watch to his waistcoat and a signet ring to his hand, made to pick up gloves and hat, then simply stopped, standing to rub his hands over his face in frustration. Nicholas knew. It had become impossible to disguise it. He had tried not to look at Nell. To touch her. To keep his distance when in the public eye. He had hoped, fought hard to hold his feelings in check. Not well enough, it seemed. Nick knew him too well. At least he could rely on his brother to be discreet. They both knew that they could not afford one whiff of scandal. If any word of an association between Lord Henry Faringdon and the newly widowed Marchioness of Burford got out to become the latest *on dit,* they would be all but destroyed. The censure of the *haut ton* would be damning indeed, for which he would never forgive himself. So he must guard his actions in future. There must be not the smallest hint of love or desire or need. He gritted his teeth. Nothing beyond brotherly affection and concern. But it was sometimes impossible when Eleanor looked so lost and weighed down by uncontrollable events. Or when she sparkled with courage and determination to fight back against the odds. Or when she smiled at him, her eyes glowing and her lips curving in just that way she had… Lord Henry groaned. In fact, it was simply impossible.

The morning visit to Octavia Baxendale at Faringdon House and her difficult but inconclusive conversation with Sarah gave Eleanor much food for thought. Sarah's protection of the child, her awareness of his needs, had been keen and instinctive. When he was in distress her response to him was immediate and loving. Quick to restore him to laughter. Whereas Octavia…she had continued her conversation after the briefest of glances towards the source of the youthful tantrum. Eleanor could not imagine being so uninterested in her son's concerns. But she lifted her shoulders in the slightest of shrugs. As Judith had been quick to point out, not everyone was blessed—or cursed—with strong maternal feelings. And, without doubt, the child was healthy and well cared for. There was no cause for concern for the well-being of Octavia's son.

The sunshine flooded the window embrasure of the little parlour at the front of the house where Eleanor stood, her own child in her arms, contemplating their uncertain future. She had been driven to rescue her son from his nursemaid in the nursery, to spend time with him, perhaps to reinforce her memories of Thomas and her marriage when the future had seemed so settled. So certain. She held the child close, enjoying the warmth of his small body, the grasp of his fingers at the neck of her gown. She rubbed her face against his, making him chuckle, so that those glorious eyes, not the dark blue with which he was born—indeed, they were now the most beautiful clear amethyst of her own— sparkled with innocent pleasure. Whatever the future would hold for him, she vowed that he would be safe. She could protect him and give him the best life that was in her power to give, whatever the outcome of Sir Edward Baxendale's assertions. And she would love him with all the fierce maternal love that flowed through her veins. The infant whimpered a little, his mouth downturned as her possessive hold tightened inadvertently. Eleanor laughed a little as she loosened her grip and turned towards the view from the window for instant distraction from tears.

'One day you will own a house as fine as this,' she told Tom. 'Finer, in fact. As fine as the King's own palace, if you wish it.' Her cheek pressed against his hair as he leaned to stretch out his hand to the world beyond the glass. 'One day you will own a splendid bay stallion, just like that one.' She pointed as a rider went past, the hollow sound of the hooves echoing on the hard surface. 'You will ride as well as your father—all style and dash and elegance. And you will look like him. I know it, even though you are still so small. I see his dark hair and straight nose.' She touched him with gentle fingers, savouring the curves of childhood that would disappear all too soon. 'Not his eyes—they are mine—but those splendidly arched eyebrows. And the curve of your jaw just there.' She ran her finger over the soft cheek. 'You will be tall and handsome and when you smile the young ladies will all want you to look in their direction. Just as I did when I saw your father. You will break many hearts, I am sure—and you do not care about one word I have said to you!' She laughed in delight as she swung him round in a circle.

Then her thoughts drifted to Thomas, her husband, as the baby dozed a little on her shoulder. The images rose before her mind, crystal clear, finely etched, a painful and difficult meshing of contentment and grief. The morning she had gathered all her courage to present herself at Faringdon House to enquire for Hal. She had expected to be turned away, but Thomas had seen her, invited her into the library to know the reason for her distress. Only to inform her that Henry had sailed two days before. She had not believed him. She remembered as if it were yesterday the icy finger of despair that had traced its path down her spine. She had felt almost faint with shock, disbelieving that he could have left her, without word, without even a formal farewell. He had simply gone, in spite of all his protestations of love,

in spite of the promise implicit in his lips warm against her own.
In spite of her giving him the proof of her own love. How empty
his words must have been. How cold his heart—and she had
never realised it until that moment when Thomas had said, 'But
he is gone. Did you not know?'

Dear Thomas. Her lips curled sadly at the memory. His compassion and kindness had been overwhelming as he led her to a
seat, helping her mop up her tears with his own handkerchief.
She could not have expected such concern for her broken heart,
but he had been open in his generosity.

And Thomas had married her. He knew that she loved Hal.
Yet he had still married her.

Oh, Thomas. How unfair I was to you! She rocked the baby
against her. *I gave you friendship and companionship, but I could
not give you my heart. I never pretended otherwise, but I pray
that you were satisfied. I think you deserved more. Perhaps you
did love Octavia…but I can never accept that you would have
treated me—or her—with such lack of respect. It was simply not
in your nature to dissemble and hide the truth. We were always
honest with each other.*

She brushed away the dampness from her eyes, determinedly
refusing to let her thoughts return to her troubled relationship
with Hal and his imminent departure. She cradled the sleeping
babe more comfortably, humming softly, her cheek resting
against his hair.

'You are so very young, still so unaware,' she murmured.
'And so you can never know your father—it will never be possible for you to grow up to experience for yourself his love and
care. But I will tell you all about him when you are old enough
to understand. I will never let you forget how splendid a man
sired you, even though you will never be able to keep his image
in your memory, and he will not know you as you grow to manhood.' Turning her face into the soft curls, she hid the anguish.
'And neither shall I forget. I shall remember him until the day I
die.' Her voice was soft, even if the words were fierce. The baby
snuffled and burrowed against her. 'You do not understand, but
one day you will.'

* * *

Henry stood in the open doorway to the parlour. He had been standing there for some little time, having been dispatched by Mrs Stamford with an urgent request to her daughter. He could not help but listen and watch, uncomfortable at eavesdropping on so private a moment, but caught up in the situation. She was so loving, so tender with the child. The picture they made together, bathed in bright sunshine, gave them the glowing mysticism of a holy picture. Otherworldly. Beyond time. He would have liked to have walked in, enfolded them both in his arms in a symbol of love and possession, but could not, dare not, break the spell. He was shut out from this relationship by present circumstances and past history. His throat dried, his heart beat with a heavy pulse as he controlled the wave of regret and longing that compromised him with its intensity. Into his mind came the memory of the woman and the babe as he had once seen them, when Eleanor had leaned over the crib in candlelight and crooned a lullaby to a restless infant. The image was sharp, clear as the faceted crystals in the chandelier, and it rocked him to his very soul. Such love and tenderness between them. Henry was forced to turn his face away from the brightness before him, to close his eyes momentarily to shut out the promise of what might have been, and yet could never be. He would have retreated, leaving her undisturbed. After all, he did not know what to say to her and in that moment could not trust his composure.

Then, as he would have stepped back, she became aware and turned her head, a little startled. He had no choice but to continue with his errand.

'I did not mean to disturb you, my lady.' Eleanor apparently did not notice his hesitation. But his voice sounded strained, even to his own ears.

'You have not.' What was he thinking? His expression was bleak, the flat planes of his face stark with an emotion held in check. She hid her own discomfort behind a polite exterior, but could not look at him.

'Your mother seems to feel that there is urgent need for you below stairs. She accosted me in the hall. Some disagreement, I believe. She would not explain, but she is not happy.'

'Oh. My mother tends to see household catastrophes where they do not exist.' Eleanor managed a slight smile as she sighed.

'I dare not suggest such a thing. I think you had better go.' Henry's appraising glance took in her discomfort, her lack of ease in his presence. He wished that he knew why.

'It will be some trivial matter that Marcle will be able to solve without difficulty. My mama has a need to interfere!'

'I am aware. But dare not say that either!'

Now she laughed, the atmosphere lightened, as had been his intent. 'If you would ring the bell for Jennie to take Tom…'

'No matter. I can watch my nephew for a few moments without danger to him or myself, I expect.'

'Are you sure?' He did not know whether he saw amusement or uncertainty on her face as her eyes finally lifted to his, but either was better than her previous withdrawal.

'No. I can but try.'

She laughed again as she walked to the door, quickly turning her face away. How much had he heard of her foolish conversation with Tom? She was intensely aware of the hot colour that stained her cheeks, embarrassed by her vivid memories of a few moments before.

'Eleanor.' His voice stopped her. 'Will you return when you have dealt with the crisis? There is a matter that I need to discuss with you.'

'Of course.' She frowned. 'Should I be worried?'

'No. Not a matter of concern—rather one of hope. But there is something you should know that Nicholas has discovered.'

'Very well.' Eleanor tucked the child securely into the corner of a chair, supported by a cushion and, with the brief instruction to watch her son, left in the direction of her mother's raised voice.

'So.' Henry eyed the child with some disquiet. 'What do we do? I know nothing of babes. I suppose I can talk to you. Or perhaps I simply leave you to sit there until your mother returns. And pray that it will not be long!'

A whimper at the loss of his mother was the only response.

'Don't cry. Not that. I shall have failed and have to face your mama's wrath. Come here.' He bent and lifted the child with definite lack of expertise, but carefully enough, to carry him to the window as Eleanor had done. 'There—that is far more interesting.' He looked at the child, noting the features, his heart suddenly clenching in his chest. 'Oh, God! Thomas. I wish you had not died. You should see your son. So much like you.' He smiled as the baby blinked owlishly at him. 'Even to that innocent stare when there is mischief afoot. I predict he will be a handful as he grows—but with all the charm in the world.' The smile faded, his features taking on an austere cast. 'And his mother is exactly what you would have wished. I will care for your son—and Eleanor, if she will allow it. For both of them, as you would have done.'

Eleanor returned, the matter of responsibilities for ordering both household and kitchen candles quickly smoothed over, to see Henry in the window, holding the child. She came to an abrupt halt, much as Henry had done earlier. The breath caught in her throat at the unexpected scene. Both dark heads close together, some ridiculous conversation going on, which had caused the child to focus on Lord Faringdon with determined concentration and an instantly recognisable Faringdon frown. The object under discussion appeared to be Henry's half-hunter repeater watch, which he had opened to chime the hours and the quarters. Tom's frown suddenly replaced by a grin in which teeth were just beginning to emerge. He giggled at the bell-like tones.

She could weep for what might have been as Henry turned his head at her approaching footsteps.

'Eleanor.' The relief was palpable. 'As you see, I am entertaining your son. Not a tear in sight.'

'Thank you.' She was unintentionally abrupt, to hide the emotion that threatened her composure.

'You had better take him. I might drop him.'

'You look very competent.' She held out her arms, then turned her back, concentrating on the child, struggling to keep her voice light. Her heart ached. 'You said you had something to tell me.'

'Yes. It will interest you inordinately to know that Octavia's name is not Baxendale. It is Broughton. Aunt Beatrice remembered.'

'Broughton!' Eleanor became very still as enlightenment came to her, her eyes widening. The unexpected news overrode her wayward emotions and her discomfort in Henry's presence. She now turned to face him, features vivid with renewed hope, but still kept her gaze fixed on Tom's face. 'And so her brother? The Reverend Julius, I presume.'

'Yes.'

'Then…' she shook her head '…why did Sir Edward claim to be her brother? Why did the Reverend Broughton lie to us?'

'The details are not yet clear. But tomorrow Nick and I will go back to Whitchurch. The Reverend has an unsavoury reputation, it would appear. Nick has traced him to some of his London haunts. Debt is an issue. It might explain why he was willing to put his hand to documents so obviously fraudulent.'

'And you do not want me there.' She nodded once in quick understanding, but still disappointment.

Henry walked to the other side of the room, to put as much distance between them as was possible. He did not want to see the wild hope in her eyes. It was difficult enough to hear traces of it in her voice without surrendering to a need to hold and comfort her—in case their investigation came to nought.

'It would serve no purpose, Nell.' His words sounded cold, unfeeling.

'I understand. Whatever you wish, of course.'

'You amaze me, Eleanor.' Those well-marked Faringdon brows arched.

'Did you expect me to demand that I accompany you?'

'Yes. Nick and I thought we would have to lock you in your room.'

'I see. So you have already discussed the possibility!' And clearly not something that he wished for. Against her will, she was touched by amusement and decided to be charitable. 'No, I shall not be so difficult and uncooperative.'

'We could have the key to the whole secret by tomorrow night.' He tried to be encouraging.

'Yes. It will be a relief.' Her voice was colourless, disguising the thoughts that jostled in her mind, destroying the hope that should have been ignited by his words. *It will all be over. I should be overjoyed. My son's inheritance is safe.* She looked at the handsome man standing by the door. Noting the distance between them. Recognising his deliberate intent. *And then he can go back. Back to Rosalind. Don't think about it. Don't think about anything but the benefit for your son. Don't hope for the impossible. He did not want you before. He will not want you now. It is finished.*

Henry was shattered by the stricken look on her face, a fleeting expression of despair, seemingly incongruous with the news he had just brought her. Perhaps he misread it. Perhaps she was simply tired. But he doubted it.

He bowed and left. There was nothing he could do for her but unmask Edward Baxendale and Julius Broughton as the villains that they undoubtedly were.

He would do that, if he could do nothing else.

Lord Henry made the journey once more by curricle to the tranquil village where a malicious plot had been conceived and put into motion, accompanied as planned by his brother. It had to be admitted that he was not sorry; it was a more relaxed journey without the tensions and enticements of Eleanor's presence. But he had been more than a little surprised by her compliant willingness to remain in London, her uncharacteristically placid acceptance of his decision. Or perhaps it had not been placid but edgy, withdrawn, an unwillingness to be in his company, and he said as much to Nicholas as the miles sped past.

'She did not wish to come.'

'She seemed very calm about the whole affair at breakfast.' So Nicholas had sensed nothing untoward. 'You did not then have to lock her in her room.'

'No.'

Nicholas thought about it. 'You can't blame her. This will not be a pleasant interview and she would learn nothing that we cannot report back, after all.'

'No.'

But it worried him. Did she dislike him so much, a renewal of the hatred and contempt that had flashed in her eyes when he had first returned to Burford Hall? And if so, what had precipitated it? Had their night together, however unwise it might have been, not been what he had thought? She had quite deliberately refused to meet his eyes when he had told her of Nick's discovery, deliberately turning her back against him, when only the night after the Sefton soirée she had shivered in his arms. Arched her body against his and cried out his name with a fierce passion that had matched his own. And yet when she had returned to the parlour to take her son from his arms her response to him had been cold and aloof. He might as well have been a stranger to her. Women! How could a man ever be expected to follow their train of thought? He snapped his thoughts back to the present, tightening the reins, as one of the lively bays took it into its head to shy at a passing pheasant.

The minor skirmish and battle of wills over, his thoughts turned back to Eleanor whether he wished it or not. It was for the best. He could leave for New York with nothing to pull him back to England. No unfinished business, no untied ends, no tangled emotions. The bitterness might have dissipated from their relationship but, whatever Nick had intimated—and he was not perfectly sure that he understood his brother's comments—Eleanor was more than willing to turn her back on him as if there had never been any passion between them. So be it. It would be better so. There were no alternatives open to them under the law and it would be irresponsible of him to even contemplate anything other than a distance between them. Time and space would allow them to forget. To heal. Memories would fade. He would settle in New York, marry, produce an heir—and think of Eleanor merely as a pleasant if complicated interlude in his past, with no power to hurt or move him to unbearable need.

Not that time and space had worked any such miracle in the past two years! But it would. It must!

What could he possibly hope for in a future with Eleanor? The

law and the church forbade any relationship between them, other
than that of brother and sister. He set his teeth and concentrated
on his horses.

They approached the pretty village of Whitchurch once more
with its Norman church and cluster of tidy cottages. Past the
Great House, still shuttered, where Sir Edward Baxendale lived
with a sister and a baby—a sister who was not Octavia Baxendale. Or Octavia Broughton. And on to the Red Lion where Jem
Abbott welcomed them, remembered his lordship and his open-
handedness, stabled their horses and offered them tankards of ale.
Henry refused and they walked the village street to where the vicarage was tucked behind the church in its leafy glade. No funeral
occupied the churchyard this day to take up the Reverend Julius
Broughton's time. It could be presumed that he would be at
home to receive them.

The door to the vicarage was opened at their knock by the
same village girl who had been present on Henry's previous
visit. Young and comely, dark haired and dark eyed, with a flash
of vivacious spirit and interest as she cast a less than servant-like
glance over the two visitors. Her lips curled in welcome, her eyes
sparkled with a sly flirtatious intent. She was very young, as
Henry remembered, an unlikely choice for a housekeeper—but
the house was undoubtedly well kept. Perhaps the Reverend had
discovered a jewel. And yet, Henry admitted cynically, in the
light of their knowledge from Kingstone, and Jem Abbot's knowing comments, perhaps housewifely duties had not been uppermost in the priest's motives when employing her.

'Come in, my lord.' The girl stepped back. 'The master is in
the library.'

'Molly, is it not?'

'Yes, my lord. I remember you.' She gave him an appraising stare
again at odds with her apparent role in the household. 'And could
this be your brother? He has the look.' She dropped a pert curtsy
and then with a swing of her hips she preceded them down the corridor and into the front parlour. 'I will see if the master is available
to see you.' And left them, closing the door quietly behind her.

Nick raised his brows. 'I see what you mean.' He grinned.

'Not my first image of housekeeper in a vicarage. She is certainly nothing like Mrs Calke at Burford Hall.'

'Nothing at all! Don't let yourself be distracted, Nick!'

'No. I would not dare! But I wager that the Reverend Julius is, between writing sermons and burying the dead. She must be a great solace to him. Especially on a cold night.'

Henry snorted in appreciation and agreement, when Molly returned to usher them into the library with the sweetest and most innocent of smiles for the two gentlemen.

The room was as Henry recalled it. Bright with sunshine, polished with the faint aroma of beeswax and lavender lingering in the air, the books arranged with neat precision on their shelves. What had he thought when he had first entered it? The room of a scholar and academic? How wrong he had been. The gentleman in question sat behind his desk, light falling on his fair hair and finely chiselled features. Appearances were deceptive—they had been well deceived by the Reverend Broughton! Lord Henry controlled the surge of bitterness that threatened to choke him when he considered the results of this man's immoral meddling.

'My lord.' The priest rose from his chair, a faint but not unfriendly enquiry on his handsome face. 'How can I be of assistance?'

'Reverend.' Henry inclined his head in a cool acknowledgement. 'Can I present to you my brother, Lord Nicholas Faringdon? Nick, this is the Reverend Julius Broughton.'

They bowed, manners impeccable.

'I believed our business to be complete, my lord. I think I can give you no further information about the affairs of your late brother and Octavia Baxendale.' The priest's forehead creased in a slight frown, but the smile remained on his lips. He looked from one brother to the other for enlightenment, causing Henry to marvel at the man's ability to pursue the charade. How could anyone suspect a gentleman of such well-bred appearance and deportment—and a priest—of deceit and trickery?

'But I believe that you can.' Lord Henry's voice was cool and flat, revealing nothing.

'Very well. I will do what I can. Please sit. Perhaps I can offer you a glass of wine?' He stretched out his hand towards the bell-pull to summon Molly.

'No. This is by no mean a social call, sir.' But they took the offered chairs.

'So, my lords.' The Reverend Broughton lowered himself carefully to his own armed chair, his pale eyes moved between the two, but with no hint of discomfort or apprehension. No premonition of what was to come.

He is very sure of himself! Will he be willing to admit the truth, when we have no firm evidence? Only gossip and supposition that will prove nothing? Henry smothered the doubts, refusing to believe that they would fail in their mission. Too much hung on their success.

'It would appear that you have something of a reputation in town, sir.' Nicholas opened the conversation.

'I don't follow…' For the first time there were the faintest shadows of strain at the corners of the priest's mouth. His lips thinned marginally.

'I should tell you that after my brother's recent visit, I made it my business to ask questions in London.' Nicholas crossed one leg nonchalantly over the other. He might have been discussing the weather. 'Your name is well known, but perhaps not in the best of circles for the most altruistic of reasons.' He allowed his lips to curve in a faint but humourless smile. 'Some of my acquaintances were very ready to gossip about you, despite your position in the Establishment.'

'I fail to see… What do you imply, my lord?' Broughton picked up the pen from the desk, turning it in his fingers, as he kept his enquiry calm. 'My acquaintance in London is small. I cannot imagine that my infrequent visits make me an object of interest to anyone.'

'The word, sir, is that you are in debt. That you have a name for gambling, for hard drinking. And for unsavoury relations with certain women. Not what one would expect from a man of the church, I venture to suggest.'

'And you would give credence to such slanders? Accuse me without giving me a hearing?' The man to whom they had so casually tossed their accusations remained cold, austere, a man of principle, with just a touch of arrogance. He raised his chin to look down his aristocratic nose, his lips thinned with displeasure. 'There is no truth in it. And what possible bearing could this…this *gossip* have on your interest in the marriage at which I officiated?' The Reverend Broughton appeared to be genuinely stunned and outraged—until it was noted that his hands had clenched around the quill, to its detriment. 'It surprises me that you, my lord, would so willingly believe the gutter-sweepings of society gossip. Mere empty-headed nothings, without proof or conscience. And what business is it of yours? What right have you to interfere in my private affairs?' Broughton suddenly rose to his feet as if he could sit no longer, throwing down the pen as he did so, regardless of the spray of black ink that spread across the sheet of paper before him. There were high spots of colour on his cheekbones now. Of ill-concealed rage.

'I am not sure what bearing the gossip has yet,' Lord Henry chose to answer, his response as controlled as the priest's was not. 'But I think it will. You lied to me, sir.'

'Lied? I think not.'

'The marriage of Octavia to my brother.' He produced a copy of the document and laid it on the desk between them. 'It never happened, did it? This is a copy of your fraudulent document—bearing your signature—of an event that never happened.'

'You have no proof of that. On what grounds do you claim that the marriage never took place?' Cold anger burned in his eyes and he kept them fixed unwaveringly on the man who challenged his authority. 'You can have no proof!'

'No. I do not.' Henry admitted the fact with bland and unnerving assurance. 'But I do have proof that Sir Edward Baxendale is not Octavia's brother. That her true name is not Baxendale but Broughton, so that her name as written in the document is a fraud. And that therefore, I suppose by pure exercise of logic, *you* are Octavia's brother. If you are prepared to lie about that, then you would hardly balk at perjury over the matter of my brother's supposed marriage.'

Broughton had not expected this. His face paled, his breathing becoming shallow as he weighed the words spoken against him in such unemotional terms, but yet his voice calmed, his self-control remaining intact.

'A ridiculous notion.' He sat again and spread his hands. *They had no proof!* 'You can see the family resemblance between Octavia and Sir Edward. It is very clear.'

'No. I disagree. It is merely a matter of fair colouring. Indeed, it is the same as your own.'

'You have no proof.' Broughton fell back on denial.

'Oh, but I have.' Nick tried not to glance across at his brother at Henry's unexpected statement. It must be a bluff! He hoped it would work. 'Did I not tell you?' There was now an unmistakable undercurrent of menace in Henry's voice. His eyes were glacial and without mercy. 'Another lady travelled here with me today. An older lady. I have left her at the Red Lion, recovering from the journey. She claims acquaintance with you, Reverend Broughton.'

'Really?' His lips curled in a sneer of disbelief. 'And who might this ill-advised lady be?'

'My aunt. Lady Beatrice Faringdon. She remembers the Season when Octavia was presented into society very well since her own daughter made her curtsy to the polite world at the same time. She remembers my brother's flirtation with Octavia. And she remembers Octavia's brother who accompanied her to London. It was not Sir Edward. It was yourself, sir.'

'I deny it. How could she make such a false statement! It was four years ago!'

'Lady Beatrice has an excellent memory. She recalls that Octavia's name on that occasion was *Broughton*. If I escort her here, I am sure that she would instantly recognise you as Octavia's brother. She certainly had no recollection of Sir Edward Baxendale. Would you care to wager against it? As much as the 2,000 guineas which you owe Spalding? It would be a far safer bet for me than any wager which you might risk on the turn of the cards in *vingt-et-un*.'

Broughton said nothing, but sank back into his seat as if he needed the support, his hands clasping the edge of the desk in a vice-like grip. He contemplated the ruin of his life, spelled out in Lady Beatrice Faringdon's words of recognition.

'I suggest that this whole sorry affair is a sham, a cunning trick to take control of the Faringdon title and the inheritance.' Henry continued to hammer the nails into the priest's coffin. 'Thomas did not marry Octavia. You put your name to a false document.'

The statement was again met with silence. The Reverend Broughton took a deep and ragged breath as failure and social condemnation stared him in the face through the implacable eyes of Henry Faringdon.

'So, do we agree? This is not a genuine document. Or do I need to escort Lady Beatrice here to convince you?'

'No. There is no need.' The response was soft but quite clear. 'The document is not genuine.'

'Then the marriage never took place? You admit it?'

'The marriage never took place.' Broughton stared at his hands as if seeking an answer that would release him from the repercussions of his actions, but found none. His lips barely moved but he spoke the words. 'It never happened.'

'And are you willing to sign a declaration to that effect, sir?'

That brought the priest's head up, his eyes narrowed, a faint wash of panic.

'And if I do not?'

'If you do not, I would make it my business to spread the details of your dubious and scandalous affairs and your lack of integrity. I doubt that your position in the Church would remain secure in the light of such damning revelations.'

'Have I an alternative?'

'No.'

'Then I must.'

He pulled a clean sheet of paper towards him, picked up the pen, dipped it and began to write. For the next several minutes, the only sound in the room was the scratching of the quill on paper. When it was done, apart from the signature, Broughton looked up to find Faringdon's eyes on him. Questioning. Stark with contempt.

'Well?'

'Why did you do it?' Henry asked.

'Think about it.' Broughton laughed, a harsh sound in the sun-washed room. 'A fool could work it out—and you are no fool, Lord Henry. I am in debt to a sum far beyond my income. As your brother intimated, there is a shadow of scandal over my life. I am not proud of it, but neither will I grovel.' He shrugged his careless acceptance, without compunction. 'But it means that I am open to blackmail.'

'Sir Edward?'

'Of course. I am not the villain in this piece, much as you might wish to believe it. Sir Edward owns this living, which brings me a meagre income. Thus he holds me in the palm of his hand. To crush or to give freedom. If I agreed to support his claim to your family inheritance, he promised me security of tenure and money to pay off my debts and keep the style of life that I enjoy. If I did not…I would be destitute. He had the whip hand and I merely bowed to the stronger force. I would do the same again tomorrow given similar circumstances.'

'But now I hold the whip hand.' The curve of Henry's lips was not pleasant. 'So which is it to be? Sir Edward or myself?'

Broughton shrugged again. 'It seems to me that I am damned if I do, and damned if I don't. An interesting position for a priest to find himself in, I think! But I know that you will carry out your threat.' He read the determination in his lordship's face and gave a brief nod. 'I will sign to repudiate my actions.'

'Then do it.'

He did, with a final flamboyant sweep of the pen across the white surface, flinging the quill down at the end as if it burned his fingers.

'Thank you, sir.' Henry stood, bowed with heavy mockery and retrieved the copy of the marriage document and Broughton's written confession, folding them carefully and stowing them in his inner pocket. 'I doubt that we will need to meet again. I fervently hope that it will not be necessary. I will leave you to work out your own salvation with Sir Edward, and wish you well of each other.'

He walked to the door. Then hesitated and looked back.

'Why did you do it?' He frowned his incomprehension and his bitter disdain. 'How could you allow your sister to be used in this plot by Sir Edward? A young girl, easily manipulated by a stronger will. How could you allow it, even with the promise of money to pay your debts and a roof over your head? In effect, you sold your sister into Baxendale's hands to be used for his own purposes. It is despicable for a man to stoop so low.'

'I had little choice in it. How could you possibly understand?' Broughton was also standing, still the epitome of the cultured, educated cleric. He laughed bitterly. 'It is true that Octavia is my sister—but that is not all. She is also Sir Edward's wife!'

'His wife!'

'His wife. And has been for some little time.' The sneer on the priest's face was heavily marked. 'Which left me with no power whatsoever over his dealings with her.'

Henry looked at Nicholas, his gaze inscrutable, then back at the priest. 'So you told us the truth! You said that you officiated at a marriage at which Sir Edward was present. He was, of course. But not as witness.'

'Edward married her. Octavia's name truly is Baxendale. And, whatever your presumption, there was no force involved in her relationship with her husband. Octavia is a biddable girl and quite content with her lot. I do not believe that obeying her husband in this affair has been difficult for her.'

Henry weighed the words carefully. They had the ring of truth. It was easy for the priest to shift the blame.

'Then God forgive you, for I cannot.' He bit out the words. 'You have no remorse and deserve to be cast into the fires of hell. You do not know the pain you have caused to an innocent woman.' He turned his back and walked out of the Reverend Broughton's library.

Chapter Nine

'**H**is *wife?*'

Eleanor was incredulous, her voice rising, brows arched in amazement. Whatever she had expected from the visit to Whitchurch, it was not that.

'Octavia is Edward's wife,' Lord Henry confirmed. 'She was never married to Thomas. Your marriage is recognised in the eyes of the church and the law. You are, without any doubt, Marchioness of Burford.'

Eleanor and Henry faced each other across the morning room in Park Lane. The hour was nearing midnight, the ladies had already been retired for the night, the house quiet with only one branch of candles left by a conscientious Marcle to illuminate the hallway for the late arrivals. But on their return from Whitchurch, Henry knew that Eleanor would need to know the truth, no matter how late the hour. It would be cruelty indeed to withhold it. So, lingering only to strip off his greatcoat and gloves, whilst Nicholas returned the curricle and horses to their stabling at Faringdon House, Henry sought what promised to be an emotional audience with his brother's widow.

She now stood before him. It was clear that she had been awaiting their return, unable to rest, unable to sleep. He had not even needed to knock on her door. Now she waited, frozen into immobility, the heavy lace robe falling from throat to floor as she

steeled her mind to hear and accept her fate. Her hair curled in
a rich bronze mantle onto her breast, ends tipped with gold by
the subdued candlelight, drawing his eyes to her soft curves. He
could imagine that hair, as he had seen it, and saw in his dreams,
pooling on his pillow, the sensuous silk of it curling onto his chest
as she bent over him to lower her lips to his. He would have given
the world at that moment to have the right to take her to his bed,
to tell her the result of his journey as she lay in his arms, replete
from the demands of his body, but pushed the thought away. Instead he stood at a little distance, watching her carefully as she
took in the import of his words. Her eyes were huge, glazed with
shock at first, but now the flicker of hope gave them an inner
glow. She stood motionless, her mind focused somewhere far beyond him, weighing the repercussions.

'I thought you would wish to know tonight. You might rest
easier for the knowledge. You can sleep again, knowing that
your son cannot be disinherited.' He took a step back, away from
the candlelight, so that she could not read his expression.

'Yes. Oh, yes. Thank God!' Without thought beyond the deluge of relief and gratitude that threatened to overturn her delicate control, she covered the stretch of Aubusson carpet between
them and stretched out her hands to him. He simply had to take
them in his own clasp. How could he possibly reject her? Drawing her closer so that their joined hands rested against his chest,
even though his instinct warned him to keep his distance. But he
could not.

'How can I ever thank you?' She tightened her grip, oblivious
to their closeness, to his own struggle for mastery of his desires,
and smiled up into his face. 'And my child? Is Tom truly safe?'

Henry took a deep breath in an attempt to restore some semblance of order to his thundering heart, without any noticeable
effect. Surely she would feel the harsh rhythm that shook him to
the core? But he kept his voice calm and unemotional in the eye
of the whirlwind that prompted him to sweep her into his arms,
to kiss her until all the sadness and heartbreak was finally obliterated. 'The child's inheritance is secure since you were Thomas's
legitimate and only wife. The Reverend Broughton was per-

suaded to put his signature to his own confession, repudiating the documents presented to Hoskins by Sir Edward Baxendale.'

'Tell me why… How did it happen? How were you able to make Julius Broughton admit to such treachery?'

Henry drew her to the little couch, pushing her gently to sit and taking his own place beside her. He might resist taking her in his arms, but he would not willingly forgo his possession of her hands, which still clung to him as if he were indeed a lifeline in a storm. Her hands were trembling with the force of the relief, but she did not let go.

Henry explained, simply and lucidly, the content of the audience with Octavia's brother, the Reverend Julius Broughton, detailing all that he had revealed.

'So there we have it.' He smiled a little as relief and triumph chased each other across her lovely face.

'So. Sir Edward blackmailed him into forging the documents.' Eleanor frowned at the news, looking down at their joined hands. 'I did not like him. But I would never have thought him guilty of that. All the pain and turmoil he has caused. I know that he has admitted his fault—but I do not think I could ever forgive him. Or Sir Edward. Or those who turned their backs on me and wished me ill.' She glanced up, a bitter little smile twisting her lips, which touched his heart. 'You have no idea how vindictive I can feel when I think of the willingness of those *friends* to listen to poisonous unsubstantiated gossip. It shames me—but I cannot resist it.'

'It need not shame you, dear Eleanor.' He encircled her wrists with strong fingers, caressing the soft inner skin where the blood pulsed against his gentle clasp. 'A great wrong was committed against you. But it is over now. You must try to forget it and live out the rest of your life, secure in your social position, as if your status had never been questioned.'

'I think it will be difficult. I feel as if my good name and my position within the Faringdon family has been called into question and I have been left feeling—ashamed and unworthy.'

'I know it. But your family—those closest to you and those who knew my brother Thomas well—they never had any doubts.'

'No. *You* did not, I know.' She glanced up at him, a little shy, a little unsure.

'No. How could I?'

'Forgive me, Hal. I could weep.' She loosened one of her hands to brush a tear from her cheek. 'Even though the relief is great, I feel sad. Perhaps it is reaction. Perhaps I should be singing with joy!' Her laugh was a little tremulous.

'You need to sleep. You will feel better tomorrow. There is one thing, Eleanor.' His words were very gentle. 'It should not be a problem, but it would be as well if you were prepared.'

'What is that?'

'It may be that Octavia's son John is indeed the child of Thomas,' he warned, eyes sombre as he waited to see how she would react. 'We know that they were attracted and spent time together. But how far did their relationship progress? It could be that she carried Thomas's child before her marriage to Sir Edward, and it was that fact which gave Baxendale the idea to pursue the claim in the first place.'

'I see. I had not thought of that.'

'John could indeed be Thomas's illegitimate son.'

'Yes. Will it alter the inheritance?'

'No. The child will have no claim on the estate—indeed, there will be no actual proof of his sire apart from Octavia's own words. And how far should we trust her? I fear that she would follow Sir Edward's instructions to the letter without compunction. And Sir Edward could use the boy's existence to stir up scandal against the family if his darker scheme to disinherit you failed—as it now must.'

'Poor child. A pawn in everyone's game. Do you suppose anyone loves him for his own sake? He is very beautiful.' Eleanor remained silent for a long moment. 'If he is Thomas's son, I think the Faringdons should recognise him as such. And arrange an annuity perhaps.'

'You are very generous, Nell, and you humble me.' It took every inch of self-control not to lean forward and kiss away the furrow between her brows. 'Your spirit is as beautiful as your face. In spite of the agony they have put you through, you can still feel compassion.'

'He is only a baby after all.'

'Yes. Listen to me a moment. I think, if you are willing, we should try to speak with the nursemaid again. If we have some evidence to prove the relationship between Sir Edward and Octavia, she may be prepared to say more of what she knows about the child. She clearly cares for him and may be prepared to tell the truth. And perhaps if we met her away from the house, away from watchful eyes and the malign influence of Sir Edward. If I speak with Eaton, he will know if the girl takes the air at a particular time of day, and where. We should be able to waylay her without too much difficulty. Would you agree?'

'Of course. I truly believe that Sarah knows more than she is saying.'

'We may be able to persuade her, if she knows that it is for the good of the child.'

Henry raised her hands to his lips and kissed her cool fingers, first one hand and then the other. He could not resist. Even less when she smiled, her amethyst eyes glowing with an intensity of colour at the sudden restoration of hope. 'You are so very beautiful.' He turned her hands to press his lips to her palms, marvelling at their softness, the slender elegance of her fingers as they curled around his.

And Eleanor? The burning heat of his mouth against her skin made her breathing as ragged as his.

'Hal,' she murmured, closing her eyes against the feather-light brush of his lips, 'you are so very kind. To me. And even more to a child who may or may not be Thomas's son.'

'Perhaps.' She felt his lips curve against her wrist where he was pressing kisses against the pulse, which beat so hard that it took her breath away. 'But I do not think that I do it out of kindness. That is too mild an emotion.'

'Why do you care so much?' A whispered enquiry born out of the yearning in the depths of her heart.

'Because I...' he hesitated, aware of the words that he might have spoken but reluctant to break the spell of that intimate moment '…because I care about your happiness. And I suppose that I hold to a belief that every child has the right to know the identity of his father.'

She stilled, froze, the colour in her cheeks and the smile on her lips draining away. It was as if her blood had turned to ice. He watched the transformation with shock. And to be replaced by what? Fear? He could interpret the stark expression in her eyes in no other way.

Abruptly she pulled back, away from him, tugging her hands free.

What had he said? What had he done?

She rose to her feet, an edgy movement quite unlike her usual graceful elegance, backing away from him. 'I must go, my lord. It is late. You have all my thanks, of course.'

She almost ran from the room, leaving him totally at a loss.

Eleanor fled up the stairs, into her bedroom. She closed the door and leaned against it, her breathing uneven, not simply from her flight. She felt very cold, all the pleasure of the past hour destroyed by that one chance comment. She must think. Must decide. Dear Thomas—he had foreseen that some moment like this might arise in the unknowable future. And now it faced her.

What should she do? She could leave things as they were, the easiest option of course, Tom secure in his inheritance. Indeed, what had changed? Only her perception of the situation. And her knowledge of what was *right*.

Guilt pooled in her blood, her breath refusing to settle, cheeks ashen.

Every child has the right to know the identity of his father.

She pushed herself from the door to go to the dressing table. Sitting on the low stool, she pulled open the lowest drawer and lifted out a number of flat jewellery cases. The dreaded diamonds and other Faringdon family pieces. Below them was a small carved box, deeper than the others. As she opened it, it released the distinctive scent of sandalwood and she lifted out a silk-lined tray of smaller jewels. Worth a fortune, a king's ransom, but they did not interest her to any degree as she laid them aside without a passing glance.

Beneath them was a letter on thick cream vellum. Not very old, it was as clean and uncreased as the day it was written, the seals intact. Faringdon seals. The inscription, as she had known, was in Thomas's erratic scrawl. And the inscription was enigmatic.

Eleanor—

This is for Hal if you should ever consider that he needs to know.

She held it in her two hands, knowing exactly what it contained, torn apart by indecision.

What do I do, Thomas? Remain silent, safe in deceit, safe in the letter of the law? Or speak the truth and risk everything on the throw of this one dangerous dice? If the dice runs true, will the winning not be magnificent, worth every risk? But if it runs against me... What then?

She really did not know what Thomas would advise. Nor did she have any presentiment of Hal's reaction if she gave him the letter.

Somewhere in the depths of the house a clock struck the hour with quiet chimes. One o'clock. Eleanor sighed. Now was definitely not the time to be making so crucial a decision. With weary fingers she replaced the letter, then the jewels, back into the drawer

Whoever said that love brought happiness and contentment, she mused, as she took herself to bed, facing another restless night in spite of Hal's good news. It had brought her nothing but indecision and despair.

Now it threatened to tear her heart in two.

Discreet inquires of Eaton, butler at Faringdon House, elicited the information that it was customary for the young maid who cared for the child to take him for an airing in the park on fine mornings, before the fashionable crowd began to gather for their promenade. Armed with this knowledge, Henry and Eleanor took the barouche on the following morning to make contact with the girl. Whatever had disturbed Eleanor seemed to have released its hold on her, Henry noted, but she kept her distance from him, mentally if not in person. Approachable enough, but cool. And the shadows beneath her eyes were stark testimony to the fact that she still was not sleeping. Whatever relief his news had brought her, there was still something that troubled her. She would not confide in him, of course. So, waging a war against frustration, Henry decided to await the outcome of their morning's task and simply engaged her in trivial conversation and observations on their mutual acquaintance as they turned into the gates of Hyde Park.

They had not far to go before sighting the two figures whom they sought. Early as it was, it was very quiet with few interested parties to watch and comment on the scandalous developments within the Faringdon family.

'Stop the carriage,' Lord Henry requested his coachman.

They pulled to a halt near to where Sarah walked along the grass at the edge of the carriage drive, trim and composed as ever in a plain dark pelisse and an undecorated straw bonnet, holding the hand of the golden-haired child who attempted to pull her in the direction of the squirrels that hopped and chased around a distant stand of trees. She was laughing at his enthusiasm and inclined to follow his lead, but turned her head as the barouche drew up along side her and instinctively pulled the boy close to her side.

'Sarah.' Eleanor deliberately kept her voice low and undemanding as she leaned to smile down at the pair. 'A lovely morning for a walk. I think John would like to run rather than walk—at least he is still small enough that you can catch him.'

The young woman looked up, a fleeting shadow of concern crossing her features, but then as she recognised the Marchioness of Burford she smiled and nodded. 'Yes, my lady. He is always full of energy.'

Eleanor put aside her parasol and reticule and descended from the carriage without waiting for Henry to assist her. 'I would like to talk to you. It concerns the child.'

Sarah immediately stepped away, casting an anxious glance at Lord Henry who also joined them on the carriageway, and swept the protesting child up into her arms as if she sensed danger. Even, perhaps, an abduction.

'Don't be nervous.' Eleanor reached out to touch the young

woman's arm in reassurance. 'I intend no harm to either you or the child. This is a public place and you are in no danger from me. I wish you nothing but well. This is Lord Henry, brother to my late husband. You must remember him from your visit to Burford Hall.' Henry bowed, deliberately remaining beside the carriage. To approach might be seen in the light of intimidation. 'Perhaps you would consent to ride with us a little way. And then we will return you back to Faringdon House. I am sure John would enjoy to ride in the barouche. My own son likes nothing better.'

'It is very kind of your ladyship, but…' Sarah's anxieties were clear.

'Please, Sarah. It is most urgent.'

'Very well.' How could she refuse a request from the Marchioness herself? Reluctantly the young woman allowed herself to be handed up into the barouche with John ensconced on her lap, looking round with wide-eyed interest.

'We need to know, Sarah.' Eleanor took her seat and turned to face her as the barouche moved off at a sedate pace. 'You must know that it will not be to the disadvantage of yourself or the child. Will you help us?'

'If I can.' She was nervous. Her eyes moved from one to the other as she waited. 'But I do not understand what you could want from me. I am only the nursemaid, employed to care for the boy. How can I possibly help you?'

Henry's voice was gentle and full of understanding as he broached the issue. 'Let us be open and honest from the beginning, ma'am. You should know that I have spoken recently with Julius Broughton.'

There was now a distinct flash of panic in her eyes. Eleanor knew that if the barouche had stopped, Sarah and the child would have fled. But it was not possible so she simply sat, her hands white-knuckled as they clasped around the small body on her knee.

'I know that he and Octavia are brother and sister,' Henry continued.

'Oh.' It was little more than a sigh.

'I also know that there was never a marriage between my

brother and the lady. That, in fact, Octavia is the wife of Sir Edward Baxendale. The Reverend Broughton has admitted as much.'

Eleanor leaned forward to touch the girl's unresponsive hand where it clasped around the child. She was startlingly pale, but made no reply. There was no need. The truth was obvious in her face, in her teeth buried in her bottom lip.

'We need to know about the child, Sarah,' Henry continued. 'Is he Sir Edward's son?'

Sarah was silent for a long moment, studying the boy's upturned face as he laughed, enthralled by the speed with which they were travelling. Then she looked at his lordship, at his stern face but kind eyes. 'No.' She shook her head, compelled to reply. His eyes and voice might be compassionate, but she knew that he was determined to learn the truth. She made the decision to tell it. 'No. He is not Edward's son.'

'Then…is he…is John the son of Thomas, my husband?' Eleanor dared to ask the next question. 'Did Octavia bear Thomas a son out of wedlock?'

Sarah transferred her gaze to Eleanor's taut features, only able to guess at the emotion that surged within her at such a question, but could find no words to reply. She snatched away her hand from the comforting grasp, to hold the child close as she hid her face against the curve of his neck.

Watching them together, the light dawned for Eleanor. How could she not have made the connection? She had seen it before, and commented on it, without understanding its significance. It was as clear as faceted crystal in the morning sunshine.

'Of course,' Eleanor said softly. 'He is yours, isn't he? *You* are Edward's sister with the baby, who lived with him at the Great House.'

'I must not say.' Sarah's voice was muffled against her son's head.

'I should have guessed days ago,' Eleanor persisted. 'You are so loving, and caring of his needs. When Octavia was so uninterested—'

'Octavia cares nothing for him!' Eleanor's words brought an instant reaction. Sarah raised her head, lips thinned in anger, her words bitter. 'He is mine! Never hers! I should never have gone along with it. It was a terrible thing to do. I am so sorry…' Tears began to stream down her cheeks, as much in anger as in grief.

Eleanor produced a handkerchief and tried to calm the girl's anguish. Henry instructed the coachman to turn into one of the quieter drives where no one would be witness to her distress.

'Will you tell us, Miss Baxendale?' Lord Henry asked, giving her the respect of her true name.

'I dare not. Edward…'

'I will do everything in my power to protect you from Baxendale,' Henry tried to reassure her as the pieces of the puzzle began to fit together in his mind. Sarah's participation in Baxendale's intrigue, willing or otherwise, would prove to be the final key to the mystery.

'But I have nothing.' Her words were clipped and despairing. 'I need his protection. He warned me that—'

'We know so much already.' Eleanor tried to hide the urgency of her need. 'You must tell us the truth. It was a despicable thing for your brother to have done. I can see that you have been given cause for great suffering. If you will trust us, we can rescue you and make it right again.'

'Why not?' Sarah sighed, closed her eyes for a moment. 'What do I owe Edward now? I am so tired of all this deceit. It is true that I am Edward's sister and that John is my son.'

'Could you tell us how it was that you allowed your brother to make use of him?' Eleanor asked in her gentle manner so as not to distress the lady further. 'It must have been very difficult for you. Why did you agree to play the role of nursemaid?'

Sarah Baxendale looked at Eleanor for a long moment. Then nodded and began to explain the events which led to the deception.

'I was married to a naval officer, Captain John Russell,' Sarah explained. 'He was killed in action in the last months of the war against Napoleon. My son was born two months after his death— his father never knew him. The pension is very small and I had no resources of my own so Edward gave me a home and an allowance to bring up my child. I was companion to Octavia. He was very kind to me, you see.'

She bit her lip as the memories flooded back.

'And then he told me of his plan: for Octavia to pretend that she had been wedded to the Marquis of Burford, who had just died. And to claim that John was her child. Her brother Julius would provide the legal evidence, lured by the promise of a well-lined pocket. Even if he is Octavia's brother, he disgusts me…' Sarah frowned as she considered the sins of the Reverend Broughton. 'I refused, of course. How could I give my child into Octavia's careless hands? But Edward said that if I cared so much, I could take the role of nursemaid so that I could be with him. He threatened to…to turn me out if I did not comply. I would be homeless and without financial provision. I have no other relatives, you see. I did not know what to do. He knew that I had no choice and had no compunction in threatening me. But he told me it would not be for ever—perhaps only a few months at the most. So I gave in—for such a short time whilst we were in London. I know it is no excuse, but that is why I allowed myself to become involved in something that has filled me with guilt and a self-disgust beyond all bearing. I have shamed my own name and that of my dear husband.'

She dashed the tears from her cheeks with an impatient hand, determined to regain some of the dignity that had been stripped from her by her wilful brother.

'I don't think I realised that it would cause so much hurt. I did when we came to Burford Hall, of course. When I saw the effect of Edward's claims on you, my lady. But I closed my heart to it because I seemed to have no choice in the matter.'

She began to weep again.

'Mrs Russell,' Henry addressed her with due formality. 'Would you consent to tell this sorry tale to my lawyer, Hoskins? That is all that would be required of you.'

'I dare not face Edward,' she whispered in broken tones. 'He will punish me if he learns that I have spoken with you.'

'There is no need to face him, unless you wish it.' He looked to Eleanor for confirmation, an eyebrow lifted. She nodded, reading his thoughts. 'Nor will he harm you. I would suggest that you owe your brother nothing. He had no consideration for your feelings when he forced you to agree to so diabolical a plot against all your maternal instincts. We will acknowledge our great debt to you. You are free to live at Burford Hall with your son. Not as an employee, but as a guest. And the estate will provide you with an income. Until you decide what you wish to do and where you would wish to live. But you will never suffer for what you have done for us today.'

'No. I cannot…'

'Will you at least consider it? For the sake of John, if not for yourself?'

Sarah sat silently, looking at her son. She ran her fingers over his fair hair, so like her own, her lips curling into a reluctant smile when he looked up into her face and laughed with childish delight, lifting a hand to pat her cheek as if he would have given comfort. She would do anything for the safety and happiness of her child.

'Very well. I think that once again I have no choice.' She looked up, her eyes now clear and determined, and addressed Lord Henry. 'I fear that sounds churlish, which was not my intention. I know that I do not deserve your gratitude or your help, rather your condemnation. I have done you and your family a terrible wrong, helping to destroy the good name and integrity of your brother and his true wife.' She inclined her head towards Eleanor. 'But for the sake of my son, I will accept your offer, and thank you from the bottom of my heart. I will speak to Mr Hoskins.'

Henry took possession of one of Sarah's hands and lifted it in formal recognition of her intent to his lips. 'You must not blame yourself, ma'am. The wrong was Baxendale's—and you have now remedied it. My family's inheritance is no longer in doubt. The guilt is not yours.'

'And you have taken a terrible weight from my mind.' Eleanor touched the lady's hand in ready compassion. 'Your courage has ensured that the future of my son, as well as your own, is safe.'

If Mr Hoskins was surprised to see his noble Faringdon clients at an hour when they might normally be partaking of a light luncheon, he did not show it, but ushered them into his office.

He was unable to disguise his amazement, however, when he was introduced to the young woman who accompanied them. Why should the Baxendale nursemaid and the child at the centre of the controversy be on such terms with the Marchioness of Burford? She apparently was under no duress, but entered his rooms with quiet composure, holding the child tightly against her. He sensed a tension within the little group. But he did not express his speculative interest—instead he found seats for the ladies and fussed over a glass of ratafia for them and a brandy for his lordship. The child seemed content, in the short term, to sit on his nurse's knee and investigate the contents of the Marchioness's reticule.

Hoskins cast a sharp eye over the tall figure of Lord Henry as he took up a position beside the hearth with its smouldering fire. His reacquaintance with his lordship since his return from New York had given the lawyer considerable cause to re-evaluate the man who dominated the small room. If he had chosen to pay a visit at this time of the day, then there must be some pressing need. He remembered a young lad with vivid features, athletic build, and more energy and charm than was good for him. Always into mischief, but with the ability to extricate himself without too much difficulty. Always ready to challenge authority, to kick over the traces, but with a smile to win over those who might condemn him too harshly.

America had been good for him, Hoskins decided. Somewhere to channel his energies, without the rigid restrictions of birth and privilege to hamper his plans and dreams. Not for everyone, of course, but Lord Henry had done well. Confidence. Authority. Determination. They sat lightly on him, but made an immediate impression. He was still elegantly sophisticated in style and dress, still dramatically handsome, still capable of the effortless charm of his youth, but there was now an edge to him. Not a man to tangle with, as Hoskins had thought on their previous meeting in these very rooms, not a man to cross. From the look on his face at this moment, Hoskins would not have cared to be in Sir Edward's shoes. And as for the business with Faringdon and Bridges in New York, which his lordship had put temporarily into his hands during his stay in London—he would lay a wager that Mr Henry Faringdon of Faringdon and Bridges would do very well and make a fortune to rival that of his noble family in England.

'Well, my lord.' Hoskins finally took his own seat behind his desk. 'To what do I owe the pleasure of this visit?' He allowed his gaze to take in the ladies, but then returned his attention to Lord Henry. There was an air of anticipation here that he did not understand. He had no good news for them. There was no doubt in his mind now that Sir Edward Baxendale's claim was genuine. He frowned, contemplating the wound that he must inevitably inflict on the Marchioness, and wished that it was on an occasion of his own making. But she was here and he supposed that a final statement from him was necessary. It would not lessen the pain by drawing out the situation. 'I expect that you have come about the inheritance. A most unfortunate business, of course, as I have previously expressed. We have, I believe, to accept the truth of the Baxendale claim.'

'No.' Lord Henry spoke with quiet certainty, and moved to sit beside the Marchioness. 'No, we do not. The truth is this. We have undeniable proof, sir, that Baxendale's proposal that his sister was married to my brother and therefore that her child is heir to the title is nothing but a fraudulent sham.'

'Proof, you say?' Hoskins's frown deepened. 'I have to tell you, my lord, that in my opinion as your lawyer, the legal documents produced by Sir Edward are without question genuine.'

'No, they are not. They are fraudulent. I think that we should begin, sir, by allowing Mrs Russell to explain her presence here today.'

So Sarah Russell, née Baxendale, laid out before the astonished lawyer the nature of Sir Edward's scheme and her own part in it. Reluctant at first, with much hesitation, she grew in confidence as the enormity of her brother's behaviour towards her struck her anew. As she spoke, the persona of family employee and nursemaid dropped away, to be replaced by the quiet dignity and pride of both a lady of gentle birth and the widow of a naval officer.

Hoskins listened in silence until she had finished.

'I have kept silent when I should have spoken out,' she stated finally, impressing Hoskins with her admirable composure. The time for tears was past and she would follow her conscience. 'John is my child, the son of my late husband, Captain John Russell. Octavia is Edward's wife, not his sister, and she is childless. That is the truth of it, sir.'

'Well.' Hoskins leaned back in his chair, looking from one to the other. 'Well! I am speechless!'

He was rendered even more so when Lord Henry produced and laid before him on the desk the written statement from the Reverend Broughton, which explained further the source of the forged documents.

'So these documents…' his lordship finally indicated the ostensible proof of marriage and birth that had caused all the heartache in the first place '…are worthless.'

'Indeed. You have been busy, my lord. And very clever in your investigation.' There was more than a hint of admiration in Hoskins's shrewd eyes as he gathered up the documents.

'Not as clever as we should have been, I fear.' His lordship gave a rueful smile. 'We asked the wrong question. Or did not ask enough of them about Baxendale's family.'

'How so, my lord?'

'When we visited Whitchurch, the people who knew Sir Edward spoke of his sister and a baby, a sister who had lost her husband.' Eleanor took up the story. 'We did not ask if he had a wife as well. Since she was never mentioned, we presumed that he was unmarried and so came to the wrong conclusion. We thought the sister was Octavia.'

'I see. We have to thank Mrs Russell for her honesty in this matter. We are much in your debt, ma'am.' Hoskins inclined his head gravely towards the young woman.

'There would have been no need for the debt if I had been honest from the beginning,' she replied with shattering honesty, unwilling to accept a lessening of her burden of guilt. 'I simply hope that I have been able to make restitution, although the pain and grief will always leave its shadow.'

'Nevertheless, ma'am, without your courage, we would be unable to thwart Sir Edward's plans quite so effectively.' Lord Henry, who had risen to his feet, bowed in recognition of her admission. He smiled at her, a smile of great charm, hoping to allay her guilt. 'Do not be so ready to take the blame that your brother should bear.'

She looked up at him, cheeks now a little flushed, in gratitude for his understanding. 'Thank you, my lord. I hope and pray that you will indeed thwart my brother. I owe it to the memory and integrity of my husband's name. I have not done well by him, allowing his son to be used in so vile a scheme.'

'We shall unmask Sir Edward.' Hoskins stated with calm assurance, then glanced at Lord Henry from under his brows. 'So what is your plan of action now, my lord?'

'We need to see Baxendale. I suggest that you set up a meeting here. He will presume that it is to ratify his sister's position and the child's inheritance, and so will come without apprehension or fear of discovery. Then we will lay the evidence before him. I wish to be present. And her ladyship, of course. Mrs Russell if she wishes it.'

'Good.' Hoskins rubbed his hands together at the prospect of the completion of the unseemly business. 'Tomorrow?'

'Yes. Let us finish it as soon as possible.'

'It will be my pleasure, my lord.'

So tomorrow it would all be over.

Mrs Russell returned to Faringdon House with her son, to take refuge in the nursery, thus avoiding her brother and his wife, and to decide whether she would wish to be at that meeting. She did not know.

Eleanor acknowledged the relief that she could finally allow to sweep through her veins, as cold and clean and sparkling as a glass of the finest French champagne. She could hold her head up in public again, although she chided herself for allowing so foolish a situation to matter so much. The rest was far more important. Thomas's good name would be restored, no longer the subject of barbed gossip and sly innuendo in the clubs and fashionable withdrawing-rooms of the town. And her son... Tom would come into his inheritance in the fullness of time, as was his right.

Her cup should be full, her happiness complete. So why was there a shadow overlying her sense of achievement? Why was there a constriction, a tightness around her heart? She asked herself the question, her eyes unseeing of her surroundings as they drove home in the barouche, but she knew the answer. It was engraved on her very soul. Hal would leave. *Let us finish it as soon as possible,* he had said. She would lose him and her heart was sore. And, whatever excuses she could make to herself to explain away her behaviour, she was forced to acknowledge that she had not been honest with him

Henry watched the Marchioness in silence as she studied her gloved fingers so intently, wrapped in her own thoughts. It was almost done. He had fulfilled his duty as his brother's trustee and his success was on the verge of completion. The moment should have been sweet indeed. His family was secure and matters could easily be left in Nicholas's more than competent hands. That was it. His life in New York called to his blood and his imagination— and there was nothing to keep him here. No matter how much he longed to hold Eleanor and celebrate their triumph. The need to touch her as she sat with her face turned from him made his fingers burn. He accepted with the innate honesty so typical of him that the fact that she had rejected him for marriage with his brother no longer mattered, had not mattered for some time. Somewhere over the past days, his anger had drained away. He had loved her then. He loved her now. He would love her to the end of his days.

Chapter Ten

As agreed, they waited in Hoskins's office at eleven o'clock the next morning. Lord Henry, Hoskins and Eleanor. They did not know if Sarah Russell would attend. Perhaps not. It would be an unpleasant interview at best, possibly vicious in its outcome, and they had to accept that she might not feel strong enough to face down her brother, knowing that she was instrumental in his failure to achieve his nefarious goal.

Eleanor was nervous. But you cannot lose, she told herself. This is merely the final act in the tragedy, to expose the evidence before Sir Edward and thus accomplish his defeat. What possible evidence can he produce to refute the claims of his sister Sarah and Julius Broughton? She worked hard to keep an outward calm as she sat before the fire, resisting the temptation to fuss with her gloves, the strings of her reticule or the carved handle of her parasol. It could be seen, however, that she occasionally found the need to smooth her palms down the skirt of her deep blue muslin gown, and her cheeks and throat, above the delicately ruffed collar of her silk spencer, were more than usually, if becomingly, flushed.

Lord Henry stood beside her, immaculate and elegant in pale pantaloons, polished Hessians and dark superfine. Eleanor glanced towards him, intimately aware of his supportive presence, and privately considered him more devastatingly attractive than any man had the right to be. But that was not the first impression sensed by any casual onlooker. His face was cold, impassive, his eyes holding the glacial chill of mid-winter, his mouth grimly set. But when the door of the outer office was heard to open, and footsteps entered from the street, he leaned down to touch Eleanor's shoulder, fleetingly but with warm comfort. She looked up, unable to disguise her nerves as the muted sound of voices could be heard. His expression softened, his smile for her alone.

'We shall win, Nell. Never doubt it.' His gentle tones, his supreme confidence, warmed her cold blood like the finest brandy.

Sir Edward arrived to the minute of the hour, bowed into the room by one of Hoskins's clerks. As he walked in, it was clear from his demeanour that he had come intending to enjoy the final success of his risky enterprise. Immaculately dressed, well groomed, his blue eyes clear and smiling, he oozed confidence in the expectation of enjoying the Faringdon fortune through the enhanced status of his supposed sister. He bowed to Lord Henry and the lawyer with polished grace, his smile expressing magnanimous appreciation that he would win and they would lose and that he could afford to be gracious in victory. Then he turned to Eleanor, who had remained seated, took her hand to bow over it and kiss her fingers. Compassion was clear in every gesture, in the sorrowful expression in his intense gaze. Eleanor found the greatest difficulty in not snatching her hand away from his light grasp. Instead she gritted her teeth and kept her mouth curved in a semblance of a smile and hooded her eyes with downswept lashes. Henry did not even try for a pleasant expression, but regarded Sir Edward with a stony expression worthy of the Medusa. Although he gave the impression of arrogant assurance, he kept his hands clenched at his sides, eyes cold and flat, momentarily sorry that duelling was out of fashion. Or even if pistols at dawn were not an option, he would have liked to spread Sir Edward Baxendale out on the floor with a fist to the jaw.

Sir Edward, unaware of the latent hostility in the room, took a seat. Lord Henry did not.

'A delicate situation, my lord, my lady.' He sat with one leg crossed elegantly over the other, supremely at his ease. 'But I am sure that we are all in agreement that it is time we settled the matter of the Faringdon inheritance. I presume that such is the reason for this meeting?' He arched a brow towards the lawyer. 'Then we can get on with our lives and allow the grief of the past weeks to settle.' So accommodating. So reasonable. Eleanor felt a sudden urge to scream her objections to her husband's name being so vilified.

'Do you plan to remain in London, sir?' Hoskins enquired with casual interest, as if nothing were amiss.

'My sister proposes to remain for a week or two at Faringdon House. Then it is her intention to repair to Burford Hall.' He turned his sympathetic gaze on Eleanor. 'Have you finally decided on your own destination, ma'am?'

'Not finally, Sir Edward.'

'And I presume that you, my lord, will return to America. So much opportunity there for a man of enterprise such as yourself. And Lord Nicholas?' His brows rose again in polite but pointed enquiry. 'I think that Octavia will not wish him to stay on at Burford Hall. Or at least not in a permanent nature. Perhaps to visit eventually… She considers that it would be somewhat…ah, uncomfortable in the circumstances. Until her position in the family has become more generally accepted, you understand. We shall make our own arrangements for the administering of the estate.'

And so all was to be very neatly arranged to Sir Edward's liking!

'And I will discuss with Hoskins the matter of the annuity for yourself and your son,' he continued with another sparkling smile in Eleanor's direction.

'How thoughtful, Sir Edward. I am sure that I should be grateful for your consideration in the circumstances.'

Hoskins cleared his throat in a little cough to draw attention back to himself. It was time, he decided, to end this cat-and-mouse scene as he bent a fierce stare on Sir Edward. 'Before we consider all these arrangements, sir, there is one small matter remaining for us to discuss.' Hoskins glanced up at Lord Henry who had remained silent, allowing the lawyer to take the initiative. His lordship could not guarantee the politeness of his words in the face of Sir Edward's overweening triumph.

Sir Edward caught the glance between them and his eyes narrowed in quick suspicion. 'Is there some problem here that I should be aware of? I cannot imagine what could now hinder the settlement.'

'There is indeed a problem, sir.' Hoskins lifted three documents from a pile in front of him and spread them on the desk. 'There is indeed.'

'Then perhaps you would explain—'

They were interrupted by a light knock on the door. One of the clerks from the outer office opened it to usher a lady into the room. 'The lady is here, sir. You said to show her in if she came.' He closed the door behind Mrs Sarah Russell.

Sir Edward turned his head in some surprise at the interruption, and then froze, the smile leaving his face. 'What is this?'

'The lady has some part in this discussion, it would seem, sir.' Hoskins rose to draw the lady into the room. 'She was kind enough to bring it to my attention yesterday.'

'I do not discuss my family's business before my servants.' Sir Edward's eyes were suddenly as icy as his insolent words, but there was a wariness in the clenching of his hands on the arms of his chair as he thrust himself to his feet.

'Then there is no problem, is there, Edward.' Sarah came to stand quietly beside her brother, to meet his supercilious stare with her own of sorrowful but calm acceptance. 'Since I am *not* your servant, the discussion can continue.'

'What is this?' he repeated, a tinge of colour now creeping into his face. 'You are my sister's companion and nursemaid for the boy. Why are you here?'

'You cannot continue with this masquerade, Edward. I have told Mr Hoskins the truth and my own shameful part in it.'

'No. It is not true.' He looked round, now uneasy, to assess the reaction of the other players in the game.

'Will you deny your relationship to me, Edward?' Sarah persisted, quietly but not to be intimidated. 'Do you deny that you are my brother and that I am no servant of yours?'

'No…no, of course not.' He looked across at Lord Henry and then at Hoskins, searching for a way out of the abyss that had suddenly opened up, dark and deadly and totally unexpected, before his feet. 'Yes, Sarah is my sister, fallen on hard times as a penniless widow. I have given her a home, as companion to my sister Octavia and nurse to the child.'

'And the child?' Sarah had no intention of allowing him to escape from the web of deceit that he had so carefully woven to catch the bright prize of the Faringdon inheritance. The web that had entrapped so many innocent people. 'Do you dare to deny that John is my son, not Octavia's?'

'You must understand.' Sir Edward grasped his sister's arm, fingers white, as if to silence her, and appealed to Hoskins. 'Sarah was overcome by grief at her husband's death. It overset her mind and she has never recovered. She came to believe that Octavia's son is her own, because she was never blessed with her own child. She needs sympathy…time to recover. The doctors tell me that there is no medical cure, only time and rest will ease her mind.' He tightened his grip so that Sarah was seen to wince. 'You should go home, Sarah. Octavia will care for you there. Let me arrange—'

'Let me go, Edward.' Sarah pulled ineffectually against the restraint, but Edward shook his head.

'Come now, Sarah. I will arrange for a cab to take you back to Faringdon House.' He would have pulled her towards the door.

'I suggest that you release the lady.' It was the first time that Lord Henry had spoken since Sir Edward entered the room. When Sir Edward hesitated, his lordship stepped forward with clear intent in his grim expression. Sir Edward allowed his hand to fall from his sister's arm.

'You do not appreciate, my lord—'

'We cannot accept this explanation, Sir Edward.' Eleanor's clear voice broke the tension between the two men as she stood to move between them. 'If Mrs Russell is indeed your sister, why should you imply that she is merely a nursemaid for the child, and treat her as such? When you first visited us at Burford Hall, you certainly gave the impression that she was a paid retainer, not a close member of the family. Besides, I have seen her with the boy. To me there is no doubt that he is her son. It could not escape my notice that Octavia appeared to have little interest in him.'

'You must not misread the situation, my lady—' Sir Edward tried to regain his composure, but his skin was waxy and sweat had begun to gleam on his brow.

'Enough!' Lord Henry intervened. 'The game is at an end, Baxendale.' He leaned forward, picked up two of the documents from the desk and tore them deliberately in half. 'These, sir, are your witnessed papers, proof of Octavia's marriage and John's birth.' Then he cast the pieces into the fire where they disintegrated in a shower of ash. 'This is what they deserve.'

'What have you done? They are legal documents.' Sir Edward looked on aghast, still unwilling to accept that all was indeed at an end.

'No, Baxendale.' His lordship held him, eyes resolute and pitiless. 'They are worth nothing. I know their true value because the Reverend Broughton admitted as much. In writing, so there would be no doubt, when he acknowledged that Octavia was his sister.' He lifted and held out the third document for Edward to read. 'I am certain that you will recognise the hand as that of your *wife's* brother. No more lies, Baxendale. I think we know the truth.'

Sir Edward's face was ashen as he stared at the incriminating admission in Broughton's recognisable hand. His lips twisted into a snarl as he witnessed the destruction of his plans and he turned on his sister. 'This is all your doing. How could you betray me? How could you show such ingratitude after I saved you from penury after your unfortunate marriage? I warned you of the consequences—'

'The lady no longer needs your support.' Lord Henry stepped forward to take Broughton's confession from Sir Edward's clenched hand. 'I believe that she would no longer choose to live under your roof. I shall make it possible for her to live with a degree of independence. Her duty to you is at an end as, I suggest, is yours to her.'

'Ha! You have come out of this very well, my dear sister. I should congratulate you.' Whipping round with a snarl, he lifted his hand and would have struck her if Henry had not intervened. With lightning reflexes he seized Baxendale's wrist and bore down, forcing him away from his sister, who had stood her ground, stricken at the unexpected attack.

'Don't give me an excuse to strike you down.' His lordship's words were low but none the less deadly. 'There is nothing I would like better, for the anguish that you have inflicted on my family as well as on your own sister.'

'Take your hand off me!' Sir Edward wrenched himself away, but made no further attempt to approach Sarah.

Shocked beyond words by the threat of violence, Sarah covered her face with trembling hands and began to sob. With a soft murmur of compassion, Eleanor moved to put comforting arms around her and to lead her to the door.

'I will take Mrs Russell to Faringdon House to collect John and then on to Park Lane. It would be better, I think. Will you…will you follow soon?' She looked anxiously from Henry to Sir Edward, caught up in the bitter mood between the two men, uncertain of the outcome.

Lord Henry nodded his agreement and smiled thinly. 'Soon. There is no need for your concern, my lady.' He strode to open the door for them, bowing with all courtesy as if he had not threatened physical violence a moment ago. 'All will be well.' So they left, accompanied by Hoskins, who would arrange a carriage for them, leaving Lord Henry and Sir Edward alone.

They faced each other across the room with its weight of law books and legal documents, the air still and heavy between them. As heavy as the unfinished business.

'Tell me one thing before we finish this.' Henry took up a stance behind Hoskins's desk. 'Why? Why Thomas? I presume your motive was money. But why choose to discredit him?'

'Of course it was money.' Baxendale had no hesitation in confession, a certain pride shining in his eyes as he expressed his illogical hatred for the family whose fortune he would have acquired without compunction. 'And Thomas Faringdon provided the perfect candidate. His unexpected death was most opportune. I knew about his liaison with Octavia when she was presented to Society. How he sought her out, and flattered her. He obviously thought her birth good enough for a light flirtation! He would have married her, Octavia believed, but he was warned off by interfering members of your arrogant family. So he rejected her because she was not good enough for him, her family not sufficiently well bred for a Marquis! He should have been whipped for his casual treatment of her! But, of course, that is not the way of the world.'

'But…' Lord Henry's brows drew together into a forbidding line. 'You would base this whole campaign, to discredit a reputation and destroy the security of my brother's wife and child, on something so tenuous as a flirtation that occurred four years ago? I find it difficult to believe any man of honour capable of such vindictive manipulation of a series of events that never even happened—that had not the slightest foundation of truth.'

'Why not? Your brother's death provided the perfect occasion for revenge. Octavia should have been Marchioness of Burford. Doubtless would have been if Lady Beatrice Faringdon had not stirred the mud in the bottom of the pool. So I would see to it that she achieved the recognition that was her due.'

'And benefit from her newly acquired status by association.'

'Of course.'

'And, had you been successful, Octavia would have had the whole Faringdon fortune fall sweetly into her lap.'

Sir Edward made no reply, eyes focused on some distant unpleasant vista, the muscles in his jaw tightening as he saw the destruction of all his hopes and intricate planning.

'With the financial reins in *your* capable hands, of course.' Lord Henry pursued the matter with the inexorable intensity of a knife edge.

'Yes!' It was a hiss of despair, of abject failure. 'Octavia should have had what she deserved.'

'So it was money. As simple as that. A desire to line your pockets with gold.'

'Oh, no.' The shrug, the sneer were unmistakable. Baxendale's eyes snapped back to his tormentor, filled with a cold hatred. 'There was nothing simple about it. Don't patronise me, my lord, with facile explanations. What do you know of genteel poverty, which grinds you under its unforgiving heel? When every coin has to be counted, but your status demands that you keep up a gracious lifestyle. Cushioned in wealth as you have been all your life, even though a younger son—what do you know of a father who drank and gambled away the family inheritance before dying in debt over a losing hand of cards and a glass of brandy in a gaming hell? A weak mother who frittered away what was left in meaningless luxuries. You have not the slightest idea!' His lips curled back from his teeth in a vicious parody of a smile. 'The house at Whitchurch will fall around our ears without an input of hard cash. The only way in which we could fund our stay in London now was through a small bequest from a distant cousin. And that is now spent to no purpose. There might be money in my mother's family, but there is no hope—' Becoming aware of the rising tone in his own voice, the uncontrolled outpouring of despair, Sir Edward snapped his teeth together to cut off the flow of bitter words.

'So you would cast the blame for your sins elsewhere. I should have expected it.'

'No. I will shoulder the blame, my lord. But necessity can drive a man to extremes.'

Henry turned his face from the harsh lines of naked greed and desperate failure. There could be no room for sympathy here. Edward Baxendale's glory would have cost Eleanor far too high a price.

'But the risk you were prepared to take was nothing short of fantastic. Did you think that no one would remember Octavia and her brother? Were you so sure that you could conduct yourselves so as to blind everyone to the truth?'

'Why not?' A gleam of sly cunning lit his face for a moment, displacing the bitter failure. 'After all, we nearly did it! If it were not for your interfering aunt, we would have carried the whole matter off in good style. People have short memories and mostly accept what they are told and what they see. No one other than your aunt thought to question my role as Octavia's brother. Scandal is the breath of life to many who would call themselves your friends. Like the vultures they are, they were more than willing to pick over the bones of the Faringdon family with gleeful enjoyment. If our luck had held, Octavia would have claimed the Faringdon inheritance and would be made welcome into society.'

And, although it sat awkwardly with him, Lord Henry had to admit to the truth of it. 'But after your confession, I can hardly believe that you were so idealistic as to do it all for your wife, can I?' He made no effort to hide the repugnance in his voice.

'Believe what you like. It no longer matters, does it? I think this conversation is at an end.' Sir Edward lifted his shoulders in an elegant shrug. 'It was worth the risk. And what do you intend to do? Drag the case through the courts? I doubt it! Think of the entertainment it would provide for the *ton!*'

'You disgust me. Get out of these rooms. And it would please me if you would remove yourself and your wife from Faringdon House at the earliest opportunity. No, I shall not take the matter further. You are not worthy of my consideration!' His lordship strode to open the door.

'Don't dare preach morality to me, my lord.' Baxendale did not move. The sneer on his face was heavily marked as he realised the depth of his failure. 'Your precious sister-in-law made sure that she ensnared your brother, did she not? She has been no better in her dealings with the Faringdons than the sins that you are prepared to heap at my door.'

'What?' Henry's hand closed on the door knob and was still.

'Don't tell me you did not know!'

'There is nothing to know.' But his eyes were watchful.

'So she has not told you? Well, I don't suppose she would. Females are always more devious than you would expect. And more mercenary, as exhibited by my dear sister Sarah, who has sold me for the price of her independence.'

'Tell me.' It took all Henry's control not to seize Sir Edward by the throat and shake him as a terrier would shake a rat, to wipe the contempt for Eleanor from his thin lips.

'Miss Eleanor Stamford was carrying your brother's child before their marriage,' Baxendale informed him, teeth glinting in vindictive pleasure. 'Of course he would have to marry her, as a man of honour, whether he wished it or not. Her birth is no more distinguished than Octavia's. A respectable gentry family, but with no claim to aristocratic supremacy. But Miss Stamford won the prize. You did not know?' He sneered again as he read correctly the tightening of muscles in Lord Henry's jaw. 'Ask her how long after the bridal nuptials the child was born, my lord. You were in New York and so would not see the clever scheme being unfolded. She and her ambitiously devious mother were determined to get the Marquis before the altar. Your dear brother was well and truly trapped by a beautiful face and the promise of a bastard if he did not act quickly. So he married her.' Sir Edward shrugged again. 'So don't talk to me about plotting and intrigue!'

'Your unsubstantiated opinions do you no credit.' There was barely a hesitation before Henry collected his scattered wits and replied, 'The Marchioness is a lady of unquestionable integrity and principle. If I discover that you have spread such gossip around town, I shall have no hesitation in making it a matter of law. Believe it, sir, before you choose to meddle further in the concerns of my family.'

He flung open the door and bowed, coldly and formally, the merest inclination of his head. But his thoughts were in a turmoil.

Hoskins returned, having delivered the ladies to a waiting cab. As he approached the open doorway, Sir Edward pushed his way past to storm out of the room.

'Get out of my way!'

They watched as he stalked to the door leading on to the street, flinging it back so that it hammered against the wall. Hoskins glanced at Lord Henry with raised brows.

'Let him go,' Lord Henry answered the silent question. 'He has no more demands on my family.' His voice was firm but a little weary as he eased his shoulders against the strain.

'What do you wish, my lord? To pursue the matter through the courts? To obtain recompense? I have to say that I don't advise it.'

'No. Let the matter die a natural death. I don't wish to provide the scandalmongers with any more salacious detail to discuss. I will make provision for Mrs Russell. The Baxendales will doubtless retire from town—I doubt that we shall see them again in the near future. They would not wish to draw further attention to themselves. And I believe that the Reverend Broughton's membership of White's will also lapse!' Lord Henry showed his teeth, more of a snarl than a smile. 'It will give me considerable pleasure to ensure that a man capable of such immoral dealings is no longer received at a gentleman's club.'

Hoskins was moved to smile at the prospect. 'It was well done, my lord.'

'Yes. And I have to thank you for your timely support.'

He left the lawyer's rooms with a lightening of the heart, but he could not dislodge a persistent worry that kept him on edge. He could not quite banish Edward Baxendale's final accusations from his mind. A sour note that spoilt his sense of completion. Baxendale had been mischief-making, of course. Eleanor would never stoop to such devious means. Surely she would never deliberately use the conception of a child to force his brother into a marriage—simply to ensure a glittering title and untold wealth. He would never believe it of her. And yet the malicious words, delivered in Baxendale's smooth, sly voice would not quite go away.

The Faringdon family chose to gather once more in the intimate family parlour in Park Lane. Sarah Russell, returning earlier with Eleanor, had retired to a guest bedchamber with her son and one of the maids who would look to their needs and act a nursemaid for the distraught but determined lady. Exhaustion had finally taken its toll. Although she had recovered from her bout of tears, she did not feel capable of sitting down with all the members of the family whom her brother had so ruthlessly pursued and exploited in his desire for wealth and revenge.

Exhaustion also laid its hand on the other individuals who came together to discuss and marvel at the recent development. There was a strange sense of emptiness, of anticlimax, Eleanor thought as she sank onto the sofa. She felt tired, but could not rest, could not quite accept that Sir Edward and Octavia no longer had any right to oust her from her home and rob her son of his birthright and herself of her widow's jointure. And there was a tension here, particularly in Henry, that she could not quite pinpoint. Perhaps she was simply tired, as were they all. Perhaps it was all imagination. The morning would bring calm and a sense of rightness and completion.

'What do you suppose Baxendale will do now?' Nicholas lounged in a chair to the detriment of his coat and yawned.

'Go back to the Great House in Whitchurch and live out his days in disillusioned reflection of what might have been, I presume.' Henry frowned as he leafed through a handful of letters that had been delivered that morning and were so far unopened. 'And his wife with him. And I expect he will find an excellent excuse to terminate the Reverend Julius's tenure of the living of St Michael and All Angels. I find that I cannot feel sorry.' His stern face was made no more approachable by the sardonic smile that touched his mouth. 'The wages of sin for our devious vicar could be homelessness and poverty.'

'And quite right, too. It is a disgrace that such a man should have a care of souls. I can find no Christian charity for him in my heart.' Mrs Stamford cast a sharp look at her companions, daring anyone to disagree with her.

No one did.

'I wonder what Octavia is thinking?' Eleanor picked up a forgotten piece of embroidery and instantly put it down again with nervous fingers. 'Nothing seemed to move or disturb her very much. Perhaps she does not care very deeply about the outcome. I doubt that she will miss John.'

'Her brother Julius suggested that she simply did whatever Edward told her to do, and was not unhappy with the situation,' Nicholas remembered with a twist of distaste to his mouth.

'I think they will not return to London any time in the near future,' Mrs Stamford gave her opinion. She was the only one of the little group with any energy about her. It burned in her face, in her eyes, a vindictive sense of triumph that flushed her narrow features with bright colour. 'Octavia will be able to return to her beloved rose arbours and trellises. I think that polite society would not make them welcome again if they knew the full story.'

'Perhaps. I think I do feel a little sorry for Octavia. Her life seemed to be so empty.'

'You should not, Eleanor.' Mrs Stamford's voice was sharp, her fixed gaze condemning. '*You* were the victim. The Baxendales deserve no sympathy, no compassion whatsoever. How can you even think it? What thought did they give for your comfort? None! They would have stripped you of your name, your title and your home.' She drew in a breath as she sought to control her damning words. 'But you are now vindicated, my love. And the dear child. What a terrible few weeks we have had, to be sure. I am quite worn to the bone.'

'I valued your support, Mama. It was not inconsiderable.'

'Of course. When would any mother not do all in her power to safeguard the future of her daughter?' Then, on a thought, 'Should we inform Lady Beatrice of the outcome? And the Countess of Painscastle? And perhaps some of our closest friends? Such as the Carstairses. We should not risk you being snubbed again, Eleanor, by those who are still motivated by ignorance or cruel inaccuracies.'

'No,' three voices answered in unison.

'I will not gossip about such private, family matters, Mama. It is not good *ton*.' Eleanor shuddered at the prospect, but her tone was decisive, all dignity. 'Let us simply leave it and forget it ever happened. I forbid you to be the source of any further scandal.'

Mrs Stamford flushed. 'Very well. If that is your wish. But I—' She caught her daughter's eye. 'Very well. But you should give thanks for your release from Sir Edward's clutches.'

Nicholas yawned again. 'We do—we do indeed.' He pushed himself to his feet. 'I feel as tired as if I have experienced a week of bad hunting, all hard runs, heavy going, a poor scent and nothing to show for it in the end.' He stretched his shoulders. 'But at least I need never darken the doors of a gaming hell again.'

'You have all my thanks, Nick.' Henry stood to grasp his brother's shoulder in gratitude.

'My pleasure.' He yawned once more and shook his head. 'I am going down to the stables—I need a ride, fresh air, easy conversation. Care to accompany me?'

'Later, perhaps.'

'I shall go and check on dear Tom.' Mrs Stamford, still a little put out, followed Nicholas to the door. 'At least he is too young to realise the dangers and be affected by them.'

Eleanor and Henry were left alone. She wanted more than anything to thank him, to express her gratitude for his strength and active support over the past days, but he seemed edgy and distant, fraught with an energy that made no sense to Eleanor. It was *not* her imagination. She did not know what to do or what to say.

'I would thank you—'

'I do not want your gratitude. We have had this conversation before.'

Eleanor flushed, remembering the occasion far too well, yet persisted. 'You have it anyway.'

Impatience lent his tongue an edge that startled her. 'Forget the whole episode, Eleanor. You have what you wanted. The title for your son. The estate is secure with the entail. The income from it will allow you to live in luxury. One day you may feel able to marry again. There is no more to be said—let that be an end to it.'

'Hal…'

She could think of no suitable reply, her mind a blank. This was not what she had expected or wanted. Why was he so brusque? What had she done? Silence lengthened between them as, with an intolerant shrug, Lord Henry put distance between them to stare unseeingly down into the remains of a fire. He tried to block out Edward's words. What the hell should he say to her? If Baxendale had intended to cause dissension between them, he was succeeding beyond his wildest dreams! Henry cursed himself silently. What a fool he was. Turning his head, he looked across at her, acutely aware of her troubled expression and confusion. And he grimaced at his own lack of finesse in handling her. He stood upright, his back to the marble fire surround and tried to put matters right between them.

'Forgive my ill temper. You are the last person who should be called on to suffer it. I have no excuse other than a surfeit of legal complications and Baxendale's sly smile!'

'Of course.' The taut muscles in Eleanor's neck and shoulders began to relax just a little. 'Don't apologise—there is no need' The weight on her heart began to lift just a little. 'Now you will go back.' A statement, not a query.

'Yes.'

'How long before you leave us?'

'I shall try for a passage next week from Liverpool.'

'Mr Bridges will be relieved to see you at last. He must have quite given you up, believing you lost to the dens of iniquity in London.' She tried to keep the tone light. A brief smile illuminated her face, forcing him to look away as he replied. Otherwise he might be driven against his better judgement to take her into his arms and kiss her until she sighed and melted against him. And then where would they be? He swore silently again, but his response was mild.

'Yes. I think he is beleaguered by business. He prefers action to figures.'

'Will Rosalind welcome you home?'

'She might.'

There was a moment of uncomfortable silence. Then,

'Tell me when you know of your departure. Otherwise I think I will take Tom back to Burford Hall. I have had my fill of London for the present, and I have no wish to live at Faringdon House yet. I will take Mrs Russell with me and see to her comfort—I expect she and the boy will enjoy life in the country.'

'Of course. Nick will see to any financial matters and your comfort.'

'He is very capable.'

'He enjoys it. If you will excuse me, my lady, I have some letters to write.'

Eleanor sighed inwardly. So coldly formal. Whatever the problem, it still troubled him. And the rift between them was as wide and as bottomless as it had ever been.

'To be sure.'

He looked at her, a searching glance that revealed nothing of his thoughts. Then, with a curt bow of the head, he turned and walked away from her, as she knew he would.

She had no right to call him back.

Edward Baxendale's bitter accusations against Eleanor refused to be banished from Henry's mind. Had she indeed trapped Thomas into an unwanted marriage with a child conceived out of wedlock? Without doubt, it would not be the first time that such a ploy had been used by an unscrupulous woman to gain a foothold into a noble family. But Eleanor? Never! And yet, how could he possibly discover the truth of it, if only to put his mind at ease. He could hardly ask Eleanor herself. Had she after all rejected him with the sole purpose of luring his brother into a far more advantageous union? Henry had decided that it no longer mattered, his love for her was absolute, no matter what had driven her to turn her back on him. But if she had used the child to spring the trap on his brother? He shook his head in disbelief. It simply did not fit with his image of her.

But sharp-edged doubts assailed him and refused to let up, and a far sharper edge that he should even contemplate questioning her honesty. He cursed himself for harbouring such doubts—but they remained. And there was no doubt, he knew in his heart, that Eleanor's doting mama would be prepared to take any step that would ensure the well-being of her daughter. He had heard such words from her own lips. How could he forget her almost unseemly delight over Edward Baxendale's fall from grace and Eleanor's social reinstatement?

He paced the morning room, self-disgust riding him with sharp spurs, his unfinished letter to Nathaniel Bridges lying forgotten on the desk as he wrestled on the one hand with his conscience, which insisted that Eleanor's honesty should not be questioned, and on the other the distrust created by Baxendale's vicious and well-aimed words. He loved Eleanor. By God, he did, beyond all thought and reason. But it might be that he had at last learned the truth behind her failure to join him on his voyage, committing her future irrevocably to his. Who could he possibly ask to gain further enlightenment? Whatever happened, he must do nothing to create more scandal, to spread any further shadow over Eleanor's name.

His head came up as he heard Nicholas's riding boots echo on the tiled floor of the entrance hall. Here was the only member of the family with whom he could share his thoughts. And even then, not totally. He opened the door and stepped out.

'Hal.' Nicholas swung round. 'Are you coming after all?'

'No.' He grimaced. 'Much as I would like to. Too much neglected business. Nat Bridges will write me off as dead!'

'Well, if you will sully your hands with buying and selling and the acquisition of something as common as money! By the by, I would not say it in front of the ladies, but…congratulations!'

Henry's brow arched in silent query.

'On burying the Baxendale plot so effectively…and without any fuss.'

'I would have dearly enjoyed burying Baxendale himself!' Henry smiled wryly at the prospect. 'You will never know how difficult it was to keep my hands from his throat when he tried to throw the blame in any direction but on himself, his own greed and ambition.'

'I expect it tapped the depths of self-control. Not something you used to be famous for!'

'It did. It was still hard. A sharp right to the jaw would have been much more in my line. Or even the use of a riding whip across his shoulders. He deserves far worse for what he did.'

Nicholas continued to head to the door, picking up whip and gloves from a side table.

'Nick…'

'Hmm?'

'Tell me…tell me about Eleanor and Thomas. Were they happy?'

'Now there's a strange question.' It stopped Nicholas in his tracks and he swung round to face his brother. 'Yes. To my knowledge. They seemed so.'

'Why did Thomas marry her?'

'An even stranger question!' He slanted a quizzical glance at Henry's face, but was unable to read the shuttered expression. 'I don't know. Speak with Eleanor if it matters. I don't advise it, though. Nell is a very…a very private person.'

'No. I wouldn't, of course.' He followed Nick to the door, unable to let the matter drop. 'It's just…'

'Something Baxendale said?'

'Yes. You are amazingly astute, little brother.'

'I am always astute, if you did but notice. But it's simply a matter of logic. Was it simply mischief-making?'

'I expect so.'

'Want to tell me about it?'

'No. I am not proud of my doubts! It will be best if I keep his poisonous words to myself, I think.'

'To share them could draw the poison. I can be a willing listener.' Nick angled his head, waiting for the reply. He had not often seen his brother so troubled.

'But not if it causes pain and even more hurt.' Henry frowned at the problem.

'True.' Nick shrugged slightly. 'Then you must perforce bear the burden alone. Do you want my advice?'

'I think I can guess.'

'Then forget it, Hal.' Nicholas for once was deadly serious. 'His intentions will have been malicious, for sure. How could you expect him to tell the truth about anything? You should not waste one moment's thought on any accusations he made. And certainly not anything concerning Thomas and Eleanor. Baxendale would be overjoyed if he knew that he had been successful in destroying your peace of mind. Don't let him!'

'Sage advice.' Henry turned as if to retrace his steps to the morning room, then with second thoughts, looked back. 'Was it a love match?' he asked bluntly.

'Well, if we are returning to Nell and Thomas…' Nick huffed out a breath and thought for a moment. 'Yes. They were attracted. The marriage was certainly arranged quickly. Perhaps not a grand passion, I would have thought. But they were happy enough together. They talked to each other, laughed together. You know…'

'And the child?'

'That's easy.' Nick smiled, a little sadly, as the memories crowded in, of happier times before his brother's death. 'Thomas doted on him. Very proud. As he should be. He was already planning when to teach him to ride and to shoot duck on the lake at Burford Levels, even though he was barely a year old. I never thought of Thomas in a paternal role, but it suited him. Why?'

'Nothing. I simply wanted to know.' Henry decide there was nothing more that he could ask.

'Problems?'

'No. Of course not.'

'Good.' On a decision, Nicholas stalked across the hall and took his brother by the arm. 'Come to the stables. Leave your letters for the afternoon—they will still be there tonight! Time you had some light relief.'

'Very well.' Henry smiled a little wearily, gave in and allowed himself to be led, grateful to have his mind taken from the suspicions that beset him. Perhaps Nicholas's remedy would push everything back into perspective for him and then he could be at ease again. At ease with Eleanor. 'Forgive me, Nick. I seem to have got into the habit of questioning everybody and everything—looking for shadows when they do not exist.'

'And very uncomfortable for us all it is, too. You need a drink and some convivial company.'

'True.'

'Easily done. Come with me.'

So much for business. Henry shut the door on the morning room and the affairs of Faringdon and Bridges and accompanied his brother to the door, more than a little reassured by what could only be described as a most inconclusive conversation.

Eleanor spent another sleepless night, thoughts in turmoil. Would she ever sleep well again? she wondered as she pushed her fingers through her hair, tangling the already disordered curls. Within a week Hal could have packed his belongings, terminated the rent on the London house and taken the mail coach to Liverpool. It was very possible that she would never see him again. Never hear his voice or feel the touch of his hands, in simple care or in passion. She stiffened her muscles to hold off the desperate sense of loss that swamped her mind and her heart and once again threatened to drown her in a deluge of helpless tears. She must not think of that. She breathed deeply and fought against the fear that stalked her through the dark hours. She must not allow it to colour her judgement. Her own loss was not the issue here.

For a little time she sat in her bed against the soft pillows with a book open on her lap, but to no avail. She could not read. The words on the page meant nothing to her when all she could see was Hal's stormy eyes, the groove between his brows when he was caught up in some matter, the utmost tenderness in his smile when he had kissed and held her against him, inflaming the needs in her body to match his own. Or the possessive fire when he had turned the key to imprison them together in his bedchamber. So she cast the book aside to pace her own room. Taking out Thomas's letter from her dressing-table drawer, she turned it over and over in nervous fingers—and then replaced it beneath the cases of jewellery. That, she decided, was not the way forward. He would either believe her on her own merits or he would not. It was a risk she would have to face. With that thought in her mind, she took herself to her son's room, to stand by the crib, silently watching him as he slept, fine lashes casting shadows onto his cheeks. How beautiful he was, what a splendid child she had been given. What a fine young man he would grow up to be.

The thought did not make her mind any easier. She had kept her secret for two long years, explaining it would be no easy matter.

By dawn, she had made her decision, for better or worse. Really, it was very simple. She did not know why it had caused her so much heartache, but her *toilette* took considerable time as she dressed with care, determined that she would look her best if she was to be on trial for her past sins. The exquisite silver-grey-and-cream-striped gown, demure and understated in its colouring, gave exactly the impression of sophistication and sobriety that she needed, the delicate ruffles at hem and neckline flattering but restrained. Her hair, charmingly arranged in ringlets, fell from a high knot to brush her white shoulders. She knew that she looked well enough, although nothing, other than the use of cosmetics that she determined to eschew on this occasion, could put colour into her cheeks or disguise the evidence of her sleepless night. No matter. It was important that she appear composed and assured, that her courage should not desert her in the face of Hal's amazed disbelief. Or his total rejection.

In spite of her clear intentions and her determination to be courageous at all costs, Eleanor could not face breakfast. She waited in her room until it was late enough in the morning for Henry to be engaged in business in the morning room.

Then she descended the stairs at last, breathing shallow, palms damp with latent panic. It was a dangerous game she was playing. She could win the glittering prize. Hold the moon and stars in her hands. Or her hopes and dreams could disintegrate, her heart broken. But she must do it. It was only *right*. Henry must not be allowed to leave England without the knowledge, without the opportunity to make a choice that could change the direction of his whole life. If she kept silent, the guilt would be too heavy and would hound her to the day of her death. She owed him the truth, even if he damned her for it and left her to face the future alone.

Henry ignored the timid knock on the door of the morning room. It would not be one of the family—they would not knock, so probably one of the servants who would go away if he made no response. He did not need an interruption. Marcle could find Nicholas if there was some urgent matter to be dealt with. The neglected business of Faringdon and Bridges still lay before him as he had left it on the previous afternoon. He must complete it. There was a sailing next week from Liverpool that he would take. With luck and a fair wind the letters could leave tomorrow and would make land before he did, informing Nat of his imminent arrival and the decisions he had made. Caught up in the planning, he did not notice when the door opened quietly and Eleanor entered.

She closed it silently and remained by the door, watching him for a little while as he sat, head bent, reading rapidly, before making a reply with firm characters on the page. There was a line between his brow as he concentrated, just as she had imagined in her thoughts the previous night. The bright sunshine kissed his raven-black hair so that it shone blue-black, but it was too dense to take any gilding. She knew its weight and its texture, its softness against her skin that made her shiver with remembered passion, and her fingers yearned to touch it again. Her mouth was dry, her pulse hectic.

'Hal.'

He looked up and immediately smiled. How could he not? How beautiful she was with the clear morning light teasing her hair with hints of gold and auburn, and bringing a jewel-like glow to her extraordinary violet eyes. He held out his hand to encourage her closer, his doubts assuaged by her presence and the fact that she had sought him out. He expected to see contentment in her face, an ease previously absent.

His gaze locked on hers. 'What is this?' He pushed back the chair and rose to his feet, approaching to take her hands in his, raising them to his lips, searching her face with instant concern. 'The Baxendale issue need no longer worry you. You must sleep and eat and regain your peace of mind. Nothing can harm you now.' He bent his head to press his lips to her forehead in a blessing, infinitely tender. 'You need not be unhappy Nell.'

Carefully, she disengaged her hands, which caused him to frown, and took a step in retreat. 'There is something I must tell you…'

Her low voice and the shadows in her eyes made his blood chill. There was something here… He set his mind and his will to remain calm.

'Come and sit,' he encouraged. 'Tell me what it is.'

She resisted still, remaining tall and straight in the centre of the room. He noted that her hands were clenched into fists at her sides, although half-hidden by the folds of her dress.

'No. I must stand… Listen, Hal. You must not go back to America without knowing…without realising…' Her words dried on her lips.

Hal's concern deepened, acquiring a sharp edge that sliced at his heart. 'Do I really need to know?' he asked gently. It was the coward's way, he knew, to prevent her opening her heart to him, but what good would it do? Was she indeed going to confess at last that she had rejected him to set her sights so much higher—and had achieved her goal through less than honourable means? He did not think that he wanted to know. He would rather live without the unpalatable knowledge of her betrayal and perfidy, rather carry the memory of her softness and sweetness as she turned to him in the night.

'I must say it,' she said simply, studying her fingers now linked before her, white with tension. 'It is on my conscience. And it could affect your future, your whole life. I must say it. By keeping silent I committed a great wrong.'

A pause. She moistened her lips with her tongue, then raised her eyes to his, a silent plea for understanding and compassion. For acceptance of a situation that had not been entirely of her own making, in which she had made the only choice possible.

'My son. Tom. He is not Thomas's child. He is yours…your son, Hal.'

The resulting silence echoed in the room, filling it from floor to ceiling with a tension that could be felt, tasted even. Lord Henry stared at her, blank shock imprinting his face, his brain repeating the words over and over again as if it might make for clearer understanding. Incomprehensibly, he could not grasp their significance.

'What?' The question was harsh, even though his voice was soft. He had suspected her of carrying Thomas's child and cursed himself for his lack of trust. But he had never suspected this.

'Tom is your child.' Eleanor never once took her gaze from his face, pinning him with her words, challenging him to deny it. 'That last night we spent together… I found that I was carrying him when you had gone…'

'My son.' The meaning took hold, searingly bright, as the implications began to leap into sharp and painful focus. As Henry recalled, suddenly with a terrible clarity, the words that he had overheard her speak to the child, his child, in the small sunlit parlour. Before he had held the infant in his own arms. *You can never know your father…you will never keep his image in your memory…* And he had not known, not understood. How could he have held his own son and not have realised? But then he had not understood her meaning. The powerful tangle of emotions threatened to choke him, but his eyes were stark, austere even, all emotion effectively buried when he turned his gaze on the woman who stood before him. 'Why did you not tell me? Why did I not know of this?'

'I did not know how to reach you. I wrote to you, but received no reply. And then it was too late—I was married to Thomas and it would have done more harm than good to tell you. And…' But there were no excuses, really. She gave up, eyes still searching his face to determine his reaction.

'Did Thomas know?' Henry rubbed his hands over his face, struggling to make sense of the incredible confession. 'When you married him, did he know that you carried my child?'

'Of course he did!' She grew pale with anger and not a little shame that she had put Thomas in such an invidious position. 'Would you accuse me of tricking him? Of course Thomas knew that Tom was your son.'

Baxendale's words returned to Henry like a blow to the gut. *Your precious sister-in-law made sure that she ensnared your brother, did she not?* This terrible scenario opening before him, revealed by the only woman whom he had ever loved, was even worse than the one painted by his enemy with such malicious intent. The shock wave rolled over him with remorseless power. It coated his next words with pitiless despair.

'Or did you allow my gullible brother to think that the child was his? Was that why he married you, to give his name to his own bastard child? Poor Thomas always did believe the best of everyone. Did you indeed trap him into marriage? Baxendale did not realise how far from the mark he was. Even he did not imagine that you would be capable of such a depth of deceit and trickery.'

Eleanor drew in her breath at the deliberate and ruthless assassination of her character. The pain in her heart was tangible.

How could he accuse her of such dishonesty? What could Edward Baxendale have possibly said to cause this volley of spiteful words?

'Why tell me now?' Lord Henry demanded, lips curled in a snarl. 'If you made so little effort to inform me two years ago, why now?'

She strove for calm in the midst of this storm of callous cruelty. There must be a way out of this maelstrom if only she could find it. 'Because with Thomas's death it has changed everything. The title is yours by rights. You should be Marquis of Burford. My son—your son—has no right to inherit before you.'

No! Oh God, no!

An icy hand closed inexorably round his heart with exquisite torture as he contemplated the one thing in life he did not want, had never wanted.

'I do not want it.' The denial was flat and instantaneous, disguising his fear. 'Neither the title nor the estate.'

'Perhaps not. But it would be wrong if you never knew, never had the knowledge to make the choice.' She swallowed against the lump in her throat. 'If you never had the choice to claim your son and recognise him as your own.'

'Do you really expect me to believe all this?' She would never have believed the flat denial in his eyes, in his voice.

'Why not? Why should you not believe me?' Anger began to replace shock in her veins and she lifted her head, drawing pride and dignity around her shoulders like a velvet cloak. 'I could have let you leave next week—without ever telling you that you had a child. Why should I make up a situation that would compromise my own honour? I have nothing to gain from this confession other than society's condemnation if it becomes known outside these four walls. It was my decision to allow you…intimacies without marriage. For that I certainly deserve censure. And how I paid the price!' She stifled a sob. She would not shed tears over this. Never again! 'I trusted you to marry me.'

Her accusation hit home, but he was too angry to give it credence, to contemplate it for more than a heartbeat. Even though a small part of his brain admitted that in all honesty she could not take all the blame for this. The child was the making of both of them in a moment of mutual love and desire. Hers had been the innocence on that occasion. How could he be so utterly selfish as to heap the blame on her? *If* the child was really his, of course, a nasty little voice insinuated in his mind. But he pushed away the uncomfortable thoughts and concentrated on the burning issue that raged, destructive and uncurbed, through his blood.

'You ask why I should accept your words. Perhaps you think your timely *confession* to be in your own interests. I suppose that it is just conceivable that, given the glad news of a son and heir, I would fall at your feet in guilt for my past actions and in gratitude marry you. That would restore all your status and wealth as Marchioness of Burford. An achievement indeed! Instead of the power being held in trust and your own income limited to that from the widow's jointure, however generous it might be.'

'Do you think so little of me, that I would deliberately lie to you?' Her cheeks were ashen, her eyes so dark as to be almost indigo as she regarded him with horror.

'Perhaps not, in all fairness.' The admission was forced from him. 'But I would not put it past your mother to lay out such a campaign! Her ambitions for you are outrageous. Whether you are compliant in her schemes or simply ignorant, I know not.'

Eleanor could find nothing to say. Her body seemed numb to all sensation. Nothing could be worse she thought, watching herself objectively, listening to Hal's harsh voice as if it were from a great distance, than this one moment in her life. She felt as if he had struck her, an open-handed slap, as indeed he had, with words if not with his hand. Her heart ached from the blow.

Lord Henry saw the effect of his attack. It had been devastating. It struck him instantly that he was in the wrong, but his disillusion was as bitter as gall, his wretchedness at being chained into a life that he detested was intemperate. Resisting the urge to enfold her close, to stroke and comfort, to fall on his knees to beg a forgiveness that he did not deserve, was almost beyond his power. Even though he raged against himself for his brutal insensitivity, Hal continued to lash out to cover his own hurt, his own vulnerability.

'Are you sure that you really know whose child it is?'

She had been wrong, Eleanor thought. This was worse. She shook her head as she struggled to find an answer to such an impossible question. 'I...I can't...'

Self-contempt now lodged in his chest to reproach him for so offensive an attack, disgust that he should make such an unwarranted accusation. Seeing the rigidity in her whole body, he reined in his temper and tried for a more moderate tone. 'Could you not have told me this any time before now, Eleanor?'

But Eleanor was beyond moderation. Fury leapt within her with all-consuming flames. She was past considering the effect of her words and struck out in her own defence. 'When do you suggest, my lord? The moment you arrived back at Burford Hall?' The sarcasm was biting, although she kept her voice low and admirably controlled. 'Welcome home, Henry. Let me introduce you to your son.' She laughed with a hint of hysteria. 'It would have put Sir Edward's news of an unknown wife, hidden away in the country, in the shade, I imagine. No, I could not. And I will tell you why. I was afraid.' She all but spat out the words. 'I was afraid to tell you. I knew that you did not want me. I could accept that—and have done so for two years. But I was afraid to discover that you would not want your son either. I thought that would break my heart.'

'Eleanor!' He had hurt her beyond measure.

'And I was right, wasn't I? You have no wish to know him or claim him and I cannot persuade you otherwise. It makes me regret that I ever tried, simply for the sake of my own conscience. It would have been far better if neither you nor my son knew. Thomas was more of a father to him than you could ever be.'

The hurt shimmered between them. Her eyes bright with unshed tears. His face ravaged with the deep lines of hard-held emotion. The abyss yawned wide and dangerous between them, impossible to bridge.

'Don't concern yourself, my lord.' Eleanor continued to pour out the anguish and the pain. 'Tom will never have to know that his father did not choose to acknowledge him, for I know not what reason other than that you doubt my honesty. From this moment,

Tom's father was Thomas, my husband. How could I have been so mistaken in my judgement? What a terrible mistake I made. And what a fool you must think me.' She laughed again, a sharp sound without humour that told him more than anything else of the depth of her despair. 'Go back to New York, Hal. Forget that Tom and I exist. I loved you to the depths of my soul and I gave you everything. I gave you a splendid child. But you are not worthy to be the father of my son. I wish Rosalind well of you.'

She turned her back on him.

Henry strode from the room, her final words, her merciless condemnation ringing in his ears. He thought that they would haunt him forever. He did not see the tears spangling her cheeks, despite all her good intentions. Or read the desolation in her face, not yet hidden behind a mask of hard serenity that would deny to the world that her heart had been ripped to pieces.

How could he have done it? How could he have been so deliberately cruel? So demon-driven, vicious as a wolf attacking its prey. Fear, he admitted. A title he did not want. A way of life that he had no desire for. But a son? The child whom he had held in his arms? He believed her, of course, every word that she had spoken. Her integrity was beyond question and she would not make up such a story. But he had hurt her so much. She would never forgive him, and rightly so. He was no better than Baxendale in his destruction of her life. Worse, in fact, since she had come to trust him and rely on him. And yet he had turned on her, cut her with taunts and vitriolic words. She had every reason to hate him. What the hell did he do now?

And he had a son.

'Hal…'

'Not now.' He strode past Nicholas with savage grace. 'Come and ride if you wish, but don't talk to me for a little while. Just don't ask. I am impossible company. I have just committed the worst sin of my life. I cannot undo the words I have said or the harm I have caused…'

Seeing the ungovernable torment and remorse in his face, Nick let him go, standing to watch as his usually impassive brother flung out of the house. At that moment, nothing would have persuaded him to restrain his brother, to question the reason for his distress. Nothing would have made him go into the room that Hal had just vacated, where Eleanor still remained. If he had needed any confirmation of his suspicions, his convictions even, it had just struck him with all the brutality of a slap to his face. Surely only two people helplessly in love could reduce each other to such devastating unhappiness as he had seen in his brother's face.

From the window of the morning room, Eleanor also watched with eyes as cold and empty as the hollow places in her heart. Could she blame him? Yes, she could! She had not deserved such condemnation, would never have believed that he would show such harshness towards her. But circumstances had conspired against her, she had kept her secret from Hal, and whatever Edward Baxendale had said to him in the aftermath of their disclosure of his deceit had borne fruit. She had played the game out to the full and must now bear the consequences of her shattered dreams and bruised heart.

But she had told Hal the truth at last. His reaction to it was within his own dominion—and, besides, he would be gone in a few days. Her damaged heart would heal, in a hundred years or so. And whatever she had told Hal in her wretchedness, in the desert of her wasted emotions, she *would* tell her son about his magnificent father. But never that Hal had rejected him, had rejected them both.

Chapter Eleven

'Nick. There is a ship sailing next week from Liverpool. I shall take passage on it.' Henry came to a halt at the bottom of the staircase as his brother was making his way down, dressed with fashionable, if unusual, flamboyance to go out.

'I supposed you would eventually.' Nicholas cast his hat and gloves onto the sidetable in the hall and followed Henry into the morning room. 'But I did not expect you to go so soon.' He took the offered glass of port. 'I shall miss you, Hal.'

'An important business deal has come to fruition—a lucrative contract that we wish to take up to ship raw cotton to the mills here in Lancashire and then return the finished textiles.' Hal made an obvious excuse. 'It is best if I am there. Besides, there is nothing to hold me here in London.' He bared his teeth in something that was not a smile and took a swallow of the port. 'Forgive me. I did not mean that as it sounded.'

'So I should hope.' Nicholas punched his shoulder in mock disgust, thinking that Hal looked as if he had spent a night of torment. No doubt the result of his conversation with Eleanor on the previous morning, the content of which still remained a mystery to him. Both parties had been at dinner, but so scrupulously polite to each other that it had been painfully unnerving to watch and listen. Like the silent shattering of fragile glass. The atmosphere had then glittered with shards of that broken glass, lurking to slice at the unwary—he had been more than glad to escape and join a party of friends at the theatre. What Henry had done he did not know and dare not ask. Eleanor had stalked from the room as soon as the meal had ended, leaving Mrs Stamford to stare with puzzlement from one to the other.

'So you are leaving me to manage the estate in your absence?'

'Yes. You will have to work for a living, for the first time in your life.' Henry put down his glass and took the seat behind his desk. 'Seriously, Nick. Would you dislike it too much? If so, it is unfair of me to leave you with it.'

'No. You know me better than that, Hal. There is nothing that I would like more. I have plans. When Tom inherits the estate in the fullness of time it will be a wonder to behold with sound investment. When he is older, I will see that he is up to scratch. He will not live off the estate, giving nothing back, if I have anything to say in the matter.'

Hal's answering smile was bleak. 'I know that he is in good hands.' *My son. My son.*

'And I know that you would not want to take it on. For you to have been born the eldest son would have been the worst possible destiny for you.' Nick grinned in some sympathy. 'Whereas I enjoy the life as a country squire. I shall not be sorry to leave town.'

Henry's smile vanished, leaving his face harsh and strained. 'Hoskins can be relied upon,' was all he said. He frowned unseeingly out of the window, arms folded before him on the desk. That was the key, of course, to his disastrous confrontation with Eleanor. Nick's comment that he would not ever want the title, the social hierarchy, the acceptance that the manner in which the world saw him should rest purely on an accident of birth. The idea that all men should have the same opportunities open to them, to construct a future for themselves dependent on their own efforts, suited him far better. And it was that which had pushed him over the edge. The title was legally his after the death of his brother, tying him into a social and class system that he was more than ready to escape. That, coupled with Edward Baxendale's vicious accusation and Mrs Stamford's determined and unseemly pleasure at the outcome, had driven him to heap the blame on

Eleanor. As if she were responsible for chaining him to a life that he detested as much as Nick enjoyed.

Not true. Of course it wasn't true. He knew it in every sinew of his body, heard it in every beat of his heart. And what had he done? He had made her cry! Humiliated her. Questioned her morality and her veracity. He deserved to be flogged. To be damned to the fires of hell.

It had not helped him when last night he had taken himself on an impulse to the baby's room. An astonished nursemaid had looked up from her seat beside the fireplace where she was sewing some small item of clothing. She leapt to her feet as if to leave the room.

'Don't go. I just need a moment.' *A lifetime.*

He looked down into the crib.

Hair, brows, nose—exact replicas of those that he saw every morning in his mirror. A sturdy frame that would become lithe and athletic. He would ride a horse with elegant grace. He would shoot with skill and accuracy. He would have dogs and horses as he grew from babyhood. He would look to Nicholas for his initiation into the rites and responsibilities of adolescence and adulthood. He would grow up not knowing his father.

The baby opened his eyes. Deep amethyst, fringed with dark lashes.

Henry held out his hand, drawn impossibly against his will to touch, to savour. The baby chuckled and clutched, delighted with the company, making contact in his small fist, drawing the offered fingers to his mouth to gnaw on them with half-formed teeth.

Henry's chest tightened, he found it difficult to swallow. His son. And Eleanor's. Whom he had rejected.

Oh, God!

What could he possibly say to Eleanor? She had borne this beautiful child alone, without him. He mentally thanked Thomas from the bottom of his heart for coming to her salvation. Knowing his brother as he did, he understood exactly what Thomas had done and why he had done it. Married Eleanor to give her the shelter of his name and consequence, so that no one need know that she had borne a child without the protection of marriage vows, and his brother's child would have all the benefits of being brought up as the Faringdon heir. Henry breathed hard against the flood of emotion that threatened to unman him, longing for that one impossible opportunity to tell Thomas of his gratitude.

And he had accused Eleanor of treachery and betrayal, of luring Thomas into a marriage to satisfy her greed and ambition. Nothing could be further from the truth.

But why had she not come to meet him, to join him on the voyage? If she had, their marriage would have legitimised the child and all the following complications would never have arisen. He would probably never know.

He stroked his hand gently over his son's hair, cupping his cheek, caressing the perfect fingers, the shell-like nails. Then turned and left the room, as quietly as he had come, with nothing resolved

'Does Eleanor know?' Nick broke into his uncomfortable musings, concerned for the stark misery in his brother's eyes.

'Yes.'

'What did she say?'

'Nothing of importance.' Henry shrugged and switched his focus back to Nick, replacing the inscrutable mask. 'Why?

Well! Nicholas hesitated, remembering. That was one statement palpably untrue if Hal's face, bleak with shock as he had exited the morning room after his conversation with Eleanor, was anything to go by. But should he interfere further? 'Nothing. Just that I had thought that you were not…not indifferent to each other.' Nicholas made his decision, for better or worse, and came to sit opposite the desk, to fix Hal with a stern expression. 'To put it bluntly, I had thought that you were more than half in love with her. That is, until whatever passed between the two of you yesterday afternoon in the morning room.' He waited the space of a heartbeat, seeing the shutters come down on any emotion in his brother's face. 'You are free to deny any or all of it if you wish, of course.'

'Ha! I wish I were free.' The words were wrung from Henry.

'What should I understand by that?'

'Nothing! Nothing at all!.' Hal sighed and drove his fingers through his hair. 'Yes, I love her. Of course I do. How can I deny it? I love her and I always will, even though I have hurt her beyond belief.'

'So why are you leaving her? Have you told her that you love her?'

'No.'

'I also thought Nell loved you. Is it because she is Thomas's widow that you have not spoken? I don't see that it has any bearing on your feelings for her or hers for you.' He frowned as he remembered their previous conversation. 'Is that why you asked me if theirs had been a love match?'

'Not really. There were other reasons at the time… But I have destroyed any hope of her love,' Hal answered quietly. 'She will never forgive me.'

'It can't be as bad as that.'

'It can—you have no idea!' *I questioned the birth of her child. I accused her of every sin possible. I humiliated her.*

'Are you going to tell me?'

'No. My feelings do not matter. Her life is here with the child. I have nothing to offer her. And—you cannot have thought…' Hal's face was bleak indeed '…there can never be any future between myself and Eleanor of that nature that has the blessing of the law. The church, little brother, in its infinite wisdom, denies the right of a man to marry his brother's widow.'

'I did not know…'

'Oh, we could find a minister easily enough, who would turn a blind eye and commit the deed. Particularly if we greased his hand with sufficient gold. Perhaps even the Reverend Julius Broughton could be persuaded on such terms!' His laugh was a harsh travesty. 'But anyone with ill intent or outraged morality could have such a union declared null and void. Imagine the scandal that would create! I will not do it, even if Eleanor would contemplate such a relationship between us. Which she would not, not after…' He shook his head and lapsed into silence.

'I see. I had not thought of that.' Nicholas decided to leap into the yawning chasm of Henry's reticence, to risk an outbreak of the banked temper in his brother's eyes. It would not be the first time that he had pushed and provoked until he had goaded his brother into disclosing what was on his mind. He might risk a firm and horribly accurate straight right to the jaw—a not infrequent retaliation in childhood when tempers had run high—but Nicholas was quite capable of holding his own, and it would be worth it if he could draw some of the pain from Hal's set expression.

'Look, Hal. I am not blind. To put it bluntly, the love between the two of you is as clear as a rising hawk at noonday. It shimmers between you when you are together in the same room.' He saw the glint of denial leap into his brother's eyes and stretched out a hand across the desk to grasp his wrist in strong fingers. 'Don't bother to deny it. She is as much in thrall as you. Why not simply take her with you? Marry her in New York where the family connection is not a matter of public knowledge. Surely it is better than committing yourselves to a lifetime of misery apart?' He hesitated, tensed his shoulders. He might as well say it. 'Do you have to be so damned noble?'

'Noble?' The icy flash in Henry's eyes heralded the expected eruption of passion. He snatched his wrist from Nick's light grasp, surged to his feet and strode to the window, his back turned against his brother's sharp gaze. 'Noble! Never that. This all started with an act of supreme selfishness on my part. Don't speak to me of nobility.'

Nick opened his mouth to ask his meaning, but did not. Too personal. Too painful. And perhaps, watching the unfolding events of the past days, he could guess at one of the problems which beset the two people he loved most. Hal could easily be Tom's father. But Hal would be protective of Nell and the child to the bitter end. It would be insensitive in the extreme for Nick to press him for an answer.

'I must not risk dragging Nell's name through the mire again. I won't do it, Nick. She will be safe here, with all due respect and honour. I know that you will care for her.'

'Of course.' His brother's anguish tightened cruel fingers in his gut. 'Are you indeed quite certain, Hal?'

'Yes.'

'You know your own affairs, I suppose.' Nicholas looked dubious but realised that he would get nothing more from his brother. Whatever had been said between Hal and Eleanor on the previous day was having a dire and lasting effect.

'Yes. I do. I shall leave for Liverpool in two days.' Henry strode to the door, opened it, thus bringing the conversation to an end.

And then I need never see her again!

As Lord Henry was engaged in deflecting his brother's interest and planning his future without Eleanor, the Marchioness of Burford was spending the day with a martial glint in her eye. Her mood alternated wildly between intense hurt and intense fury, the latter being in the ascendant. Sparkling anger ran through her veins, intoxicating in its effect, instilling her with magnificent energy. She railed silently at the pig-headedness and insensitivity of all men, and Lord Henry Faringdon in particular. So! She had lied to him, lied to Thomas, had she? How dare he accuse her of such perfidy—and without one scrap of evidence? How dare he believe that she had acquired wealth and a title through a devious and unscrupulous manipulation of Thomas? What had she done to deserve such an attack? Not that she cared! And what could possibly have driven Lord Henry Faringdon to use such cruel taunts towards her? Not that she cared about that either! She did not want an explanation from him. Or an apology. Or anything at all, ever!

Eleanor would not listen to the hurt of her broken heart. She would dearly like to break his lordship's head instead, with a particularly ugly Sèvres vase which stood on the mantelpiece in her bedchamber. Except that it would be a waste of the vase.

So she spent the day in a ferment of anger and bad temper. She contemplated throwing her breakfast cup of hot chocolate at the wall—except that Marcle would think that she had taken leave of her senses, as well as having to deal with the resulting sticky consequences. She thrust the pins to hold her curls in place with a savage turn of her wrist as if she were skewering Lord Henry's vital organs. She even snapped at her mother in unusual temper. No. She did not wish to go to Hookham's circulating library. If her mama wished to do so to exchange the latest offering from Walter Scott, then she must go alone. When Nicholas attempted to draw out the rigidly controlled lady by offering to escort her to eat ices at Gunter's in Berkeley Square, he was met with a coldly formal refusal and a flash of amethyst eyes, hardly the reaction he had anticipated for such a compassionate gesture and such an agreeable way to spend a morning. Eleanor noted the surprise, but she would not feel guilt—not even the slightest twinge. Presumably *all* Faringdon men were similarly obtuse and insensitive as Lord Henry Faringdon! She informed Lord Nicholas, in similar style to her conversation with her mama, that if he did indeed wish to stroll through Mayfair on so trivial an errand, he was free to do so, but without her. She was sure that he could pass the time far more profitably without her assistance. And then she turned her back on his amazed stare, leaving Nicholas to consider that perhaps ices had not been the best offering for so glacial a lady. And relieved that he did not have to spend any length of time in her company until her usual good humour had been restored to her. Whenever that would be. He bowed and retreated in poor order.

On meeting by chance Lord Henry himself, the chief culprit in the drama, Eleanor gratified him with an icy inclination of the head, the tiniest of movements, certainly one of her more effective set-downs, and then proceeded to walk past him into the parlour as if he were invisible, and closed the door in his face with considerable satisfaction.

Still restless and with time hanging heavily, she took herself off to spend a pleasurable interlude with baby Tom in the nursery. But the infant was tired and fractious with teething. When denied his own way over the delicate but potentially dangerous issue of cuddling the grey kitten who had accompanied them from Burford Hall, he wailed and fussed, his cheeks flushed with frustration and damp with tears. His mama kissed him and mopped up the tears, with fruitless efforts to deflect Tom's attention from his heart's desire, until she shut the kitten out of the room. The baby eventually fell into an exhausted sleep after another outburst of heartrending sobs, leaving Eleanor with the

cynical observation that he was entirely like his father, bad tempered when thwarted to any degree. But his father need not think
that *he* would receive any such sympathy from her, she vowed,
as she crooned a soothing lullaby to her son and smoothed his
ruffled hair.

By this time Eleanor felt the need to do something outrageous.
She contemplated the possibilities with enjoyment. She could
perhaps walk down St James's Street without her maid, under the
ogling eyes and raised quizzing glasses of the bucks and beaux
of the Bow Window Set. An action of complete impropriety that
would surely damn her utterly in the eyes of the polite world and
ensure that no one would be willing to receive her. What did it
matter? Lord Henry Faringdon had believed the worst of her even
when she was innocent!

The sooner Lord Henry Faringdon left these shores the better! Even if the rift in her heart throbbed with pain and widened
a little further at the prospect!

Perhaps she should stroll along Bond Street, she mused, toying with the light luncheon served by a wary Marcle, who was
more than a little aware of the remarkable unpredictability of his
mistress's mood. She could fritter money extravagantly on any
number of fashionable articles that she did not want and did not
need. But perhaps not. In the end she took herself off to the
Countess of Painscastle's *at home* where she regaled and entertained her hostess with a somewhat selective and censored ac-
count of the events of the previous day and her difference of
opinion with Lord Henry. Judith's instant sympathy was balm to
Eleanor's damaged soul, especially that lady's willingness to
rise to her defence against all men, in particular her hapless
cousin, Lord Henry Faringdon.

All in all, in spite of the satisfaction which she undoubtedly
felt, it was one of the most exhausting days of Eleanor's life.

Later that same afternoon Henry returned from an equally exhausting visit in the company of Lady Beatrice Faringdon. She
had insisted on hearing all the details of the Baxendale scandal,
word for word, commenting at length and with much pride on

her insight into that gentleman's perfidious character, and equally that of the disgraced Reverend Julius Broughton. Henry felt wrung out and decidedly irritable. And so groaned inwardly when Mrs Stamford accosted him in the hall, obviously lying in wait for his return. He had had enough of managing females to last a lifetime.

'I need to speak with you, my lord.' She saw his reaction, his inclination to retreat, and knew that he would make an excuse. She stretched out a hand to touch his sleeve in unexpected intimacy, but her words were all formality. 'Urgently, my lord. Or I would not trouble you.'

'Very well, ma'am.' They climbed the stairs, Henry wishing that he were anywhere but here, and he bowed the lady into the small parlour where a fire had been lit for his return.

She looked at him as he walked past her into the room, shocked by the weariness that he could not hide.

'I think I will ring for some tea. You look tired, my lord.'

'If you wish.' He would have much preferred a brandy, but it did not really matter. Nothing seemed to matter when he had so deliberately and callously broken Eleanor's heart and refused to recognise his own son. Nothing else mattered at all in comparison.

Mrs Stamford busied herself ringing the bell and informed Marcle of their needs. Then settled herself into a chair. Henry stood with his back to the fire, determined to hear her out and make his escape as quickly as possible.

'I have a confession to make, my lord.'

Not another! He stifled a sigh and raised his brows in polite enquiry.

As he cast a glance down at her, his attention was caught for the first time by her appearance. She was uncomfortable in his presence, not at ease. A deep line was engraved between her brows and she worried at her bottom lip with her teeth. She anticipated this conversation with even less pleasure than did he. A sharp suspicion crossed his mind.

'Did Eleanor send you?' he asked bluntly.

'Eleanor? No!' He imagined that she shuddered as a cold chill swept her skin. 'Eleanor knows nothing of this.'

'So. Tell me of this *urgent* matter, ma'am, which cannot possibly wait until tomorrow.'

They fell silent as a footman entered and positioned the tea tray on a small table to Mrs Stamford's right, placing the tea caddy at her left.

'Eleanor is very unhappy,' Mrs Stamford stated when they were once more alone, as if she had learned her words during the long wait through the afternoon. 'So are you, my lord, if I may presume to comment.' Lord Henry's gaze sharpened, but he forbore to reply. She had, it appeared, more sensitivity than he had previously given her credit for. 'I do not know the reason.' She held up her hand as she sensed his interruption. 'I know. It is not my concern. But I should tell you what I did. I think that I must. One moment, my lord.'

She opened the silken strings of her reticule and searched its contents, producing eventually four folded sheets. Clearly letters.

'I am not proud of this, but you have given such generous service to my daughter. And there is such unhappiness between you. You deserve to know the truth. And I think it would be wrong if this event from the past should cause further dissension between yourself and Eleanor. I think it casts a long shadow.' She wet her lips with the tip of her tongue. 'I think these speak for themselves, my lord.'

She held them out.

He took them without a word, turned them in his hands. He knew what they were, did not need to read the inscriptions. There were two letters in his bold hand, curled and much travel worn. Two were in Eleanor's writing, as clean and neatly folded as the day they had been written.

'You intercepted them.' It was a statement, not a question. Suddenly everything was very clear, inscribed with diamond brightness, the answer to all his questions and doubts.

'I did. I do not deny it.' Her eyes for the first time made contact with his, a challenge in their depths, daring him to condemn her, much as her daughter had done over the paternity of her child. 'I would probably do it again tomorrow in the same circumstances. Any mother would. I did not want Eleanor to commit herself to you—a younger son—and a risky life in the colonies. She was so young and I knew so little of you…so I intercepted the letters. Eleanor's never left the house. It was so simple—and Eleanor was so trustingly naïve. It was an easy matter to bribe her maid into handing them over. And equally simple to prevent yours from ever falling into Eleanor's hands. That was the reason she never joined you when you left the country. She believed that you had never written to her, had forgotten her, or deliberately rejected her.'

'As I believed that she had rejected me.' His voice held a weight of sadness.

'Yes, my lord.'

He turned the letters again in his hands, reading Eleanor's clear inscription of his name. Mrs Stamford awaited his response.

'Did you read them?' he asked finally.

'No.' Mrs Stamford flushed at the implied criticism. 'You might give me credit for some honour in my dealings with my daughter.'

'Why should I? You have no idea how much grief and pain you caused by your actions. Nor the present repercussions from your ill-judged decision.'

'Perhaps not.'

'Were you not aware of how much unhappiness you caused your daughter? How could you do it to her?'

'I knew. But I believed that she would forget.' Mrs Stamford raised her shoulders in elegant dismissal of her fault. 'Eleanor would soon meet someone else who would prove to be a respectable husband.'

'I blamed her, you know. And she blamed me. It has caused so much bitterness between us. How could you justify that to yourself, if you loved her?' Mrs Stamford had the grace to flinch from Lord Henry's accusation, but she stood her ground.

'A parent will do anything for her child.' Mrs Stamford rose to her feet to face him, as fierce as a vixen defending her young. 'I thought that she would be happier making a more stable marriage here. Settling in a comfortable house with husband and children. Not so far away—so that I could see her and enjoy her happiness and that of my grandchildren. She is all I have and I want only the best for her. But I do not expect you to understand, of course.'

But perhaps he did after the revelations of the past days, he thought. Acquiring a son gave a man a different angle on life. He would never have the right to enjoy his son's happiness other than from a distance and without recognition. Too many obstacles stood in the way. For the first time he understood in part Mrs Stamford's dedication to Eleanor's happiness.

'One thing.' He looked up from the letters, still folded in his hands, with a keen glance. 'When I had gone, did you throw Eleanor into Thomas's path?'

'No, I did not.' Mrs Stamford folded her lips in some indignation. 'I am no fool, my lord. I wanted her to marry well. She was a beautiful débutante, but not even I could look as high as a Marquis for her. It was a great surprise when he offered for her.'

'Had she known Thomas long?'

'No. A mere matter of weeks. What does that matter?'

It all fit together in his mind, with a sharp click of certainty, the final pieces in the puzzle. Thomas had indeed rescued Eleanor, a victim of his own thoughtlessness and her mother's meddling. His heart went out to Eleanor, who had been unaware of the forces that had worked so successfully against their union.

'It does not matter at all,' he now admitted. 'I am grateful for your telling me. And returning these.'

'I regret the pain I caused. She was devastated when she thought you had left her. And she is distraught now'

'Yes. I imagine.'

'I know not what will ease her pain. Will you tell her of the letters? Of my part in it?'

'I must.'

'She is at Lady Painscastle's now.' Mrs Stamford walked to the door, the tea forgotten, her errand complete. 'Judith is holding an *at home*. Eleanor will not be back until late. I doubt that she will choose to stay the night—not with the child here.'

'Then I must wait.'

'I am very sorry, my lord.' Mrs Stamford waited for a reply, but there was none, Lord Henry's concentration being fixed on the letters, the answer to all his uncertainties, held tightly in his hands.

Eleanor returned at a late hour from the Painscastles' town house. Word had begun to spread, discussing with intense enjoyment the Baxendale débâcle in every salacious detail. Eleanor had known as soon as she had been bowed into the room by Judith's butler, aware of the lightening of the atmosphere. Whispering, yes, but no hostile glances. Discreet asides behind fashionable fans, but no one thought to snub her. Judith had hugged her in delight, demanding a thorough gossip when time and opportunity allowed. Lady Beatrice had descended on her in full sail of mulberry silk and old lace, and had kissed her cheek. *So pleased, dearest Nell! And so brave of you to face all the past unpleasantness with such composure and assurance.* Eleanor had felt a sudden urge to shriek her fears and hurt to the room at large. How shocked they would be! But of course she did not, playing the role assigned to her of gracious lady of impeccable lineage and connections. She was back in the fold, after all. Accepted as Marchioness of Burford. Welcomed by the *ton* as one of their own as if her integrity had never been questioned, never been in doubt.

She knew that she should be rejoicing.

She returned to Park Lane, exhausted after her emotional day. By now her righteous fury had calmed to leave her aware only of the wretched emptiness that had assailed her since Hal had stalked from her presence, having accused her of disloyalty and trickery and malicious deceit. Nothing could fill the hollowness, just as nothing could prevent his words from circling over and over again in her brain. A headache lurked behind her eyes. She looked in on the baby, who slept in innocent ignorance of the impossible rift between his parents, then rang for her maid to help her disrobe. She was in process of stripping off a pair of elbow-length lavender kid evening gloves when a light knock was followed immediately by Lord Henry's entrance without further ceremony into her bedchamber.

Maid and mistress both looked up in amazement at the lack

of ceremony. Eleanor's anger found reason for instant and tumultuous rebirth. To be accosted in her own bedchamber! Whatever he had to say, she did not wish to hear it! She tightened her lips, but such sentiments were vividly expressed on her lovely face and in the dignified lift of her head—if her visitor had been in any way sensitive to appearance and atmosphere. Lord Henry simply ignored the accusing stares, wasted no words of greeting. He had been waiting far too long.

'I need a word with your mistress. Meg, is not it? If you would leave us.'

'I am tired, my lord. Can it not wait until tomorrow?' Eleanor was anything but accommodating.

'No.' Neither was he.

'Thank you, Meg. You may go to bed.' Eleanor bowed to a stronger force. 'I will undress myself.' Meg curtsied, a nervous glance at his lordship, and left.

'You should not be here.' Eleanor smoothed the gloves and placed them carefully in a drawer, relieved to have something to do with her hands.

'Do you wish me to leave?'

'Yes.' She would not look at him, but gave her attention to folding a spangled gauze stole with long fringes.

'This is the only place where I can be sure of your undivided attention—if you will put away that damned stole!' The frustration of the long wait surfaced, to be ruthlessly suppressed. Now was not the time for show of temper. This was going to be just as difficult as he had expected.

'I cannot think what you have to say to me, my lord. You have already destroyed my character and my morals. I think that is enough! I would be grateful if you would leave my room—now, my lord.'

Eleanor turned her back to sit down at her dressing table, raising her hands to remove her necklace.

Henry strode across the room to stand behind her, setting his teeth against her rigid formality. But, of course, he deserved no less. He deserved that she slam the door in his face!

Eleanor's hands froze in mid-air at his sudden proximity, at the stern set of his features, but she gave no quarter. There was not one spark of encouragement in her severe expression, brows simply raised in frigid enquiry.

'I will play lady's maid, if you will allow, my lady.' He was in control again, equally formal if that was her game, and bent with clever fingers to discover and release the gold catch on the string of sapphires. 'Not the diamonds, I see.'

'No.'

He laid the gems on the dressing table. Gently removed a pair of sapphire drops from her ear lobes to join them. Then, as she continued to sit, in frozen immobility, began to remove the clips from her hair until it tumbled in a profusion of curls and waves to her shoulders.

He resisted the urge to touch it, lowering his hands.

She wished that he had not resisted—but would not admit it, to him or herself.

'I do not need your help.'

His eyes connected with hers in the mirror. What she read there made her heart turn over in her breast, her throat tighten. Regret, certainly. A depth of self-disgust for his previous treatment of her, that too. But also lust. Desire. A fierce and burning passion that threatened to sweep away his careful command of words and actions.

But it did not.

'Turn around, Nell.' His voice was gentle. He took a step back from her, allowing her some space.

She watched him in the candle-lit reflection, considered refusing—but feared the result if she did. She would turn to face him as he asked, but did not have to listen or respond or cooperate. She did not have to listen to her senses that whispered intoxicating words of love for this man, that spilled jewels of heat and longing through her blood.

So she turned on the stool, hands folded on her lap, chin raised, her eyes pure ice, mouth set and unsmiling. No—she would not make this easy for him. The pain was still too sharp to be set aside. She doubted that it would ever be healed.

'What do you want, Hal? We have nothing more between us

that needs to be said. Your views of me were made perfectly clear yesterday. Nothing has changed that I am aware.'

'Nothing is clear between us, Nell.'

She would have risen to her feet, but he put out a hand, the lightest of touches on her arm, to stop her.

'Eleanor…'

'I don't want to know.'

'I know. And I can hardly blame you, can I? But will you at least hear me out? There is so little time left before I leave.'

There was no change in her expression. She was astounded at her ability to dissemble, to hide her thoughts. He was left uncertain and perhaps for the first time in his life a little afraid of a woman's response to him.

'If you must.' She shrugged a little, pleased with the result, as if it were of no consequence at all.

Taking one of the riskiest gambles of his life, Hal bent to lift Eleanor's hands from her lap, holding tight when she would have pulled away. And startled her when he sank to one knee before her.

'No!' she gasped.

'Yes! I must. What I said to you yesterday was unforgivable. I would give the whole world to retract those words, but I cannot.' For the first time in their relationship, she sensed his lack of confidence where she was concerned. 'This may seem overly dramatic, but it is the only way I can think of to gain your attention, other than throwing myself under the wheels of a passing cab.' There was no humour in his face, none of the arrogant assurance that the world might see. 'My words must always lie between us, to my intense regret. I know that I don't deserve your forgiveness, but must beg it none the less.'

'Please…' She tried again to pull her hands from his clasp. And failed.

'Will you at least listen? That's all I ask. Then I will leave you and embarrass you no longer.'

He waited, dark head bent, then looked up as she was silent. A little nod of the head was all the encouragement he got. He lifted her fingers to his lips. They were cold against her skin, she noticed, cold as ice.

'I accused you of so many things. I don't wish to repeat them. It shames me to think of what I allowed myself to say. I must have been out of my mind to even consider such things.' His hands tightened on hers, unaware of the strength of the pressure as he remembered his bitter accusations with undiluted horror. 'I know that Tom is mine. I know that Thomas married you in full knowledge, to save your reputation and cherish the child within the family. I know that you were innocent in all your dealings with him, that to trick or to manipulate is not within your nature. I also know, beyond doubt, that you did not reject me in favour of my brother's title and wealth. I was so wrong.' He sighed a little. Forgiveness seemed an impossibility.

'But why, Hal? Why did you do it? Why did you say all those dreadful things? I had surely given you no cause for such suspicions.' Eleanor frowned, mouth still set in an uncompromising line, but at least she was listening.

'So many reasons. None of them good. The worst is that…I allowed Baxendale to colour my view of…of events. He said that you had trapped Thomas by claiming to carry his child. And then when you told me…'

'I see.'

'No. I don't think you do. My reactions were appallingly, dishonourably self-interested. There is no excuse. I did not want the title. Or the weight of responsibility of the family estates. My initial response was to reject them. So I accused you of setting a trap to bind me to you and the inheritance. And by doing so harmed beyond repair the one love of my life.'

'So rather than be Marquis of Burford, you accused me of dishonour.' She would not let herself think of his last remarkable statement. But she kept it close, in her heart.

'Yes.'

'Oh, Hal! How could you? How did such divisions come between us?'

'Nell… Can you find it in your heart to forgive me?' As he felt a trembling in her fingers, he decided to put it to the test, to lighten the painful tension that held them so relentlessly apart.

'I would not wish to kneel at your feet all night, but will do so if it will give me half a chance.'

The resulting half laugh, half sob, gave him the merest touch of hope.

'Can you not give me the smallest crumb of comfort?'

'You do not deserve any!'

'I know it.' He was instantly sober again, but the painful weight in his chest, which had tortured him and compromised his self-control since their bitter quarrel, loosened a little. 'Anything that you say to me will not be any worse than the words I have used against myself. Yet I would ask that you have mercy. To know your hatred and contempt is unbearable.'

She made him wait a little longer. Not out of wilful cruelty, but because she needed to know her own feelings before she laid bare her soul. But she would do it. The time was past for hiding thoughts and feelings and she could bear no more secrets. There had been enough in past weeks to last a lifetime.

'Hal…I love you so much. Nothing will change that.' His eyes snapped to hers, not expecting such generosity, hardly able to believe it. He held his breath as she continued. 'How can I not forgive you? I swore that I would not. That if I had to suffer, so would you.' She laughed, a little sadly. 'But I love you and need to forgive you. I should have been more open with you… I accused you of rejecting me and your son…'

'No, Eleanor. You must not take any of the blame here for my irresponsibility towards you. My shoulders are broad enough to take the weight, as they should.'

She stood then, pulling him to stand with her. She did not let go of his hands, as if they were her only link with the reality of the moment.

'What now?' she asked, unable to see the future.

'You should look at these.' He released her hands, reluctantly, to take the slim bundle of letters from his inner pocket and handed them to her. With one accord, they moved to sit on the day bed in the window embrasure.

'What on earth…?' She turned the pages over, much as he had done earlier that afternoon. She needed no telling what they were.

'Can I guess where these came from?'

'I think you might.'

'My mother. I did wonder…but never really believed that she would do something so deceitful and wounding. Something that would hurt me so. She would, of course, if she believed it to be in my own best interests.'

'Yes. She did, with the willing conspiracy of your maid who thought you needed to be protected from my unprincipled schemes to snatch you from the country.'

'How did they come into your possession?'

'Your mother gave them to me. A fit of guilt. I think she felt that I had earned the truth after my efforts on your behalf. And because I had not seduced you and jeopardised your reputation when you were under my roof, under my protection.' He watched the immediate flush of colour in Eleanor's cheeks. 'She wanted to sever any connection between us, to see you comfortably established in England where she could take enjoyment from your success and your children. America was too far away for her to contemplate.'

'Oh, Hal. So much pain.' Eleanor pressed the letters between her palms.

The urge to draw her close in his arms was strong, but he could not. Not until the air between them was cleared. Not until he had fully understood the depth of her pain.

'Tell me about it, Nell. Tell me what happened when I left you.'

'You can guess, I am sure. You knew Thomas so well.' A sad smile tugged at the corners of her mouth. 'I came to Faringdon House. I had heard no word of you for days, weeks almost. And I knew by then that I carried your child. I was desperately unhappy…'

'I am so sorry, Nell. How supremely selfish I was, how arrogant, to take advantage of you as I did. I had the experience to know better when you did not.'

She shook her head but continued, the memories of those difficult days flooding back. He saw the lines of strain, the tightening of the muscles in her jaw, and knew that she would not tell him the full story of her sense of betrayal. 'I plucked up the courage to call at Faringdon House. What was I going to ask when I got there? I have no idea. But the butler would have been able to tell me where you were.' She brushed away a stray tear. 'I was not thinking very logically, you understand. When I arrived Thomas was there, in the entrance hall. He invited me in, sat me down in the library, and told me that you had sailed for America. Had been gone for some days. I cried. He dried my tears and…and before I realised, I found that I was telling him everything. I was so afraid. I didn't know where to turn. I did not dare tell Mama… And Thomas was so…approachable.'

'I know it. So Thomas offered you marriage.'

'Yes. He cared for me and did all he could to make me comfortable—for my sake and for yours. We had not heard from you—and he did not want scandal to touch either of us, or the child.'

'He would. Nell—I am so sorry that I accused you of wanting him before me—for his consequence only.'

'Oh, no. Thomas was so kind, so generous. He had no obligation to rescue me from my own stupidity.' Her innocent comment, unintentional in its power, made him flush, a twist of a knife in his heart. 'I told him everything. It was such a relief. I had no idea that he would… I refused his offer at first, but he persisted. And then I felt that I had no choice…I had the child to consider.'

'Can I ask one thing?'

'Of course.'

'Were you happy together?'

'Yes. He was the most caring of men. We were the best of friends.'

'I think you married the best of the Faringdons!'

'He loved Tom, you know. For himself as well as because he was yours.' In the resulting silence she stretched out her hand and touched Henry's cheek, sensing his heartache. 'He left something for you.'

She rose to her feet, moved to the drawer and extracted the letter, handing it to Hal. She stood before him as he read the inscription.

'Do you know its contents?'

'No. It is for you, if I deemed it necessary.'

He broke the seal and smoothed open the single sheet. It was very brief and typical of his brother.

Hal—
If Nell has given this to you, there must be a good reason for it. The child is yours. You have only to look at him to see it. He is a delight and I have looked to him as to my own. As I know you would do if our situation were reversed. Nell had been everything I could desire in a wife. It was your loss but I cannot regret it.
Ask her about the boy's name.
Thomas

Hal looked up to where Eleanor still waited, eyes sparkling with unshed tears and compassion, his own narrowed in anguish.

'Tell me about the child's name,' he asked quietly.

'Henry Thomas, of course.'

'Of course. I should have known that he would think of that.'

He laid the letter carefully on the seat and stood. He did not touch her now.

'You said that you loved me. Would you accept my own avowal of love in return? Despite all I have said and done, deliberately or otherwise. Despite the hurt I have caused you.'

'Yes.' Her eyes were wide and clear, allowing him to read every thought.

'You make it sound so easy.'

'I think it is—if we can put aside the past and trust each other.'

'Ah, Nell. I don't deserve such love. And the future for us is not a simple matter at all…'

'I didn't think you would ever love me again.'

'I have never stopped loving you.'

As one, they moved together, drawn by invisible bonds. Placing her hands, palms flat, against his chest, Eleanor marvelled at the strength of Hal's heartbeat, a heightened pulse that echoed her own. When she smiled at him, he accepted the final loving benediction from her and framed her face in his hands, pushing back the tendrils of hair that he had loosed, caressing her temples and fine cheek bones with gentle thumbs.

'You are so beautiful. Your face would torment me in dreams, the violet depths of your eyes would enclose me. I would wake, longing to wind my fingers into your hair, holding you so that I could not possibly lose you again. How could any man not love you?'

'It only matters that *you* do.'

'I do. I do.' For a long moment he rested his forehead against hers, to savour her closeness. Then, sure of his ground, he slid his hands down the graceful column of her throat to her shoulders, to clasp and pull her close, to allow his lips to touch hers. Gently, tenderly, as if she might resist such intimacy. but her lips were warm, soft and responsive under his. And he knew that they would open and welcome his invasion with little enticement from him.

He pulled back a little on hearing a soft murmur in her throat, but could not mistake the flush of pleasure in her cheeks, the glow in her eyes.

'Kiss me, Hal,' she whispered. 'Show me that you love me.'

'If you will kiss me, my lovely Nell. And show me that I am forgiven.'

She stepped into his arms, raising hers to lock behind his head, drawing him close. 'I love you.' She murmured the words against his lips. It was the flame to light the fire, the candle to singe the moth, and he needed no further invitation to show her with his body where words seemed so inadequate. He dragged her close, even closer, angling his head to fit his mouth more perfectly with hers and her lips opened to allow him to stroke and caress, claim her breath, swallow her shivers of delight. It was as if they had never been parted, never separated by the terrible rift of time and space and malicious intervention. Her body moulded to his, breast to breast, thigh to thigh, a fusing of flesh as their minds joined in demand and counter-demand. As he had dreamed, Hal wound one hand into her luxuriant curls and held her in his power—aware of nothing but her essential appeal to his senses, her total surrender. Eleanor felt his power and gloried in it, in his firm muscled flesh, in the hard length of his body.

When he finally released her, they stood, shaken by the emotion that thundered through their blood, their breathing laboured and uneven. Her eyes were blurred, swamped with love, lips soft and parted. He could not take his gaze from her.

'I love you, Eleanor.'

'And I, you.'

When Eleanor smiled up at him, her eyes shining with such joy and hope, Hal battled against his doubts and fears to draw her close again, unable to resist the overwhelming allure of the beautiful woman in his arms. He would kiss and hold her, convince her of his love for her, if only for a little time. She must not be left in any doubt, when he finally left her, that she meant more to him than life itself.

Eventually he put her from him, when the anguish in his heart grew too great to push aside.

'Nell. You are my beloved—my heart and soul.' His words were all that she had ever wished to hear, but the lines of his face were taut and stark. The intense grey depths of his eyes, cold and bleak, did not speak of love but fear.

'What is it, Hal?' She touched his face, the crisp outline of his lips, fingers trembling with the lingering aftermath of passion and with equal fear of the unknown.

'I said that nothing was simple between us.'

'I remember. But you love me. And you know that I love you.' She frowned a little as she tried to envisage the problem.

'Yes. And yes.'

'Tell me then. That I may understand.'

He held her again, resting his cheek against her soft hair. Arms enfolding strongly around her, his fingers spread wide to press her close. As if their proximity would take away the pain which he knew he must inflict.

'I cannot publicly acknowledge Tom as my son.' The statement was blunt, the tone flat, without inflection, not open to disagreement. 'I must not, whatever the temptation.'

'Why not? If—'

He withdrew a little from her, placed his fingers gently over her lips, desperately aware of the hurt in her eyes, but unable to prevent it, not if decency and principle had any meaning for him. Nor, God help him, the weight of the law.

'Think about it, Nell. Once, in despair, you told me that if Baxendale's claim was upheld before the law, they would brand you a whore and your child a bastard. I remember your choice of such brutal words and so should you.'

'Yes. Oh…' Enlightenment came to her, distressing in its clarity, a bright sword edge in her heart.

'If I acknowledge Tom as my son, will it not do the same as you feared? It will destroy your reputation as surely as any action on Baxendale's part, if I acknowledge that your son is mine, conceived out of wedlock. And it will make my brother a cuckold. It will proclaim to the world that you were my mistress and that my son was foisted on my brother, with or without his knowledge. Can you not imagine the consequences of such an admission from my lips? It is too terrible to be contemplated.'

'Hal!'

'I cannot do it, Nell—to Thomas or to you. I have too much honour to bring disgrace to you and to my family name.'

'You would put honour before love?' She might ask the question, but she already knew the answer, as strongly and assuredly as she knew Hal.

'You do not know what you ask.' Suddenly releasing her, he walked away so that she might not see the dilemma which tore him apart. 'I cannot risk your social and very public degradation. It is too much to ask.'

'Then let us come with you to New York.' Her mind sought furiously, feverishly, for some alternative to the living death that he proposed. 'No one will know. If you do not wish to marry me, I can accept that, but we could be together.'

'No. You must not say such a thing.' He regretted his harsh tones and gentled his voice, explaining the obvious but with little assurance that she would accept his reasoning. 'I have nothing to offer you, Nell. A new company that might fail as easily as succeed, with all my financial resources tied up in it. I have some responsibilities to my partner. I live in rented rooms. Law and order is still sketchy. And life is nothing if not dangerous and full of risks. Even the voyage has its dangers.' He walked back to her, to stand beside her again, sensing her resistance. 'It is not the life I would give you, darling Nell.'

'So we stay here—Tom and I—and you return to New York.' Her heart was cold. Her voice was cold.

'Yes. Your life is safe here. Tom will grow and learn, inherit the title and, when he reaches his majority, he will take on the Faringdon estates. Nick will be an excellent trustee, of course. You will live in style and comfort as befits your rank—and an untarnished reputation. That is what I would want for you.'

'You offered me marriage once—at the Red Lion in Whitchurch,' Eleanor reminded him, fighting against the wave of despair that threatened to engulf her. 'When I had nothing but a ruined name and an illegitimate child.'

'I know. I was wrong to do so—but allowed my heart to rule. You had nothing to lose then, Nell. Now you have everything to lose.'

'I would give up everything—'

'Nell.' He tilted her face up to his with gentle fingers. 'Listen to me, Nell. It is not simply a matter of my own wishes. We cannot marry, can never do so.' The words were forced from him. 'The church condemns it. You are my brother's widow. And unless there are grounds for an annulment of your marriage to Thomas, on the grounds of non-consummation…?'

She shook her head as she took his meaning. 'No. There are no grounds for annulment.' Bright colour flared in her cheeks. 'Thomas and I were truly man and wife. He…he came to my bed…'

'That is as it should be, my dearest one.' He stroked her cheek, the lightest of touches. 'Of course Thomas would want you. What man of flesh and blood could not?' Hal's smile was infinitely understanding. 'But it means that we cannot marry. My love. My life.'

'Would anyone have to know? If I came with you to New York—'

'Eleanor, listen to me.' His voice was gentle, but the words were cold and would brook no dissent. They lodged in Nell's chest with an unbearable weight. 'Yes, I could marry you. We could hide the true facts, find a minister who would carry out the ceremony. But what then would life be for us? For you? Flinching at every shadow, wary of every stranger who might know of our past and from either malice or outrage drag our affairs before the law. Our marriage could be declared illegal by anyone who discovered the truth and found a reason to stand in public and declare it void. Do you wish to live the rest of your life in fear that we shall be discovered? With all the resulting horrors of public speculation and condemnation? I will not tie you into a relationship that could bring you such shame and humiliation. Or even, quite simply, cause you to regret that you had ever chosen to walk that path with me.'

'I do not want to live the rest of my life without you.' She knew that she had lost the battle, but still could not let it go. 'I could never regret it.'

'I will not do it. I will not risk the possibility of more scandal attached to your name—or the children that we would have together.'

Henry took her hand, to link Eleanor's fingers with his own, as if it might force her to accept the weight of his argument. But she did not, would not. Not even in the face of such a final and irreversible judgement. The tender symbolism held no meaning for her.

'So my loss will be Rosalind's gain.' Eleanor could not disguise the bitterness. Indeed, she did not even try. Hal drew in a sharp breath at the lethal weapon that she had chosen to use against him in her distress. She had chosen well.

'Don't ever think that.' He lifted their joined hands to his lips. 'You should understand about Rosalind. We have an understanding. She gave me companionship, friendship, a human touch when I was alone and needed it. She is under no illusions. I never lied to her about my feelings for her, nor she to me. She knew that my heart was already given.'

'I see.'

'You have nothing to fear from Rosalind. But I cannot take you with me.'

'Hal…' How could she persuade him? She feared that his will would withstand any argument of hers. 'I would live with you in a gutter, with or without the blessing of the church, if I loved you enough.'

'And you do, of course.' He smiled, not doubting her for a moment.

'Yes.'

'But I will not ask it of you. It is too big a sacrifice for any man of principle to ask the woman he loves.' The smile vanished, leaving his face severe. 'It is enough to know that you love me. It has to be enough.'

She could not push him further. The set of his mouth and the sharpness of his cheekbones, where skin was tightly stretched, warned her that it would do no good. Her heart was banded with iron, unyielding and painful, her breathing difficult. Would it be like this for ever? Was there nothing she could salvage for them both from this morass of loss and despair? Perhaps…

'Will you do one thing?' She curled her fingers more tightly around his, willing him to look at her.

He did so and could refuse her nothing. 'If it is in my power.'

'If I have to live out the rest of my life without you, will you give me this one night together?'

'Nell…' For a moment he turned his face away from her in an intensity of emotion. 'How hard you make our parting.' Then turned to hold her eyes with his own, held fast by the passion of dew-drenched violets. 'Do you know what it is that you ask of me?'

'Yes,' she whispered. She would not back down from this one promise of shared glory. 'I can be thoroughly selfish—and will be if you would divide us asunder.'

Hal hesitated, acknowledging her strength of purpose. 'There could be consequences, as we know too well. Are you willing to accept that?'

Her amethyst gaze was implacable. There was no going back, not after offering herself to this man so blatantly, and without even the trace of a blush. 'There could.' She inclined her head in acceptance. 'I will face them if it should be so.'

'How can I resist such an offer. You know it. You are my only weakness.' His smile was a little wry, a little sad and he took a breath. To take her to his bed would make their parting so much more difficult. To know the satin glide of her skin beneath his, her softness moulding to the hard planes of his own body. To feel the intimate heat of her close around him in both possession and submission. It could destroy all his best intentions, unless he exerted his will to the utmost.

But he owed her that much, after all the grief in their past. And he would fulfil his obligation with every muscle and sinew in his body, with grace and finesse. 'Very well, lady. I will give you this one night with all the love and tenderness within me. I will leave you with no doubts about my need for you. I will promise that when we are apart you will remember this night with every waking and sleeping thought. You will know what worship and adoration, of a man for a woman, can be.' He bent to touch her lips with his own in recognition of his promise. 'I will give you this one night of love.'

And he would take it for himself.

So, because he was unable to give her any hope for a future together, Henry gave her the night she asked of him. Regardless of the bitter-sweet pain of separation, which a night of love-making would prolong almost beyond bearing, he could not refuse her. Nor, in all honesty, did he wish it. They would proclaim the glory of their passion and devotion one final time—and exalt in it.

Wrenching despair, soul-searing desolation, both were kept at bay, forbidden to encroach even though they knew that Hal's leaving would come to them as assuredly as the lightening sky of dawn. Such emotions would not be allowed to intrude into their room, into their bed, banished by the supreme quality of exquisite care that he lavished on her through the darkest hours. Love in every touch, in every caress, in every heated kiss. A tender wooing to construct an unbreachable barrier between the lovers and the approach of cruel reality.

Clothing was not permitted to be a hindrance, thus quickly shed. They had completed and overcome a long and hazardous journey through lies, deceit and deception, deliberately placed obstacles. Nothing should now come between the celebration of their mutual desire. Eleanor consented that Henry lift and carry her to the bed where the curtains were drawn back, the covers folded away and the pillows banked in soft invitation. Once there, she opened her arms to take him in, enclosing him to her breast, to imprint the essence of him on her mind and body for ever.

Slowly, thoroughly, Henry made love to her. There was no hurry, no demands on their time except to give and receive a precious gift. As if their lifetime stretched before them where they might sleep and wake together in joyous intimacy every night and morning for the rest of their lives. Eleanor had asked for a memory. Henry set himself to create one, as bright and as mystical as the beams of the moon that illuminated the room for them in its soft light. No candles were required to add to the glamour. Only silvered shadows, soft glimmering highlights on shoulder and thigh, hard-edged curls of hair and turns of hand, the deep velvet of secret, intimate places.

She was a man's dream, a fantasy of enchantment and fascination. Henry could not eat or drink his fill at the banquet offered in her arms. He touched and tasted, all those satin, seductive curves that tempted and beckoned, holding back when her immediate response, slim body arched against him in potent demand, would have driven him too precipitately to immoderate action. He framed her face with his beautiful hands to press gentle kisses on temple, eyes and finally her parted lips as her breathing quickened. Leisurely kisses possessed her, cleverly rousing her nipples to hard desire, tracing the soft hollows at her waist to make her shiver, anointing the tender skin between her thighs, which made her cry out. The taste of her skin, the perfume of her hair were branded into his memory for all time. Gentle but deliberate, he pursued the path that he had set himself, to awaken her senses to delight as he moved his body languorously against and over hers. Until his weight held her in thrall, aware of nothing but her allure as she smiled, a smile that stirred his body and blood as a sorcerer would create and use irresistible powers. Until he drove her to forgetfulness with skilful mouth and experienced fingers so that she shuddered in his arms, the heat becoming too great to withstand.

Eleanor felt the power ripple through her veins, turning her blood to red-hot gold as she stretched her body over his, hair falling on his chest so that he gasped, muscles tightening. She allowed her breasts to brush against the hard planes, delighting in the immediate response of his erection. As he had pleasured her, so she reciprocated with growing confidence and assurance. Her fragrant breath whispered against his skin. Soft lips, allowed to roam at will, dragged him to the very edge of reason. How amazing, she discovered, that she could reduce this powerful man to such weakness, that his body should quiver with such need as he strained hips and thighs against her in a gesture of dominant possession. How miraculous that she could compromise his proud self-control, as he could rouse her to mindless dependence. She stroked and smoothed, familiarising herself with the firm contours of muscle and sinew, lest in the endless years apart she should forget. As if she ever could forget.

She would not allow him to forget her.

No emotion, no passion was permitted to remain unawakened between them as the hours ticked inexorably past.

At last they came together in mutual demand. She opened to him and he slid gently into her, held deep in her tight velvet softness where he belonged. Slowly filling her and claiming her for all time. Eyes locking in pleasure beyond all words, drowning in the depths of love and a need to give and receive. He moved slowly to draw out the glory of it, until nerve-endings sang, blood raced, breath seared in lungs, pulses hammered with demand for release. But he would not. He kept the rhythm slow, hers matching perfectly, thighs clasping his hips, body arched to take him even deeper.

'Love me, Eleanor. Want me,' he murmured against her mouth, his lips a burning brand, breath ragged.

'I love you. I want you.' The stretching of her body beneath him echoed her words. Responding, he thrust deeper yet.

'No one will ever love you as I do.'

'Nor as I love you.'

Until passion grew too great. He waited until she reached the crest, hands tightening on his arms, nails digging crescents into his skin. Until she cried his name. Then thrust to hurl them both from the mountain peak, from where they fell together into hot darkness.

Afterwards she lay in his arms, head resting against his shoulder, but did not sleep. Time was too precious to be wasted without sensation, without awareness. Time enough for oblivion when she was alone. So she sensed his breathing, the steady rise and fall of his chest against her cheek. Absorbed his warmth and strength that wrapped her around to hold her safe. She would remember the splendour of loving and being loved with such intensity, with such unbearable tenderness, and rejoice through the pain of a future alone.

Eleanor wept a little, despite her intention to remain strong. For herself. For Hal. For their inevitable loss. For Thomas, whom she had not been able to love as he had deserved, but who had given her so much in full knowledge of her predicament. She had indeed been blessed. And Hal had given her a son.

Hal caught her tears with his mouth as they tracked down her cheeks into her hair, but said nothing, allowing her the luxury of weeping in his arms. Then, as desire built, he moved to take her again. And again.

Now he whispered words of love. Foolish words and avowals that reduced her to laughter and tears. All the words of love and care that had gone unuttered on the tempestuous and passion-rent night of the Sefton soirée were now given free rein. Whispered mouth against mouth, against silken skin, against scented hair. Every nuance expressed that neither might be left in doubt for all eternity. But no promises were made for the future. No words, no future. And she accepted it with a courage and fortitude beyond his imagining. His love for her was as boundless as the ocean that would soon divide them. As sure as the law that would stand in the way of their union.

Hers for him was as bright and durable as the stars that glittered in the night sky beyond their window.

In that one night of love they celebrated their eternal love—but also set each other free for a future alone. To make separate lives. To exist alone. Without the intimate knowledge of the other's thoughts and desires. Without a familiar touch or caress. The night was both a confirmation of love and a terrible sacrifice.

'I will love you until death, Eleanor.'

'Yes. Until death.'

With daybreak, they would never see each other again.

Chapter Twelve

Eleanor slept late. Exhaustion, mental and physical, had finally laid its irresistible hand on her. Henry had loved her, kissed her, held her, possessed her. Set her ablaze in a night of aching tenderness and overwhelming passion. Sleep had been far from their thoughts. Until they had fallen, deep under its calm surface, replete, at some little time before dawn.

But now she knew that he was gone.

Left London more than two days before he needed to catch the sailing. To lessen the agony and anguish of a drawn-out parting, for them both. He would think of that, of course.

The bed was cold. She ran her hand over the empty space beside her. No colder or emptier than the spaces in her heart. She buried her face in the pillow, breathing deep, to catch the lingering scent of him. How quickly it was gone. How impossibly short the night had been. And now her life stretched before her, impossibly long without him. Only one thought hammered in her mind, beating its message through her blood, through every vein. He loved her, but she must learn to live life without him again.

It drove her to rise from her bed. There, on the dressing table, were the letters where she had left them the previous night. Hers and his, hidden away by her mother all those months whilst she had craved news of him. She would read them one day. But not now. They were not important. She knew what was in Hal's mind and did not need words of two years ago to convince her of his love.

She simply stood in the middle of the room, remembering. A night of such splendour and magnificence. The glory of it still sent shivers over her skin, still tumbled through her veins with the cauterising heat of volcanic lava. She could taste his lips on her own, feel the brush of his hands against her skin, as if he were there with her. Whatever the future would hold, she would never regret this night. He had touched her soul and she knew, beyond doubt, that his heart was hers. It was enough.

It had to be enough.

And she had her son. Their son. To cherish and raise to manhood, as she and his father would wish.

On that thought Eleanor pulled on her robe and made her way to Tom's nursery. He was awake, gurgling with incomprehensible words when he saw her, pulling himself up by the sides of the crib to bounce on urgent feet. Soon he would walk. Soon he would run through the vast rooms at Burford Hall. And Hal would never see.

She lifted him, smoothing down his linen smock, crooning to him as he wriggled and pulled on her loosened hair.

'He has gone. But how he loved us,' she informed the infant in serious tones as if he would understand every word. Tom patted her face, fussing to be set down. 'He would not take us with him. He thought only of the dangers. I wish he had not been quite so honourable…'

She would have walked to the window to look down on the street where sparrows twittered in the cherry tree, but stopped when her attention was caught. The small night stand beside the crib. Beside the night candle.

She smiled then, although the glitter of tears was there if anyone looked closely. He had been here. He had been to say farewell. She closed her hand on the precious items and carried them and the child to the light of the sun streaming through the window.

Henry's gold half-hunter, which had entranced Tom as it repeated and chimed the hours and quarters, lay on her palm. And a seal, which she had never seen before, to be worn as a fob on a chain of gold. The body was amber, glowing in the light with yellow and deep ochre, tiny leaves trapped for all time in its depth. A beautiful object, of some history, beyond price to her. Its setting was chased gold, intricate, delicate, holding the resin securely with elegant claws. And carved into its flat surface was the Faringdon crest. Hal's own seal, left for his son.

'Look, Tom. This is for you.' She held out the seal to Tom, who immediately grasped the golden chain, transferring the links to his mouth.

'He left this for you. And the watch. But I don't expect he thought you would eat it!'

She laughed—and then on a sob, quickly swallowed, pressed her lips to the soft curve of his cheek.

Eleanor made the decision to return to Burford Hall. As she had told Hal, she had had enough of London and the shallowness of polite society to last her for some weeks, if not years. A lifetime even.

She must stop thinking about him! And dreaming. Waking to sense the brush of his fingertips against her cheek. The cool pressure of his lips, heating to an intensity of demand that caused her to shudder with longing. Expecting to see his tall figure every time she entered a room, his smile that illuminated all the dark places on her soul. Devastated when she realised anew that he would never be there. She was alone and must accept it.

The house in Park Lane was hers until she wished to leave. Nick would see to the rent and its eventual termination. She would not go back to Faringdon House yet, even though she believed that the Baxendales had departed for enforced seclusion in Whitchurch. It was all so empty without Hal. Her life was empty…

She must not think about him!

So they were packed, her clothes and all the many necessities for the baby, ready to depart on the following day. The ladies of the household gathered in Henry's morning room at three o'clock for tea and a final parting exchange of news and gossip as Cousin Judith joined them. Mrs Stamford planned to stay on in London for a few days with some distant relatives. Sarah Russell, more relaxed and at ease in her new surroundings, would go with Eleanor. Her guilt had begun to dissipate. She smiled more. Did not feel the need to apologise to Eleanor every day for her brother Edward's sins. Did not feel the need to watch John with an eagle eye every moment of every day. So she would go to Burford Hall and take up residence there. Eleanor had come to like the quiet, gentle girl. She thought she would be glad of her company in the empty hours and days ahead.

Eleanor had deliberately made no mention to her mother of the letters that now rested in a jewel case, replacing the one from Thomas that Hal had taken with him. What use? Nothing of the past could be changed and what could Eleanor possibly say that her mother did not know already? The confiscation of the letters had wrought a bitter rift between the lovers, as was intended, but Eleanor had made her peace with Hal, and he with her. No point in raking over cold ashes.

Mrs Stamford watched her daughter, wondering at her brittle composure, her dry-eyed determination to arrange her future to her own liking with no reference to her mother's opinion. Here was a young woman, chilly and aloof, with none of the softness of the past. Mrs Stamford eyed her askance when Eleanor kept her silence, but for once she did not dare broach the matter of the wayward letters. These days the Marchioness of Burford had a steel-edged maturity, a cold decisiveness, and had drawn a line of privacy over which her mama felt it unwise to cross.

Eleanor had read Hal's letters. And re-read her own naïve pleas for a word from him, a simple recognition that he had not forgotten her. An explanation for why he had sailed without her. She had wept a little. He had not forgotten her. She pressed his words to her heart. Regretted Hal's final decision to the bottom of her soul, and then put the letters away. She knew that he would not write again. Nor would she.

The chatter as the ladies drank tea was light, mostly inconsequential news of their mutual acquaintances. Judith promised to visit Burford Hall in the summer months. Mrs Stamford expressed the opinion that she might take herself to Brighton. Or perhaps to drink the waters in Bath. Sarah expressed her pleasure at the prospect of country life and fresh air. Open spaces for John to run and grow. Eleanor played her part. Yes, she anticipated the slow pace of life at Burford with calm approval. Unaware that her companions were concerned for her overbright eyes and pale cheeks. That she ate little and slept less. Unaware of their urgent conversations about her state of mind and the possible remedy. The only remedy. She would have been horrified if she'd known the depths of their concern, if she had realised that they could read her so well. She had been determined that she would not mope! She would rebuild her life and be perfectly content.

Of course she would.

Hal's departure had been accepted with little comment. He would be missed, of course, but it was no surprise that he had gone. It had always been his intention and his commitment to Faringdon and Bridges could not be overset. Perhaps he had not been expected to leave quite so precipitately, but then Hal was always a man of action and impulse. He had said his farewells to Nicholas and that was that. There was nothing more to discuss. And besides, such a conversation invariably brought a tightness to Eleanor's lips, an added pallor to her face.

As Nick had announced, 'It was always Hal's nightmare that he would ever be called upon to be Marquis of Burford. I wager he is plain Mr Faringdon in Faringdon and Bridges.'

And Eleanor knew that he was right.

'A visitor, my lady.' Marcle entered the room, disturbing the feminine chatter.

'Who is it, Marcle?'

He coughed, a warning. 'Lady Octavia Baxendale, my lady.' The butler's eyes and face remained amazingly bland, given the extent of knowledge below stairs. 'She is alone and requests a moment of your time.'

'Octavia!' Startled, Eleanor looked around the circle of faces. She was the last person who might be expected to pay a formal visit to Park Lane. 'I thought she had left London. They are no longer at Faringdon House, I know.'

'What on earth can that woman want?' Mrs Stamford was immediately hostile. 'I would have expected the lady and her despicable husband to have slunk back to the country. Will you indeed see her, dear Eleanor? I don't advise it. You should say that you are not receiving visitors—she will undoubtedly understand the snub.'

'Yes. I will see her.' Octavia's visit was intriguing and there was nothing to fear from it. 'Alone, I think. Would you perhaps give me a little time?'

The ladies withdrew to a parlour, reluctantly, wishing they could do something so lacking in gentility as to listen at the door.

Marcle, all cold arrogance and affronted dignity for the past treatment of his mistress, showed Lady Baxendale into the morning room, offering her the smallest of bows. Eleanor stood beside the fireplace, waiting with interest. How would the young woman react? What on earth was it that she wished to say? Eleanor had no idea.

'Lady Baxendale, my lady.' Marcle withdrew, as reluctant as the ladies in the parlour.

'Forgive me for encroaching on your time, my lady. You are very kind and...very kind to see me.'

Octavia was just as Eleanor remembered her at their last meeting in the garden of Grosvenor Square. Calm, placid, apparently unmoved by the unusual circumstances of this visit, showing neither embarrassment nor undue emotion of any description. She was carefully groomed, her fair hair in smooth, well-ordered ringlets, her dress fashionable—no longer black but in a youthful shade of eau-de-nil, her straw bonnet with feathered trim becoming, her gloved hands clasped lightly on the handle of her parasol. Her blue eyes gazed at her hostess with a strange guileless innocence, brow smooth, lips relaxed. She could pass for any young woman of respectable birth and independent means. Not one who had been integral to a dangerous game of fraud and deceit.

'I am at a loss to know why you should be here.' Eleanor broke the silence that had descended on Marcle's departure. She remained standing and did not immediately invite Octavia to sit.

'No. Of course you would wonder. I could hardly be welcome in your home.' Octavia's voice was light and pleasant, her expression accommodating. They might have been discussing the fashions of the day.

Eleanor mentally shrugged. There was no understanding this young woman who could stand before her with such apparent lack of awareness of the hurt she had wittingly caused. 'Please sit.' She gestured to the sofa.

Octavia did so, supremely composed, laying aside her parasol and removing her gloves with calm intent. She folded her hands comfortably in her lap and looked once more at her hostess.

'We will leave London tomorrow for Whitchurch. Edward does not know I am here. He would not be pleased.' A tiny frown creased her smooth brow. She looked, Eleanor thought, ridiculously young, little different, she imagined, from the débutante who had made her curtsy four years ago and caught Thomas's passing interest.

'I had to come,' she continued. 'I have tried to see Sarah, but she would not.'

'You cannot blame her.'

'No. I think that we did not deal well with her. Perhaps some time in the future…'

'I don't know. She will stay with me for the present, at Burford Hall.'

'Yes. I liked Burford Hall—I remember thinking how pleasant it would be to live there when I first visited you.' Such an ingenuous comment almost made Eleanor smile. 'I came here to say that I am sorry. I caused you much pain. And I remember Thomas with much fondness. It was wrong of me, perhaps, to pretend that he was less than honourable.' For the first time Eleanor caught a flash of discomfort on the delicate features.

'It was. Why did you do it? Why did you go along with such an outrageous charade? It could have worked, of course. But would you have been content, happy knowing that you had stolen what was not yours to take?'

'No. I don't think so.' Lady Baxendale appeared to give it some thought.

'So why?'

'It was Edward's decision. His plan.' The lady lifted her hands, then allowed them to drop back into her lap, as if her answer explained everything.

'But if you were uneasy with the lies and deceit, why did you not refuse?' Eleanor frowned her lack of understanding. 'I find it impossible to believe that you could be so…so accepting.'

'It is very simple, my lady. I love Edward. And I will do what he asks. It has always been so. I have known him all my life, you see.'

'And what will you do now?'

'Go back to Whitchurch, of course. It is my home. It will not be unpleasant to go back.' Octavia's reply was immediate and accepting of her changed circumstances, accompanied by the slightest of shrugs. 'It is Edward's decision. And I do not think that we will be made welcome in London when the truth is known. But Edward will take care of me, whatever the future might hold.'

With such an explanation, there was nothing more for Eleanor to say, nothing more for Octavia to add.

On that acknowledgement, Octavia stood. 'I have outstayed my welcome. I cannot expect forgiveness from you. Edward would say that I should not even offer my regrets. But I felt it right.'

'I admire your sense of justice. Your recognition that your actions were the cause of great harm and sorrow.' Eleanor's tone was a little dry as she too rose to follow her guest to the door.

'Oh, no.' Octavia admitted. 'I am sorry that I hurt you—but I would do the same again tomorrow if Edward asked it of me.'

She turned at the door, replacing her gloves, drawing them over her wrists with neat precision. 'I know that you will condemn me for my actions. But it seems to me that when your heart is engaged, then nothing else in life seems as important.' She gave another elegant little shrug, which sat quaintly on her young shoulders. 'Edward is everything to me. I would follow him to the ends of the earth if he asked it of me. It is not an excuse, my lady, just a fact. And I thought that you should know.' She dipped the slightest curtsy with impeccable grace. 'I doubt that we shall meet again. Good afternoon, my lady.'

Octavia Baxendale opened the door and left the room, closing it quietly behind her.

Eleanor found herself staring at the closed door, an arrested expression on her face.

'What did she say? What did she want? Was she indeed repentant for all the lies she told and all the misery she caused?'

Octavia had no sooner stepped out of the front door, escorted by a still disapproving Marcle, than the ladies quitted the parlour to return to the morning room, questions tumbling from their lips. To find Eleanor standing as Octavia had left her, eyes a little glazed, rigid tension in the set of her shoulders.

'What did she say?' Eleanor repeated, her thoughts clearly elsewhere. 'That she loved Edward more than anything in her life, had always done so. That she would follow him to the ends of the earth if he asked it of her.' She repeated the words as if they were engraved on her heart.

Mrs Stamford instantly bristled. 'Had she no shame? Could she not even offer the semblance of a heartfelt apology? Any true remorse? To you and to dear Sarah. When I think how she was prepared to use a child to achieve their fraudulent claims… A colder woman I have never had the misfortune to meet. She would appear to have no sense of right or wrong.'

'No.' Eleanor shook her head, turning away from the little group. 'I think she knows very well. She was sorry to cause hurt, she said. But in her eyes her devotion to Edward excused everything. Even though she knew that what she did was wrong.'

'And I suppose you accepted her explanation, expressing your admiration of her fortitude.' Mrs Stamford stepped up to her daughter to take her arm in a firm hold, exasperation clear on her face. 'And probably sent her on her way with your blessing, if I know you! Eleanor, how could you!'

'No, Mama. Admire Octavia? How could I? But I do understand her—her love for Sir Edward…'

'And I suppose you told her that, too!'

'No. I...I did not... Octavia expressed her regret. Then just explained why she had done it...and left. I don't think she wanted my forgiveness. It did not seem to matter to her. Edward was the only one who...'

To the shock of everyone present, and to her own, Eleanor promptly burst into tears, covering her face with hands that shook. All the pent-up anguish flowed out, all her carefully constructed self-possession, held in place since Henry's departure, was obliterated in a storm of weeping. She sobbed uncontrollably, one thought only in her mind. She could not admire Octavia. But the lady's affirmation of unconditional love for Edward had touched her heart.

Judith tutted in sympathy, rushed to take her in her arms and to lead her to the sofa so recently vacated by the unrepentant Octavia.

'I am so sorry.' Eleanor sniffed as she tried to stem the sobs. 'What must you think of me?' She dabbed ineffectually at her tears with a small scrap of lace-edged linen.

Judith produced her own handkerchief and added it to the flow, making soothing noises and patting her shoulders. Until the sobs gradually abated.

'Nell. Look at me.' Eleanor raised her tear-ravaged face at the masterful demand from a usually easy-going lady. 'This cannot go on! Tell me what you most want in life. Be truthful!' Judith added as she sensed Eleanor begin to withdraw behind her habitual shield. 'What would you wish for, if any wish could be granted at this moment?'

'To be with Hal.' Tears threatened again.

'We thought as much.' Judith looked round to meet the eyes of the other interested ladies, a curl of satisfaction in her smile. 'Now don't cry again!'

'We knew that was the way of it.' Sarah nodded in agreement.

'But he has left me.' Desolation refused to loose its hold on Eleanor.

'Then follow him!' Judith gave her a small shake in frustration. 'Do it. Go to him!'

'I can't. He does not want me.'

'Nell—this is not like you. Where is your strength and

courage?' Judith's vivid Faringdon features, so like Henry's, were afire with determination on behalf of her friend. 'Of course you can. Being a man, he probably does not realise what he wants.'

'Oh, but he does. Indeed he does, Judith. But he must not marry me. The law forbids it…' Sobs threatened her returning composure again.

'There now. Such a little thing!' The Countess of Painscastle snapped her fingers in casual dismissal of the laws of man and God. 'You say that you love Hal. And yet you would live the rest of your life without him? Go to him, Nell. Anything is better than needless loss and regret.'

'What if he refuses to take me with him?'

'Are you going to give him the chance? I had thought better of you!'

Eleanor looked across to where her mother now sat. The lady's features were carefully schooled when she spoke. 'You love him, Eleanor. I should have known… I too did you a great wrong, as you know… And I suppose I would make recompense.' She winced a little at the sheer surprise that Eleanor could not disguise, but continued none the less. 'I don't like it. It breaks my heart to lose you and the child—but I can see in your face that you would be with him.' Mrs Stamford's eyes were bright, but no tear was allowed to escape, no expression of weakness. 'If you want him, Eleanor, then take Judith's advice. I will not put my weight of argument against it.' But she turned her face away.

'Octavia would do it.' Eleanor considered her previous conversation with that lady. *I would follow him to the ends of the earth if he asked it of me.* 'She would allow nothing to come between her and Edward.'

'There now. If she can, insipid creature that she is, so can you. It is settled.' Judith was now triumphant. 'And Sarah will go with you, won't you, Sarah?'

'Sarah?' Eleanor felt as if she were being swept along by a veritable hurricane, all her arguments ignored, all her reasoning disputed and thrown out. And even her mother… She felt momentarily helpless, but the feeling could not compete with the sudden surge of hope in her heart. *I can do it. I can go to him and insist that I go with him!*

'I would go with you.' Sarah's face lit at the prospect and she nodded towards Judith. 'We have talked of it and decided. I believe that Captain Russell might have liked the idea of his son to be brought up in America. I have a mind to see it for myself. Will you let me accompany you?'

'Oh, Sarah!' Eleanor dabbed once more at her eyes.

'Don't anyone say anything else to reduce her to tears again!' Judith instructed with a frown. 'Sarah—go and tell Nick that it is all decided. He will know what to do.'

Eleanor laughed softly. 'I have stopped weeping—I do promise you. What has Nick to do with it?'

'All your possessions are packed,' Judith explained. 'It seemed to us that you will have just enough time to take the coach to Liverpool and catch the sailing. Nick will arrange it, of course.'

'Have you been scheming behind my back?' Eleanor's fine brows rose at the extent of her family's duplicity.

'Yes. But only for your good.' Judith leaned to kiss her on both cheeks. 'It broke my heart to see you so unhappy. Go to Hal and make a new life for both of you, and for Tom.'

They left her alone with Nicholas.

'I see that Judith has been arranging everyone's life, as usual. And yours in particular.' He walked across the room to take her hands in his, lift them to his lips in formal salute, much as Henry was wont to do. The resemblance had never been so strong.

'Do you disapprove, dear Nick?'

'No. How could I?'

'Hal cannot marry me. Any union between us will not be legal.'

'I know it.' There was no condemnation here.

'Even if I take Tom with me? Out of the country?'

'Eleanor.' Nick's voice was gentle as he released her hands. 'He is Hal's son. Am I right?'

Bright colour suffused Eleanor's cheeks, but she would not deny it. 'Yes. Oh, yes. I did not realise…'

'No one gives me any credit for any percipience. You are as bad as Hal!' He huffed out a breath in mock annoyance. But smiled at her confusion and was quick to reassure her. 'I guessed long ago. Watching the two of you, it was not difficult to see the connection between you and Hal. The love that neither of you could deny, no matter how hard you might try. And Tom is as much like Hal as he resembled Thomas.'

'Oh.'

'And Thomas, being the honourable man he was, made you his wife and gave Tom a father because Hal did not know. Am I right?'

'Yes.' She sighed at his quick understanding and his calm acceptance of what many would have condemned out of hand.

'And Hal knows,' Nick continued, 'but fears taking you into hardship and danger.'

'Yes. That is it. You know us very well.'

'So it seems. You will join him in Liverpool and Sarah will accompany you. Or that was Judith's plan.'

'Yes. But what about the estate, Nick?'

'I will run it, with Hoskins dealing with all the legal business. When Tom comes of age, he can claim it. He can choose to live where he wishes.'

'But—'

'Before you ask, it will not be a burdensome task to me. I shall enjoy having a free hand.' Nicholas took her shoulders to shake her, much as Judith had done. 'Look, Nell. Do you love Hal?'

'More than life itself.' She found herself deliberately echoing Octavia's words, a tender smile touching her lips, leaving Nick in no doubt of the power of her love. He was quick to banish the sharp twinge of envy and turn his mind to the practical.

'Then go to him. You will catch the sailing. Everything is arranged.'

He took her hands once more and pressed a light kiss of farewell to her forehead, his smile a little sad at the anticipation of loss for himself.

'Thank you. Dearest Nick. I can never express my gratitude enough.'

'You do not have to…' But he spoke to an empty space. Eleanor had turned on her heel, to collect her son and begin her journey to Hal.

'Poor Hal.' A sudden grin lightened Nick's rather sombre expression as he envisaged the meeting in Liverpool. 'He does not know what fate has in store for him.' Then followed the Marchioness of Burford from the room to arrange the travel documents and the stowing of the luggage in the travelling coach.

Chapter Thirteen

In Liverpool, the days passed slowly for Lord Henry as the *Sea Emerald* made ready to sail. He put up at the Black Bull, a small but comfortable establishment close to the docks, and tried without success to exert some patience. Captain Armstrong and the ship's officers set about the supplying of the vessel with food and water, and the careful stowing away of trade goods, mostly cutlery and domestic hardware from Sheffield and the Black Country. Henry's impatience did not make it happen any quicker, but the ship's company was soon used to his interested presence on board. After all, the experience, invaluable in itself to a man newly engaged in trading contracts, took his mind off other issues. Or at least that was his plan.

He had done the right thing. Of course he had. He must not allow his impeccable reasoning to disintegrate into so much smoke and dust in the dark hours of early morning when sleep evaded him, to torment him over and over again with visions of impossible loss. He had made the only sensible decision. Taken the only honourable course. If he allowed himself to question his logic, he would begin to regret. And then it would be the easiest thing in the world to reject all honour and take the next coach back to London. Or Burford Hall. Or to wherever he could find Eleanor. No, he must not even consider such action. It was desperately important that she be kept safe in a life of cushioned luxury, her reputation untarnished, their child secure to inherit as was his right.

He cursed fluently as he watched the sun rise to herald a new painful dawn.

What had he done? His mind refused to listen to the sensible advice, his senses refused to be swayed by clear, cold argument, his blood refused to run quietly in his veins when he remembered their final night together. Her willing submission to his demands, her unquestioning response to his every caress, of hands and mouth and body.

He had been given his heart's desire. And wilfully turned his back on it. Not coldly, not with calm acceptance of the inevitable. By God, it had torn him apart. And continued to do so with the vicious claws of a predator, laying in wait with diabolical cunning for every moment that he allowed his defences to fall. But it had been madness to think that it was ever possible to take and to keep Eleanor at his side. And yet he could not get her out of his mind. Soft and naked and pliant in his bed. In his arms.

He groaned as he tossed and turned, sleepless once more, despite the renowned comfort of the Black Bull accommodation.

At least when the *Sea Emerald* sailed, there would be no going back. The decision would have been made, finally and irrevocably.

On the day before the proposed sailing, Lord Henry transferred his meagre luggage on board. It was a less than spacious cabin, but he had paid for the privacy it offered, and for that he would willingly tolerate the cramped surroundings as they sailed out of sight of land.

Later that night, before they would sail at dawn, he returned to the vessel after a final glass of wine with a group of associates at the Black Bull.

'Evening, sir.' Captain Armstrong touched his hand to his hat as he stood waiting on deck.

'Captain Armstrong. A clear night. Good weather for sailing.' The last thing Henry desired was a lengthy conversation, but resigned himself to it. He would spend many weeks in the Captain's company.

'Indeed, indeed. There's been a delivery for you, sir. I have sent the package to your cabin. A matter of urgency, I was given to understand.'

'Then I must go and investigate.' Henry bowed his departure and made for his cabin. He could not think what might have arrived with urgency. Letters forwarded from London? Had he mislaid something of importance that Nick had posted on with such speed? He shrugged, unable to guess. It really did not seem to matter. With such preoccupation, he did not notice the amusement in Captain Armstrong's face, or the knowing gleam in his eyes. Nor had he noticed the bustle on the dock. The smart coach and four, dusty from fast travel. Or the luggage being manhandled on board the *Sea Emerald*.

He went below, treading carefully in the ill-lit gangways below decks. It was well enough now, he thought idly, but what would it be like in a major storm after weeks at sea? His muscles tightened at the anticipation of such discomfort as he opened the door of his cabin. Stepped in and closed it behind him.

And halted, heart picking up its beat, breathing shallow. He was unprepared for this. The room—little more than a space—was small, dark and cramped, made worse by his recently disposed luggage. But someone had entered and had lit a half-shuttered lantern, which cast a circle of light onto the narrow cot against the bulkhead. The rest of the cabin was in deep shadow.

But on the cot, swathed in a soft shawl and blankets, and making every attempt to escape, sat a baby. A child with Faringdon features. A child who looked up at the opening of the door and blinked disconcertingly at him with amethyst eyes.

Henry halted, shocked into immobility by the totally unexpected. It was as if he had been robbed of all breath, of all power of thought and action. Then behind him, to his left, there was the smallest of movements.

He turned his head.

Eleanor.

She wore her fashionable travelling costume, high waisted, shawl-collared, eminently practical, a straw bonnet, feathered and be-flowered, and kid gloves, standing hands clasped before her, waiting for him. As if she had just stepped out of the house in Park Lane with nothing more important on her mind than to stroll through the gardens or to visit the expensive shops to spend a little money on fripperies in Bond Street. Her face was calm, her mouth relaxed and unsmiling, but her eyes were watchful. And fixed on him.

'Eleanor…' The words would not come.

'Lord Henry…' Now she could summon a slight smile at his obvious confusion, but her heart was beating fast, as fast, if she had but known it, as his.

'What have you done…?'

'I am coming with you.'

'I told you that it is not possible…'

'I do not accept your reasoning.'

She was so damnably calm, so assured and certain of the step that she had taken! He immediately sensed danger here. His gaze went to the baby, who appeared to be watching the scene with utmost fascination, and back again to Eleanor. Should he rage and curse? Or take her in his arms? Shake her or kiss her? Or simply ask her to leave, to take herself and the baby back to London. Perhaps that would be too cruel. But if she stayed… He knew well the limitations of his own control where she was concerned.

Eleanor could not read his face. It was severe. Harsh, even, with deeply engraved lines around his stern mouth as the consequences ran through his mind. Had she made the wrong choice when she had gambled everything on his needs being as great and all-consuming as hers? Icy fingers of dread began to tease their path down her spine, but she held them at bay. She would not make it easy for him to reject her again. She would trample on Hal's principles if she had to. But his honour was another matter…

'Nell…'

'If Octavia can follow Edward to the ends of the earth, then I can follow you.'

'Octavia? What has Octavia got to do with it?'

'Nothing, really.' With carefully controlled fingers, casually and without haste, she unfastened the ribbon bow of her bonnet, removed it and placed it on the cot with her gloves. Then unbuttoned her coat and disposed of it likewise. 'I have arranged everything and am here with the blessing of Nick and Judith.'

'Nick?'

'Yes. And you should know that Captain Armstrong has found a cabin for Sarah and John.'

'Sarah!'

'Even Mama waved me off,' she continued, smoothing down her fine woollen skirts, 'almost with good grace.'

'Your mother! Oh, God!' Henry ran his hands through his hair. 'It seems that within the last minute, lady, you have turned my world upside down and my wits have totally deserted me.'

'So I think. You sound like a demented parrot, my love.' She came to stand before him. But not too close. Not to touch. The ultimate decision here must be his.

'I will not take you with me.' The words were forced from him, but immediate.

'Hal. Look at me.' Still she did not smile. There was a challenge in her eyes. 'The only reason for me to leave this ship is if you tell me that you do not want me—that you do not love me enough to spend the rest of your life with me.'

He looked at her, a brooding quality in his eyes. How unfair that she should have done this, using his one weakness. But how magnificent. He was aware of nothing but her grace and beauty and the love that shone in her eyes. The love that he knew, without doubt, was for him alone. And he knew that she intended to fight for her happiness. He stifled a groan at the prospect.

'I cannot. You know that I cannot say that.' It was the only answer he could make in all honesty.

'Well, then.'

'It does not solve anything, Nell.' A hint of desperation crept in. 'It does not negate any of my reasons for leaving you in London. I have nothing to give you compared with what you have here.'

'My son needs his father far more than he needs a title and an estate.' Now there was the faintest snap of temper. 'And when he is old enough, he will tell you the same. You are not free to reject him, Hal. Nor me.' She played her final cards, flinging them

defiantly at his feet. 'If you love me indeed, you must in all
honour take me with you.'

'I should send you back.' Desperately, aware of his resistance
crumbling before her deliberate and irresistible provocation, he
held back.

'What? With my reputation even more besmirched, after joining you on board ship? What would the Princess Lieven say? I
shall be banned from Almack's for ever! I cannot believe that you
would do that to me, Hal.'

'Blackmail, Eleanor?' Now there was a spark of appreciation
for her tactics in his sombre eyes, matching the glint in hers.
Against his will, against all his intentions, he felt the tight knot
of despair that had constricted his chest with tight bands begin
to dissolve, replaced by an insidious warmth and hope.

'If it is necessary.' She raised her chin, accepting the blame,
if blame there must be, but the flush that tinted her cheeks fluc-
tuated deliciously. 'But I would rather you took me willingly,
than under duress.'

'Your reputation is inestimable,' he stated, dropping his gaze
because hers was too bright, too certain, with the faintest of
sighs. 'It always will be. There is no duress for either of us.'

Suddenly, aware of possible disaster of a domestic nature,
Henry turned from her with a rapid movement to scoop up Tom,
determinedly attempting to crawl to investigate the space over
the edge of the cot. With gentle hands and remarkable efficiency
he smoothed the ruffled curls, then wedged the baby back into
safety behind the barricade of a small travelling bag and the
blankets, thoughtfully removing the enticing prospect of Eleanor's feathered bonnet out of reach.

She watched and smiled and waited. Perhaps the battle was
almost won. When he turned back to her, she stretched her arm
across the void still separating them, to touch his cheek in the
lightest of caresses. Much as she might have stroked her son's
cheek—but the result was intoxicating. Fire and heat sparked between them across the space.

'Do you love me, Hal?' Eleanor noticed with interest that she
was suddenly breathless.

'Yes. As God is my witness. Yes.' All the doubt and uncertainty seemed to smooth from his face as he took a deep breath. 'I do not need to ask if you love me. If you have thrown in your lot with me, you must indeed be besotted, you foolish girl.'

'Will it be so bad?'

'Desperate.' Still he did not approach her. 'You will be Mrs Faringdon and live in a two-roomed garret above a business premises. You will have to learn to cook and clean and take care of money—no frivolous spending on gowns and kid gloves.' A faint sardonic smile tugged at his lips as he took in her stylish and expensive gown. 'We shall be forced to live on bread and soup—or something of that nature.'

'As bad as that?' It would be all right! Her pulse throbbed, her senses swam with relief. 'Should I change my mind, after all.'

'Oh, no.' He took one step closer. 'You had your chance and deliberately threw it away. You are in my power now, my lady.'

She veiled a satisfied gleam with long lashes, fighting to hold back tears. 'Thank God for that.'

Then he took another step. And she was in his arms. Held as he allowed his lips to claim his own. Hair, eyes, temples, lips, he kissed her with intense deliberation and growing urgency, halting only to murmur her name, to seek out the impossibly soft skin at the base of her throat where the pulse beat in tune with his. And Eleanor clung to him as the warmth in her blood was so effortlessly ignited into heat, to cleanse and burn, to obliterate all doubts for the future, all pain from the past.

'Hal—oh, Hal. I thought you might send me home,' she whispered as he tangled his hands in her hair, the better to seek and take possession of her mouth, slanting his head to capture and demand.

'You are home.' Drunk on heady passion, he tightened his hold, hands fierce, mouth scalding. 'You will stay with me! You no longer have a choice.'

His lips made their searing pathway along her elegant shoulder—then came to a halt as they brushed against a fine gold chain. He raised his head to look down at her, immediately lost in the shining depths of dew-sprinkled heart's-ease, but his desire was reined in and lightened with humour.

'I thought you would have brought the diamonds.'

She choked on a little laugh, putting up a hand to her breast. 'No. They are not mine to bring. But this is. It was given to me a little while ago. By an admirer. An admirer whom I choose to remember.'

'With fondness? With a little charity, perhaps?'

'With ecstasy!'

He lowered his lips to her breast, to press them against the fine amethyst jewel in its diamond setting, in recognition of the past before they put it from them for ever.

'I would give you more than this. I would give you my name, Nell.' His laugh was, for a moment only, heavy with irony, muffled against her hair. 'But you already have it.' His fingers encircled and tightened around Thomas's diamond and sapphire ring that she still wore, that he himself had replaced on her finger that night at the Red Lion with a silent promise to love and care for her. 'And you already have the Faringdon bridal ring.'

'You gave it back to me when I would have rejected it, Hal.' Eleanor bent her head to touch her lips to his hand, as it still enfolded hers, in recognition of that gesture.

'It is where it belongs. And where it will stay.' Hal's expression was stern as he spoke, his words a confirmation of his promise at the Red Lion, so that Eleanor might hear and know. 'I would give you the protection of my body. The worship of my soul. The adoration of my heart. Is that enough for you, my love, my heart?'

'I will accept all that.' She spread her palms against the solid beat of his heart, absorbing the comfort and the promise.

He put her from him, taking her hands and lifting them to his lips, first one and then the other, before looking down into her lovely face. 'Then this is all simply unfinished business, awaiting its completion for two long years. Your mother kept us apart. But Thomas kept you safe for me. Now you are mine. It is our destiny. And I would reclaim my own. In the eyes of God you, and Tom, are mine. With or without the sanction of the law, I claim you. I will love and cherish you to the end of my days. Will that be enough for you, my dearest and only love? It is all I have to give—and it is yours to take, if you will have it.'

Now Henry's hands folded around hers, encircling them in a gesture of strength, both comfort and protection. And the most tender expression of love.

'I accept, my lord.' Eleanor allowed her hands to rest in his as the heat spread urgent fingers to tint her skin with a blush of becoming rose. How splendid he was, how aware of her needs and anxieties, the weight of the past on her heart. How could he think that any woman would refuse such an offer? How could she possibly refuse?

'I will construct for you a house in New York. And build a life for you, worthy of you.' But he knew that she was now his, whatever the future would hold.

'I will live with you, Hal. With joy and contentment, assuredly. I will give you all the love that fills my heart and soul.' She hesitated, but only for the length of a heartbeat. 'And, Hal, I will give you back your son.'

His breath caught, moved unbearably by the generosity of her offer after all that had passed between them.

'A man could ask no more. Eleanor, my love.'

His lips once more took hers and sealed their future together.

* * * * *

A BRAND-NEW BOOK IN
THE DE WARENNE DYNASTY SERIES
BY *NEW YORK TIMES* BESTSELLING AUTHOR

BRENDA JOYCE

On the evening of her first masquerade, shy Elizabeth Anne
Fitzgerald is stunned by Tyrell de Warenne's whispered suggestion
of a midnight rendezvous in the gardens. Lizzie has secretly
worshiped the unattainable lord for years. When fortune
takes a maddening turn, she is prevented from meeting Tyrell.
But Lizzie has not seen the last of him....

Tyrell de Warenne is shocked when, two years later, Lizzie
arrives on his doorstep with a child she claims is his. He
remembers her well—and knows that he could not possibly
be the father. Is Elizabeth Anne Fitzgerald a woman of
experience, or the gentle innocent she seems?

The MASQUERADE